TRACEY JANE JACKSON

The Bride Price

Civil War Brides Series Book #1

Sale of this book without a front cover may be unauthorized. If this book is coverless, it may have been reported to the publisher as "unsold or destroyed" and neither the author nor the publisher may have received payment for it.

The Bride Price is a work of fiction. Names, characters, places, and incidents are the products of the author's imagination and are used fictitiously. Any resemblance to actual events, locales, or persons, living or dead, is entirely coincidental.

2010 Tracey Jane Jackson
Copyright © 2010 by Tracey Jane Jackson
All rights reserved.

Published in the United States

"Tracey Jane Jackson will enthrall you with her talent for vivid storytelling, and her gift for creating real characters that will make you ache and sigh. Prepare to be swept off your feet and carried away to another time and place!"
Julianne MacLean – USA Today Bestselling Author

For other titles in the Civil War Brides Series, visit:
www.traceyjanejackson.com

Like Tracey's page on Facebook:
www.facebook.com/traceyjanejackson

And follow her at Twitter:
@trixiejaxn

For Mama Robin
You took my period and showed me where to stick it

For Gornitzky, Beitschy & DebM
You are the women of my tribe who keep me sane

Most especially...for my husband
You will forever be my Jamie

CHAPTER ONE

**Portland, Oregon
January, 2007**

JAMIE FORD LEANED against the frame of the solid pocket door and tried to focus on something other than the vision of his beautiful wife dozing on the chaise in the library of their historic 1870's Victorian home. The wires of her Left Ventricular Assist Device were covered by the book laid flat over her stomach...she'd obviously fallen asleep in the middle of her read.

He sighed and dragged a shaky hand over his face, wincing as he encountered three days worth of stubble. He must look like hell. It couldn't be helped. He'd managed to grab a quick shower, but shaving took more time and energy than he had at the moment.

Sophie's condition was deteriorating and he coveted every minute of each day God saw fit to give them. Her doctor had decided it was time for her to be hospitalized until a matching heart could be found. She was scheduled to be admitted in the morning and Jamie didn't know what the future held for them. He'd sold his Internet company a year ago, and although he still held a seat on the Board, his CEO days were behind him.

Sophie mumbled, drawing his gaze. He swallowed hard, sending up another silent prayer that a heart would be found in time. Crossing the library's thick Oriental rug, he pulled a chair close and sat next to her. Weight loss and shortness of breath were the only external indications she was sick, and his eyes swept over her once-voluptuous body.

He picked up the book and smiled. *Team of Rivals: The Political Genius of Abraham Lincoln.* Even sick, she couldn't get enough of her hero. She was obsessed with all things Civil War related, and Jamie believed the worst part for her about getting sick was the inability to travel and participate in reenactments. They'd turned down two invitations in the last year.

Lifting her hair, he stroked a golden curl. The myriad of colors, much like the ribbons of caramel taffy, slid through his fingers.

Sophie let out a quiet sigh and turned her head in her sleep. "Jamie?"

"Hi, baby."

Her eyes fluttered open. "Hovering?"

Jamie inhaled deeply, relishing the sound of her voice as he leaned over and kissed her forehead, a subtle attempt to check her temperature. "How are you feeling?"

"Hmmm...how am I feeling? Give me a dose of Dilaudid and ask me then."

"Are you in pain?" His voice shook as he stood.

She grabbed his arm. "A joke, sweetheart. I'm sorry. No pain, just a bit groggy—and thirsty."

Jamie poured a glass of water and handed it to her. "Are you hungry at all? Do you think you could try to eat something? Alex cooked again."

"Is she still here?"

"No. Luke picked her up about an hour ago. She'll be back tomorrow morning."

Their closest friends, Lucas and Alexandria, were daily companions at the Ford house. They cooked, cleaned, and did anything they could to take the pressure off Jamie. The help allowed him to spend every available moment with Sophie.

Sophie rubbed her forehead. "Where's Emma?"

"Out with Hannah. She'll be back in a couple of hours." Truth be told, Jamie practically had to force Sophie's sister out the door.

"Ooh, so we have the house to ourselves?" Sophie raised her eyebrow.

Jamie chuckled. "Yes we do."

Sophie dragged her legs over the side of the couch and stood. Jamie wrapped an arm around her waist. "Careful."

"Jamie, I'm fine," she insisted. "Besides, I'd really love a shower."

"All right, sweetheart, I'll take you upstairs."

Jamie lifted her in his arms. Carrying her up the narrow stairs and to their bedroom, he set her on her feet in the adjoining bathroom.

"Where's the shower pack?" she asked.

"I have it." Jamie helped her undress and switch over to the waterproof pack. He started the shower and waited for her to step inside.

"I'm perfectly capable of showering without you, love. Jeez, you'd think I was dying or something." She gently pushed him away and pulled the glass door closed.

Jamie left the bathroom, but didn't go far. He was gathering clean clothes when he heard Sophie's soft cry. He rushed into the bathroom, somewhat panicked. Sophie could never be described as graceful, her clumsiness somewhat endearing to him, but with a heart that didn't work correctly, this trait was now more of a concern.

Jamie found her sitting on the floor of the shower, her knees drawn up to her chin. "What happened?"

"I felt a bit lightheaded."

Turning off the water, he grabbed a towel and reached in to lift her into his arms.

"You're gonna get wet," she whispered as she wrapped her arms around his neck.

"There are worse things in life than getting wet holding a beautiful woman in my arms after she's showered." Sophie burst into tears. He pulled her closer. "Sophie, what?"

She wiped the back of her hand across her eyes and muttered, "I'm useless. I can't even shower without feeling like I'm going to pass out. I can't believe you're going to have to do everything for me. You didn't sign up for this. I think you should just leave me. I don't want you to have to deal with me wasting away."

Setting her on her feet, he wrapped the towel around her and then cradled her face in his hands. "Sophie Jane, who peed in your cereal this morning?"

She glared at him, fire lighting her dark blue eyes. "Apparently, the same person who gave you your sense of humor."

Jamie chuckled. "With your temper, you'd think you were born a redhead."

"Oh, you're funny."

"I think we need to set some ground rules here."

"Ground rules?" she asked.

"First of all, I'm not going to leave you. You don't get to make that decision for me." She tried to interrupt but he held up his hand. "Second, you are not useless. Third, I love you, so you don't get to escape. Not that you could. If you can't take a shower without me, then it's a sure bet you can't run away from me."

Sophie let out a quiet snort.

"I can't believe you'd even think that I wouldn't want to be here. No matter what happens, I'm here, with you and for you. Leaving you would be like losing my right arm. I couldn't do it. Got it?"

"I'd totally understand. You know that, right?"

"In sickness and in health. I took my vows seriously, did you? It's all encompassing. Your sickness and mine." He smiled gently and kissed her nose. "You're my ten-cow woman. Even at your worst, there's nobody better for me than you. I'm afraid you're stuck with me until the very end—and even if you die before me, I'll figure out a way to find you. Don't ever doubt it."

Sophie patted his chest. "Okay, okay, no need to get so melodramatic."

"Let's get you dressed and I'll check your monitor so we can eat."

She nodded, but by the time he settled her into their king-sized bed, she slumped against the pillows and waved away his offering for food.

"You need to eat, Sophie."

"I'm too hot to eat."

Jamie stroked her cheek. Her skin was beaded with sweat. "I'm calling Chrystal."

"Seriously?"

Their neighbor, Chrystal Gornitzka, was a registered nurse who'd been a wealth of information and comfort since Sophie's diagnosis. Jamie picked up the phone and dialed her number. "Hi, Chrystal, it's Jamie. Sophie's fever seems to have spiked again. I'm not sure what to do."

"I just pulled into the driveway. I'll grab my bag and be over in few."

Jamie let out a sigh of relief. "Thanks, I really appreciate it. The door's unlocked—just come on in." He hung up the phone, and poured Sophie a glass of water. "Drink this, baby."

She took the glass from him and sipped. "I probably just need some Tylenol."

"Perhaps. Let's wait for Chrystal and then go from there."

Sophie groaned. "That poor woman must have a life outside of me, Jamie."

"Well, I don't." He forced a smile. "So humor me."

Before she could protest further, they heard the slam of the front door and then footsteps on the stairs. "Yoo-hoo."

"Up here, Chrystal," Jamie called.

Chrystal walked through the door, her shoulder-length brunette hair slipping over her cheeks as she set her bag on the bed. "Hi. Does someone have a fever?"

Sophie's eyes flashed with mischief as she smiled. "Next you'll be asking me how *we're* feeling."

Chrystal opened her bag and pulled out a thermometer. "How are we feeling?"

"Everyone's a comedian today."

"You know the drill." Chrystal pushed the thermometer between Sophie's lips.

Sophie mumbled something.

"Ten-Cow, shhh," Jamie admonished at Sophie's attempt to talk.

"She's doing fine. And you should probably stop calling her a cow. She's well below her normal body weight." Crystal pulled the thermometer from Sophie's mouth.

Sophie met his eyes, a sweetness in them that could always render his heart liquid in his chest.

"Oh, he can call me Ten-Cow." She winked at him.

"Really?"

"It's a romantic story of undying love," Sophie said. "Tell her, Jamie."

"Undying love, huh? Does that even exist?" Chrystal's arched brow popped in question.

"I'm going to be sick." Sophie sat up suddenly.

Jamie grabbed a bowl and held it under her chin.

"Give her some Tylenol and then call the doctor." Chrystal's eyebrows puckered.

Jamie felt the color leave his face. "Is it serious?"

Chrystal shook her head with a gentle smile. "Honestly, I think it's just the flu, like the doctor said yesterday. The Milrinone drip is at the dosage set, her pic line is working, and the LVAD is doing its job, so her lethargy is because of the fever. The antibiotics will kick in soon and she'll probably feel better in the next day or two."

Jamie stroked Sophie's cheek.

"I'm fine, Jamie." Sophie turned to Chrystal. "Thanks for checking on me."

Chrystal patted her hand. "It's my pleasure, Sophie. Call me if you need me. Even if it's the middle of the night. You can tell me the story later." Jamie stood but Chrystal held her hand up. "I'll let myself out. Tylenol, cold compresses, doctor, and she should be good as new."

Jamie nodded. "Thanks."

Once Chrystal left, Jamie gathered the Tylenol and a cool washcloth. He waited until Sophie took the pills and then sat beside her.

"Jamie? You need to stop worrying. The LVAD is doing its job and tomorrow I'll be monitored constantly by people who know more than you and me."

He frowned. "Sophie, your immune system is lowered and you're weak. I can't help but worry."

She squeezed his arm. "Okay. I can't make you not worry, but there are people who live for years with this device. I'd have been dead within weeks without it, and now I'm 1A status, guaranteed the next matching heart."

"If your flu goes away."

Sophie sighed. "It will."

The peal of Jamie's cell phone interrupted their discussion and he glanced at the screen with a scowl. He answered the call, leaning back in the chair with a sigh. "Hey Brian."

"Hey Jamie. We got push back from the Cary camp."

Jamie shook his head. "So? I'm not taking money from them. Get legal involved if you have to."

"It's a lot of money," Brian argued.

"I don't care if it's all the money in the world, it's not worth it."

"Okay, okay. I'll talk to the lawyers."

"Thanks. I have to go." Jamie hung up before Brian could respond.

Sophie raised an eyebrow. "Someone wants to give you money?"

"Don't worry about it. It's nothing."

"Everything okay?"

Jamie nodded. "Yes. Brian's just having a difficult time without me there to hold his hand."

Sophie smiled. "If you need to go into the office after you get me settled tomorrow, you can. I'll be fine."

"Not going to happen." He reached for his guitar.

Sophie chuckled. "Ah, yes, the other woman. Will you play me a lullaby—provided she doesn't mind, of course." She smoothed her blankets and gazed at him.

"Well, Ten-Cow, that depends on you." He paused, the hollow sound echoing through the chamber of the guitar as he tapped his hand against it. "One song for two bites of food, that's the deal."

Sophie sighed through tight lips. "I'll take a bit of the orange."

Handing her a wedge, he waited for her to eat it, and started to play quietly. Sophie hummed along with the melody, and Jamie paused, midstrum. "I miss your voice."

Sophie smiled. "I miss singing."

Jamie reached over to the nightstand and opened the drawer.

"What are you doing?"

Jamie grinned. "I'm reminiscing." He pulled out an old playbill from the production of *Grease* she'd starred in. "You were the perfect Sandy."

Sophie chuckled. "If only you could have been my Danny."

Jamie snorted. "I'm not going to justify that statement with a remark."

Sophie rolled over and wrinkled her nose. "Well, you would have been better than Justice Wright."

Jamie shrugged. "He seemed okay. He played the role well."

"You try kissing a gay man and make it look real."

Jamie laughed. He leaned over and kissed her quickly, before handing her another wedge of orange. "That should settle your stomach enough to eat something substantial." Sophie rolled her eyes and Jamie responded with a raised eyebrow in challenge. "You're gonna eat, Ten-Cow."

Sophie scrunched her nose up in disgust. "I'm not hungry."

"You have to strengthen your body in order to fight—"

"The infection that will tax my failing heart even more," she interrupted and slid further under the blankets. "I know, Jamie but my heart's gonna stop whether I eat or not. Daddy's did and I couldn't make him live."

Jamie froze, a quiet hiss escaping between his teeth.

"Sorry, baby," Sophie whispered. "I shouldn't have said that."

Jamie shook his head. "It's fine."

She smiled.

"Why the Cheshire?" he asked.

"I just remembered a weird dream I had about one of our reenactments."

"Really?"

"Do you remember the haunted house?"

Jamie laughed. "Not haunted, simply a case of faulty wiring."

"Right. Go with that."

Three years ago Sophie had taken part in a Civil War event that was filled with mishaps. Little things like a power surge that caused a television, hidden behind an antique painting, to turn on. "Your team had fun explaining the noise coming from behind the artwork. Didn't one of the old ladies faint?" Cradling the guitar on his knees, Jamie picked up the fork again, speared a small piece of potato, and lifted it to her mouth.

She shook her head. "That was Miss Olive. I personally thought it was a stroke of pure genius on her part to fake a swoon. She distracted people until we could shut off the breaker."

"Sophie, you need to eat."

"I'm too hot to eat." She pushed the blankets away from her body.

Jamie helped pull the blankets further down the bed. "Imagine *you* in the nineteenth-century without air conditioning. God forbid the temperature went above seventy degrees and you're stuck in a gown like Mary Lincoln's." Jamie leaned over her and settled his palm on her forehead. Sophie winced and let out a quiet moan. "Are you in pain?"

"No, just feel sick. And hot." Sophie reached for his hand. "I'm fine, Jamie. Really. I just need to sleep."

Jamie watched her eyes close and her breathing grow even. Taking Sophie's frail hand in his, he stroked her arm. "Remember when we met? The frat party. I'll never forget the moment I saw you. You were yelling at some frat guy who'd just slapped your butt, explaining the pitfalls of displaying chauvinism in your presence. I wondered if you were a law student."

He lifted her hand to his mouth and kissed the inside of her wrist, drawing in her scent. "I couldn't take my eyes off you. You were pissed, and it made me hot. I'd never seen anyone put someone in their place the way you did that guy."

The headlights of a car flashed through the window as it drove by, illuminating the room and drawing shadows across the wall. "I knew I had to meet you." Jamie squeezed her hand. "When we talked, I felt like my life had just started and there was no way you weren't going to be in it. I knew you'd be mine—forever." He couldn't continue. Tears escaped as he laid his head down, her hand still in his, and closed his eyes.

* * *

Sophie's eyelids felt like lead weights. She wanted to wake up, *needed* to. The bedroom grew cold, despite the roaring fire in the corner. Sophie tried to get her bearings, forcing her eyes open. Her gaze fell on the shelf that held her favorite Lincoln biography, and she stared in disbelief. The wood grain faded away, becoming the trunk of a very large tree. Beyond the tree, all she saw was an expanse of snow and forest.

Sophie squeezed her eyes shut and then looked again. The books and shelves were back. Sophie's focus pulled back to Jamie, but as she stared down at him, the sheets melted away, becoming a mound of fresh snow. Her body frozen, Sophie shivered, and then the bed was back. She tried to force her body to move again, but couldn't reach the blankets. Sophie's head fell back onto the pillow.

The ceiling disappeared. White sky met her gaze; drops of cold water feathered her face. She shivered again and glanced back down at Jamie. He lay still next to her, his hand covering hers. Her vision blurred.

I'm hallucinating. This must be what happens with a raging fever. Jamie, wake up. I need you.

Sophie's heart stuttered and pain coursed through her chest.

No, not hallucinating. Dying! Am I dying?

The snow returned and she tried to reach out to the strange vision. Before she could do anything else, the room spun, and her world went black.

* * *

Jamie jerked awake at Sophie's shiver. Leaning over the bed, he put his hand to her mouth, then her cheek, and relief slicked through him as heat bloomed against his skin.

"Sophie? Honey, wake up." His voice shook as he whispered her name again. Her shaking worsened, and he pulled the covers to her shoulders, just as he heard the front door slam.

"Jamie!" Emma called from the foyer. "I'm home."

Jamie jogged down the hall and peered down from the landing. "Up here."

Emma's straight blonde hair slid behind her shoulders as she lifted her head. Deep blue eyes so much like her sister's narrowed in concern as she peered up at him. "You sound weird, what's wrong?"

"Sophie's fever spiked, and now she's shaking. She's freezing."

Emma took the stairs two at a time. "Did you give her anything?"

"Yes, Tylenol. I don't know if it's helping though."

Emma ran to the bedroom as Jamie grabbed a couple of blankets from the hallway closet and followed her. "Emma?" Jamie scanned the room and found her standing over the empty bed holding Sophie's LVAD wires. *Wait—empty?* His heart raced.

"Where is she?" Jamie moved to the side of the bed and ran his hands over the sheets.

Emma dropped the wires. "I don't know. Did you see her leave the room?"

"It would have been impossible."

Emma grasped his shoulders and turned him to face her. "Did you check the bathroom? She probably just went to splash water on her face."

Jamie pushed her hands away. "Check downstairs." Without waiting for Emma to agree, he ran through the upper floor, yelling Sophie's name. He lingered in each room just in case she might appear at his call.

Emma met him back in his bedroom. "She's not downstairs...or in the basement."

Jamie pulled at the sheets on the empty bed and dropped to his knees, shaking hands digging into his scalp. "Where is she? Where is my wife?"

CHAPTER TWO

AMMONIA. SHE HADN'T expected heaven to smell like bleach. And voices? No, yelling. *God allows yelling in heaven?*

Then wet, bone-chilling cold pressed into her skin, her bones, her mind. *Why's it cold...and why am I wet? If my bedroom has central heat and a fireplace, certainly heaven does, too.*

Most of all, the pain had vanished...the expected burn as she breathed no longer clutched her chest. She took in a deep breath, and forced her eyes open.

Light made her blink even as she swatted at the stench. "What—?"

"Betty, get Dr. Wade, quickly!" a female voice yelled.

A form bent over her. A pretty woman, her hair whisked under what looked like a bonnet. She wore a woolen gray coat and not a stitch of makeup, as if she were some sort of religious conservative. The woman removed a dark glove and pressed a warm, soft hand to Sophie's head. "Miss, can you hear me?"

"Yes, I can hear you. Why am I cold?" Sophie asked.

"You've fainted in the snow. We're going to take you to my home. My husband will help you. He's a doctor."

Snow? This is heaven, right? Why is there snow in heaven?

Sophie tried to sit up but before she could manage, a pair of strong arms lifted her. Her head snapped up, and she stared into warm, brown eyes.

Not Jamie's. These belonged to someone unfamiliar.

"Put me down!" She pushed at his shoulders. "Where is my husband? Where's Jamie?" Wriggling her body in an effort to dislodge herself from the stranger, she only managed to skew her all too inadequate clothing.

"I don't know a Jamie, ma'am. I think you may have hit your head." His deep-set gaze assessed her. A lock of sandy blond hair fell over a wide forehead. His face, weathered and sun-beaten, cradled a gentle smile as his eyes met hers. Not quite gentle enough, however, to stop the nervous shiver that coursed through her body.

"My head is fine. Put me down."

With his wide shoulders, he carried her without trouble, and her efforts to get him to release her failed. Although she had lost quite a bit of weight over the past year, she certainly didn't feel as waifish as she had moments ago.

"Ma'am, quit your wrigglin'. No harm will come to you."

Something in the softness of his southern drawl eased her fear – albeit slightly. He shifted her in his embrace, but there was no sense that he might set her on her feet. "What's your name?"

"Richard Madden, ma'am."

His name dropped away as her surroundings came into view. Snow-covered trees surrounded them. The sound of crunching under his feet distracted her focus as he carried her toward a home that looked like something out of a Benjamin Franklin restoration. Sophie looked everywhere, trying to take it all in.

The brick Federal style manor loomed ahead; seven steps led to a cobblestone porch, housing two large white doors and an iron doorknocker. Sophie guessed the heavy iron would echo through the entire house.

I'm hallucinating. Isn't that what brain tumors do to you? Great! A brain tumor and a failing heart!

"Are you the doctor?"

"No, ma'am, I'm a neighbor of the Wades. I'm going to take you into the house."

She pushed at his shoulders again. "No, wait. I don't know these people. I don't want to go into their house."

"Ma'am. No one will harm you. The Wades are good people."

She allowed herself to relax slightly at his words. *This must be what they call Stockholm syndrome. I'm trusting my kidnapper.*

"Who are the Wades?" she whispered.

Before the man could answer, she heard a deep voice ask, "Nona, what's amiss?"

She turned toward the sound and saw a tall stranger come into view. A glance revealed dark blond hair graying at the temples and a quick smile.

"Michael, this girl appears to have fainted out by the stables. I found her when I went out for my morning constitutional."

Sophie's heart raced, the sensation alien to her after so much time with one which barely beat. Her mind reeled, trying to make sense of what happened.

"Richard, bring her into the parlor," the deep voice bellowed. "Nona, have Betty get some warm blankets. She's probably frozen to the bone."

Richard walked up the front steps and into the large foyer. Sophie's gaze couldn't linger on the surroundings of the entrance as he carried her into the room just to the right of the front door. Richard laid her gently on the sofa and solid muscles constricted beneath his thick, woolen jacket. When he exhaled, she smelled a hint of alcohol on his breath.

The man he called Michael hovered over her with kindness in his light gray eyes.

The doctor?

"Now, young lady, let's have a look at you. How did you end up by the stables?" He turned to Richard. "Was she with you last night?"

A look of offense flashed over Richard's expression. "The lady wasn't with me, Michael. I've never seen her before."

Darn right, Skippy. I was with Jamie.

"Who are you guys? Am I dead? Is this heaven?"

"Heaven?" Michael chuckled. "Nona has often referred to our home as heavenly, haven't you, Mrs. Wade?"

Sophie shot a frantic look around the room. "But – uhh, I think I died." Sophie's hand pressed against her stomach as she whispered, "Why are you all dressed in costume?"

Nona disappeared, returning a moment later followed by a large, dark-skinned woman wearing a gray dress and crisp, white apron. "Here are the blankets."

As the doctor's wife moved to her side, Sophie took in her appearance. Nona had removed her bonnet and strawberry blonde hair, streaked with light strands of gray, reminded Sophie of many of the women's hairstyles in her collection of nineteenth-century photographs: parted in the middle and secured at the nape of her neck. Tiny in stature, no more than five feet tall, and in constant motion, Nona flitted around the room.

Sophie's gaze drifted over the deep blue of the woman's intricate, velvet dress. She had discarded her plain gray coat, revealing pearl buttons and frilly lace at the neck of the gown. It looked like something out of *Gone With the Wind*. "What a beautiful dress."

"Thank you. We have a wonderful seamstress in town." Nona fingered one dainty button proudly. "Madame Desmarais is a wonder with a needle and thread."

"Oh, I thought perhaps you'd made it."

Nona chuckled quietly. "I have several that I have sewn. However, this one is a favorite, and today is a special occasion."

Sophie wondered what the special occasion could be.

Perhaps a costume party?

"Richard, thank you so much for carrying her in." Nona turned away from Sophie.

"No harm. She doesn't weigh anymore than a bag of cottonseed." Richard's southern accent came out thick and heavy.

Sophie darted a glance in his direction.

A bag of cotton seed? How much does that weigh?

She assumed it must be some kind of southern expression and shook herself from her fog. "So, if I'm not dead, is this an hallucination?" She rubbed her forehead with her fingers. "I must be dreaming."

"Excuse me, dear?" Nona asked.

Sophie sat up further and caught a reflection of herself in the gilded mirror hanging low on the wall. Standing slowly, her legs shaky from months of bed rest, she was surprised to find that in every other way, she felt fine. Her heart beat normally and her breathing was no longer labored. Despite her weakness, she felt as though she could run a mile.

She glanced into the mirror and let out a rather inelegant snort. Still dressed in her pajama bottoms and one of Jamie's old sweatshirts, she ran her hands over her waist. She stared at her appearance, not recognizing the young woman staring back at her. Her heart disease had caused more weight loss than even she had been aware of. The pants, once a bit tight over her full figure, now slipped low on her hips.

I look sixteen.

Lifting the pant legs so she could see her feet, she heard a gasp from Nona. Sophie pressed her frozen toes into the lushness of the Oriental rug on the floor and looked around at the strangers. "Where are my shoes?"

"Ma'am, you should sit down," Richard said.

"And cover your ankles," Nona whispered.

Suddenly embarrassed, Sophie nodded and sat back onto the sofa.

"Michael, is she all right?" Concern marred the woman's otherwise flawless features.

Doctor Wade turned to Sophie. "Young lady, what's your name?"

"My name is Sophie—Sophie Ford. Where am I?"

"My wife found you lying out by the stables. I'm Dr. Wade, and of course, Nona, whom you've met, and the gentleman there is Richard Madden, our neighbor." His eyes grew serious. "Where is your family, and why are you unattended? A young lady should not be unattended."

"I don't know. I think I...died." Even as the words left her mouth, she realized how crazy she sounded. "At least, I was supposed to be dying, but then I had this strange vision..."

Oh, yeah, vision *makes you sound so much saner.*

The tall man in the corner raised his eyebrows at the doctor, and Sophie felt Michael's fingers squeeze her wrist slightly as he took her pulse. He raised his eyes in concern and then repeated what he'd previously said, enunciating each word a little more forcefully. "My wife found you out by the stables. I am Dr. Michael Wade, this is my wife Norine, whom we all call Nona, and the gentleman over there is Richard Madden."

"Yes, you said that, I just don't understand why..." Her words fell away as she stopped a sob with the back of her palm. Sophie tried to breathe in an effort not to hyperventilate.

Where is Jamie?

"Where is your family?"

"My family?" She narrowed her gaze. "I ...uh...well, see, I was at home, and then everything got sort of fuzzy, right after Jamie fell asleep. I know he gave me a dose of....where is Jamie? Did I die? This just can't be real. Jamie would never let me go. He promised me forever."

"No, ma'am, you are alive, I assure you." He patted her hand kindly and then checked for broken bones. "Where are you from? Is there somewhere we can take you? You have family in these parts?"

Nona frowned. "Michael, does it look like she hit her head? She seems very confused."

When the doctor probed Sophie's head at his wife's urgency, she swatted his hand away. She'd had enough invasive examinations during her life, and no way would she accept probing in her afterlife. Sophie screamed on the inside.

"No bumps. No physical injuries."

Sophie shivered, unsure if it was from the cold or the confusion, as she began to recognize this wasn't heaven. Where was Jamie?

"Look at the poor dear, she's shaking," Nona murmured. "Michael, the blankets."

The doctor gently laid blankets over Sophie, and she fingered the delicate fabric of the top cover.

"Do you live nearby? Is there somewhere we can take you?" Michael asked.

"I live in Portland, but I don't know how I got here." Frustrated, Sophie sat up. Nausea hit her with force. She remembered she hadn't eaten more than the oranges Jamie had insisted on earlier.

Earlier...or a lifetime ago...or in my subconscious. What the heck is going on?

Nona bustled over, sat down next to Sophie, and laid a gentle hand on her arm. "Don't worry about anything. You must have lost your memory. Just lie back and relax. You're safe here with us. You couldn't have shown up at a better, safer place. You are welcome to stay as long as you have need. With a little rest, perhaps your memories will return."

Sophie rolled her eyes. "I haven't lost my memory. I'm Sophie Ford. I'm married to James Ford, and I'm supposed to be dead." Then under her breath, "Or, not, apparently."

She had to admit, she felt relieved that she wasn't dead. But still— *where is Jamie?*

"You're married? Where is your husband? Is he one of the soldiers working with Richard?" Nona frowned. "Michael, why would her husband leave her in the snow?"

"My husband isn't a soldier, he's an artist and musician, and he would never leave me in the snow. Wait a minute." Her hand flew to her forehead. "Snow? Where am I? There wasn't any snow in Portland yesterday. Just rain."

Richard frowned and Sophie didn't miss his patronizing tone as he drawled, "You couldn't possibly have been in Maine yesterday, ma'am."

"Maine?"

"Yes, ma'am. It would have taken you several days to travel here to Harrisburg, especially in this weather. Not to mention it wouldn't be safe," Richard said.

"Harrisburg?" Sophie's stomach roiled. "As in Pennsylvania?"

"Yes ma'am."

Pennsylvania? What is going on?

"What's the date?" Sophie asked.

"January 31."

Okay, same date. Why are these people in costume?

"It's been a mild winter this year, although not mild enough for you to be in what you're wearing." Nona sounded a bit like her old pastor's wife, who insisted on dresses and hair pulled away from the face.

"I was sleeping." Sophie didn't know why she should feel defensive about her pajamas.

"We are in the middle of a war, and one of the soldiers could have seen you in your state of undress." Nona shuddered. "Who knows what could have happened."

Sophie's panic raised its ugly head again. She laid her hand over her stomach, in an effort not to puke. "War?"

"Excuse me?"

"You said, 'war.' What war?"

Nona whipped her head toward her husband. "What a strange question. Michael, she *must* have hit her head. Are you certain you checked her thoroughly?"

Sophie pushed herself up with limited breath. "What war?"

Nona tsked and said slowly, "The War between the States."

Unable to stop the screech that escaped her lips, Sophie squeezed her eyes shut and whispered, "The 1860s War between the States?"

"Well, it's 1863. Of course it's the 1860s War between the States." Nona turned back to Michael. "You must check her again."

"If I'm not dead...am I dreaming? I must be dreaming. How long have I been here?"

Nona's eyebrows knitted together. "We just found you...in the snow."

Sophie's throat closed and her eyes filled with tears. Taking a deep breath, choosing to limit her words, lest men in white coats suddenly arrive to take her away, she decided to work out her confusion later. "I think I'm all right, Mrs. Wade. Perhaps I do just need to rest."

"Please, dear, call me Nona."

Sophie took a moment to appraise her surroundings. The parlor appeared exactly as she had always envisioned an authentic nineteenth-century room would look like. Right down to the American Federal sofa she lay on. Sophie noticed the man who carried her in standing in the corner. He seemed to be brooding.

Wait. Brooding? I wouldn't have a dream with the quintessential brooding male. Okay, Sophie, think. In my world, what would the large man be doing right now? Smiling? Joking? Dancing? This is my dream...or my heaven, and I refuse to have anyone brooding. Of course, the fact I'm concerned about someone brooding, just goes to show how crazy I am. Maybe this is the entrance point to a padded room.

If she closed her eyes, counted to ten, maybe she'd wake up. Squeezing her eyes shut, Sophie slowly counted the seconds off then looked again at the man in the corner.

Nope, still brooding.

"Betty, prepare the blue room for our guest," Nona instructed.

Sophie held her hand up. "I don't think that will be necessary. I'm sure my husband will be here any time now. He must have just gotten lost, or detained. Yes, detained. That must be it. He can't be far away. He would never leave me. We're usually joined at the hip."

"Joined at the hip?" Nona lowered her voice. "Perhaps we shouldn't speak of those things in mixed company."

Sophie swung her legs around and settled them on the carpet. "Oh, sorry. Um, it's an expression...from home. Um, we spend a lot of time together."

The doctor laid his hand on her shoulder. "Why don't we just take you on upstairs? You can lie down for a little while and Nona will find you something decent to wear. I'll have Richard make some inquiries about your husband. We'll make certain the two of you are reunited as soon as possible."

"That's very kind of you. Thank you, Nona." She stood and faced Richard. "Thank you, um, Mr. Madden, is it?"

"Yes ma'am. There's not much of a chance a man can get lost in this town. If he's here, someone will know where he is. You said his name is Jamie?"

Sophie nodded. "His name is James—actually, we call him Jamie. James William Ford is his full name."

Richard raised an eyebrow. "What does he look like? I'll ask down at the field office and see if I can't locate him for you."

"Tall, blue eyes, short dark hair, goat—" Sophie stalled, he didn't appear to be listening.

His eyes met hers. "He has a goat with him?"

"No, sorry. He has a goatee—no, he had one, but now he has a beard."

When Richard nodded, Sophie turned to follow Nona up the stairs, her hands grasping the tie at the waist of her pants, now threatening to fall below her hips. Richard stepped behind her and bent to lift her, but Sophie pushed him away. "No, I'm fine. I can walk up the stairs."

"Ma'am, you've had a nasty accident—"

"*Please,* don't touch me," she interrupted. She put more distance between them, and waited for him to step back before following Nona. Sophie felt as though they walked past more than a dozen doors before arriving at the one Nona referred to as the 'blue room.'

As she followed the doctor's wife inside, Sophie's mouth dropped open. A large four-poster bed dominated the room. A roaring fire in an elaborately carved fireplace made the space feel warm and welcoming. Sophie crossed the hardwood floor to admire a beautiful mahogany highboy and matching vanity that flanked a large window. The furniture shone with a deep luster that could only have come from elbow grease and copious amounts of beeswax. She shook her head in wonder.

Her love affair with all things Civil War era had not prepared her for the opulence she was encountering. Who would have thought people could have such beauty and civility amidst the destruction of war? The snow outside was a blinding white and it sparkled like fairy dust, vibrant and alive. The wooden floors gleamed like honey, and the room she stood in was awash in vivid blue.

Blue floral wallpaper covered the walls, and the china bowl and pitcher matched the design. A primrose blanket and an embroidered quilt covered the bed. The items that didn't have some shade of blue in them seemed right at home, despite their hue challenge. Everything about the room projected comfort and welcome. It would be a perfect B&B and just the kind of place she'd want to spend a cozy weekend snuggled in bed with Jamie. Tears pricked her eyes as she thought of Jamie.

I need him here. Where is he? Does he know where I am or does he think I'm dead?

She drew a ragged breath and allowed Nona to help her change into a nightgown. Nona had also located a robe and, although it was several inches too short, it was warm, which was all Sophie cared about at the moment. Sophie got settled in the large bed and clasped her hands together, uncertain what to do.

"You should sleep and get your strength back."

Sophie stared at her plain gold wedding band and ran her finger over it. "I'm fine, Nona. My husband will find me."

"I'll tell you what. As soon as your husband arrives, I'll wake you." Nona patted her hand.

Sophie took a deep breath. "I suppose I am rather tired. Please promise me you'll wake me as soon as he gets here. I'm sure he's frantically trying to find me and is worried sick."

As soon as Nona left the room, Sophie slid from the bed.

Wake up, Sophie. You are not in the middle of the Civil War. You are not in the middle of a real life freakin' reenactment. This is a dream.

She pinched her leg. "Ow." Slapping her hand over her mouth, hoping Nona wouldn't investigate the noise, she stood on shaky legs for several seconds. Nothing.

She stepped to the fireplace and reached her hands toward the amber flames.

Um, yeah, those are hot. What the heck is going on? I have to find Jamie.

CHAPTER THREE

SOPHIE PACED THE room for what seemed like hours. She investigated every inch of it, not that it helped. The warmth of the bed beckoned to her, so she finally forced herself to climb back under the covers. She tried to nap, without success. She sat up, tossed back her thick mass of curls, and brought her palm to her chest.
I can still breathe without pain.
Raising her head to the ceiling, she took a deep breath.
How is this even possible?
Sophie eased out of the tall bed and grasped the post to steady herself. Her weak legs protested the sudden activity. She made her way to the mirror and slipped the borrowed robe open, studying her torso. She still had the scar from her open heart surgery, but it was faded significantly, and her chest tube scars were no longer there. She ran her fingers over the smooth skin and leaned forward to get a closer look at the scar.
It just looks like a scratch! Jamie's going to freak when he sees my body back to normal.
Pulling the borrowed robe tighter around her, Sophie moved to the bedroom door. She poked her head out, listening for sounds, before making her way down the hall. Where was the bathroom? She tried a few doors but only found other bedrooms.
She hoped she wasn't going to have to use a chamber pot. Dream or no dream, the idea was gross. Hearing noise coming from downstairs, she paused on the landing. The sound of laughter and clinking glasses wafted through the foyer.
Sophie slunk down the stairs and made her way toward the dining room, uncertain exactly what she would find, but following the sound despite her racing heart. As she turned the corner, she stopped, and a fork dropped with a loud clutter.
Sophie's mouth came open as Richard stood, nearly knocking his chair over in the process. He made a beeline for her. "Mrs. Ford, ma'am, you shouldn't be down here without any clothes on."
"Excuse me?"

Richard grabbed her arm and pulled her into the foyer.

Sophie's skin crawled as she yanked her arm away. "Let go of me."

"Ma'am, people shouldn't see you like this, it's not decent."

Sophie narrowed her eyes. "What do you mean by 'not decent'?"

"You're almost naked."

Sophie glanced down to make sure another button hadn't popped open. "I'm fully covered!"

"You're not fully covered. Your ankles are showing, among other things," Richard whispered.

Feeling a gentle squeeze on her elbow, Sophie turned her head to find Nona, her expression full of motherly concern. "Sophie, dear, what are you doing down here?"

Michael stood behind Nona and moved to block Sophie's view of the dining room.

"Where's Jamie?"

Nona shot a frantic look toward Michael.

"Mrs. Ford. Turn around and go back to your room." Richard pointed to the stairs.

"Where is my husband?"

"Sophie, dear, he isn't here." Nona wrapped an arm around her shoulders. "Let's get you back upstairs."

"Please." Sophie shook her head. "I want my husband."

"We can speak privately upstairs," Richard replied.

"Please tell me now."

This must be a nightmare. Any minute, I'll be back in the Jamie's arms, back in our bed.

Nona tried to lead her to the stairs but Sophie refused to budge. Without warning, Richard picked her up, and Sophie let out a squeal. "What are you doing? Let me go!"

"Ma'am, we need to get you back into bed. You're making a scene and upsetting Nona. We'll explain everything once you're settled." Richard moved toward the stairs.

"Mr. Madden, put me down, I can walk by myself." Sophie pushed at his chest. "Jamie is *not* going to be happy with you man-handling me." He didn't comply, so she tried a different tack. "Mr. Madden, please, put me down. Seriously, this is ridiculous."

Reaching the bedroom door, Richard pushed it open with his shoulder. He lowered Sophie onto the massive bed, and the top of her robe popped open. Catching Richard's leer, she grabbed for the quilt to cover herself. As Nona and Michael rushed into the room, Sophie turned a crimson face toward them. "Where is Jamie?"

Nona stood in front of her and settled a hand on Sophie's shoulder. "Sophie, Richard has spent most of the day looking for him. There simply isn't any record of a James William Ford anywhere in the Union Army."

"I told you. He *isn't* a soldier. Where else did you look? Did you check the hospitals? Maybe he's been mugged. Did you check the airport? Maybe he went looking for me there."

"Airport? What's an airport?" Richard asked.

"What do you mean, what's an airport? This dream is really getting lame."

"Lame, dear? Do you have a horse that went lame? Is that how you ended up at the stables? Were you thrown?" Nona asked and then turned to Richard. "You shouldn't be in here, Richard. It's inappropriate."

He gave her a reluctant nod and stepped into the hallway.

These people are out of their minds. Wake up Sophie, WAKE UP.

Taking a deep breath, Sophie fisted her hands in her lap. "Look, something's not right here. No, I did not get thrown from a horse. I'm Sophie Jane Wellington Ford, married to James William Ford." Her voice rose in volume. "I'm twenty-six years old. We've been married for five years. I'm from Portland, Oregon. I need Jamie. *Please.*"

Nona wrung her hands and turned to her husband. "Michael, please, there must be something you can do for her."

"I'll return shortly."

Sophie let Nona wrap her arms around her. "Nona, please, I need Jamie. He can't have just disappeared. *I* can't have just disappeared! I don't understand. I'm supposed to be dead. I should be dead."

"Is it possible your husband died in the war and you're forgetting? Maybe you think it should have been you?"

"He's *not* a soldier. I haven't lost my memory." Sophie swallowed. "And I'm not crazy." Her eyes moved skyward in desperation. "Oh, God, please help me, please, please help me."

Michael returned with his medical bag in hand and moved to her side. "Mrs. Ford, I have something for you that will calm you. I would like you to drink all of this for me, please."

"What is it?" Sophie asked suspiciously.

"Laudanum."

With a frantic shake of her head, Sophie pushed the covers away and threw her legs over the side of the bed. "No. Definitely not laudanum. I don't want to be drugged."

"Mrs. Ford, you need to calm down. You'll give yourself an apoplexy," Michael warned.

Obviously hearing the argument, Richard stepped back in the room and crossed his arms.

"Who are you people? This isn't right."

"What's not right, Mrs. Ford," Richard asked.

She glared at him. "Trying to drug innocent people, man-handling them, and throwing them onto beds."

Richard stalked toward her and leaned down. "Mrs. Ford, you need to get back into bed. The Wades are good people. They are simply trying to help. I would rather not have to hold you down while the doctor forces the medicine down your throat."

Her body leaned away from his threat of its own accord and, cursing her fear, she ground out, "Why are you using your brute strength to hold me against my will? What are you even doing in my bedroom? When Jamie gets here, you're going to have a lot of explaining to do! He's gonna kick your ass."

"Mrs. Ford, I don't have a donkey, but if I did, I don't know why your husband would want to kick it. Perhaps you hit your head a little harder than we originally thought."

"You're the donkey!"

Oh, good one, Sophie. That told him.

"Get back into bed, sit still, and take the medicine Dr. Wade is offering—or I will make you," Richard threatened.

As the tension in the room thickened, Sophie stopped fighting. After downing the bitter laudanum, she drank the water Richard offered, all the while imagining him in a floral dress, lying helplessly as she tied him to railroad tracks and twirled her waxed moustache. The visual made her feel a *little* better.

Nona took Sophie's glass and set it by her bedside. "There's a sweet dear. We'll get you back to sleep and things will look better in the morning. You'll see."

Sophie groaned at the positive pronouncement over the worst predicament she'd ever been in. As the laudanum took effect, her limbs grew heavy and sluggish and her eyelids drooped. She smacked her dry mouth a few times as she watched the doctor and Richard make their way from the room. Sophie barely noticed Nona linger at the bedside for a few minutes before tiptoeing out into the hall.

Sophie heard voices just outside the door but they trailed as the group moved away. She tried to roll onto her side, without much luck. Her body felt like a lead weight. *Why won't my butt follow my shoulders?*

Taking a bigger swing with her leg, she finally ended on her side but realized she wasn't comfortable there either. She rolled onto her back before trying to sit up and climb out of the bed. Inching her body toward the edge of the mattress, she reached her hand out to steady herself on the side table but only managed to knock the glass onto the floor with a loud crash. Before the sound even registered in her cloudy mind, the door opened with a bang. Gasping in fright, she turned toward the light.

"Sophie, dear? What happened?" Nona rushed to her side.

Just before her feet hit the floor, Sophie's dizziness overwhelmed her. A quiet groan escaped her as she swayed toward Nona.

Nona laid her hand on her shoulder. "There is broken glass at your feet. You need to be careful." Nona gave a gentle smile. "Why are you trying to get out of bed? I was certain you were asleep when I left you."

"I have to—that is, well, I need to—" Sophie tried to put aside her humiliation and think through the confusion for the right words.

"I know what you need." Nona pulled out a porcelain bowl from under the bed.

Ugh, chamber pot.

Nona helped to steady Sophie as the laudanum coursed through her system. "I apologize about the primitive chamber pot." Nona patted her back. "I'll have a proper commode moved in here in the morning. I'll send Betty in to pick the glass up, once you're asleep."

Commode. Morning. Yes.

Sophie twirled the words through her cloudy mind. "Thank you."

Nona helped her back into bed before quietly leaving the room. Sophie tried desperately to fight her drug-induced lethargy, but she was unsuccessful.

* * *

Sophie forced her eyes open and grabbed her pounding head. She focused her gaze on the ceiling, and several minutes passed before she realized she was still in the blue room. As she lowered her hands to her sides, her fingers touched the soft fabric of what she assumed was a homemade quilt; the ridges of the stitching rising like tiny hills under her fingertips.

Sitting up carefully to get a better sense of her surroundings, she eased out of the tall bed, made her way over to the window, and pulled the floor-to-ceiling curtain aside. The sun hid behind a mass of dark clouds. However, morning beckoned, and she noticed fresh snow on the ground. Sophie couldn't help but smile. She'd always loved the snow.

Leaning her forehead against the windowpane, she sighed. Her breath left an oval-shaped fog ring on the glass, and she drew a question mark in it with her finger.

What am I going to do? Am I in a coma and this is an hallucination?

Am I dead and in heaven? Maybe it's hell and I am destined to be without Jamie forever.

A quiet knock at the door interrupted her thoughts. She grimaced. "Come in."

"Good morning, dear."

Squeezing her eyes shut for a last, brief second of solitude, Sophie pushed herself away from the window and turned. "Good morning."

"How did you sleep? I didn't want to wake you too early, so I told the staff not to disturb you."

"Thank you." Sophie bit her lip. "I want to apologize for my conduct last night."

"Don't give it another thought. You were overwrought. I'm confident that we will find your Jamie and you'll have some answers." Nona laid mounds of fabric on the bed. "Are you hungry? I can have Betty bring you a tray."

"No, thank you, Nona. I'm not really hungry right now." Sophie turned to look out the window again.

"Dear, you really should eat. You need to get your strength up. My sister, Elizabeth, brought a few dresses and personal things over this morning for you."

Sophie let Nona fuss over her, pleasantly surprised that Elizabeth had provided several gowns that fit her. Uncertain how long it would take her to get used to wearing a corset for extended periods of time—she had a difficult time wearing them with her reenactment costumes—she tried to remember how to breathe without hyperventilating.

The combination Nona chose for Sophie consisted of a deep blue skirt with a simple white bodice. The jacket, a lighter blue, was adorned with piping that matched the skirt. Elizabeth sent ribbons for each of the dresses, and Sophie used one of them to pull her long hair back and tie it securely at her neck.

Sophie forced a smile. "Nona, thank you so much for your kindness."

"It's my pleasure, dear. I know things seem frightening right now, but I hope you will consider my home your home. You are welcome to stay as long as you have need."

"Thank you."

Nona led Sophie downstairs and into the large dining room. The buffet had a simple but abundant breakfast arrangement. Smelling the savory aroma of the sausage, pancakes, and fried potatoes, Sophie filled her plate, her stomach rumbling in anticipation. She avoided the final concoction, a dish that looked positively disgusting. Her stomach rolled as the beady eyes of a fish stared at her from beneath the sauce.

Sophie and Nona were in the dining room for only a few minutes when the butler showed a beautiful, petite woman into the room. Her strawberry-blonde hair framed a heart-shaped face, and wind-blown cheeks illuminated larger-than-life blue eyes. She appeared a younger version of Nona.

"Christine, what are you doing here so early? Weren't you scheduled to be at the hospital today?" Nona stood quickly and made her way over to the woman. She folded her into one of her motherly hugs.

The younger woman removed her winter cloak and gloves to reveal a dark blue skirt. Her matching jacket was buttoned all the way to her throat, and Sophie assumed it was a uniform of some type. She handed her outerwear to the butler hovering behind her and laughed. "A very good morning to you, too, big sister."

"My word, where are my manners?" Nona turned to Sophie. "Sophie, this is my youngest sister, Mrs. Martin. She volunteers at the local hospital, taking care of wounded soldiers." She turned back to her sister. "Christine, this is Sophie Ford. She landed on our doorstep yesterday, for lack of a better word."

"It's a pleasure to meet you." Christine shook Sophie's hand and then turned to her sister. "Liza came by to see Mama and me after she dropped the dresses off to you this morning, so I've heard part of the story. I thought I would call on you and see if you needed anything."

News certainly travels fast around here without the use of cell phones.

"You look lovely in that dress, Mrs. Ford. Much better than Elizabeth would have. Just don't tell her I said that," Christine said.

"Thank you." Sophie fingered the fabric. "Has your sister never worn this?"

Christine chuckled. "No. None of the ones she gave you have been worn."

"Wow—I mean, my goodness."

Nona glanced at the clock on the dining room wall. "Oh, my, look at the time. I must get the menu organized for tomorrow night's soiree. Christine, would you please keep Sophie company while I talk to Cook?"

"Of course." Christine sat at the table and turned to face Sophie with a warm smile.

"Chris—" Sophie wrung her hands. "Um, may I call you Christine?"

"Of course."

"What is this soiree Nona referred to?"

Stirring sugar into a cup of coffee, Christine explained, "We have spent the past week honoring officers who have made it home for a brief sojourn. The soiree will cap it off. Many will leave again in the coming weeks, as new marching orders are being delivered as we speak."

"Oh," Sophie squeaked.

Christine laid her spoon aside and looked at her in concern. "Are you all right, Mrs. Ford? Can I get you something?"

"Um, no, no, I'm fine. I just thought about all those people." Sophie took a deep breath. "I guess it freaked me out a bit."

Christine furrowed her brow. "Freaked you out? What does that mean?"

Sophie internally smacked her hand to her forehead.

"Oh, right, well, it means, kind of scared me." Sophie smoothed her hands across her skirts and then settled them on her lap. "I hope it will be all right to stay in my room with the door locked tomorrow night."

Christine laughed. "Why would you want to do that?"

"I just don't feel up to a party, I suppose."

Christine took a sip of her coffee and set her cup gently in the saucer. "Mrs. Ford, I understand you've lost your husband."

"Please, call me Sophie. And, yes. I have no idea where Jamie is. I'm choosing to think he's misplaced, but everything's a bit of a confusing mess right now."

"Well, let's try and focus on the positive." Christine dropped another sugar cube into her coffee. "Now, let's discuss gowns. I know one in particular that Elizabeth had made. She disliked the color, so never wore it. It would look incredible on you. We'll have Madame Desmarais alter it for you before the party. Elizabeth has influence with her." She added in a conspiring whisper, "She should, with the amount she spends there."

Sophie waved a hand in the air. "Please don't go to any trouble, Christine. The dresses Elizabeth has already provided are beautiful. She has been more than generous."

"Don't be silly, it's our pleasure." Christine set her coffee cup down. "Now, I must get to the hospital. I'll return at three and we'll go down to Madame's together. I'm on my way to pick up a few things from Liza's, so I will also get the dress."

Christine gathered her outerwear and Sophie walked her to the door. "Thank you for spending some time with me."

"My pleasure, Sophie. I'll see you later."

Watching as Christine climbed into her little buggy, Sophie remained in the open doorway as the horse trotted down the long driveway.

CHAPTER FOUR

SOPHIE CLOSED THE door and leaned against it in silence, turning when she heard Nona's familiar footsteps tap over the foyer.
"There you are, dear. Did Christine leave?"
Sophie nodded. "Yes, just now. She said she'll be back at three to take me to Madame something or other?"
"Madame Desmarais. She's a miracle worker with a needle and thread. She makes all of Elizabeth's gowns and believe me, Elizabeth keeps her working day and night."
Sophie smiled. "So I've heard."
"Oh, Sophie, you have such a lovely smile. I look forward to seeing that more often. Now perhaps you should rest before Christine collects you. She can be a bit overwhelming if you're not prepared for her."
Must run in the family.
"Thank you. Do you have a book I might borrow? I'd love to read something."
"Yes. Come with me." Nona led her to their library and when Sophie stepped into the room, she sighed in awe. Three walls had floor-to-ceiling bookshelves; the dark mahogany showcased intricate carving. Two high-backed chairs faced a large, stone fireplace. A hearth raised it three feet off the floor and offered a warm place to rest your feet. This could only be described as her dream room. "This is perfect, Nona. Thank you."
"You're welcome, dear. I'll have Daniel add wood to the fire and you can rest in here, if you like. I'll collect you at three. Richard will be joining us for dinner, so I have requested Elizabeth send over an appropriate gown."
Sophie smiled her thanks and searched for something to read. There were many medical books, which shouldn't have surprised her, and she thought she might be disappointed, until she came across "*Lady Audley's Secret,*" written by Mary Elizabeth Braddon.
Curling up in one of the chairs, she tucked her feet under her and settled in to read. But she found she was unable to concentrate, and the pages swam before her. Turning her head, she stared out the window.

Where are you, Jamie? She felt tears slip down her cheek and wiped them away with the palm of her hand. *Please, God, I need some answers here. As grateful as I am to be healthy, I want my husband back. I think I'd rather be dying with Jamie, than healthy without him.*

With her chin on her palm, she continued to stare out the window.

Almost an hour into her forced rest, Sophie was grateful when she heard the rustle of fabric behind her. "Miss Sophie?"

"Hmm?" Sophie peeked around the high-backed chair.

"Miss Nona says her sister will be here soon."

Sophie stood, lightly running her fingers over the fabric of her skirts to smooth them, and followed Betty out of the room. She arrived in the foyer just as the butler was opening the front entrance door. Thinking Christine had come a few minutes early, Sophie hurried forward to greet her new friend.

She froze mid-stride and felt her face heat with indignation.

Richard Madden handed his hat and gloves to the expectant butler. "Good afternoon, Mrs. Ford. How are you feeling today?"

"I'm fine, thank you, Mr. Madden." Sophie clasped her hands tightly behind her back. "Have you found something out about Jamie? Is that why you're here?"

Before he could answer, Nona bustled into the entryway and greeted Richard with a big smile. "Richard, what a nice surprise."

"Good afternoon, Nona." He gave her a slight bow.

Sophie turned back to Richard. "Mr. Madden was just going to tell me what he found out about my husband."

Richard stood in silence.

"Well? Mr. Madden?" Sophie ground out, a little more pointedly.

Richard turned and spoke directly to Nona. "Is Dr. Wade still here? I thought I'd try to catch him before left for the hospital."

"Or, you could answer my question." Sophie didn't like being a shrew, but this man's arrogance irritated her. Call it a fault of hers, but she always felt the need to put male chauvinists like him in their place. That, and she desperately wanted to know where Jamie was.

"Ma'am, I don't have anything to tell you at present. I really should speak with Dr. Wade before I go any further."

"Have you found him, then? Is he hurt and you don't want to tell me? Is that why you need the doctor? It is, *isn't* it?" Panic bubbled up and threatened to spill over. "Why are we just standing here? Take me to him." She moved toward the front door.

Richard didn't budge.

"Why are you looking at me that way? Take me to Jamie! Please."

Nona let out a quiet sigh. "Sophie, calm down. I'm certain Michael will tell us everything, once he and Richard have a chance to talk."

"Please, Nona. I need to see him." Sophie turned back to Richard. "Where is Jamie? Why are you just standing there?"

Michael rushed in. "Richard, Nona? What is going on here?"

"He won't tell me where Jamie is!" Panic had been replaced with anger, and Sophie turned back to face Richard. "*Please*, Mr. Madden. Where is he? If you don't tell me, I'll make your life a living hell. Do you hear me? *A living hell!*"

She registered, barely, Nona's stifled, "Oh, my!"

"Yes, ma'am, I heard you." Richard made a sweeping motion with his hand. "In fact, I believe the entire countryside heard you."

Sophie was beside herself. "You are the most irritating, arrogant, subspecies of a human being I have ever come across."

"Sophie, I don't think that's particularly fair to Richard. He has been trying to help find your husband, and I think you need to be a bit more appreciative." Nona fluttered to her side and patted her hand.

Sophie took a deep breath in an effort to calm herself. "You're right, Nona, I should apologize." Turning to Richard, Sophie forced a smile. "Mr. Madden, I am sorry for calling you a subspecies of a human being. Now, please tell me what you have found out about my husband."

"What about the irritating, arrogant part?"

"Excuse me?"

Richard smiled. Smug and infuriating. "The irritating, arrogant part. You only apologized for the subspecies human being part."

She clenched her fists at her sides. "I did that because I didn't want to insult any other subspecies. I withdraw my apology. Where is Jamie?"

"Richard, stop torturing the poor girl. Tell us what you have found out," Michael said.

Richard turned his back on Sophie and once again spoke directly to Michael. "A new group of wounded have been brought to the hospital. One of the men resembles the description Mrs. Ford gave me, and I hoped you could have a look at him. He's unconscious and severely wounded."

Or you could speak to me directly and stop pretending I'm not here. She glared at Richard, but kept her thoughts to herself.

Turning to the doctor, Sophie begged, "Please Dr. Wade, you have to take me. I'll be able to tell you if it's Jamie right away."

"His wounds are quite gruesome, Mrs. Ford. I'm not sure it would be a good idea for you to see him like that," Richard interjected.

Sophie continued to seethe. She couldn't help herself, her hand flew to her breast, and she did her best Scarlett O'Hara imitation. "Thank you for your concern, Mr. Madden. I don't know how I'd survive all of this without it." She then turned to Nona. "Please make them take me. If it's Jamie, he's going to need me. I have to be there. I don't want him to wake up alone, wondering what's going on."

Before Nona could respond, a knock at the door interrupted them. Richard reached out and opened it and Christine sailed through, with another woman in tow.

"Well, doesn't this look like a party?" Christine chuckled. She looked around at everyone, and her eyes lit on Richard. "Good afternoon, Richard, what a nice surprise seeing you here."

He gave a slight bow. "Good afternoon, Christine, I hope you are well? Elizabeth, once again a pleasure."

Christine urged Elizabeth forward, towards Sophie. "Sophie, may I introduce our sister, Mrs. Whitman?"

Sophie shook her hand. "It's nice to meet you."

"Nice to meet you, too," Elizabeth said.

"Are you ready for Madame's?" Christine raised her eyebrows in question.

Sophie grabbed her arm. "Will you please take me to the hospital, Christine? Jamie's there and he needs me."

"Ma'am, I'm not certain it is your husband," Richard reiterated.

Sophie bit the inside of her cheek to keep from screaming. "Please stop ma'aming me."

Christine and Elizabeth looked at each other like they had just come into the middle of an intense play and missed the entire first act.

"Please, Christine," Sophie begged.

"Well, of course I will. If your Jamie's there, I'll help you find him," Christine promised.

"Thank you." Relief washed through Sophie. Finally, someone would take her to Jamie.

"The carriage is right outside. We'll stop at the hospital and then go from there to Madame Desmarais'," Elizabeth said.

Sophie could only stare at her. Who could think of shopping when Jamie could be lying, mortally wounded, in a hospital bed?

* * *

When they finally pulled up to the hospital, Sophie shuddered, speechless. This truly was no more than a glorified tent. She had seen photos and read descriptions about what Civil War hospitals were like. She'd been aware tents were often used, but nothing prepared her for the overwhelming sight and smell of blood and dirt. The stench hit her full force, and only by breathing through her mouth was it bearable.

Sophie followed Richard past rows of soldiers in various stages of injuries and consciousness before he paused at a cot in the back corner of the tent. Once Richard stepped aside, Sophie took a deep breath, inched closer to the young man—and nearly passed out. Feeling Richard's firm grip to her elbow, Sophie forced herself to look.

A gash from one side of his forehead to the other didn't appear to have been cleaned and was left open to the air. From what she could see, under the inadequate coverage of another bandage, his right eye appeared to be bulging from its socket. A makeshift binding on his arm barely covered his missing right hand.

Sophie covered her mouth with her fingers. Her heart broke for the young man left to die in the corner of a filthy tent. Richard pulled her into his arms and held her as she wept into his chest, and although the faint scent of alcohol wafted from him, she was too upset to care. "I've lost him. He's gone. How did I get here? What am I going to do without him? I can't *live* without him."

Christine rushed over and pulled her gently away from Richard. "Sophie, it's all right. He's not dead, can you see? He's breathing. Your James is alive. Michael will have a look at him, and we will all take care of him so that he comes back to you quickly. Shhh, Sophie, look. He's alive. You need to believe he's going to be all right."

But he wasn't Jamie. He was someone else's husband, son, brother. Someone else's friend or lover. He wasn't hers.

Her stomach churned at the realization she was somewhere Jamie might never find, and her breath left her body at the thought that they might be lost to each other, without hope. She was in 1863, and he was stuck in the future to mourn her death—or disappearance—or whatever.

Her hand found its way to her chest as her step faltered, and she bent at the waist in agony from the pain. Christine held her steady, and Sophie took a deep, ragged breath. "Christine, it's not Jamie. It's not him. He's truly lost to me. He's gone."

Sophie took the handkerchief Christine offered and wiped away her tears. Christine wrapped her arm firmly around Sophie's waist as she took a deep breath and tried to take a measure of the comfort Christine offered.

Turning, Sophie addressed them all, "Thank you, everyone for bringing me here, and for the patience and kindness you have shown." She took a deep breath. "Christine, would you mind terribly taking me home? I don't feel up to shopping at the moment."

"Of course, Sophie."

Sophie followed the women out of the hospital and into the carriage, although she saw nothing as she slid the curtain aside and stared off into space. She had to figure out what to do from here. In the 1800s, women were vulnerable. Men made the rules and kept women housed and fed. Women didn't work for a living, unless they "worked" for a living and that was something Sophie would never do.

Only God could help her now, and He just *had* to direct her home.

Arriving at the house to find the butler, Daniel, waiting on the porch, Sophie allowed him to assist her from the carriage. She followed everyone inside and absently removed her gloves and bonnet.

"Sophie, let's get you upstairs and then you can rest, all right?" Nona asked.

Sophie nodded and climbed the stairs, grasping the exquisitely carved handrail until her knuckles were white. Christine, Nona, and Elizabeth followed.

"Is there anything I can get for you?" Elizabeth asked.

Sophie shook her head.

"How about some water?"

"No, thank you," Sophie whispered.

"Nona, Elizabeth, why don't the both of you go downstairs and I'll sit with Sophie for a little while. It will give us some time to talk."

As Elizabeth and Nona reluctantly left, Sophie paced the room, chewing on her thumbnail as tears streamed down her face.

"Sophie?"

"Hmm?"

"We will find James."

Without looking up, Sophie shook her head, stalled briefly, and then started to pace again. "We must take care of that young man, Christine."

"We will."

Sophie grabbed her arm, her heart racing with an unnamed fear. Something about this soldier was significant. She didn't know what, couldn't put it into words, but knew she had to do something. "Will you please ask Dr. Wade to take personal care of him. I can't tell you why it's important, because I don't know, to be honest. But it is."

"Of course." Sophie started to pace again, and Christine laid her gloves on the side table. "Is there something else?"

"Like?"

"Something you're not telling me?"

Sophie's head whipped up. "Why would you say that?"

Christine sat slowly in one of the chairs near the fireplace and smiled up at Sophie. "I'm certain I couldn't say."

Sophie watched Christine through narrowed eyes for several seconds, her heart racing as she assessed the woman. "I can't tell you."

"You can't tell me what?"

"I can't tell you that—" A quiet snort escaped and Sophie stalled. "Nice try."

Christine folded her hands in her lap. "Sophie, you can tell me anything."

"Not this." Sophie rubbed her forehead with her palm.

"Why not?"

"I just can't tell you," Sophie stressed.

"Sophie, you can. Will you trust me?"

"Christine, it's far more than you could ever comprehend. You'll never believe me and just think I'm crazy."

"What if I promise to believe you no matter what?"

A groan escaped as Sophie stopped pacing briefly. "You really think you could do that, no matter how farfetched you might think my story is?"

"I really think I could do that, Sophie. Will you try?"

Sophie took a deep breath and said a quick prayer. Squeezing her eyes shut, she turned away from Christine and whispered, "I'm from the future. The year 2007, to be exact."

"I'm sorry?"

Sophie faced her again. "I'm from the future, Christine. I was born in 1981…"

Christine stood with a gasp. "That's impossible."

"I truly wish I was." Sophie took a deep breath and shared her story.

Sophie didn't go into detail about planes or automobiles, but did fill her in on almost everything else. Including her love and knowledge of the current war.

"My word," Christine muttered.

"Yes, my word."

"Can you prove it?"

"I can tell you something that will happen in the future, if that will help."

"Like?"

"Um…An act will be passed called The First Conscription Act. All men aged twenty to forty-five will be drafted into the military. They can pay their way out or find a substitute, but the poor will protest and riots will break out in New York. But that doesn't happen until March." Sophie rubbed her forehead. "There isn't anything significant happening until then, so I can't really prove anything until then."

"Well, perhaps I'll reserve judgment until March."

"Truly?" Sophie kneeled in front of her and took her hand. "Do I see an asylum in my future?"

"It's quite an extraordinary story, Sophie, but I do believe you."

Sophie let out the breath she'd been holding. "You do?"

"Yes. And my instincts will be proven in March, I expect."

Sophie raised an eyebrow. "You're not just saying that so it lulls me into a false sense of security?"

"If I were?" Christine had an evil glint in her eye.

"Men in white coats aren't going to come in the middle of the night and carry me off on a stretcher, are they?"

Christine giggled. "You have quite the imagination. I don't think we should spread this information to the masses but I also don't think you're lying or mad."

Sophie stared at Christine, eyes filling with tears. "Thank you, Christine. You have no idea what this means to me."

"Well, enough of that. I want to know everything that's going to happen with this war. Don't leave out any details." She clapped her hands in excitement.

"I won't—on one condition."

"Anything."

"You cannot tell anyone about the war. I don't think the outcome should be altered."

Christine nodded. "I'll keep your secret, Sophie."

"Also, you must help me find my way home. I have to go back."

* * *

Bernadette Desmarais sat with her husband, Philippe, in their spacious, modern kitchen in Portland, Oregon – present day. "This is not going well," Philippe said as he ran his hands over his beard.

"*Oui,*" Bernadette replied. "But what choice do we have? She's the one."

"He will die without her, *cherie.*"

Bernadette stood and paced. "*Oui.*"

"They must be reunited."

"He was not part of the plan, Philippe."

"I understand that, however, she will waste precious time trying to find her way home. James must join her, or she will be unable to guide the others to stop the threat."

"She is strong."

"*Oui*, however, that strength is not focused where it should be."

Philippe stood and wrapped his arms around his wife. "Imagine living without me. You would not fare so well."

Bernadette playfully slapped his arm. "It is you that would not fare so well without me, husband. Don't forget that."

Philippe chuckled. "You're probably right."

"I'll visit him tomorrow, but at the very least, he goes within the week."

CHAPTER FIVE

"You realize it has been weeks with no word." Pacing the floor, cell phone gripped in his hand, Jamie rubbed his forehead with his other, his voice low and lethal as he spoke to the FBI agent on the other line. "No, she would not have left me. She couldn't leave the room without losing her breath. She would never have made it out of the house, let alone far enough away for me not to find her!"

"Jamie?"

Turning to find Emma standing in the doorway of the library, a frown on her face, he raised his finger and watched while she crossed her arms and leaned against the frame.

"Yes, fine." Jamie snapped his cell phone shut.

"What did they say?"

Bracing his hands behind him as he leaned on the desk, he let out a growl. "What they always say. A whole lot of nothing."

Emma moved further into the room. Her hand reached for him but dropped quickly at his deflection. Jamie didn't want to be comforted. He wanted his wife back.

"I'm sorry," she said.

"Not your fault, Squirt." The peal of the doorbell interrupted any further conversation, and Jamie made his way to the door.

"Hi, Jamie," Chrystal said from the porch.

"Hi. What are you doing here?" He stepped aside. "Come in."

"Thanks. Is Emma here?"

"I'm here," Emma called as she made her way into the foyer. "Sorry, Jamie, I told Chrystal to stop by."

Jamie nodded but didn't comment as the nurse stepped inside.

"I wanted to introduce you to one of our grief counselors. She should be here any minute." Chrystal hugged Emma.

"We don't need grief counseling, Chrystal," Jamie said.

"I asked her to come, Jamie." Emma dropped her head, face red.

He raised an eyebrow. "Why?"

"I think it might help."

Before he could argue, another knock sounded on the door, and Jamie was forced to put aside his opinions. He opened the door, and a tall woman, with dark auburn hair swept up into a simple chignon, lifted her chin as she held her hand out to Jamie. *"Bonjour.* You must be James. My name is Bernadette." Her deep-set blue eyes shone kind and bright.

She spoke with a strong French accent, her voice deeper than expected for a woman. Jamie smiled. The only person who called him James was Sophie—when she was angry with him. "Please come in."

"Merci."

"Also, please, call me Jamie. Nice to meet you." Jamie shook her hand, his eyes drawn to Emma, who appeared contrite. Bernadette's warm, firm grip pulled his focus back to her.

"Jamie. I am here to help."

"Thank you," he said gruffly.

Despite his reservations, Jamie forced himself to sit with the women and, if it were just for Emma, talk about Sophie's disappearance and feign acceptance for her absence. It was ridiculous, but Jamie tried to nod at all the right times and appear to be grateful for their interference. He tried to keep his relief hidden when his phone rang, and he excused himself to take the call.

Sequestering himself in the library, he took another call from the authorities, all the while trying not to punch his fist into a wall. Slamming the phone down, he dropped his face into his hands.

"Jamie?"

Raising his head, he forced a smile. "Sorry, Squirt, the FBI was returning my call. Are the ladies still here?"

"No, they left almost an hour ago. I tried to find you…"

"Sorry," he interrupted.

Emma snorted. "Right. You were hiding, admit it."

"I admit nothing." Jamie smiled.

She raised an eyebrow. "You weren't on the line with the FBI this entire time, were you?"

Jamie shook his head. "No, only part of the time. A courtesy call from the man who's been put in charge. He's investigating a few other disappearances."

"Like Sophie's?"

Jamie nodded but didn't want to elaborate. "You're all dressed up. Are you going out again?"

Emma slid her hands down her hips, across tight-fitting jeans. "Yeah, Hannah and I are going to check out a new club in the Pearl."

"Do you think that's wise? It's the third time this week."

"Um, hel-loh, you're not my father, and it's not like you're in the frame of mind to be good company—" and then, "Oh, Jamie, I'm sorry. I didn't mean it."

Jamie gave her a sad smile. "I know, Emma. We're all under stress. Just be careful, okay? Call me if you need me to pick you up."

"We'll take a cab, but thanks."

Jamie walked her to the door before returning to the library and grabbing a glass and a bottle of Patrón Silver. He climbed the stairs and headed towards his bedroom at the end of the hall, unchanged since Sophie's disappearance.

Stalling at the threshold, eyes scanning the familiar scene, he forced himself to walk inside and inch toward the antique sleigh bed. He set his glass and bottle on the nightstand, and scratched at his beard as he stared into space. Hitting play on his iPod, he lowered himself onto the mattress and buried his face in the soft down of Sophie's pillow. The familiar scent of peach, apricot, and sandalwood, the one distinctively Sophie, invaded his senses as he hugged it to his chest and reverently ran his hands over the satin pillowcase. "I miss you, sweetheart."

An hour and six shots of Tequila later, he stumbled to his closet, wanting to hold something else that smelled like Sophie. He yanked the door open, his seventh drink teetering dangerously at the rim, and watched in horror as Sophie's wedding dress slipped from its hanger and pooled onto the floor. He swore.

"Sophie's gonna kill me." Then, a pathetic laugh, followed by a scowl and the sound of glass shattering against the wall. He stared down at his empty hand, registering he'd thrown the tumbler.

Wiping the splash of liquor from his hands, Jamie reached inside the closet and lifted Sophie's wedding gown from the floor. He fumbled with the hanger in an attempt to get everything put back together. Eyeing his own wedding attire, he reached for it. He held the Union Army uniform at arm's length, her gown forgotten. In homage to his wife's obsession with the War Between the States and her unwavering attention to detail, Jamie had made sure it was period correct to every last element.

Because of Sophie's love of horses, Jamie learned to ride soon after they met. As a surprise for their wedding, he chose to have this cavalry officer's uniform made and relied on Alex to help make it authentic. To this day, he didn't know what Alex said, or did, so that Sophie never caught wind of his plans, but it worked.

Pulling the light blue pants on, he smoothed the yellow stripe down the side, surprised they still fit. His unstable fingers fumbled with the buttons and a growl escaped. "A zipper would have been better," he slurred into the air.

He grasped the silken rope around his neck that held Sophie's engagement ring, anniversary band and a New Zealand bone carving Hannah had given him for his birthday one year, and slipped it into his undershirt. He'd found Sophie's rings the night she'd disappeared, but there was no sign of her wedding band. He took a modicum of comfort knowing that wherever she was, she still wore it, along with the ring that matched his.

His Civil War shirt, although in the style of a nineteenth-century army shirt, was better made and much more comfortable, but the jacket was authentic. Dark blue wool, with nine brass buttons in equal distance down the breastplate. Alex had found antique shoulder boards for a 1st Lieutenant and added them as a little joke.

Jamie asked her at the time why she didn't make him a captain, and Alex had laughed. "Because you don't ride well enough to be a captain."

Buttoning the jacket as he sang along to their favorite Tonic song, Jamie could barely hold back the desperation as he forced memories aside and tried to forget – just for a day. He stared at his reflection in the full-length mirror. Satisfied with his appearance, he grabbed his cavalry hat, the tequila bottle from the nightstand, and stumbled down the stairs and into the library.

He froze. "What the—?"

Turning around, he stared at the railing of his staircase, but when he turned back to the library, he gazed upon a vast field, hazy with smoke, and the smell of gunpowder overwhelming. No hint of Sophie's beloved library remained.

Before he could make sense of anything, excruciating pain spread through his side and then, blackness.

* * *

"Sir? Sir? Can you hear me?" Amelia Powell frantically whispered. "Oh, please, please wake up." She turned toward the house, and called out, "Daddy, come quick, there's a soldier out here."

"Amelia, there's been no fighting around here, how can there be a soldier on the field?" a deep voice bellowed from a distance away.

She let out a quiet huff before calling back, "I understand that, Daddy. Nevertheless, there *is* a soldier lying here and he's bleeding." Amelia turned back to the soldier and tried tapping his cheek again. "Sir. Please wake up."

His eyelids fluttered open and Amelia was taken aback by the dark blue orbs staring at her in confusion. He squeezed his eyes shut again briefly and then grimaced.

"Don't try to move, sir. You appear to have been shot. My father is coming to help. If you would just lie still." He groaned and moved his hand away from his side. Amelia pushed it back. "You need to keep pressure there. Can you tell me your name?"

He licked his lips and frowned. "James."

"What's your last name?"

"Uh..." He shook his head. "I don't know."

Amelia raised her head at the sound of her father's heavy footsteps. "Meely, run and get David and John. We're gonna need to get him into the barn."

"The barn, Daddy? He's a Union soldier. I think we should offer him refuge in the house."

Her father knelt beside James and studied him briefly. "All right, Meely. We'll take him into the house. Now, go fetch David and John."

"Yes, sir." Amelia picked up her skirts and ran for the fields.

There weren't many men left to work their dairy farm. Anyone healthy and willing was fighting, but the Powell's had been lucky enough to gain loyalty from a few of the slaves that Amelia's father had freed years ago.

Many wealthy landowners had begun to free their slaves, but it took a while for her father to agree—truth be told, it took a while for her mother to agree, which in turn, influenced her father's decision. But her brother, Samuel, had been right and her father finally saw the wisdom in his suggestion.

Two of the men chose to stay and work the farm, even after many of the others had joined the Union. Amelia had suspected her brother may have offered them a financial incentive to stay on, but she doubted she would ever know for sure.

She caught sight of them moving the herd from the lower pasture. David was larger than life with an easy manor and quick sense of humor. He stood at least a foot taller than Amelia and had scared her when he'd first come to the farm. That all changed after he'd risked his life to save her from a nasty run-in with an angry bull when she was nine, and now she viewed him as her own personal protector.

John had been raised on the Powell farm, and he and Amelia had played as children. He was two years her senior and as Amelia blossomed into a beautiful young woman, her mother forced him to keep his distance. Amelia had defied her at every chance. She considered John one of her very closest friends, and she'd been his shoulder to cry on when the girl he'd loved had been forced to follow her family after they were freed. Amelia had secretly taught him to read and write, something her mother would have surely stopped if she'd ever found out.

"David, John, come quick. There's a wounded soldier up near the house. Daddy needs him brought inside."

John waved back and the two men came running. David removed his hat and gave Amelia a warm smile. "Where's he at, missus?"

"In the back paddock, just past the garden."

Amelia led them to where her father knelt over James. It appeared he was speaking to him, but Amelia couldn't figure out if the soldier was answering.

Mr. Powell raised his head. "Oh, good. Move him into the south guestroom upstairs, and then one of you go for the doctor."

"Yessuh," David responded. He and John picked him up and did as they were instructed.

Amelia followed them inside and heard the sputtering of her mother from behind David. "What do you think you're doing with that man?"

"Mama, he's a wounded soldier. Daddy told them to take him up to the south room."

"Oh, for goodness sake." Her mother waved her hands towards the stairs. "Make it quick, then."

"Yes'm," they mumbled and hurried up the stairs.

When Amelia tried to follow, her mother grabbed her arm. "You will not be alone with them."

"Mama, he needs help."

"Young lady, you're barely sixteen. You may not go into a room alone with a man and two Negroes. What would people think?"

Amelia wanted to scream. "That I'm a good Samaritan, and willing to help a soldier who has obviously put his life on the line for our Union."

Her mother huffed. "Well, you'll wait until the doctor has seen him and then you'll let Della tend to him. John may assist…he is her son after all."

Amelia lowered her head. "Yes, mama."

CHAPTER SIX

CHRISTINE WAS A willing hostage for well over two hours as Sophie regaled her with stories of the future. "Do you think you could help me find my way back?"

"I have no idea where to begin," Christine said.

"Perhaps where Nona found me?" Sophie widened her eyes in hope. "By the stables?"

A knock at the door interrupted their conversation and brought Nona, followed by Betty and another servant, laden with trays. Sophie and Christine moved to help with the food.

"You both missed dinner."

"Thank you," Sophie said. "This is very thoughtful."

Nona ushered the servants from the room and then turned to Sophie. "I'll leave the tray. You should eat and then rest. You've had a very emotional day."

Sophie nodded and then Nona left the girls alone again. Christine prepared two plates and, with a sigh, Sophie forced herself to choke down a few bites of chicken and fruit.

"Tell me more about Jamie." Christine wiped her mouth with her napkin.

Sophie's heart warmed as her thoughts wandered to her husband, and she couldn't help but smile. "He's the most amazing man."

"How did you meet?"

"We met at a college function. He was singing, and I was instantly lost."

"He sings?" Christine asked.

"Yes, incredibly. We used to sing together, actually."

"I'd love to accompany you on the piano sometime."

Sophie grinned. "I would like that."

"Sorry, I've veered from our topic. Please, continue." Christine sipped her drink.

"Well, Jamie took me bowling on our first date."

"What is first date?"

"A first date." Sophie chuckled. "I suppose it would be similar to a ride in the park, or a private dinner, once courtship has been offered." Christine nodded, so Sophie continued, "It was *the* perfect date. Especially when we said good night."

Christine raised an eyebrow in question.

"I was beyond excited because he'd asked me out again, and we had plans to see a local band the next night."

"What is a band?"

"Right. Um, a performance with musicians. People pay to see musicians perform, but we don't dance to the music—well, not the way you do in this century."

"You can explain that another time."

"Thank you." Sophie smiled.

"So, after you said good night, what happened?"

Sophie's hand found its way to her chest. "I had just closed and locked my apartment door when I heard a knock." Sophie blinked back tears as the moment came rushing back. "I opened the door and suddenly he was there, arm around my waist, and a hand stroking my cheek as he kissed me."

"The scoundrel!"

Sophie sat forward. "No, no, he wasn't. He was the perfect gentleman. It's just different in my time."

"How different?"

"It's hard to explain. Sex before marriage is acceptable, even expected, so Jamie and I were considered strange."

"What do you mean?"

"Well, we chose to wait until marriage to consummate our relationship."

"As it should be," Christine said.

Sophie smiled at Christine's pursed mouth and blushed cheeks. Her expression was reminiscent of Jamie's very proper, very Baptist, grandmother. "Is this too much information?"

"No, just unfamiliar. I've never witnessed affection between a man and a woman, and we certainly don't discuss it. Please, continue."

Sophie chuckled sadly. "Jamie's kiss was amazing. I had never been kissed like that before and, believe me, he never disappointed in that regard. Even five years later, his kisses can make my legs weak."

A quiet squeal brought Sophie's eyes back to Christine, who was bright red and fanning her face with her hand. "Oh, my, my."

"Sorry, Christine, I've talked your ear off."

"Nonsense. It's refreshing."

Sophie laughed out loud. "I can see how refreshed you are. Your face is beet red."

Christine cleared her throat. "Well, we'll just need to find a way for you to move on."

"No, Christine, you don't understand. I *can't* live without him. I am his Ten-Cow woman."

"He called you a cow?"

Sophie nodded. "Reverently."

Christine settled her head against the chair as Sophie shared the fable.

"There is a story of a farmer with three daughters. One was fair-haired and lovely, and her hand in marriage was exchanged for a high price of seven cows, eight chickens, and five pigs. His second born was equally pretty as the first, but her hand came for far less a price at five cows. Then the youngest, a quiet young maiden, not particularly pretty, but sweet. The old farmer feared his youngest daughter would never marry and he'd be stuck with her. So he set her price at one cow and the runt of a sow's litter."

Christine wrinkled her nose. "She sounds positively homely."

Sophie chuckled. "One day, a young man came to the farmer and told him he had fallen in love with his youngest daughter and he would do anything to marry her. The farmer informed him of the bride price and the suitor left without comment. A year went by, and although both his other daughters had married, his youngest remained at home, pining for her young man."

"You'd think she would have married someone else by then."

Sophie raised an eyebrow. "Is romance lost on you, then?"

Christine lifted her cup to her mouth. "Sorry, continue."

"Anyway, the farmer and his wife weren't sure how they were going to break it to their daughter that, obviously, her young man just didn't feel she was worth the one cow and piglet. When the maiden had lost all hope, her young man came. With ten cows in tow. He'd also brought with him, three goats, six pigs, and twenty chickens. The girl's father met him at the door, and the young man said, 'I believe you have highly undervalued your daughter. Here are ten cows, which is what I believe she is worth.'"

Tears slipped down Christine's cheeks, and she pulled a handkerchief from her cuff to wipe them away. "My word, Sophie. How romantic."

"I know. I feel sometimes I take that for granted." Sophie frowned. "His love for me is overwhelming at times."

"I also lost my husband."

Sophie gasped. "You did? Oh, Christine! I'm so sorry."

Christine held a hand up. "I'm only telling you because I'm proof that life will go on."

"How did he die?"

"He was killed at Shiloh."

"April 1862," Sophie whispered.

Christine's eyes widened. "Yes, that's right."

Sophie gathered her dishes and set them on the bureau as Christine continued her story.

"A wonderful man, handsome and kind. Peter became my world. We were married for three years before the war started, and when it did, I truly thought it would be over quickly and he would come back to me. My brother, Andrew, was his closest friend, and they decided to join together." Christine got a faraway look on her face. "Such a difficult time." With a sad smile, she faced Sophie again. "Our little girl, Eleanor, had just died from influenza. She was only two years old and the grief was overwhelming. I think Peter tried to forget, so when the opportunity came to join the Union, he jumped at it."

"That makes sense," Sophie said as she turned from the bureau to face Christine.

"A few days after the battle at Shiloh, I volunteered at the hospital and received word that Andrew made it to Charleston, despite severe wounds. I convinced Michael to travel to him, and harder still, persuaded him to take me. I was still quite surprised we were even notified."

"How did they know about him, or for that matter, you?"

"Andrew and Peter purchased disks they wore around their necks. They had their personal information engraved on them. We had never heard of anything like that before but were grateful."

The first dog tags.

Sophie leaned forward. "What happened?"

"They brought my brother in unconscious, his face badly bloodied and shrapnel in both his knees. Apparently, he'd escaped a group of Confederates who captured several of his unit. He stole a horse and made it to safety."

Sophie gasped. "Incredible."

"Or, stupid." Christine clasped her hands in her lap. "Andrew remained unconscious for several days after we arrived, but when he woke, it fell to him to tell me Peter had been killed. Andrew told me that as he rushed to Peter's side, a canon ball exploded in front of him, and his legs were so damaged, he couldn't move fast enough to get to Peter. Andrew still feels guilty about it. The physical limitations from his injuries are a constant reminder. He also has some scarring on his face and walks with a limp."

"How sad," Sophie whispered.

"Oh, there's nothing sad about my brother. He's the strongest man I know."

"What happened to Peter?"

"All I have is a letter and medallion that Andrew managed to grab. I had to say goodbye to a ghost."

"Christine," Sophie said sadly.

"My only regret is that we didn't have any other children. When Ellie died, the thought of getting pregnant and losing another baby was just too much. I have a marker for Peter next to Ellie's grave on the little hill, overlooking Mama's house."

Sophie and Christine sat in silence for several minutes and then Christine stood. "I should take my leave."

Sophie stood as well. "Thanks again for the great talk."

Christine smiled. "Try to get some untroubled sleep. You deserve a reprieve."

"If I can find a way back to Jamie, that just might happen."

"We'll try tomorrow."

"Thank you."

Sophie changed and climbed into bed. Her head spun with too much information, her heart beat with too much emotion. As she closed her eyes and forced herself to think of happier times, she melted into the memory of Jamie.

* * *

"Good morning, Miss Sophie. Time to rise and shine." Betty opened the drapes, waking her later than usual to help her dress.

Do they make everyone chipper in this century?

"Good morning, Betty."

Nona poked her head in. "Good morning, dear, did you sleep well?"

"Like a baby."

"Oh that's wonderful." Nona smiled. "Would you like to join me for breakfast?"

"Yes, Nona, breakfast would be lovely."

Sophie finished dressing and then followed Nona, who appeared to be in a fine frenzy this morning, downstairs. They ate a quick breakfast, then Nona dragged her along for what she called her morning constitutional.

A tour of the grounds revealed an expanse of land Sophie had never experienced, and she wondered how long someone could be lost on their property before they were found. Nona explained that Richard Madden shared a certain section of acreage and Sophie listened distractedly. At that precise moment, he appeared before them, sitting on a beautiful Thoroughbred gelding, no less.

"Good morning, ladies. What a pleasant surprise seeing both of you here."

Sophie ignored him.

"Good morning, Richard. I'm showing Mrs. Ford the grounds. I thought she might like a brisk walk to start the day. Are you off to the hospital?" Nona enquired.

"Not right this minute, but I'll be meeting Michael there later to check on a few of my men," he replied as he continued to stare at Sophie, who covertly observed him as he conversed with Nona.

He wore a tan pair of breeches, a basic white shirt, and nicely tailored jacket. His hat was tilted slightly over his eyes and she couldn't help but notice strong hands outlined beneath soft, kid gloves. Since he didn't make an effort to speak directly to her, Sophie chose to stay quiet. She didn't particularly like him, and every time she opened her mouth in his presence, she said something unpleasant.

Once Richard finally rode away, Nona and Sophie made their way back to the house. It was past time for lunch and there was still a lot to do before the party. Sophie, emotions still raw from the day before, tried to figure a gracious way out of the event but had no luck coming up with a viable plan.

Michael surprised them by joining them for a late lunch and just as the three of them were finishing up, the butler showed Christine and Elizabeth into the dining room.

"Good afternoon, family."

Both women wore smiles from ear to ear.

"What are you up to, Teeny?" Suspicion hovered in Nona's voice.

"Whatever do you mean, Nona?" Christine feigned innocence. "I'm not up to anything."

Nona's eyebrows puckered. "Well, my dears, I don't have time to figure out exactly what you two are up to, as I have a party to plan. Just try not to make a mess. That's all I ask."

"Us?" Elizabeth and Christine said, in unison.

Christine grabbed Sophie's hand and pulled her from the dining room. Elizabeth seemed as giddy as a teenager. Sophie was intrigued and slightly worried at the same time.

"What *are* you two up to?" Sophie asked as they entered her bedroom.

"Nothing, really. Trust us," Elizabeth replied.

"Famous last words, as they say."

"Who says?"

"Never mind." Sophie pulled Christine aside. "We're supposed to look for that place, remember?"

"I have already been there, without luck. However, we haven't much time to prepare for the party. We'll look again tomorrow."

Sophie sighed in frustration but didn't feel as though she had much choice, and nodded her agreement. Christine had Betty prepare a tub for Sophie and poured scented oil into the water just as Elizabeth came into the room carrying a load of packages.

"What have you got there?" Sophie asked.

"A surprise. Now climb into the tub like a good girl and stop asking questions. All will be revealed in due time."

Sophie felt a bit squeamish about undressing in front of virtual strangers, but they turned their backs and waited for her to get into the tub. The water covered every inch of her and she decided her momentary exhibition was well worth her embarrassment. She hadn't had a proper bath since her arrival, and this was heaven.

The girls helped Sophie wash her hair. There was so much of it, after all, it took the three of them to manage it. Faster than Sophie would have liked, Christine held up a huge towel for Sophie, and she stood reluctantly and stepped out of the tub, before sitting in front of the fire so that Elizabeth could style her hair.

The girls had a blast. They talked and giggled like teenagers and Sophie felt like she had two new sisters. She just wished Emma could be here to join in the fun. She would love Christine and Elizabeth.

Sophie took a deep breath. For whatever reason, she was now in 1863, preparing for a night of fun without Jamie. She thought it strange how she started to comprehend all of this from that first moment of true pain, when she saw the soldier that wasn't Jamie, and now she was in the midst of an intense moment of pleasure that couldn't be dismissed.

Once Elizabeth was done with Sophie's hair, Christine opened the package on the bed and pulled out the most exquisite ball gown Sophie had ever seen. Burnished copper silk caught the light from the fireplace as Christine shook the skirts out and Sophie was in awe – until Christine held up the bodice. With a low neckline and what appeared to be a very tiny waist, Sophie let out a nervous giggle. "I can't honestly see how that will ever fit me."

Christine smiled. "That is why we have this."

When she held up the corset, Sophie groaned. Wrapping the contraption around her waist, Christine tightened it, and Sophie declared she was more evil than Betty, once the deed was done. The girls helped Sophie get into the dress and then pulled out the matching slippers.

Elizabeth led her to the full-length mirror and Sophie didn't recognize herself. The bodice came to a point over the full hoop skirt, and was off the shoulder, with short sleeves. She giggled a little when she looked at her cleavage, spilling over the top of the dress. She and Emma always called cleavage, 'Cleveland.' Her mother was a bit embarrassed about discussing breasts with them and made up the nickname.

Well, mom, this is Cleveland, Columbus, Cincinnati, and all surrounding areas.

Elizabeth created a masterpiece with Sophie's hair as she wove copper ribbon in and out of her curls. Sophie knew Elizabeth wasn't sure what do to with the front of her hair, since unlike women in the Civil War period, Sophie had bangs. Elizabeth ended up sweeping them to the side and it created such a soft effect around Sophie's face, she felt somewhat ethereal. She was too afraid to move.

How would everything stay like this without Aqua Net?

Elizabeth and Christine had brought their gowns over to join in the fun of them all getting ready together, so Sophie helped them dress. Elizabeth's hair was a deep, rich, auburn and perfectly straight. Women in the twenty-first century would have been envious. She chose an emerald green velvet dress, with matching satin slippers, and was also well endowed, so Sophie didn't feel as self-conscious, since Elizabeth seemed to be spilling out of her dress too.

Christine's periwinkle blue satin gown complemented her strawberry-blonde hair and the dress fit her to a T. However, she didn't appear to be spilling out anywhere, which seemed a bit unfair to Sophie.

There was a knock at Sophie's door and Nona poked her head in. "Elizabeth, Adam is here. Are you ready?" And then, "Oh girls, you all look beautiful."

"You do too, Nona," Sophie said.

Nona wore an ivory gown with blue flowers embroidered around the neckline and hem. Her dark strawberry blonde hair was pulled up into a simple style, with matching blue ribbon woven into her chignon.

Sophie's heart raced with excitement, despite her earlier reservations. *What woman didn't like a good occasion to get dressed up for? It's always fun, especially when you have girlfriends to share in the night.* She froze, suddenly terrified.

She couldn't dance. She had tried to learn for the reenactments but was hopeless. Two left feet and all that. The team would give her some other responsibility when it came to demonstrate the old dances. What was she going to do? Would she be expected to dance? Now she really did just want to shut the door and lock out the world.

"Sophie, what's amiss?"

"Will I have to dance? I'm really bad at it. I have two left feet and I'm always tripping over my partner's feet, or stepping on his toes. Seriously, I suck at it."

"Suck? What does sucking have to do with dancing I wonder?" Nona asked.

Christine nodded toward the door. "Nona, we'll meet you downstairs in a few minutes."

Nona followed Elizabeth out of the room and gave the girls a few minutes of privacy.

"Sophie, don't concern yourself. You won't have to dance. I don't typically like to dance at these functions either. It's just not the same without Peter. You can be my partner tonight and we will both refrain from any dancing."

"Thanks, Christine, I really appreciate it." Sophie took a deep breath. "I think I'm ready now. Are you ready?"

"I'm ready."

"All righty, then. Let's hit it!"

Christine frowned. "Why do we need to hit anything, Sophie?"

"Never mind. Let's join the party."

CHAPTER SEVEN

SOPHIE, DEEP IN conversation with Christine as they descended the stairs, hadn't noticed anyone yet, however, when she raised her head, she frowned. Consciously forcing the scowl away, she replaced it with what she hoped was a serene smile, as Richard made his way toward her.

"Good evening, Mrs. Ford."

Sophie dipped her head in response.

"Christine, you look stunning." He took Christine's hand and gallantly bowed over it.

"Thank you, Richard."

Sophie followed Christine to where Michael and Nona stood. They greeted a handsome young man with red hair reminiscent of Christine, and Sophie knew he must be Andrew. He stood next to a woman, an older version of Nona, so she could only be their mother. Andrew turned, leaning on an ornately carved cane, and welcomed the girls with a huge smile.

"Teeny, how are you?" He grabbed Christine and chastely kissed her on the cheek. Andrew then turned toward Sophie. "This must be Mrs. Ford. How are you handling my sisters?" Leaning down, he added in a whisper, "They are notorious for being bossy, so please don't let them push you around." Taking her hand, he kissed it gently, and Sophie loved him instantly.

"I'm holding my own, thank you for asking. And please call me Sophie."

Andrew reminded her of Lucas and her heart caught at the memory of her husband's closest friend. The goofy class clown, always up for a good time and ready to play practical jokes on anyone within a five-mile radius.

"Sophie, this is our mother, Miriam." Christine greeted her mother with a kiss on her cheek and then turned back to her brother. "Andrew, thank you for collecting Mama. I knew she wouldn't get back from her afternoon tea with Martha before I needed to be here."

"I'm not dead, dear," Miriam admonished, and Sophie caught the siblings' silent amusement.

The group walked through the foyer and down a long hallway. Sophie had only been as far as the library and was surprised at how long it took to get to their destination. The hallway fanned open to reveal another foyer of sorts, and Sophie tried to stay silent as she took it all in.

Marble tile, alternating black and white, covered the floor. A wide stairway hugged the west wall and led to a u-shaped balcony jutting out from the upper landing. Two large doors on the opposite side of the stairway, and well over eight feet tall, were open, and music wafted from the interior. Sophie was swept with the group into the room and stood momentarily in shock.

Standing on a large landing, she surveyed the room. Easily able to hold a hundred couples, it was exquisitely decorated. The woodwork ornate, but not overly so, complemented the light blues and golds on the walls. Alcoves had been built strategically around the room in order to provide a modicum of privacy or rest, if guests needed.

A crush of people in beautiful costumes danced below, laughing in celebration of the soldiers risking their lives for the cause. Some of them would never fully grasp that risk. This was Sophie's happy place, a room full of Union soldiers and beautiful women. The music, louder than Sophie would have expected without a PA system, showcased a group of highly talented musicians. Jamie would fit right in.

Christine distracted her by taking her arm and didn't leave her side all night, both of them managing to avoid the dancing. Andrew was their ever-present escort and introduced Sophie to everyone at the party, while acting the perfect gentleman. Christine was also a wealth of information, having met many of the men through her work at the hospital. She assisted Sophie with a few of the more personal introductions.

Sophie survived dinner and enjoyed the speeches honoring the men who were so bravely fighting the Union's cause. She wished there was a way to warn them all of what lay ahead, but she knew it would be futile.

An hour into the celebration, Sophie began to relax. Unsure how much of it was the wine, she decided not to analyze it too closely, relieved that, for just this one moment, she didn't feel as though the world was closing in on her.

She stood off to the side to get a brief moment alone and gather her thoughts, when all of a sudden a glass of champagne appeared in front of her. Believing it was Andrew, she turned to thank him, a huge smile on her face. Her smile fell. "Have you slipped laudanum in this drink, Mr. Madden?"

"Sophie," he whispered.

"Mrs. Ford to you." She handed him back the glass and started to walk away from him. Richard stopped her by gently taking her arm. "Let me go. Now."

"I have acted badly, and I want to apologize."

She glanced at his hand. "I smell something harder than champagne on you. Perhaps that has loosened your behavior."

He dropped his hand and gave her a slight bow.

Christine made her way over to them, a concerned look on her face. "Richard," she said with a warning voice.

Andrew also joined them, placing a hand on Sophie's elbow. "Sophie, have you met the Quinn family? Douglas and I served at Shiloh together. He and his wife Gretchen are right over here."

Turning to him, Sophie smiled her deepest smile. The one Jamie said could bring a man to his knees. "Why, no, Andrew. I don't believe I have. I would appreciate the introduction."

Taking his arm, she turned her back, quite pointedly, on Richard, and heard Christine admonish him as she walked away. "Richard, what are you doing?"

Richard took a deep breath. "I was trying to apologize. Please forgive me."

* * *

The party wound down a little after midnight. Despite the small hiccup with Richard Madden, Sophie felt energized and could honestly say she'd had a wonderful time. Michael and Nona said farewell to a few of the stragglers at the front door. Elizabeth and Adam stood with them.

"Andrew, thank you for being my ever-gallant escort. I couldn't have made it through the night without you," Sophie said.

Andrew beamed. He took her hand and bowed over it as he placed his lips gently on her fingers. "It was my pleasure, Sophie." He kissed his sisters and then gathered up his mother, leaving behind the last set of guests.

Sophie laid her hand on Elizabeth's arm and smiled. "Elizabeth, thank you so much for this incredible dress. I don't know how I can ever repay you. It is exquisite."

"I believe it's you that made it exquisite. I'm so glad it got some use, it would have sat at the bottom of my wardrobe otherwise. In fact, I believe I may have a few more I can donate."

"Elizabeth, I couldn't. You've been so generous already."

"Nonsense, Sophie, it would be my pleasure." Addressing the group, Elizabeth said, "I think Adam and I are going to make our way home. I wonder if the children have given the nanny an apoplexy yet."

Adam chuckled behind her and the family said their good-byes. Christine decided to stay behind and help Sophie with her dress, so the girls hugged Nona, said goodnight to Michael and then made their way upstairs.

Entering her bedroom, Sophie froze, hand flying to her chest as her face grew warm. The orange glow from the fireplace enfolded her as she moved closer to the bed. The shadowing on the walls from the lit sconces reminded her of the power outage that hit her neighborhood during her first Christmas with Jamie.

"What's amiss?"

Sophie smiled. "Oh. Nothing, just memories."

"Good ones, it would seem."

"Most definitely." Sophie walked the room, taking everything in as Christine stood quietly. After a few minutes, Sophie shook herself from her fog and let Christine help her with her clothing.

Once Sophie's corset and gown were removed, Christine made her way out of the room. Pausing at the doorway, she smiled. "I'll be in the guestroom down the hall if you need me."

"Thanks." Sophie climbed in between warmed, soft sheets.

* * *

Richard Madden sat in his office, staring at the dark amber liquid beckoning to him from behind the glass. Memories slammed through his mind, despite his earlier attempts to vanquish them, but the Wades served nothing stronger than champagne, and that just wasn't doing the job. Wrapping his long fingers around the neck of the bottle, he stood and made his way to his bedroom. Sleep would not elude him tonight. Removing his clothes between swigs of whiskey, Richard stumbled into bed and closed his eyes. Sleep came, however, not without dreams.

"Richard!"

Turning, he saw sandy blonde curls bouncing as his sister skipped toward him and threw herself into his arms. "Hello, Lillian."

Memories of fifteen years ago rushed back. Caught between little girl and little lady, his ten-year-old sister was his complete joy. Never without a smile, especially for him, she worshiped him. "You're home early."

"I am. Did you miss me?"

Lillian nodded. "So much. Mama's been sick, did you know?"

Richard frowned. His mother was never sick. "No, little bean. I didn't. Let's find her, shall we?"

Slipping her tiny hand into his, she pulled him back. "No, we can't."

"Why not?"

"We will get sick."

Richard's heart raced. "We will?"

"Yes, Mrs. Johanson died already."

"Son."

Richard turned at the sound of his father's voice. "Mother's sick?"

"Yes."

Richard stepped onto the porch and followed his father inside. "What is it?"

"Typhoid. She's not going to live."

"I must see her."

Before his father could answer, they heard a call from upstairs. "Mr. Madden!"

His mother was gone. Less than two weeks later, his father met the same fate and Lillian lay in bed, fever ravaging her tiny body. Clayton had returned from school for their mother's funeral and stayed for their father's, and now the young men were forced to wait for their sister's. Richard sat vigil at Lillian's bedside as Clayton paced the tiny room.

"Dickie," Lillian rasped.

"I'm here, little bean."

"I am too, love." Clayton sat on the opposite side of her.

Lillian handed each of her brothers one of her ribbons.

"What's this, sweet?" Clayton asked.

"Please keep them and remember me."

Richard choked back tears as he nodded and took one from her.

"When you lay me in the box, will you put Lucy in with me," she asked, referring to the rag doll she was holding. "I don't want to be by myself."

"Lilly," Richard whispered. "Of course we will. Don't be afraid."
They were well past the hope that she might recover.
"Clay?"
"Yes, love, I'm here." Richard watched his fifteen-year-old brother gently lift their sister's hand and lay her palm against his cheek. He'd grown up so much in the past few weeks; they'd both been forced to.
"Tell Rosie not to cry for me and that she should stay away until this is done. I would hate for her to get sick." Rose Johanson was Lillian's best friend and had been sent away as soon as the threat had started.
"I will," Clayton whispered.
"I'm really cold."
Richard gathered her into his arms and held her against his chest. "Is this better?"
She never said another word.

* * *

Richard woke with a start and swore. Sitting up, he reached for the bottle and drank deeply, before climbing out of bed and making his way to his bureau. Sliding open the top drawer, he noticed the ribbon still sat on top of his pocket watch, and he pulled it out and lifted it lovingly to his lips. Tears streamed down his face as he let it slip through his fingers back to its hiding place. As he turned back to the bed, anger overwhelmed him.

Once they buried their sister, Richard and Clayton sold everything off, freed the slaves that hadn't already purchased their freedom, and made their way to Pennsylvania. Away from the south, away from the memories. In the midst of making their new life, Clayton found God and Richard found rage—and whiskey.

Richard pulled his pants on, grabbed the bottle, and stumbled down the stairs back to his office. He stayed there, barely lucid, until the sun rose.

CHAPTER EIGHT

SOPHIE WOKE IN a cloud. *Too much champagne, I think.*

Easing her way out of bed, she made her way to the corner of the room and, as promised, Nona had moved what she considered to be a modern commode into the room. It looked like a dining room chair with arms, but when Sophie lifted the hidden lid, she stared down at the porcelain bowl nestled inside.

Still, seriously gross.

She heard Christine speaking with Betty outside her door, and then a quiet knock.

"Come in."

"Good morning, Sophie, how are you feeling after the late night?" Christine asked.

"A little groggy but otherwise fine. How about you? What time is it?"

"Nine o'clock. Is there anything you'd like to do? I'm not scheduled to volunteer today, so I can show you around if you like."

Sophie slipped a wayward lock behind her ear. "You know what I would really love to do?"

"What's that?"

"Ride. I haven't ridden a horse in a really long time, and since Nona and Michael's stables are full of beautiful equine flesh, it seems a shame not to."

Christine nodded with a smile. "I'll have our groom saddle them for us. I think Elizabeth put a riding habit in the pile of clothes she brought over yesterday for you."

Locating the habit in the bottom of the wardrobe, Christine helped Sophie dress. The girls made their way out to the stables. As they rounded the corner, Sophie froze.

Dang it! Sidesaddle. How did I forget about sidesaddle? Of course, women in the nineteenth century wouldn't ride any other way. How am I going to get out of this one?

Sophie was a proficient rider, having won several ribbons in competition, but she'd never tried sidesaddle before.

"Is anything amiss?"

"I have never ridden sidesaddle," Sophie whispered.

Christine frowned. "I thought you were experienced."

"I am. However, I ride astride."

Christine let out a quiet gasp. "Well, you cannot ride that way here."

"I'm aware of that." They stood for a few minutes, Sophie's mind racing with what to do, her need to ride superseding her trepidation of a new saddle. "How hard can it really be?"

"I have never ridden any other way, so I can't answer that," Christine admitted.

Sophie shrugged. "Well, I need to ride. It's been too long."

Christine led her to where a groom stood with their awaiting horses. Christine mounted from the mounting block first and then the groom led Sophie's horse over so that she could climb on. Standing next to a magnificent chestnut gelding, her palms sweating and heart racing, Sophie slid onto the saddle, hooked her leg over the pommel, and arranged her riding skirts as the groom held her stirrup. Taking a deep breath, she slipped her foot in and then took up her reins.

"Are you ready?" Christine asked.

Sophie nodded. "As ready as I'll ever be."

They took it slow, riding leisurely over the vast countryside, Sophie in awe of a land that could very well soon be ravaged by an unfinished war.

She felt free. To Sophie, there was nothing like the elation she felt when riding. The troubles of the world just seemed to disappear when she was on the back of a horse. She decided she wanted to go a little faster but without "thigh power," she wasn't completely sure how to get the horse moving. She gave it a good swift kick and nothing happened, so used the crop to get him moving from the other side.

Bad idea.

All she could think about as the landscape flew by, was *how the heck do I stop this thing?* She pulled on the reins, but that didn't work, and she didn't want to cut the horse's mouth up with the bit. She couldn't place her rear in the right position without the use of both of her legs to stop him, so she just hung on for dear life and hoped the horse would eventually tire.

Hearing pounding hooves behind her, and hoping she hadn't scared Christine's horse, Sophie gasped when a very strong arm grabbed around her middle, and she was pulled onto someone's lap. Looking back, concerned for the horse, she let out a sigh of relief when she saw him slow down and turn back toward the group, reins dragging on the ground.

Once both horses had stopped, the strong arms gently lowered her to the ground, and she looked up. Into the face of Richard Madden.

Of course.

She really shouldn't be surprised.

Christine rushed up, her horse panting with the exertion used to try and catch her. She quickly dismounted and came over to check on Sophie. "Are you all right, Sophie?"

"Yes, I think so. I'm really sorry if I scared you." She smiled at Richard. "Thank you so much for your help."

"What did you think you were doing, if you didn't know how to ride?" Richard snapped. "Samson is a difficult horse and you had no business riding him."

Sophie's hackles rose. "I *can* ride Mr. Madden, I'm simply unaccustomed to a side-saddle."

"A proper lady wouldn't ride any other way."

"Well, then I suppose I'm not a proper lady," she snapped. "Not to mention, Mr. Madden, if you truly thought I was, you wouldn't continue to manhandle me at every turn."

Richard smiled slowly, a little like a shark, and stared, fixated on her chest. Glancing down, Sophie noticed the bodice of her habit, slightly askew and missing a button. She couldn't stop the blush stealing her cheeks as she attempted to fix her clothing.

"Mrs. Ford, perhaps you might want to take a few riding lessons to help you feel more comfortable on a horse. If you'd like, I would be happy to oblige."

The muscles in Sophie's shoulders crawled, and she felt as though steam would escape from her head like a cartoon character as she fisted her hands at her side in an attempt not to hit the man. "I bet you would, Mr. I'm-a-Big-Man-and-I-Need-to-Save-the-Poor-Weak-Women-of-the-World. Well, you know what? You can just take a flying leap off a very high—"

"What Sophie means, Richard," Christine laid a hand on her arm, "is that she is very grateful you came along in the nick of time. I'm certain that thank you is on the tip of her tongue, isn't it, Sophie?"

Sophie's unladylike grunt received admonishment from Christine in the form of raised eyebrows.

"Well, Mrs. Ford, the offer stands if you would like instruction in the equestrian arts. I'm available on most Tuesday and Thursday afternoons and would be happy to assist."

At his continued appraisal of her chest, Sophie turned her back on him and stomped back towards the Wades house.

"Mrs. Ford?" Richard called.

"What?" Sophie snapped but didn't break stride.

"I believe you have forgotten your horse, ma'am."

Patronizing, son of a ...

She knew he threw that little ma'am in there to irritate her. What she really wanted to do right now was throw a good temper tantrum and perhaps find a doll she could draw his face on and poke pins into. Turning around, she made her way back to Richard and Christine, snatched the reins out of his hands, and stomped back towards the stables as she muttered under her breath. Richard and Christine followed at a slight distance. She felt somewhat vindicated when she heard their conversation.

"Richard, is it really necessary to antagonize her so?" Christine asked.

Richard bowed his head in contrition. "I cannot seem to resist."

Christine rolled her eyes. "Well, it's unseemly—and entirely unlike you." She frowned up at him. "Since when did you become so ungentlemanly?"

Richard sighed. "I apologize."

Once they arrived at the Wades barn, Richard spoke with the groom, and asked him to rub down Sophie's horse. As the young lad made his way to tend to the horse, Richard cornered Sophie. "Mrs. Ford, I am truly sorry if I offended you. It was not my intention. Could we please call a truce?"

Sophie glared at him.

"Mrs. Ford?"

"I'm *thinking*!"

"I see." Taking a deep breath, he smiled – less like a shark this time, as he folded his hands behind his back. "I have an idea."

Sophie continued to glare at him without comment.

"Tomorrow is Tuesday, and I happen to have the afternoon free. Why don't you and I go for a ride? I promise I'll be on my best behavior."

"I'm not sure that would be a good idea."

Christine took Sophie's arm. "Richard, give us a moment, please?"

She pulled Sophie further into the darkened stables. "Sophie, I don't want to tell you what to do, but you will be alone tomorrow afternoon. Richard has been a friend of our family for years and I have to admit, he's acting somewhat out of character at the present time, but I have the utmost faith that you would be safe with him. You might even enjoy his company."

"I *highly* doubt that."

"I know things are confusing at the moment. I know you miss Jamie, but at some point you have to realize that you're here, and I don't know if that will change."

Sophie paced the small space. "I know. But why do I have to spend any time with him? I'd be happy to read a book and hang out at home."

Christine clasped her hands in front of her and let out a quiet sigh. "Richard would be a great champion, Sophie."

Sophie's stomach dropped. "A champion? Why would I need a champion?"

"You are a young woman alone. Beautiful, but without a past," Christine whispered. "You won't make it far without a husband to protect you."

Sophie's gasp echoed the rafters. "Are you saying that I have to marry that horrible man? I'm already married."

Christine took her hand and squeezed it gently. "You must be realistic, Sophie. You don't know where your husband is. He could be dead or lost to you forever, and without a man to protect you, you are at the mercy of someone who may not treat you as well as Richard Madden."

Bile rose unbidden. She couldn't do it. She could never marry someone she didn't love, even if she'd not already married the love of her life. And she certainly couldn't marry someone she despised. "I will not betray my husband."

Christine shook her head. "I'm not asking you to. I am simply suggesting that Richard would be a great protector. Will you give him a chance while you sort out your personal business?"

"I don't want, or need, a protector. You don't have one and seem to be doing fine."

"I've lived here most of my life and have my family. I also have Andrew. No one would cross my brother or do anything to offend Peter Martin's widow."

Sophie's eyes filled with tears.

"You have Michael's protection, Sophie. I don't want to suggest he wouldn't defend you. However, there were several men asking after you last night, and I think it concerned Michael."

Sophie rubbed her forehead, a headache rapidly approaching. "Why were men asking about me?"

"Because you are beautiful and very young, Sophie."

"I'm not that young," Sophie whispered frantically. "I'm twenty-six."

"But you look much, much younger, dear. There are many lonely men who have been at war for too long. None of whom are near the caliber of man that Richard is."

Sophie shrugged. "Just tell them I'm married."

"That will work for a time, but I still think you should get to know Richard. He's wonderful company."

"Then you date him—or marry him—or whatever!"

Christine chuckled. "He has never had any interest in me."

"But he has interest in *me*?" She couldn't understand why the thought upset her so violently.

Christine slid her arm around her shoulders. "Sophie, don't fret. You don't need to make any decisions right now."

"There is something not right about him, Christine."

"Whatever do you mean? Richard's a wonderful man. If you spend any time with him, you'll see that as well."

Sophie wondered if her feelings were due to her emotional upheaval, rather than fact. She didn't really know the man, but Christine did. So she tried to approach the situation objectively. Perhaps Christine was right and she was overreacting. Taking a deep breath, she straightened her spine and made her way out of the stables. "All right, Mr. Madden, tomorrow will be fine."

"Wonderful, Mrs. Ford. I'll see you at two."

Sophie nodded, and she and Christine made their way back to the house.

Miriam joined them for dinner and Sophie enjoyed her immensely. She was a woman in her mid-sixties and full of energy. Christine had moved in with Miriam after Peter died, and it seemed to work out well for both of the women.

The rest of the evening was spent in the parlor, the same room she was brought to after she was found. Was it really only a few days since she arrived in the nineteenth century?

As the night came to a close, Christine and Miriam said their goodbyes. Sophie wasn't sure what she was going to do until two o'clock the next day, having already finished her novel, so she snuck back to the library for another look and then made her way to her room.

Once inside, Sophie tried her best to concentrate on her pages swimming before her, but she had miscalculated exactly how much light a candle actually gave off. Not quite enough to read—actually, not quite enough to do anything other than avoid tripping over one's own feet. After about thirty minutes, she gave up.

Blowing out the candle, Sophie climbed into bed and stared at the ceiling for what seemed like an eternity.

CHAPTER NINE

THE SOLDIER HAD been closed away in the south guestroom for four days and Amelia thought her head would explode with curiosity. Her mother watched her like a hawk and she hadn't had the chance to sneak away.

Today would be the day. Her mother was going into town to do some shopping, and Amelia planned to feign a headache and a cough. She stood by the fire and made certain she was close enough for the heat to form sweat on her brow, just in case her mother needed further convincing. She heard the knock at her door and buried herself further under her quilt. She started to cough, quite convincingly if she did say so herself, just as the door opened.

"Amelia?"

Cough, cough.

"Dear? Are you coming to town?"

Cough, sniffle, cough. "Mama, I don't feel well," Amelia rasped.

Her mother hemmed quietly and made her way to the bed. Amelia felt the cool hand on her forehead. "Dear, you're burning up."

Cough.

Mrs. Powell sighed. "I don't think you should come with me today. I'll let Della know she needs to tend to you as well."

Sniff.

"You'll stay in this bed, Amelia."

"Yes, Mama," she rasped.

Mrs. Powell stared down at her for several seconds before turning and walking out the door with a swish. Amelia waited for as long as she could before throwing the covers off. She eased out of bed and tiptoed to the window. Her mother's carriage was already halfway down the road and would be out the front gates within minutes. She was safe.

A knock at the door had her flying back under the covers just as Della came in with a tray. "You's mama said you's sick, Miss Amelia."

Amelia poked her head out from under the sheet to see the raised eyebrow of a woman not at all convinced she was telling the truth. Amelia giggled and jumped out of bed. "I never can fool you, can I, Della?"

Della set the tray on the bureau. "What you up to, chil'?"

"I want to see the soldier and Mama won't let me."

Della crossed her arms over her thick chest. "I don' blame her."

"Did you find out anything else? What's his name, Della? Where's his unit?" Amelia pulled off her nightgown. "Oh, and did the doctor get the bullet out?"

"Your daddy said he's a lieutenant 'cause of the bars on his jacket, but the man only remembers that his name is James Emerson." Della picked up Amelia's discarded nightgown. "He don't know where he from or nothin' else about his life. He's healin' jus' fine. He don't talk much, but he's polite when he does."

Amelia clapped her hands. "So, he's a mystery."

"Yes'm."

"Please help me dress, Della. I want to see him." Amelia started to pull clothing from her drawers and then paused with a sigh. "He's so handsome."

Della gathered hoops and skirts for Amelia and turned to face her. Amelia slipped her corset on and Della pulled the ties. "Now, Miss Amelia, don't you go doin' nothin' reckless. That man's far too old for you. He's got a ring on, so's he mus' be married."

Amelia wrinkled her nose. "Oh. Well, I don't mind, Della. I can still look at him."

"Miss Amelia!"

Amelia giggled. "Perhaps he'd like me to read to him."

Della tied off her corset and helped her with the rest of her clothing, all the while mumbling warnings that Amelia had no intention of listening to.

* * *

"Wake up, beautiful girl."

"Jamie?" Sophie's eyes fluttered open, and she stared at the vision of her husband standing over her bed. "Where have you *been*?"

"I've been here, sweetheart. What do you mean?"

"No, you haven't been here. I've been looking for you." Sophie tried to sit up but felt frozen to the bed. "Why can't I move?"

"Ten-Cow, I've been here the whole time. Have you forgotten me already?"

"What? No!"

"Then why haven't you found me?"

Tears streamed down her temples and she shook her head. "Jamie, I couldn't *find* you."

"I don't know why you couldn't find me; I have been here waiting for you. I thought you'd never come."

Sophie felt both relief and frustration as she stared up at him. "Why can't I move? I need to touch you. I need you to hold me."

"I can't do that, sweetheart."

"What? Why not?"

Sophie's eyes flew open and she sat up, sobs racking her body. "No, no, no! Jamie, come back." Jumping out of bed, she made her way to the window and drew the drapes back, with the silly hope that maybe Jamie was behind one of them. "Where are you?"

She stared out the window and let out a little sigh at the scene. Unfolding before her was the most incredible sunrise she had ever seen. Truth be told, it was the *first* sunrise she had ever seen. Sophie and Jamie were not morning people, so were more likely to see a sunset. Oranges and yellows filtered over the ground, contrasting the stark white of the snow, and it was almost as though the sun were painting the landscape in front of her.

Sophie stood for several minutes, praying for wisdom as she watched God's artistry before her and then walked to her door and popped her head into the hallway to listen. The house was eerily quiet, indicating everyone must still be asleep.

Grabbing her book, she made her way over to the window seat. Pulling one of the curtains further open for light, she managed to get through the first five chapters before movement out the window caught her eye. Several men, including Richard, worked with the horses, putting them through what appeared to be military movements.

Sophie stayed glued to the window in utter fascination for close to twenty minutes. He really was a good-looking man. She just couldn't put her finger on what irritated her so much about him. Just as she was ready to go back to her book, Richard looked up and seemingly straight at her. Sophie doubted he saw her from so far away but pulled herself away from the window just the same. The last thing a man with a big head needed was someone staring at him. He might think she cared.

Hearing the household slowly rising, she turned as Betty knocked and came in to help her dress. Once she was finished, Sophie made her way downstairs. She joined Nona for breakfast and then she was left alone. The clock in the foyer read a little past ten, and Sophie didn't really know how she was going to the kill the next four hours. With the house empty other than the hustle and bustle of the servants, she knew she would have to provide her own entertainment.

Gathering borrowed outerwear, Sophie took off down the side path that led to the stables and the soldiers practicing their military movements. Hearing the commotion of hooves and men's raised voices as she approached, she fought the urge to peer inside the arena. Unwilling to draw attention to herself, she snuck into the dark tranquility of the barn and smiled as a few of the horses stuck their heads out to greet her.

She recognized the gelding that had taken her on the ride of her life the previous day, and she made her way to his stall and pulled a sugar cube from her pocket.

"You are a beautiful boy, aren't you, Samson?" She ran her hand over his muzzle. "I'm sorry I confused you yesterday. I wish I could ride you the right way so that we could really become acquainted. But that would be entirely too risqué in this day and age, I'm afraid."

Immaculate lines, unusually tall but still, no doubt Arabian somewhere in his lineage, Samson was larger than life. Muscular and lean, with a quiet disposition, he nickered his pleasure as Sophie held her hand flat for him to take the sugar. Hearing a slight rustle to her left, Sophie turned to find Richard in the open doorway of the barn, looking as arrogant as ever.

"Mrs. Ford, I didn't mean to startle you. Is anything amiss?"

"Of course not, Mr. Madden," she said a little more forcefully than she intended.

His hands went up in surrender. "I'm sorry. I didn't mean to offend. And, please, call me Richard. I saw you slink into the stables and wanted to make sure you didn't need anything. I also wondered if you would like to watch some of the training."

"I don't believe *slink* is entirely accurate, Mr. Madden." He raised an eyebrow at her and she took a deep breath. "Sorry. I must have gotten up on the wrong side of the bed this morning. Yes, I believe I'd enjoy watching the training."

"Wonderful. Why don't you follow me—ma'am."

Richard led Sophie out to the large open arena filled with magnificent horses working in perfect unison. Each man worked with his own mount so that both animal and rider could form a trust-bond. She spent the next two hours watching the men and horses put through their paces. It was invigorating.

Richard made his way over to her at about noon. "Mrs. Ford, the men are going to stop for something to eat. Would you like to join me for lunch?"

"They may be expecting me back at the Wades, so I should probably get going."

"I'd be happy to escort you to the house, and then perhaps I could join you?"

"All right, Mr. Madden." Sophie clasped her hands in front of her instead of taking the arm he offered. Touching him just didn't feel right, somehow.

Finding no one around when they entered the doctor's home, Sophie led Richard to the dining room and discovered a spread of cold sandwiches and fruit, along with hot tea and a pitcher of water. "I'm not quite sure what to say. Is it okay to invite you to stay for lunch, or is it something I need to run by Nona?"

Richard smiled. "Knowing Nona, if you invited the entire Union army, she would welcome them."

"Right." They perused the buffet and then Richard held her chair for her once they filled their plates.

"How is it, Mr. Madden, that you are home in relative luxury, rather than on the front lines?" Sophie dropped her eyes to her plate. "Sorry, I didn't mean that as rude as it came out."

"It's quite all right, Mrs. Ford. It's a rather long story."

"Apparently, I have almost two hours to kill before a rather overbearing man collects me for our scheduled appointment."

Richard chuckled. "He must be terrible."

Sophie grinned and took a bite of bread.

"Andrew, Adam, and I had a successful merchant business up until the war started. I have been training horses most of my life, so when it came time that the army needed a mounted cavalry, they approached me to train the men and the horses. Andrew, along with Christine's husband, Peter, enlisted at the start of the war, and Adam was left to run the business. Adam isn't in favor of the war, perhaps because he's British and has managed to stay out of the fight. Now that Andrew is home permanently, he has been a great support to Adam and, despite the war, they are prospering."

"So what is your association with the hospital then?" She lifted her fork to her mouth.

"Many of the men I have trained come back through the hospital, so I am called upon from time to time to notify next of kin, or simply let them see a familiar face. Recently, President Lincoln requested I train more men, as we've been losing so many."

"President Lincoln, himself? Not your commanding officer?"

"Technically, I'm not part of the army. My brother, Clayton, is quite close to the President, both personally and professionally, so I report directly to Mr. Lincoln. Unconventional, yes, but convenient for our leader."

Sophie sat dumbstruck. She was speaking with someone who knew her hero—personally. She was one degree of separation from one of the greatest men who ever lived. Shaking away her thoughts, she asked, "Has that been hard? Training so many men who don't make it?"

"I try not to dwell too heavily on the losses. Luckily, we've had many more successes, so I try to focus on that."

"Where does your southern accent come from? Do you have any family, Mr. Madden?"

"Richard, please. If you won't call me Richard, I'll continue to call you, ma'am," he threatened.

Sophie pointed her fork at him. "I *knew* you were doing it to irritate me. Yes, fine, I'll call you Richard. I think you should still call me Mrs. Ford, though." He raised an eyebrow at her and she folded. "Okay, fine. Call me Sophie."

"Sophie," he acknowledged. "In answer to your question, I am originally from Virginia. I don't have much family left. My parents and sister died from typhoid several years ago. Clayton is my only family now and currently stationed in Washington. His plan is to settle here when the war is over, as neither one of us feel Virginia is our home any longer. Although, I have a feeling his interests may be better served in D.C."

"Do you see him when you're called to Washington?"

"Yes. I usually stay with him."

Richard lifted a glass to his lips and Sophie noticed his hand shaking. She felt a warm flush start its way up her neck. She had no idea why, but she suddenly felt awkward.

Richard lowered his glass. "Would you like to go for our ride now?"

"I think that would be fun. I'll run and change." Sophie made her way upstairs and tracked Betty down to help her dress. She found the riding habit, clean and hung up in the freestanding wardrobe.

It took her thirty minutes to get out of her skirts and into the riding habit, and once again she wished for a split skirt. She wasn't really looking forward to the sidesaddle again but knew she didn't really have a choice if she wanted to ride.

Just as Sophie stepped into the foyer, Richard walked back through the front door. "I took the liberty of having Samson saddled for you. He's with my horse, right outside."

"Thank you."

Taking her hand, he placed it on his sleeve and gallantly led her outside. She noticed his hands no longer shook. She didn't linger on her thoughts as he helped her mount and held the horse while she tried to maneuver her skirts. Once she was settled, he mounted and they took off at a slower pace than he was probably used to, but she was grateful, still not completely comfortable in the saddle.

"Why did you decide on living here, Richard?" Sophie asked after a few minutes of riding.

"I met the Simmonds family years ago, shortly after my acquaintance with Michael. I purchased the property partly because it was next to the Wades, and partly because the horse facilities were so new. I think that might have been why Lincoln asked me to train the cavalry. I already had the perfect land, which meant the Union didn't need to look for or purchase anything."

She nodded and they lapsed into silence again. The countryside overwhelmed her senses and she took several deep breaths, almost in an effort to remember the clean smell of fresh snow. She had never seen so much and the vastness of the trees held her in awe. She couldn't imagine this beautiful place destroyed, and although she didn't remember a whole lot about Harrisburg, she hoped and prayed it stayed intact.

A man-made lake straddled both properties, and they rode the perimeter in easy conversation. Sophie was surprised when Richard brought their visit to a close. "We should really get back. I have to go to Washington tomorrow to meet with the President, and I'll need to get an early start."

Sophie nodded. "How long will you be gone?"

"I'll be gone for a few weeks, I'd imagine. Meetings with President Lincoln are never short."

Returning to the Wades without any casualties or runaway horses, Richard helped her dismount and, as he lowered her to the ground, she noticed the smell of alcohol.

Probably why his shaking has stopped.

She wondered how much he'd had to drink, and how he'd imbibed without her notice, as he walked her to the door.

"Thank you, Sophie, for a wonderful afternoon. I enjoyed your company immensely."

"I really should be thanking you, Richard. I'm sure you had a lot to do today and yet you took the time to show me around. That was very nice of you and I appreciate it."

She was a little embarrassed at her earlier treatment of him, but he was gracious enough not to mention it as they walked inside. They nearly bumped into Nona, who looked as though she was on her way out. "Oh, Richard and Sophie, what a nice surprise."

"Good afternoon, Nona," Richard said.

"Richard, Michael mentioned you were off to Washington tomorrow. We would love it if you would have dinner with us tonight. Six o'clock?"

"Yes, Nona, dinner will be appreciated. I'll see you both at six o'clock."

CHAPTER TEN

BETTY COLLECTED SOPHIE at five-thirty and helped her dress. Sophie chose a dark floral skirt with a simple white blouse and a jacket that complemented the skirt. Deciding to do her own hair, she attempted a simple chignon, but working with hairpins was a bit past her skill level. More hair ended up cascading down her back than staying in the bun.

What I wouldn't do for a scrunchy right now.

She went downstairs to see if there was anything she could help with. A funny question to ask the wealthy with servants, but her mama taught her right and she couldn't help at least asking. The house was alive with activity. Sophie didn't want to be in the way, so she made her way to the parlor. Inside she found two boys sitting on the floor playing jacks and marbles.

She was about to say something to them, when Elizabeth bustled through the door. "Boys, it's time to get ready for dinner. Please put your toys away."

"Yes, Mama."

She turned to Sophie. "Good evening, Sophie. Have you survived your day without any of us? I hope you weren't bored."

"Mr. Madden took me riding today."

"How nice." She turned back to her boys. "Thomas, Ambrose, come and meet Mrs. Ford. Sophie, I'd like you to meet my sons, Thomas is eight and Ambrose is six."

The boys jumped up and bowed gallantly. The introduction was made, and then, just as quickly, the boys took off to get ready for dinner. Elizabeth laughed as they left, hoping aloud they didn't break anything in their haste to eat. She linked her arm through Sophie's and moved towards the foyer. The butler stood at the open door, welcoming Miriam, Christine, and Andrew. The group made their way back into the parlor. Adam, having managed to corral the two young boys, joined everyone a few minutes later.

Richard arrived promptly at six and was shown into the parlor. He placed a lingering kiss on Sophie's fingers, and she blushed, embarrassed with the show of affection and somewhat dismayed by the scent of alcohol on Richard's breath, heavier than earlier in the day. She sighed in relief when she was saved by the butler, who informed everyone that dinner was ready.

The group settled into relaxed conversation as dinner was served. Adam and Andrew filled everyone in on what was happening with the business, and Christine updated everyone on life at the hospital. The family started grilling Richard about what he was going to do while in Washington and he did his best to provide as much detail as he could.

"Has the President said what he needs you for, or for how long?" Michael asked.

"I believe it's a strategy meeting. I imagine I'll be gone for several weeks."

"I'm sure Clay will be glad to see you. It has been a long time, has it not?" Nona sipped her wine.

"Yes, almost a year. It will be good to see him."

Sophie nearly dropped her fork when she felt a hand on her leg. Richard's hand. She pulled away and raised an eyebrow in warning but he simply smiled serenely as though nothing untoward had taken place. He made no further advances and Sophie almost wondered if she'd imagined it.

Almost.

When dinner was over, the men retired to the library and the women went to the parlor. Sophie was roped into a game of jacks with the boys and found herself on the floor laughing at how bad she was at it. The ball kept getting away from her and so, rather than picking up any jacks, she was forced to catch the ball. Hearing a noise at the doorway, she looked up to find Richard staring at her strangely. She didn't have a chance to ask why as Adam and Elizabeth gathered the boys up and took their leave.

Andrew had escorted Christine and their mother, so when Miriam was ready to go soon after, he took them both home. Richard was the last to leave, and despite the early morning wake-up call, he lingered and waited for everyone to leave.

"Sophie, would you join me on the porch for a few minutes?"

Sophie gave a slight nod. "I suppose."

Richard escorted her to the front porch and settled her in one of the big chairs. He sat next to her, and they spent a few minutes staring at the perfect winter scene in front of them.

"What time do you have to get on the road?" Sophie asked, breaking the silence.

"I'll be leaving at four."

Sophie raised an eyebrow. "In the morning?"

"Yes."

"Whew, that is early. Are you riding or taking a carriage?"

"I'll be taking the train."

Sophie didn't really know what else to say. She felt a bit awkward and wasn't altogether sure why Richard asked her to sit and talk with him. Rising to her feet, Sophie faced him. "Well, you should probably get going. Four o'clock is not very far away."

Richard stood as well. "Yes, you're right. I should go."

Grasping her upper arms, he leaned down and placed his lips on hers. Sophie pushed him away, nauseous by the overwhelming stench of yet more alcohol on his breath.

Where is he finding this stuff?

"What are you doing?" she screeched.

"I'm simply saying farewell," he slurred.

Sophie wiped her mouth with the back of her hand. "Well, I did not give you leave to accost me."

"I simply want to declare my intent."

"Mr. Madden, please. I'm married to someone I love deeply. It doesn't really matter what your intent is. I will not break my vows to my husband."

"Your husband is probably dead, Sophie."

Sophie blinked back tears. "Well, that was cruel."

"I apologize." He took both her hands, and placed a kiss on each of them. "I won't stay any longer than absolutely necessary and when I return, I would like to speak further in-depth. If your husband is in fact lost, I will help you in any way I can."

"I don't need your help, Mr. Madden." She pulled her hands from his. "And I won't in the future."

"We'll see," he said, tipped his hat and left her.

* * *

James Emerson sat up and turned his head at the sound of his door creaking open. A young woman shuffled inside and he had a flash of memory.

She smiled and made her way to the bed. "Good morning, sir. How are you feeling?"

"You're the one who found me, right?" he asked.

Her light blonde head bobbed up and down. "Yes. I wasn't sure if you'd remember. My name is Amelia Powell."

Her ice-blue eyes crinkled at the corner and James thought she looked like...

Who? Who does she look like?

He swore and rubbed his forehead. Nothing. He couldn't remember anything.

"Sir? Are you all right?"

James nodded slowly. "Yes, sorry. I'm feeling much better today."

The black woman who'd been looking after him brought a tray and set it on the bed. "The doctor says you's needs to get outta bed an' walk around today."

James smiled with relief.

"You jus' need to eat an' get ya strength back. You be back on your way in no time."

Back on my way to where, though? I don't even know who I am.

He nodded and picked up a piece of toast. A liberal portion of jam had been spread on top and he grinned up at Della. "You remembered exactly."

"Yessuh. It's my job to knows."

James swallowed. "Well, I appreciate it. I don't think I've ever had a better piece of toast in my life."

Della's cheeks reddened as she turned to gather the supplies to change his bandage.

"Daddy says you're a lieutenant," Amelia said.

Was he? He didn't know. The decorations on his military coat indicated he was, but he would be hard pressed to tell the difference between the bars of a lieutenant, a colonel, or Captain Kangaroo.

James shrugged. "Yes, I suppose I am."

"Of the cavalry."

Cavalry...that means horses, right?

James nodded. "Yes."

Amelia smoothed a hand over her skirts. "Did you lose your horse?"

"Miss Amelia," Della admonished. "The po' man don't know what end's up, chil'. Let him alone."

James sipped his coffee and smiled gently. "I don't know what happened to my horse. I don't know what happened to my unit, either."

Or my mind, for that matter.

"Daddy has three horses hidden in the barn."

Della dropped the bandages with a thud. "Miss Amelia!"

"Della, he's trying to keep them from the Rebels, not the Union. I think if Lieutenant Emerson needs one, Daddy should give him one."

James kept himself from laughing at Della's expression. "Don't worry, your secret's safe with me. Mr. Powell need never know we had this conversation."

Della pushed Amelia toward the door. "Shoo, missie. I nee' to change his bandages."

Amelia left the room and James slid the sheet down just enough for her to work. "Does you nee' me to get my son to help you dress?"

James shook his head. "No, thank you. I think that once you have me all fixed up, I can manage."

"Yessuh."

Once his bandages were changed, Della left the room and James climbed from the bed. His freshly washed uniform had been laid out on the chair next to the fireplace, so he pulled on his pants and paused to catch his breath.

Even though the bullet had caused a small hole and settled just under his skin, the wound the doctor created removing it was worse. He guessed the scar would be unsightly. He slid his hands down his face, surprised by the prick of stubble. He was used to being clean-shaven.

Am I?

He glanced in the mirror and vaguely remembered the face staring back at him. His beard seemed entirely out of place, but he couldn't pinpoint why. Shaking away the confusion, he put his shirt on and awkwardly pulled the suspenders over his shoulders.

On the dresser lay an unfamiliar chain with two diamond rings and the intricately carved ring he'd been wearing. Della had insisted he remove the band two days ago, concerned that if he caught a fever or his fingers swelled, he'd never get it off. He'd read the inscription half a dozen times in the last two days, trying to jog his memory. *"I love you more."*

Who loved him more? He couldn't remember and whenever he tried, he ended up with a nasty headache. He figured the best he could hope for was to heal quickly and get to wherever it was he needed to go. Maybe that would make him remember.

* * *

"Baby, where have you been?" Jamie trailed kisses down her neck as he whispered, "I have missed you."

"I can't find you," Sophie said. "Where are you?"

"I'm here, sweetheart." His hand stroked her cheek as he leaned over to kiss her. "Have you even looked, or have you forgotten me already?"

"No, never. Tell me where you are."

He drew her lower lip into his mouth and sucked; the familiar warmth pooled in her belly as he said, "I'm here. Why can't you find me?"

A groan escaped at her frustration. "You are *not* here, Jamie. Where are you?"

"Right here." Jamie slid the buttons on her nightgown and slipped his hand inside.

Sophie's body reacted instantly and her breath came in short bursts as his hands seem to be everywhere – and then nothing. She woke with a start.

That's all I get? SERIOUSLY?

Frustrated—on so many levels, Sophie punched her pillow. It was the middle of the night and she was dreaming of things that would never come to pass again. She needed to get a hold of herself. It was difficult enough to know she was no longer in the twenty-first century. Now she was dreaming of a life once lived, fully and in love.

Not fair!

* * *

Sophie woke the next morning with a plan forming in her mind. She would not wait another minute to find him. She had to get back. Jumping from the bed, she dressed quickly, foregoing the corset, and rushed downstairs.

"Good morning, dear."

"Hi, Nona." Sophie tried to keep the frustration from her voice.

"Breakfast is ready. Will you join me?"

"I need to get over to the barn."

"Nonsense. Nothing's more important that a good meal, dear." Nona slipped her arm around her waist and let out a gasp. "Mrs. Ford, are you not wearing a corset?"

Sophie rolled her eyes. "I was in a hurry."

"Well, that is absolutely no excuse to appear in public unclothed. Come. I'll assist you."

"Thank you," Sophie grumbled and followed her up the stairs.

Sophie forced down breakfast and a cup of coffee, her smile tight in an effort to keep from snapping in frustration at her hostess.

"Why don't I walk out to the stables with you?" Nona offered.

Sophie took a deep, calming breath and forced another smile. "That would be lovely."

"Sophie! Thank goodness you're here."

They turned to see Christine bustling down the hallway.

"What's amiss, Teeny?" Nona asked.

"Sorry, Nona." Christine held her hand out to Sophie. "I need Sophie to come with me, if you don't mind me stealing her away."

"Not at all." Nona turned to Sophie. "I'll see you at lunch, dear."

"Yes. Thank you. I look forward to that," Sophie answered somewhat stiltedly as Christine took Sophie's arm and guided her down the hallway. "How did you know I needed your interference?"

Christine chuckled. "I promised you that we would look for answers, so here I am."

"Thank you. Let's hurry."

Sophie rushed toward the stables, but the snow crunching under her feet slowed the attempt. Her feet began to tingle, and she stopped briefly to stomp her feet in both an effort to circulate the blood and allay her frustration.

"The buildings aren't going anywhere, Sophie."

"I need to know, Christine. I need to find something, anything."

Christine led her to where she had been found, per Nona's information, and they began to push snow aside and kick anything that might be in their way. There was no sight of a disturbance in the ground and no apparent change in the air surrounding the area. Of course, Sophie didn't really believe she'd find something so obvious as a trap door that opened to the future, but she thought perhaps there might be something to give her a clue at least.

"Ladies?"

Straightening her spine, Sophie pasted a serene expression on her face. "Andrew! What a lovely surprise."

Andrew crossed his arms, and his mouth turned up in a half-smile of suspicion. "What are you doing?"

"Sophie thought she may have lost a button," Christine said.

Sophie nodded. "Yes, exactly. A button."

"May I assist?"

"No!" Sophie rushed to say. "I mean, no, we're fine, Andrew."

"Thank you, Drew, but I don't think it's here." Christine pushed at the snow with her foot. "We were just getting ready to go back to the house."

"We were?" Sophie asked and then turned quickly back to Andrew. "Right. We have been unsuccessful, so we're going back to the house."

Andrew shook his head with a chuckle. "You two have been acting quite strange lately."

Christine linked her arm with Sophie's. "Drew! What a strange thing to say."

"The truth is a strange thing to say?" he challenged.

"No, no, we're fine, Andrew. Really." Sophie smiled. "Just looking for my button. Nothing untoward or strange going on."

Andrew raised an eyebrow. "Very well. I'll leave you to your button search. Find me if you require assistance."

"Thanks, Andrew." He stood for several minutes before finally walking away, and Sophie let out a sigh of relief. "That was close."

Christine frowned. "He's suspicious."

"Well, it's not like he could possibly guess what we're looking for, Christine, so I think we're somewhat safe from discovery."

She giggled. "True."

"Do we really need to go back to the house? I feel like we should look more."

Christine shook her head. "Sophie, there's nothing here. I'm not certain what we should be looking for, anyway."

Sophie sighed. "You're right. It's useless. I'm never going to find a way home, am I?"

"Perhaps you aren't meant to return."

"Christine!"

Christine laid her hand on Sophie's arm. "Would it be so terrible? To stay here? You have a place to live, and we are committed to helping you."

"I know. Don't think I don't appreciate it, really." Sophie's eyes filled with tears. "But I need Jamie. I can't live without him. I'm not strong like you."

"I'm not saying we have to give up entirely. I just think you should try to relax and see what you can make out of your time here. Is that too much to ask?"

"No," Sophie whispered. "It's not too much to ask. I'll try. But I'm not going to stop looking for a way back to him."

"I'll do everything I can to help you. I promise."

Sophie nodded and followed Christine back to the house. Christine linked her hand in Sophie's arm. "Why don't we visit your soldier?"

"When did he become *my* soldier?"

"When you insisted Michael take over his care, which in turn usurped Dr. Palmer's orders, which in turn, made him puff up like a peacock and challenge Michael."

Sophie's hand flew to her mouth. "He *didn't!*"

Christine giggled. "He did. However, Michael handled it beautifully, and your young soldier is now under careful watch and attention."

"Oh, dear. Did I make it difficult for Michael?"

Christine shook her head. "No, as a matter of fact, it was a beautiful sight. I've never liked Dr. Palmer, and watching him get set down by Michael was exceptional entertainment for us."

"Us?"

"The nurses."

Sophie nodded. "Ah."

"So, why don't we visit him and you can see for yourself."

"Sounds great."

Sophie followed Christine back to the house, and they climbed into her buggy and drove to the hospital. Sophie tried to hide her surprise when they pulled up to a different area than previously and entered through a separate door, surprisingly more substantial than the tent flap she'd entered in before.

CHAPTER ELEVEN

Warmth greeted her and she surveyed the freestanding fireplace and chimney built in the middle of the large tent, reminding her of a teepee. A hole had been cut into the roof of the canvas for the brick and the heat from the fire warmed the space quite adequately.

"This way, Sophie." Christine pulled her toward one of the rows of neatly set cots.

"Mrs. Martin?"

The ladies turned to see a handsome man moving toward them and Sophie felt Christine stiffen next to her. "Dr. Paxton."

Sophie noted that Dr. Paxton, tall with light blond hair and a clean-shaven face, only had eyes for Christine. His smile was quick and deep, and Sophie felt instant comfort. She glanced at Christine and raised an eyebrow. *Was that a sigh from my very proper friend?*

Sophie watched Christine closely and nearly laughed out loud. She suddenly had a dreamy expression covering her face.

"You aren't on the roster today, is anything amiss?" he asked.

Christine shook her head. "No, not at all."

A moment. Another sigh.

"Sorry, where are my manners? Dr. Paxton, may I introduce Mrs. James Ford? Sophie, this is Dr. Stephen Paxton."

Sophie reached her hand out and shook his. "It's nice to meet you, Dr. Paxton."

"Nice to meet you as well, Mrs. Ford. Is there anything I can assist with?"

"We came to visit the young soldier moved here by Dr. Wade."

Stephen smiled. "Ah, yes. He's just come out of surgery."

"Is he awake?"

"Not yet. I believe he'll be out for a while." Stephen smiled in Sophie's direction. "You must have made quite the impression."

"I'm sorry." Sophie blushed. "I hope I didn't cause any trouble."

Stephen leaned forward and whispered, "Anything that will bring Grant Palmer to his knees cannot be construed as trouble."

Christine let out a quiet gasp. "I didn't know you had an evil side, Dr. Paxton."

Sophie's head whipped up.

Is she flirting with him?

"Dr. Paxton? Oh, doctor."

The group turned at the sing-song sound of a woman moving toward them. Sophie heard Christine groan, albeit under her breath, as the pretty young woman waved at the doctor.

"Miss Sylvester? Is something amiss?"

The woman stalled briefly. "Uh, no, nothing amiss. I had but a simple question."

"I bet you did," Christine muttered.

Stephen smiled. "I'll be happy to answer it later, if that's agreeable."

"Of course," she said, although Sophie noticed her frown when she looked in Christine's direction. "Christine, you're not on the roster today."

"No, Lila, you're correct. We are here to visit with a patient. This is Mrs. Ford. Sophie, this is Lila Sylvester. She's one of our volunteers."

"It's nice to meet you," Sophie said.

Lila nodded but didn't repeat the sentiment. A minute of awkward silence ensued before Stephen turned his focus back to Christine, effectively ignoring Lila, and Sophie nearly snorted at the look of derision the woman sent Christine.

"I'll take you to the young man," Stephen offered and turned Christine towards the cot.

"Do you know his name?" Sophie asked.

"No, he hasn't spoken, mostly due to his state of consciousness. Even when he seemed awake, he wasn't coherent." Stephen stopped at the bed closest to the fire. "Here he is."

"Oh!" Sophie said.

"Something wrong?"

Sophie shook her head. "No, not at all. He looks so peaceful and very well cared for."

Stephen smiled. "We were given strict instructions."

Sophie sat in the chair Stephen pulled up next to the bed and inspected the young man's wounds. "His eye looks much better."

"Without going into detail, we were able to repair it without cutting, which lowers the risk of infection."

Sophie gently stroked her fingers over the soldier's forehead. "Remarkable. He looks so well. How is the wound at his wrist?"

"I closed the skin around his lost hand, but time will tell how quickly he will heal. My focus at the moment is to keep it from infection. The rest of his injuries were easier to repair, so I'm hopeful that if he wakes up soon, he should make a complete recovery."

"I'd like to sit with him, if that's all right," Sophie said.

"Of course." Stephen's gaze lingered on Christine. "I'll leave you to it, then."

Sophie saw Christine blush as she nodded and her eyes followed him as he walked down the aisle. Sophie grabbed her hand. "What the heck was that all about?"

Christine shrugged. "I'm certain I have no idea."

"You like him," Sophie insisted in a whisper.

Christine snorted. "Don't be silly."

Before Sophie could continue her barrage of questions, the soldier began to thrash. Christine moved quickly to hold him down, surprising Sophie with her force. "Hold him, Sophie but watch his arm."

Sophie placed her hands on his shoulders and pressed as hard as she could. The boy was strong and obviously experiencing fight or flight mode.

"Shhh," Sophie whispered. "You're okay. We're here to help. No one will harm you."

Christine rushed to find the doctor, leaving Sophie to figure out how to calm him alone. All she could think to do was sing, so she began to hum "Amazing Grace" as quietly as she could. It took a few minutes but he began to settle. Stephen arrived back at the cot, Christine and Lila close behind, and Sophie moved out of his way so that he could examine him.

"Son? Can you hear me?"

A groan sounded from the soldier and his tongue darted between chapped lips.

"He looks thirsty," Sophie said.

"I'll get some water," Christine offered.

"Son? Can you open your eyes for me?" Stephen spoke softly as he took the soldier's pulse and tried to rouse him. "You need to try and wake up if you can." Stephen lowered his wrist then slipped an arm behind his shoulders. "I'm going to sit you up."

Christine returned with a tin cup and handed it to Stephen, who tipped the rim between the soldiers lips. Sputtering, the soldier's eyes flew open and he tried to push Stephen's arm away. "Get away!"

"You're safe," Stephen assured. "Drink."

Sophie was surprised the soldier acquiesced so quickly. Stephen was able to get him to drink the entire cup of water and stay calm enough for Stephen to check several of his wounds. Sophie insisted on sitting by his cot for another hour, although the man never spoke. She knew he was awake but couldn't coax his name or any other information out of him.

Although the rest of the day was a series of motions, Sophie faked her way through it and fell into bed, hoping the next few days, weeks, months, might bring answers.

* * *

The next morning, Sophie stepped off the bottom stair and almost ran into the doctor.

"Just the lady I needed to see."

Sophie smiled. "Good morning, Michael."

"May I have a word?"

"Of course." Following him down the hall toward his office, Sophie's heart began to beat a little faster. She felt as though she was being called to the principal's office.

"Please, have a seat."

Michael waited for Sophie to sit down and then sat in the chair behind his large, walnut desk. He sat back and pinched the bridge of his nose. Sophie squirmed in her seat, growing more and more uncomfortable.

"Christine explained to me that you were insistent on a young soldier's care."

Sophie nodded. "I was. I'm sorry, Michael if I overstepped my bounds."

He held his hand up. "You didn't." He took a deep breath. "What I am unclear on, is if you know who he is?"

"No. None of us do. He hasn't spoken."

"He's my nephew."

Sophie's head whipped up. "What?"

Michael nodded stiltedly. "My youngest brother's boy. He's sixteen years old."

"*Sixteen?*" Sophie stood. "How did he get into the army?"

Chuckling sardonically, Michael slapped his hand on his knee. "He lied about his age, I would imagine."

Sophie started to pace. "Wouldn't he need paperwork for that?"

"I imagine it wouldn't be difficult to forge."

"Oh, Michael. I'm so sorry. What did his parents say?"

"My brother, Robert, has been at war for over a year now. He probably doesn't know. My sister-in-law, however, sent me a missive several months ago. Topper disappeared with his older brother, Tracker, and she asked me to use my influence to find them. I have been unsuccessful." Michael leaned forward. "Until now, of course."

"Topper?"

Michael chuckled. "When Christopher was born, Travis was two and could not say Christopher. He was forever Topper after that."

Sophie smiled. "Where do they live?"

"New York. I made some enquiries, and a Christopher Wade is listed as Private, 2nd Regiment, NY Vet Cavalry Company A. He is listed as eighteen years old."

"What about Tracker?" Sophie chewed her thumbnail.

Michael took a deep breath. "A Travis Wade, also Private, is listed as deceased."

"Michael," she whispered. "I am so sorry."

He turned wide eyes to her. "How did you know, Sophie?"

Shaking her head, she rubbed her temples. "I can't answer that, Michael. There was just something that drew me to him. Maybe because Richard thought he was Jamie. I just felt he should be tended to."

"Well, young lady, if it weren't for you, he'd have been lost."

"How did you know who he was? He was so beat up. Did he have dog—I mean, information disks?"

"No. I knew him as soon as I saw him. Nona and I visited with the family not so long ago, and he and I were able to get to know one another. He is the spitting image of his father, and he also has a mark on his shoulder that helped to identify him."

"So, what now?"

"Well, he's going to come home. Here, rather. I have sent a wire to Sarah, and I would imagine she'll arrive in the next few weeks, but I'm going to suggest he stay with us."

"Will she be all right with that?"

Michael chuckled. "We'll find out, won't we?"

Sophie sat down again.

"I'm going to visit with him today. I was hoping you might join me."

Sophie raised an eyebrow. "Me? Why?"

"I understand you have a lovely singing voice."

Sophie blushed crimson. "Christine likes to exaggerate."

"It wasn't Christine who told me. The hospital is abuzz with stories of the lady who calmed him with a song."

Sophie waved her hand dismissively. "Oh, please."

"Will you join me?"

"Well, of course. I'm not sure how much help I'll be, but I'm happy to try."

Michael smiled. "Excellent. I'd like to leave just after lunch."

Sophie stood and left his office. Wandering the halls of the house, she pondered the young man, and what kind of event would have made him leave his home at such a young age. Without answers readily available, she decided to visit Samson. He might not be able to talk to her, but he certainly made her feel welcome.

Approaching the stables, she waved to a few of the soldiers she'd gotten to know over the past few months and then made her way into the darkness of the barn. She let out a whistle and smiled when Samson's trumpet of welcome came and then the familiar sight of him poking his head out of his stall. Sophie grabbed a brush and let herself into his stall. "Hello, boy. You are a sight for sore eyes this morning."

Michael found her in Samson's stall over an hour later and let her know lunch was ready. With a final pat, she bolted Samson in and followed Michael back to the house. They grabbed a quick bite and then took off for the hospital.

They pulled up to the front of the hospital, and Michael lifted Sophie down from his buggy. He followed her inside and they were met by Stephen. "Michael. He is awake and agitated."

"Is he lucid?"

Stephen nodded. "Yes, as you requested, we've given him nothing for the pain."

"Thank you." Michael turned to face Sophie. "Follow me, please."

They walked down the wide aisle toward the cot that held Michael's nephew. He wasn't hard to find, as he was the one yelling obscenities at "the bastards who took my hand." Sophie couldn't quite comprehend Michael's calm. She didn't know the young man, and her heart broke for him, tears already forcing to spill from her eyes.

One of the nurses tried her best to hold him still, but he fought her, and managed to clock her in the face with his stump. He screamed in agony, and Michael and Stephen rushed to assist. Sophie followed close behind.

"Topper." Michael grasped the boy's shoulders. "Calm down."

Sophie checked on the nurse, relieved to see she was fine, and then made her way to Topper's cot. He continued to resist Michael so Stephen lent a hand—and brute strength.

"We could give him laudanum."

"No!" Topper bellowed.

"Topper, listen to me. Listen to my voice. You are safe here." Michael sat next to him.

Sophie watched him calm, and then his eyes opened, sudden recognition flashing across his face. "Uncle?"

"Yes, Topper, it's me. You are safe here."

Topper broke down, and Sophie watched Michael pull him into his embrace. The soldier, now reduced to a frightened little boy, took comfort in the arms of the large man.

"All is well, Topper. You'll stay with us, and Nona will take good care of you."

"Not safe, uncle."

"What's not safe?"

Pushing away from Michael, Topper wiped his face with his hand and took a deep breath. "This..." he held up his stump, "did not happen on the battlefield."

Sophie gasped and drew the attention of the young man. Michael turned and motioned her forward. "Topper, this is Mrs. Ford. She found you."

"Well, I didn't find you so much as I was brought to you." Sophie smiled.

"Sophie understates her involvement. She is the reason your care has been so thorough."

Topper nodded, his face still racked with fear. Michael stood and checked his pocket watch. "I'll discuss your current status with Dr. Paxton and then we'll take you home."

"No! Uncle, you can't."

"Topper, whatever it is that you think is so dangerous is no longer a threat. You'll be safe at our home."

Michael walked away, leaving Sophie standing by the cot. She watched as Topper dragged the blanket over himself.

She pulled a chair up beside the bed and sat facing him. "Michael's right, Topper. You're safe now."

"You don't know anything," he snapped.

Sophie clasped her hands together in her lap. "Probably true." She smiled. "But it seems as though your uncle is determined, and I don't think you have much of a choice."

He let out an expletive.

"Son, if you use that language in front of a lady again, I'll take you to task."

Sophie turned to see Michael had returned, a look of irritation on his face.

"Sorry, Uncle." Topper then turned to Sophie. "Ma'am."

"We're ready to go." Michael's expression softened, but his warning still hung in the air. "The nurses are gathering the items you came in with, and we'll continue your care at home."

Topper scowled but didn't comment as he pushed himself off the cot. Unsteady, he reached for the wall, forgetting about his injury but Sophie grabbed his bicep before he could hurt himself. She saw embarrassment register in his expression, so she quickly said, "Oh, Topper, I'm sorry. I lost my balance there for a second. I appreciate your assistance."

His eyes widened in surprise, but he nodded and didn't pull away as she slipped her hand in the crook of his arm. "Can you walk?" she whispered.

"Of course I can walk. I'm not an invalid."

"Right. Of course not."

Sophie led Topper down the aisle, all the while assisting without looking as though she were assisting. They met Michael at the entrance and then they made their way out to the buggy. Michael waited for Topper to pull himself inside before taking Sophie's hand. She climbed in beside him and tried to give him an encouraging smile. It didn't seem to work.

* * *

February and March passed without much progress. Sophie spent as much time as she could with Topper but without answers as to who the threat was. He never said the name of the man who had caused him so much fear, he woke up screaming in the middle of the night. He refused to speak about his injuries and how he got them, and Sophie did her best not to push.

* * *

"Eyes open, men," James yelled. He glanced to his right at Sergeant Mitch West. Mitch had rapidly become a confidant and ally. "You, too."

Mitch chuckled and gave him a mock salute. "Yes, sir."

Brigadier General William W. Averell, mounted to his left, moved forward and James followed. It was the third attempt to cross the Rappahannock, but trees and a unit of Confederate sharpshooters stood in their way.

"I'll take twenty." Major Samuel E. Chamberlain moved out in front him and broke away with the closest group of men.

James and Mitch pulled their horses back and sat with Averell while Chamberlain advanced toward the river. James pushed his hat back for a better view. "He'll never make it."

How do I know that?

Averell crossed his arms over the pommel of his saddle and leaned forward slightly. "You never know."

As James watched the major lead the group, he reflected on the last two months and his unusual journey to his current location in Kelly's Ford, Virginia. He'd spent another week with the Powell's and then out of nowhere, a group of cavalry officers had passed through and allowed him to ride with them until he could meet up with his own.

Of course, he never would.

In February he'd pulled Mitch out of a sticky situation with a married woman, and ever since then they'd been partners. Mitch knew about his memory loss and covered with the higher ups to keep him in their unit.

Heavy fire brought his focus back to the present. James followed Mitch into cover and then he didn't have much time to think. A shot rang out and Chamberlain was thrown from his horse.

"Let's go, men!" Averell yelled.

"Is he out of his mind?" James groaned as Averell started to cross the river.

Mitch dug his heels into his horse. "Come on."

They followed Averell, the water running a little faster than James liked. In the end, it took over two hours to cross. Mitch let out a holler as the last man made it to shore and James mirrored his relief—internally.

"Just think, Jimmy, my man. We'll be in Harrisburg before you know it. I heard there's pretty ladies and the best horses in the nation, all within ten miles of one another."

James laughed and shook his head. "Are you sure they're not saying that the horses *are* the pretty ladies?"

Mitch swore with a frown. "What do you take me for, Jimmy?"

James shrugged. "I'm just sayin' I'm not sure which one you're more excited about mounting first."

Mitch managed to catch James over the head with his crop. James laughed louder.

CHAPTER TWELVE

RICHARD DIDN'T RETURN to Harrisburg until the beginning of April. The flowers, sprouting out of the earth as the snow melted, reached for the sun that shone a little longer, indicating the beginning of spring.

Although the days were still quite cool, the absence of subzero temperatures seemed to put a skip in everyone's step. Everyone but Sophie, who still hadn't found anything to indicate how to get home. She was beginning to believe she may be stuck in the nineteenth-century for good.

On an unusually warm morning, Sophie made her way out to the stables to visit the horses, as she did as often as she could before starting her day. Her heart swelled as she called Samson's name and he whinnied for her. As she stood outside Samson's stall, she heard her name, and turned to see Richard walking towards her.

Sophie smiled. "Mr. Madden, you're home."

"Yes, ma'am, I am." He smiled as he strode over to her, took her hand, and placed a kiss gently on her fingers.

Pulling her hand away from him, she slid it behind her back. "How was your trip?"

"It went very well, thank you. How have things been here? Have you been surviving?"

"Yes. I started volunteering at the hospital. It helps the days go by quicker. You must come up to the house. The Wades will be thrilled you're home."

"I actually have several things to do before I settle back in. I thought I might visit later today once everything is completed. Would you please let the Wades know that I'll come by at six o'clock?"

Sophie chuckled. "Dinner time. Convenient."

Richard grinned. "I thought so."

He appeared reluctant to leave her, and once again, Sophie felt off-kilter. "I should get back to the house. Christine will be by shortly to take me to the hospital."

"I look forward to dinner."

"I'll see you later." Sophie made her way back to the house.

Christine pulled up in her little carriage as Sophie stepped onto the front porch, so the girls let Nona know about Richard and then rushed off to the hospital.

Sophie was glad the day passed quickly.

Word got around that Richard was home, so the entire Simmonds family, sans children, planned to converge on the Wades for dinner.

Elizabeth arrived just after five o'clock, followed closely by Christine and Miriam. Adam and Andrew were detained with some import issues, so were going to be a bit late. The girls were having wine in the parlor when the butler showed Richard in.

"Good evening, ladies. Am I the first to arrive?"

"Yes, as a matter of fact, you are," Christine said. "May we offer you a drink?"

"Yes, that would be nice, thank you." He made his way to Sophie and drew her hands to his lips. As he leaned closer, Sophie noticed the smell of alcohol again, and pulled her hands behind her back, shying away from the smell, relieved when Adam and Andrew arrived a few minutes after six and they were shown into the dining room. The table was alive with animated conversation. The hot topic, of course, was Richard's meeting with the President.

"Richard, we're all dying to know. What's the news from Washington?" Michael asked.

"Yes, Richard. Do tell." Adam's sarcastically laced comment drew a smirk from Andrew.

"Lincoln has his eye on a First Lieutenant, James Emerson, who's under Grant's leadership. Despite being wounded a few months ago, the man has shown himself to be not only a great leader of men but exceptional at strategic fighting. Lincoln has ordered that he and a few of his men make their way here. They will arrive tomorrow. Lincoln believes that he and I can partner to train more men. I'll concentrate on the horses and Lieutenant Emerson will focus on the men."

"So, what does that mean for you? No more front lines?" Andrew sipped his whiskey.

"For the time being, I'm home, with no orders to do anything differently at present." Richard stared at Sophie.

"That must be a relief." She gave him an awkward smile.

"Yes, I have to admit, it is."

Everyone was in great spirits and once dinner was over, the women retired to the parlor while the men went to the library.

The moment the girls walked into the room, the ladies begged Christine to play for them. She chuckled and sat down at the piano, insisting Sophie sing with her. It took Sophie a little longer to acquiesce. She should have known it was futile to try to bow out of it.

Christine started a tune that Sophie was familiar with so she sang along. Finishing the song, Sophie turned to see Adam leading the men back into the parlor, clapping as they entered the room.

"Sophie, that was astounding," Richard said.

Sophie blushed. "Thank you."

"Where did you learn to sing like that?" Christine asked.

Sophie shrugged. "I guess I have always sung. I never really thought about it."

"Well, you and Christine will need to play again!" Elizabeth said.

"Yes, I agree." Richard smiled.

"Thank you, that's very nice." Sophie lowered her head.

The evening wrapped up shortly after the impromptu performance by Sophie and Christine. As everyone made their good-byes, Richard hung back. Once the rest of the guests left, he insisted Sophie join him on the porch. "Sophie, you have a wonderful voice."

"Thank you, Richard."

"I missed you while I was gone."

He leaned down to kiss her, and Sophie had to hold back a snort of disgust as she deflected him, the smell of alcohol once again overwhelmming. "Richard, please, I'm not sure that this is entirely appropriate."

"I know you missed me." Reaching inside his pocket, he pulled out a long velvet box. "I have a gift for you."

"No, really, it's unnecessary."

"I took the time to choose it for you, Sophie. Open it."

Sophie held her hands up in protest. "I don't think it's appropriate."

"I'll open it, then." Richard lifted the lid, and Sophie let out a gasp of both admiration and horror. Nestled in a bed of silk lay a diamond bracelet, the likes of which Sophie had never seen before.

Three large baguettes were separated by smaller, round stones, and Sophie thought it was the gaudiest thing she'd ever seen.

"Richard, no. I can't take this. Absolutely not."

"Of course you can. It's a gift."

Richard handed the box to her. Sophie pushed it back. "No, I'm sorry. It's too extravagant and I cannot accept it."

"I don't understand. I thought we had an understanding."

"What kind of understanding?"

"A long-term one."

"Richard, I think I need to make myself clear. Despite the fact that Jamie isn't here, I am still deeply in love with him." Sophie pressed her arm against her stomach. "I don't know if that will ever change. I'd like to continue our friendship, but if you cannot accept that it will never be anything more, it might be best if we didn't see each other."

Richard looked disappointed, and she thought she caught a glimpse of anger in his expression, but his voice was even when he said, "We'll sort this out, Sophie. Take things slowly."

She didn't want to take anything slowly. She didn't want to take anything anywhere, but she wasn't in the mood to argue with him. He may never fully understand her feelings for Jamie. Exhausted from the busy day, she quickly made work of undressing and getting into bed. She had to admit she was somewhat frustrated with Jamie. She knew it was illogical, but she wanted him with her, not just to scare off the likes of Richard, and she was put out by his absence. Only Jamie could make things right.

* * *

Sophie woke the next morning, dressed quickly, and arrived downstairs to find the house in an uproar. Sophie caught Michael sneaking off to his office and cornered him. "Michael, what's going on?"

"Nona has decided to have a ball this evening for Lt. Emerson."

"Is there anything I can do to help?"

"I have found the best thing to do during times like these is to stay out of the way." Michael chuckled and continued to his office.

The front door opened a few seconds later, and Elizabeth walked in, her hands full. "Good morning, Sophie."

"Good morning." Sophie rushed up to help relieve her of her burdens.

"Thank you." Elizabeth handed over a few of her packages.

"Where would you like me to put these?"

"Let's find Nona and we'll ask her where she wants them. There is something in there for you, but I'll show that to you once we put these other things away."

They found Nona in the ballroom. She took the packages from the girls and, after a few minutes of small talk, hustled off to organize and plan the last-minute event. Elizabeth and Sophie made their way up to her bedroom.

Sophie's curiosity was overwhelming. "What have you done?"

Elizabeth turned, looking like the cat that swallowed the canary. "I haven't done anything," she said as she opened the box previously laid on the bed.

Sophie gasped as Elizabeth pulled out the most beautiful ball gown she had ever seen. Cobalt blue velvet, her favorite color, off the shoulder, and with a plunging neckline that incorporated an intricately embroidered border in ivory satin, which was also at the bottom of the skirt and sleeves. Tiny ivory pearl clusters were strategically placed around the neckline, and the buttons to close the dress matched the clusters.

"This is incredible, but I can't take this from you. You should wear it," Sophie said as she tried to hand the gown back to her.

"Actually, Sophie, it's not mine. Christine commissioned Madame Desmarais to make it when we altered the copper dress. She was going to surprise you with it on your birthday, but we both felt this would be perfect for tonight."

"This is magnificent. I can't believe how incredibly wonderful you and your family have been to me. Thank you so much for everything."

Elizabeth hugged her and chuckled. "Well, we've decided we adore you and we're going to keep you. Now, I must get back to the children. Christine will be over early tonight to help you with your hair and I believe she's also planning on dressing here. I'll see you tonight."

Once Sophie walked her out, she made an attempt to help Nona, realizing relatively quickly it was a losing battle.

Since she needed something to do, Sophie decided to take Topper lunch. Several weeks had passed since the Wades had taken in Topper and it had been tumultuous at best. Sophie saw cracks even in Nona, the woman who never lost her composure.

Carrying a tray up to his room, she knocked on the door. No answer. She tried again. "Topper? I have lunch for you."

"I'm not hungry."

"I'm coming in." She pushed the door open and frowned. "What happened here?"

"None of your business."

The tray from breakfast lay face down on the floor, oatmeal stuck to the wood, and milk souring around it.

"This is just great, Topper." Sophie laid her burden on the bureau and bent to pick up the mess. "Did you do this all by yourself? Hmm? Did it make you feel better to throw a tantrum?"

Topper grunted.

"This is ridiculous! You need to eat."

He held up his stump with a scowl.

"What?" Sophie snapped. "Are you trying to tell me that you can't eat because your hand is gone?"

"I can't do *anything* because my hand is gone," he yelled.

"You have another hand, Topper." He let out a curse. Sophie chuckled sardonically. "You don't offend me, bud. I know you'd like to, but it won't work."

"Leave me the hell alone!"

Sophie slammed the bowl onto the tray and stood. "No! I won't. Everyone in this house has been tiptoeing around, worried about the poor boy who has been injured. How young he is to have seen so much and experienced so much pain."

"Well, I have."

Sophie shook her finger at him. "It was your choice, Topper! You made the decision to lie about your age and join the adult fight. Now, you're dealing with adult consequences. I'm sorry you lost your hand. I know it hurts and makes your life difficult, but you have your other hand—and your life." She slammed her fist on the nightstand. "Look at me when I'm speaking you!" He turned eyes full of anger on her. "You have your life, Topper. Your brother wasn't so lucky, and I cannot imagine he would want you to spend the rest of yours angry and pitiful."

"You don't know a damn thing about my brother," he snapped.

"Then tell me! I want to know all of it. The good, bad, and indifferent! I'm a great ally to have, and I'm here to listen without judgment to whatever it is you want to say. But I will not sit back and let you wallow in self-pity."

"Sophie?" Michael stood in the doorway, breathing heavy as though he ran up the stairs. "Are you all right?"

"Yes, Michael. We're fine."

He glared at his nephew. "Did you do something to offend Mrs. Ford?" Michael's tone was laced with warning.

Sophie shook her head. "No, not at all, Michael. We were simply having a healthy debate." She turned back to Topper. *"Weren't we?"*

Topper nodded and turned his head toward the window.

"What happened here?" Michael bent down to help Sophie pick up the discarded dishes.

"Nothing we can't handle." Sophie stood and set the tray on the nightstand. "*Right*, Topper? He actually just asked if I could find a wet cloth so that he could wipe up the mess. Didn't you, Topper?" Topper grunted but Sophie wouldn't give up. "In fact, Michael, perhaps you could take the tray back to the kitchen and get us a few rags?"

"I'll send Betty up."

Sophie held up her hand. "No, no. Topper's going to clean the mess up. He *insists*." She nearly laughed out loud at Michael's baffled expression.

"All right. I'll return shortly."

Michael left the room and Sophie crossed her arms. Topper turned his head back to her and glared. "I'm not cleaning anything."

Sophie snorted. "Oh, yes, you are, you ungrateful little cretin."

"Who's going to make me?"

"Really? We're going with that?" Sophie turned to the bureau and poured a glass of water. "We can play this game all day long, little man, but you *are* going to clean that mess up. You're also going to start treating the staff with respect."

"They're *servants*."

Sophie turned slowly and stared at him. "No, they are not. They're hard working men and women who are paid to do a job. No more or less than you."

"I'm nothing like them."

"You're right. You're a spoiled brat."

Michael returned with a metal bucket filled halfway with soap and water, and several rags.

"Thank you." Sophie turned back to Topper. "Up and at 'em. Time to clean up your mess."

Michael set the bucket down. "Perhaps, I should get some assistance."

"No, Michael. Topper made the mess. Topper's going to clean up the mess. Now." She raised an eyebrow in Topper's direction. "Get your skinny butt out of that bed and start."

She watched him sit up, throw his legs over the side of the bed, and then push himself off the side. He let out a loud, pathetic whimper, and she had to physically push Michael out of the room to stop him from rescuing Topper. "Oh, that was really quite convincing, bud." She crossed her arms and smiled. "You've refused pain meds from the start, you don't get to pull that card when it's something you don't want to do. Now, grow a pair and start mopping up your mess."

"Sophie? A word?"

She stepped into the hallway and faced Michael, knowing exactly what was coming. "The boy is wounded. He should not have to clean when we have staff to handle it." Michael slid his hands into his pockets. "This is all too much for him."

"Michael, he threw a tantrum and that's why there's a mess to begin with. He's horrible to the staff, rude to Nona, rude to me, and an all around pain in the butt. He has to learn to live without a hand, and we need to help him do it with a good attitude."

Michael's brow puckered into a V, and Sophie reached over and squeezed his arm. "Trust me. He's angry, for very valid reasons, but he can't go through life like this."

He took a deep breath. "I'll give you some time, Sophie. I just pray it doesn't take long."

Sophie smiled. "It won't. Don't coddle him. Give me that much. The rest you can leave up to me."

With a stilted nod, Michael turned and left her. Sophie made her way back into the bedroom and found Topper had in fact cleaned up the mess and now sat on the bed, fuming.

"Good job." Sophie smiled. "Dr. Paxton is arriving in an hour to check your wounds. Right now, though, you need to eat."

"I'm not hungry."

Sophie chuckled. "Oh, I can't imagine that's a true statement. You didn't finish your breakfast."

"Has anyone ever mentioned your instability?"

"Was that a jest, Master Wade? It's a good one." Sophie picked up the tray and set it beside him on the bed. "Let's just say that my specialty falls to angry young men who like to make others miserable in order for them to feel better." She handed him half the sandwich. "Now, eat."

CHAPTER THIRTEEN

SOPHIE WAITED FOR Topper to finish his lunch and then decided to rest before the party. She knew tonight was going to be a late one and she didn't want to miss any of it. She wanted to be alert and enjoy every minute.

Sophie had been asleep for what felt like less than a minute when a scraping noise woke her, and she opened her eyes to find Christine leading Betty into the room with a bathtub. "Good afternoon, Sophie. Time to wake up and get pretty for the party."

"Ugh, Christine, what time is it?" Sophie groaned.

"It's about four thirty." Christine closed the door. "Come and take a warm bath, you'll feel better."

Sophie eased out of bed, disrobed, and climbed into the tub. As the water flowed around her body, she inhaled deeply, the scent of oranges filling her nose, and she smiled as her lethargy left her body. She couldn't think of anything she loved more than oranges. Christine was right. She did feel better. "Ah." Sophie sighed. "This is heaven."

The lit fire made the bedroom almost too warm, so Christine opened a window, just a crack.

"Can I just stay here all night? I'm not sure if I'm up for a crowd tonight." Sophie stretched her legs and settled her feet on the edge of the copper tub.

Christine laughed. "I share your feelings. But for now, let's get that hair of yours washed. If we don't start now, we might miss the party," she joked—sort of. "I don't think I've ever seen anyone with as much hair as you."

Once Sophie's hair was washed, Christine wrapped it in a towel, and then Sophie stepped out of the tub and grabbed another towel for her body. She decided not to get dressed completely and stood behind Christine, who had slipped out of her day dress and into a robe.

Styling Christine's strawberry blonde locks into a simple chignon, Sophie placed a ribbon over her crown like a headband, leaving the ends trailing down her back. Christine's hair was all one length, but instead of parting it in the middle, as was the style of the day, Sophie swept it straight back off her forehead.

"Sophie, it's beautiful. I've never seen anything like it before. Where did you learn to do this?" Christine gushed.

"I used to wear my hair like this all the time."

Sophie didn't mention that it was how she would control her locks when she competed in horse shows. She had to be able to set her riding helmet or top hat on her head, so had to have a style that worked for both.

"Your turn." Christine stood to trade places with Sophie. "Where are the ribbons that Madame sent over with the dress?"

"I think Elizabeth put them in the wardrobe."

Christine collected the velvet ribbons and styled Sophie's hair by pulling her hair loosely up and slightly away from her face. Leaving a few long curls cascading down her back, she stalled when she couldn't figure out what to do with Sophie's bangs, as they had begun to get quite long. In the end, she swept them to the side, which softened Sophie's face.

It was now time for the gowns, so Sophie tightened Christine's corset first, then helped her step into a pink chiffon dress, with layers of material that gave the skirt an almost ruffled effect. The top was a criss-cross style, off the shoulder and came to a V at her waist. With Christine's hair and skin, it suited her perfectly.

Once Christine was ready, she tightened Sophie's corset and helped her on with her skirt. Sophie yanked at the top. It gave them a bit of trouble, particularly because it was even more revealing than the copper one. She was thankful her sleeves weren't as tight across her shoulders. They lay on her arms in a droop fashion that gave her more room to move, but she still felt a bit exposed.

Sophie tried a few windmills with her arms and everything stayed where it was supposed to be, so she decided not to worry about falling out. She went over to the full-length mirror and took a deep breath. If she could have designed her perfect dress, it would have never come close to the magnificence of this one. She felt beautiful.

"Christine. It's incredible." She twirled around. "I love my hair, I love the dress, I love it all. I don't know how to thank you."

"Nonsense, it's an early birthday present. You look beautiful and that's the best thanks I can receive."

The girls left the room and headed downstairs. Sophie's stomach fluttered in anticipation as they made their way to the ballroom. They took their place in the receiving line, outside the large double doors, along with Michael and Nona, and greeted guests as they arrived.

"Where's Topper?"

Michael rolled his eyes. "He refused to attend."

"Oh, well." Sophie shrugged and turned to greet the new wave of guests. Richard arrived a little past six o'clock and as he made his way to the receiving area, he smiled deeply. Sophie smiled in return. "Good evening, Richard."

Lifting her hands to his lips, he kissed each one. "Sophie, you look exquisite."

"Thank you. You look very nice yourself."

As they continued to make small talk, they heard voices and booted footsteps in the hallway. A group of soldiers entered the anteroom where everyone stood. Richard turned and walked over to the group. Sophie and Christine continued to greet guests and as the crowd lulled, they talked for a few minutes about the hospital and one of their favorite patients.

Their conversation was quickly interrupted when Richard walked back to them. "Sophie, Christine, I'd like you to meet 1st Lieutenant James Emerson."

The soldier walked forward to greet the girls, and Sophie grabbed Christine's hand, squeezing it in panic. "Oh!" Sophie raised a gloved hand to her mouth.

"Sophie?" Christine asked, concerned. "Are you all right?"

The man stared at her like he recognized her but couldn't quite place her. Sophie's eyes filled with tears.

"Jamie." Pitching forward, she dropped like a stone.

The lieutenant reacted instantly and caught her before she hit the ground.

"Bring her into the parlor," Christine suggested. "Nona, you and Michael stay here and continue to greet people. I'll tend to Sophie. I don't want to draw attention if we can avoid it." Christine walked into the parlor. Richard followed.

The lieutenant laid Sophie on the sofa and then reluctantly stood back as Christine moved to sit beside her. "Sophie?"

"Hm," she mumbled and slowly opened her eyes. "What happened?"

"You fainted."

Sophie waved her hand dismissively in the air as she sat up. "I don't faint, Christine."

Before Christine could comment, Sophie turned her head and with a smile a mile wide, she stood and made her way to the lieutenant. "You look amazing. A little scruffy...but, still, amazing." She wrapped her hands around his waist and laid her head on his shoulder. "Jamie." She sighed and closed her eyes.

The lieutenant stood stiff with his arms out, obviously uncertain how to react.

"What's wrong?" Sophie looked up at him.

"I don't know you."

Sophie snorted. "Don't joke, Jamie."

"Ma'am, I'm sorry, I don't know you."

Sophie let out a nervous giggle. "It's me, baby."

At his sad look, she dropped her arms quickly, humiliation overtaking her as tears filled her eyes. Wiping her hands nervously over her skirt, Sophie swallowed. "Sir, I'm so sorry. You look identical to my husband." His hair was longer, and he had a full beard, but he still looked exactly like him.

"I'm sorry."

She put her hands over her face, mortified. "You must think I'm crazy."

Richard pulled her into his arms. "James, I must apologize for Sophie. She has recently lost her husband and the grief has been overwhelming."

Sophie pushed her way out of his arms. "Don't you dare apologize for me, Richard Madden. I am perfectly capable of speaking for myself." Turning back to the lieutenant, she forced a smile. "Lieutenant, again, I am very sorry. I just cannot get over your resemblance to my husband, Jamie. You even sound like him."

"No need to apologize, ma'am. It's perfectly all right. It's not every day that a beautiful woman walks up and puts her arms around me."

"Shall we make our way into the ballroom?" Richard asked.

"I need a minute." Sophie, unable to drag her eyes away from the Lieutenant, grabbed for Christine's hand.

Christine stayed with her as the men left the room and headed for the party. "Are you all right?"

"No, I'm not. That man looks exactly like Jamie. How is that even possible? He could be his twin."

"If he was Jamie, he would know you—wouldn't he? From what you've told me about him, if he knew you were close by, he wouldn't hesitate to find you. It can't possibly be him."

"But he even has the same name." Sophie pulled away and began to pace. "That can't be a coincidence."

Christine smiled. "Sophie, there are many men named James in the army. It's a common name."

Sophie sighed. "You're probably right. His hair is quite a bit longer than Jamie's and he has a full beard. Jamie was always a stickler with the razor. I have never seen him with a beard, or hair not perfectly trimmed."

Christine nodded. "There you go. I bet if he cut his hair and shaved off the beard, the lieutenant wouldn't even look like Jamie."

Just then, Richard strode into the parlor. "Sophie, are you feeling better?"

Sophie rolled her eyes. "Yes, Richard, I'm fine. Sorry I snapped at you. I know you were only trying to help."

"Are you ready to come back to the party?"

Sophie forced her feet forward and walked with Richard and Christine out of the parlor. Just before they entered the ballroom, Sophie took a deep breath, put her shoulders back, and tried to conjure up courage she simply didn't feel. She could do this. She had to.

* * *

James stood with Mitch and watched Sophie walk into the room with Richard. Tall and curvy, she was just about perfect in his opinion. He'd almost lost his composure when she'd walked up and put her arms around his waist. As she crushed her full breasts to his chest and laid her head on his shoulder, he'd had a flash of a memory and felt overwhelming love. He just had no idea what it meant.

"Who do you think she is?" Mitch asked.

James narrowed his eyes. "I've no idea."

"She's magnificent."

James turned his head slowly with a warning scowl. "You'll go nowhere near her."

"Hm. No, I don't suppose I will." Mitch chuckled. "Come on, Jimmy. Let's get a drink."

James let Mitch drag him to the refreshment table and slid back into his thoughts.

Whoever this Jamie fellow was, he was a lucky man. James focus drifted back to Sophie and he felt a small flutter of jealousy when he noticed her hand gripping Richard's arm. He had to admit, he was surprised by the emotion. He'd just met this woman. He laid no claim. Yet he couldn't shake the feeling that she was significant somehow. He had every intention of investigating that significance. He just had to figure out how.

James watched as Richard released Christine's hand and then turned to Sophie. Sophie looked up at him with a small grimace and James's ire rose as Richard took his free hand and placed it over hers with a reassuring pat. She looked like she was trying desperately not to flee.

Sophie and Richard joined the Simmonds family, who were sitting at one side of the large ballroom. Andrew rose as they approached and offered Sophie his chair. She sat down and Richard laid a hand on her shoulder.

James wanted to be Richard. He needed to be near her.

* * *

Sophie ran her finger over her wedding band, despite the fact that it was covered by a silk glove. The action gave her comfort, even if it was minor.

What am I supposed to do now?

As soon as she felt as though she was coming to grips with what happened to her, there was a wrench thrown in for good measure. She was lost in her thoughts when the Lieutenant approached the group. Richard introduced him to the family, and Sophie couldn't do anything but stare at him. She didn't know what to say. He could seriously be Jamie's identical twin. Maybe he was a distant relative.

She did notice that he darted several looks in her direction. She lowered her head slightly so he wouldn't catch her gaze.

The poor man probably thinks I'm a loon and should stay very far away from me.

Her thoughts were interrupted by warm breath in her ear. "If I leave you briefly, will you be all right?" Richard asked.

Wanting to smack his face away, Sophie stifled a growl. "I'm fine, Richard, really."

"I can stay."

Sophie gritted her teeth. "Go," and then under her breath, "*away.*"

Watching the men as Richard left her to introduce James to a few key people, her stomach churned. Every time the lieutenant shook hands, smiled, or quite frankly, moved any part of his body, she had flashes of Jamie. She turned when Christine walked over to her.

"How are you?"

"I'm fine." Sophie stood before Christine could sit down. "Do you think we could step outside and take a little walk? It's stifling in here."

"Yes, definitely."

The girls left through the side door and with linked arms, started walking. The night air was cool, and a breeze created a slight bite to the air, so Sophie pulled her shawl closer to her shoulders as the girls let out a collective sigh, enjoying the breathing room.

"This is so much better. I didn't know if I could have stayed in that ballroom for much longer." Sophie sighed. "And not just because of the heat."

Christine smiled gently. The girls ended up at the stables. Sophie always seemed to find herself here whenever she was deep in thought. There were a few lanterns lit as she led Christine into the barn and, as was her habit, towards Samson's stall. The horse popped his head out and nuzzled her hand.

"Are you feeling better, Sophie?" Christine made her way to Gentle Ben's stall.

"Other than total and complete confusion, you mean? I'm great."

"Sophie."

Sophie kissed Samson's muzzle. "Just when I thought I could start to let Jamie go, his look-a-like walks through the door just to mess with me." She laughed a little at the absurdity.

"Yes, it is strange." Christine handed her horse a sugar cube.

Hearing noise to their left, the girls turned to see two men staggering towards them. They appeared to be dirty and very drunk.

"Well, well. Good evening ladies, you appear to be all by yourselves. Would you like some company?"

Christine and Sophie darted nervous glances at each other.

"We were just leaving." Sophie grasped Christine's hand.

"Aw, now, come on, ladies. We can offer you something that the party can't," said the larger of the two.

"No, thank you, we'll take our leave now." Christine started to pull Sophie towards the barn doors. They had to pass the men to leave the stables, and as they walked by the large one, he reached out and grabbed Sophie's arm.

"Don't hurry away on our account." He yanked her toward him.

"Let go of me!" Sophie tried to pull her arm away from him. He wouldn't let go.

"You're real pretty. I bet you never had anyone like me before."

"You're real right. I've never had an ugly, smelly drunk before and I have no intention of having one now. Release me."

Despite her bluster, Sophie's panic rose as the man held her tighter. She and Christine stupidly hadn't told anyone where they were going. Despite Jamie's intensive tutelage in basic mixed martial arts training, she didn't know if she could defend herself in her heavy skirts. She tried to think of a way to get out of this.

Christine started to pull her toward the barn doors, when his just-as-ugly friend grabbed her and pulled her away from Sophie. He held her arms from behind so that she couldn't get free of him. Christine screamed but with the music and laughter in the ballroom, Sophie didn't think anyone would hear them. Samson whinnied loudly, visibly upset. Pounding his hoof, he kicked out and managed to kick a hole in his stall door.

The big smelly one pulled Sophie in front of him and pushed her up against one of the stalls. Leaning his head down, he tried to kiss her, the smell of his rancid, alcoholic breath turning her stomach. Moving her head away, she deflected as much as she could and felt bile rising in her throat as he tried to kiss her again.

"Get your hands off me, you moron." Sophie slammed her head against him. She tried for a head-butt, however only managed to clip him on the chin and give herself a headache. She tried to kick as hard as she could but she couldn't get any momentum in her hoop skirt and tight bodice.

Slapping her hard across the face, he fattened her lip and she could taste blood. "Quit fightin' me, bitch! You might be uppity and rich, but you're all the same in the end. You're going to like this."

Squeezing her eyes shut, Sophie closed her mouth tight and tried to keep him from kissing her. All of a sudden, she felt a tug and then he no longer held her in his filthy grip. She opened her eyes when she heard flesh connecting with bone and turned to see the big smelly drunk passed out on the floor of the barn. The lieutenant stood over him, shaking out his hand.

She turned to see Richard pull the other one off Christine and grasp her upper arms. "Are you all right?"

"Yes." Christine braced herself against his chest. "Thank you both for the assistance."

"What the hell were you thinking coming all the way out here by yourselves? Have you lost your minds? Why didn't you tell anyone where you were going? Why didn't you come and ask me to escort you?" Richard ranted.

"Richard, you were otherwise engaged and neither one of us came here alone. We had no reason to think anything like that would happen." Christine stepped away from him.

CHAPTER FOURTEEN

RICHARD NARROWED HIS eyes. "You are *never* to do anything like that again, do you hear me? If you hadn't come out here alone, this would have never happened. From now on, you are to tell me what you are doing at all times." He grasped Sophie's shoulders and squeezed. "You are never to do anything that stupid again."

"Leave me alone, Richard. You don't own me." Sophie pushed at his chest.

He crossed his arms. "You're a woman, Sophie—*my* woman. You need to remember that, and act accordingly. You're my responsibility, and I have every say in what you do and don't do."

Sophie rubbed her temples. "I am most definitely *not* your woman, Richard? I don't understand why you can't get that fact through your thick head."

"Sophie, I'm your protector and therefore, you need to adhere to my direction."

She fisted her hands at her side. "My protector, Richard?" Sophie threw her arms up. "You're an ass!" Stomping out of the barn, she didn't make it to the doors.

Richard pulled her back to him, roughly grabbed her upper arms, and shook her.

"Get your hands off her," James warned.

"Let go of me," she ordered.

"Not until you do as I say."

He squeezed harder and she whimpered. "Richard you're hurting me."

Richard didn't budge. James walked over to him and physically removed him from her, staying between them. "I said, get your hands off her. You have no right to touch her like that."

"Lieutenant, it's none of your business," Richard snarled.

"It became my business when you started man-handling her. I understand you're upset, but it's never acceptable to touch a woman in anger. Why don't you take some time to pull yourself together and then you two can talk when you're calmer."

Sophie stood behind James and glared at Richard.

He grimaced and reached his hand out to her. "Sophie, I'm sorry."

"Just go away, Richard. You've had too much to drink. Again."

Christine approached and laid her hand on Richard's arm. "Richard, why don't we walk back to the house? Sophie will be fine with Lieutenant Emerson."

Richard looked at Sophie, nodded at Christine, and they left the barn. When they were alone, James turned to Sophie. "Are you all right, ma'am?"

Her quiet groan echoed through the space. "Lieutenant Emerson, please call me Sophie, or even Mrs. Ford. I abhor ma'am."

He cocked his head to the side. "There's a little bit of blood on your lip. Let me wipe that off for you."

Pulling out his handkerchief, he reached out to touch her lip, but she put her hands over her face and stifled a sob. He said nothing as he removed his jacket, settled it over her shoulders, and then gently pulled her into his arms. As she cried harder, he stroked her hair and held her closer. "Shh, it's okay."

Sophie let him hold her, drawing comfort from him.

He even smells like Jamie. What am I going to do?

Sophie took several deep breaths, stifled by hiccups, and then forced herself from his arms. "I'm so sorry, Lieutenant. I'm not normally this emotional."

"You've had a rather terrifying experience. I'd be more surprised if you weren't upset." He cupped her cheek gently. "And please call me, James."

"Thank you." She looked up at him and gave him a small smile.

"Are you ready to go back to the house? I'm sure they're concerned about you."

"Yes, that's probably a good idea." She smoothed the front of her skirts and adjusted her bodice. "This night was meant for you and your men, and here I am keeping you from it. I apologize."

"Don't. It's fine, truly." Taking her hand, he gently folded it into the curve of his arm. She felt safe as they made their way out of the barn.

He patted her hand and Sophie gasped at the sight of his swollen, red knuckles. "Your hand! We need to get you some ice."

He fisted and un-fisted his hand. "It's fine."

"Just how hard did you hit him?" Sophie's eyes searched his.

He grinned. "Not hard enough. He's still breathing."

Sophie felt a flutter in her belly at the impish grin, so familiar to her. Taking a deep breath, she let him take her hand again and they made it back to the house to find Richard pacing the foyer. He turned as soon as he heard the door and started towards her. James quickly put himself between the two of them and Sophie smiled as she laid her hand on his back.

"It's fine." Removing the borrowed jacket, Sophie handed it back to James and watched as he moved to the corner of the foyer but not out of sight.

"Sophie, I apologize for raising my voice. Everyone was concerned when we were unable to locate you. At first I wasn't as worried, thinking you were visiting Samson but when we got to the barn and heard you antagonizing that bastard and then saw him hit you, I just lost my mind. If James hadn't acted so quickly, I think I might have killed him."

Sophie scowled. "So, I was antagonizing him and that's why he hit me?"

"That's not what I said," Richard argued.

"Actually, it's exactly what you said. Why is it, Richard, that regardless of the situation, you jump to the conclusion that I somehow brought it on myself? You have this attitude that women are weak and incapable of doing anything without a big strong man around to guide us. I don't know where you got the impression that you are my protector. I have never asked for that, nor promised more than friendship. I expect my friends to respect me. You seem incapable of that."

"Sophie, that's absurd." He ran his hands through his hair.

"Which part, Richard? The part that you should respect me or the part that you think I am weak?"

"You're blowing this out of proportion. That man was drunk and extremely aggressive."

"*You're* drunk and aggressive!"

Richard put his hands to his head in obvious frustration. "There was no way you could have fought him off."

Sophie pointed at him in accusation. "Maybe not, but it doesn't give you the right to rule over me."

Richard reached out to touch her but she deflected him. He lowered his hand and closed it into a fist at his side. "I just want you to be safe."

"Richard, I am safe." She settled her palm over her chest in earnestness. "Look, I'm sorry if we scared you, and I will admit that we should have at least told someone where we were going, but you don't own me and I certainly don't answer to you. If you want this friendship to continue, I need you to remember that. Right now, I'd appreciate some space. Do you think you can do that for me?"

Richard nodded. "I don't want to fight with you, Sophie. Truce?"

"Yes, truce. Now, why don't the three of you go back in, and I'll join you shortly."

"I'll stay with you." Christine followed Sophie to her room. "Is everything all right? Well, besides the obvious?"

Sophie closed the door and took a deep breath. "Yes, I just needed a minute. Richard drives me crazy. I don't understand where he gets off thinking he owns me. He's so intense and I don't always know how to react. The way he grabbed me tonight scared me, but it also made me angry, because I hate that he's ruining our friendship."

"What happened after we left the barn?"

Sophie shrugged. "I embarrassed myself by crying all over the poor lieutenant's jacket and looking like a totally unbalanced female."

Christine grimaced. "It was a frightening experience. I had a moment myself on the way back to the house. I thought Richard was going to have an apoplexy. He's not accustomed to a crying female. Did the lieutenant understand?"

"Very much so. He was wonderful. Sweet and totally understanding. He held me and stroked my hair and made me feel protected and loved." Sophie sat down on the trunk and put her face in her hands. "He reminds me so much of Jamie."

"Well, we should go down to the party and try to forget this upset, have a pleasant evening, and put all of this behind us. What do you say?"

"All right, Christine, I'll try. I have a wicked headache from trying to head butt that man and I'm sure the crying didn't help."

"I'll bet Michael will have something. We'll ask him."

"Sounds good." Sophie stood and followed Christine back downstairs. Walking through the foyer and down the hall to the ballroom, they saw James turn and look straight at Sophie. He was standing just outside the doors, and the vision of him took her back to her wedding. She didn't know why she hadn't noticed before, but he was wearing an exact replica of the uniform Jamie wore that day. She grabbed Christine's hand for stability.

"What's amiss?" Christine whispered.

Sophie took a couple of deep breaths to calm herself. "Memories."

They continued to the doors of the ballroom.

"Lieutenant Emerson, shouldn't you be inside?" Christine smiled.

"I was taking some air and preparing to go inside when I saw you. I thought I'd wait and escort you in."

"So, you weren't waiting to make sure we were all right?" Sophie asked.

"Wouldn't even think about it," he said with a huge grin.

"Good answer." Her heart beat double-time and she laid her palm over her chest as if to calm it.

James suddenly seemed nervous. "What's wrong with your heart?"

"My heart?" She lowered her hand. "Nothing. I just do that sometimes, it's an old habit."

His stare lingered briefly but he didn't comment further.

"Did you get ice for your hand?"

James studied the bruises. "No need."

Sophie turned to Christine. "I'm going to take the Lieutenant to the kitchen, go on in without me."

Christine's eyes widened. "Is that wise?"

Sophie frowned. "Why wouldn't it be?"

Christine pulled her aside. "You shouldn't be alone with a man."

"How am I alone? The house is full of guests, not to mention staff. I promise I won't find an empty room and kiss him senseless—tonight."

Christine's face turned beet red. "You are terrible."

Sophie giggled. "I know. Now, go join the party." Sophie walked her back to the doors of the ballroom and waited for Christine to let herself inside before facing the Lieutenant. "Follow me, please."

"Ma'am, it's really not necessary."

Her head whipped up. "If you call me 'ma'am' one more time, I'll convince Michael to amputate that hand," she threatened as she led him down one corridor and then another on their way to the kitchen.

James laughed. A loud, deep, belly laugh, and Sophie nearly lost her mind. It was the same. The exact same.

"You have quite the vicious sense of humor, ma—I mean, Sophie."

Sophie grinned. "Good save."

Voices and smells wafted through the hallway as the couple arrived at the kitchen, and Sophie led him inside, a smile covering her face when she saw the cook directing everyone in her matronly voice.

When Sophie had first met Mary, she was taken aback. The woman was taller than she was—and thinner. She reminded Sophie of a flamingo, however, her countenance was that of a strict governess and her dark brown hair, peppered with gray, didn't fit Sophie's idea of what a nineteenth-century cook would look like, but she instantly loved her all the same. Sophie had always been drawn to the older generation, the crankier the better, and Jamie used to tell her she could charm the socks off anyone over the age of fifty.

"How's my favorite cook?" Sophie asked as she approached the woman.

"You stop right there, Missie. You're not allowed in my kitchens."

"As you've said, Mary. However, I have a soldier with a nasty bruised hand and I was hoping you might have some ice for him."

Mary stared at James, suspicion in her eyes. "Why does he have a bruised hand?"

Sophie leaned over and whispered, "He was defending my honor."

A grunt was Mary's only reply as she turned and found a block of ice and an ice pick. Sophie watched James's expression as the woman picked off a mound of ice and nearly giggled as he stepped back slightly. Mary was quite adept at using the ice pick—a little too adept.

Wrapping the shavings into a sackcloth, Mary handed it to Sophie and then shooed her from the room but not before Sophie caught her quick wink. Sophie led James down the hall and to a small alcove that housed a bench perfect for the couple to sit on before joining the party. "Sit."

He did so, and Sophie pulled his injured hand toward her. She laid the icepack gently over his knuckles, holding it in place as she sat and settled his hand on her lap. Raising her head, she caught his expression, and her heart stammered at the confusion she read in his eyes, but then he smiled and the look was gone.

"Better?" Her voice was gravelly with emotion.

"Much." His smile deepened. "Thank you."

"Miss Sophie?"

Sophie looked up to find Betty walking quickly toward them. "Hi, Betty. Did you need something?"

"I was asked to retrieve you, ma'am."

Sophie stood and tried to keep the irritation from her voice. "*Retrieve* me?"

James stood as well and Betty stepped back slightly. "Yes'm."

"By whom?" he asked.

Betty cleared her throat but didn't answer the question.

"Betty?" Sophie crossed her arms. "By whom?"

Betty studied her shoes. "Mr. Madden."

"Thank you, Betty," Sophie said through gritted teeth. "I'll be along shortly."

Betty didn't budge. Sophie narrowed her eyes. "What?"

"I'm sorry, ma'am. I am to escort you."

"Are you *kidding* me?" Feeling a hand gently touch her back, Sophie took a deep breath and forced a smile. "Betty, you don't work for Richard Madden, so please don't worry about getting into trouble. I'll be along shortly."

Before Betty could respond, heavy footsteps echoed in the hallway and Sophie glared as Richard approached. "You are supposed to be in the ballroom."

"And you are supposed to be giving me space," she countered.

"What were you doing?"

"None of your business."

Richard turned his gaze to the lieutenant. "Missing your mama, James? Has the ice helped?"

James chuckled but Sophie moved to strike. "You are such a jerk!"

"Sophie," James whispered in warning under his breath, sending a shiver down her spine.

"Sophie, come back inside, and we'll dance." Richard's tone was laced with warning.

"I'm not dancing with you, and I'm not coming back inside until I know my guest is comfortable."

"I'm perfectly fine, Mrs. Ford." James handed the ice to Betty. "Shall we return?"

Sophie shook, anger coursing through her veins, as she tried to get her emotions under control. "Yes, lieutenant. Let's join the party."

Richard offered his arm but Sophie glanced at him before wrapping her hand in the crook of James's elbow. Catching the flash of anger in Richard's eyes, she glared at him in response and swept her hand in front of her. "After you, *Mr.* Madden."

Richard paused for several seconds but eventually made his move toward the ballroom. Sophie held James back for a few extra seconds and then let him lead her in the same direction.

"You are poking the bear, Mrs. Ford."

Sophie gasped at the use of one of her favorite expressions. She used to warn Jamie the same way when Luke was angry. For whatever reason, Jamie liked to push his best friend almost to the point of physical altercation and Sophie never understood why. "Where did you hear that?"

"I'm sorry?"

"That expression. I didn't realize it was common in, uh—these parts."

James's eyebrows puckered. "I'm not certain. I don't believe I've ever used it before, but it seemed appropriate in this situation."

Sophie chuckled. "Most definitely. And yes, I'm poking the bear. He's being a jerk and I don't care for it."

They arrived at the doors of the ballroom, Richard standing sentry and glaring in James's general direction. James escorted Sophie inside, the moment was forgotten, and the rest of the evening passed without incident.

The party wrapped up just after midnight and Sophie couldn't have been more relieved. Exhausted and wanting to curl up in a ball and sleep for a year, she waited with Christine in the foyer and said farewell to the final guests with Michael and Nona, as Richard and James both walked up. Michael and Nona said their goodnights and then the girls walked the men out to the front porch. James said farewell to Christine and turned to Sophie.

"Mrs. Ford, it was very nice to meet you. Thank you for a lovely evening." Her stomach somersaulted as he took her hand and kissed it.

As he lowered his hand, she noticed something on his palm. "Lieutenant, how did you get that scar on your hand?"

He stared at it briefly before answering, "I don't remember."

"That's quite a nasty scar not to remember how you got it."

Richard interrupted any further conversation by taking both Sophie's hands in his. He kissed them, lingering a little longer than was perhaps necessary, and forcing her to smell his alcohol-laden breath. "Sophie, I'll see you tomorrow. Sleep well."

Sophie and Christine went upstairs, helped each other out of their dresses, and then went to bed. Sophie, too emotionally drained to dwell on the bizarre night, fell into a deep sleep.

* * *

"Ten-Cow, are you remembering now?"

"Jamie?" Sophie opened her eyes, but it wasn't Jamie standing over her bed. "James?"

"Remember the cut?"

Sophie thought back to the night Jamie made dinner and the shout she'd heard from the kitchen. Rushing into the room, she found blood everywhere, and Jamie standing over the sink with a bloody towel wrapped around his hand, his face pinched in pain.

"Baby, what happened?" Sophie asked.

"I sliced open my hand. Damn, it hurts. If I can just get the bleeding stopped, I think it'll be fine. We'll wrap it tight and I'll be good to go."

"Let me have a look."

A trip to the hospital ended with eight stitches and a scar that was a constant reminder of how close Jamie came to losing function in his left hand.

* * *

Sophie jerked awake and sat up slowly.

James.

Jamie. Looks like him, sounds like him, has identical scar. If I could just get him to show me his chest.

"For more than just confirmation," Sophie said aloud, her body suddenly aroused.

CHAPTER FIFTEEN

SOPHIE WOKE UP late, her face and lip smarting from the night before, and the dream about Jamie's hand feeling more like a nightmare.

Well past nine o'clock when she finally dragged herself out of bed, she splashed water on her face in an effort to wake up. Walking over to the windows, she opened them, allowing the breeze to freshen the room.

A beautiful spring day greeted her, and she took a deep breath. The smell of wild flowers was better than any Glade Plug-In she'd used in the future.

Observing activity over at the stables, she noticed James almost immediately, speaking with a few of the men and laughing. His jacket had been discarded and he wore a light shirt and a blue pair of pants.

Yum, aren't you magnificent?

Settling her elbow on the windowsill, Sophie sighed as she watched him direct, and then stand back and observe as the men worked with the horses. She stood up and pushed her hair away from her face.

Maybe I should take a little walk to visit Samson.

Sophie dressed and stepped across the hall to check on Topper before she made her way downstairs. He wasn't in his room and when she arrived in the dining room, no one was around, so she grabbed a quick bite of food before gathering her outerwear and making her way to the stables. The sun was bright despite the slight chill, and she kept her head down as she rounded the corner into the darkened interior. She ran into a solid wall of muscle. Strong arms gently grasped her arms to steady her. "I'm so sorry, excuse me."

"Pardon me, I'm sorry," Sophie said at the same time. When she looked up, her heart skipped a beat. "Oh, Lieutenant Emerson. Good morning."

After studying her for a brief moment, he smiled. "Good morning, Mrs. Ford, how are you this morning? How's your lip?"

"Much better, thank you for asking. It's still a bit sore, but I think I'll live." She smiled without thought, and grimaced slightly as her lip smarted. Putting her hand to her mouth, she chuckled quietly. "Ow."

His eyes flashed with concern, but he smiled gently. "Careful."

He was staring at her as though she was the most important person in the world, reminiscent of a man she was not ready to forget. Sophie lowered her head shyly. "I'm fine."

"Sophie, is that you?"

James stepped away from her and Sophie rolled her eyes. "Hi, Richard." She turned towards his voice coming from the barn, irritated at the interruption.

"Is everything all right? What are you doing here?"

"I came to see Samson and ran into Lieutenant Emerson."

"Literally," James said under his breath so that only she could hear him.

Sophie glanced up at him and he winked. She felt warmth in her cheeks as she looked back at Richard. He had moved to her side in an obvious attempt to put himself between her and James. She tried not to scowl.

"Lieutenant Emerson!" The group turned to see Topper jog from the arena. "I think I did it."

James turned and reached out to take the rope Topper held out to him. He turned it over in his hands a few times and then yanked the edges to test its strength. "This is well done, Private. I dare say I couldn't have done better."

Sophie's heart melted at the look on Topper's face. His countenance changed in an instant and she could see the pride in his eyes. She smiled. Jamie was great with teenagers; it would appear his doppelganger was as well.

Richard squeezed her elbow. "Would you like to watch the training this morning?"

No, I don't want to watch the training. I want to watch the lieutenant. Preferably without clothing.

Sophie shook off her fantasies and glanced up at Richard. "Um, sure. Let me just check on Samson and then I'll join you in a moment."

"All right." Richard nodded towards the arena. "James, if I could speak with you for a moment?"

"Certainly." Giving Sophie another quick smile, he followed Richard. "Topper? You coming?"

Sophie shook off her irritation and made her way over to Samson's stall. He poked his head out to greet her and she spent a few minutes with him. It gave her time to pull herself together before walking back to the arena. Although she spent over an hour watching the training, Sophie wasn't really paying attention, drawn to the lieutenant who stood to her left working with a group of about ten men. She had a difficult time taking her eyes off him.

Realizing she couldn't stand and drool over the Jamie clone forever, she turned to Richard and let him know she was leaving. Walking towards the house, waving to James and Topper as she left, she gave way to the emotions of the night before. By the time she got home, she felt raw and emotionally exhausted.

Sophie made her way to the library and tried to distract herself with a book...or three. Rather than take them to her room, she curled up in her favorite chair in front of the fireplace and prepared to read before lunch was served, figuring she had an hour or so to kill. The time went entirely too quickly.

"Sophie?"

Sighing in frustration, she looked up from her book and toward the familiar voice. "Richard, what are you doing here?"

"Nona invited me for lunch. I offered to tell you that it was being served in the dining room."

I'll bet you did.

Following him down the hall—at a distance—she suppressed a scowl as he waited for her to catch up. As they entered the dining room, he placed his hand possessively on her back. She gave him a warning glare, not understanding why he wasn't grasping the concept of giving her space. Then she saw who sat at the dining room table.

James, Topper, and Michael stood when she entered the room and she realized that Richard was obviously trying to mark his territory. Moving away from Richard, she approached James. "Lieutenant Emerson, what a nice surprise."

James gave her a deep smile and nodded.

"Topper, you look well." Sophie smiled and almost died of shock when he smiled back.

"Shall we eat?" Nona suggested and everyone took their seats.

During the meal, Richard attempted to sit by, speak to, or monopolize Sophie at every turn. She was still tired from the night before and didn't know how much longer she could hold her temper. Every time she'd start a conversation with James, Richard would interrupt with something inane.

The meal passed too quickly, and the men had to go back to work. Sophie walked James and Richard to the foyer, wishing for some time alone with James. "Lieutenant, thank you for spending lunch with us today."

"We really need to get back to the training, Lieutenant," Richard interrupted.

"Yes, we should get going."

Although Sophie was annoyed with Richard's interruption, she let it drop, entirely too tired to get into it with him again. Topper followed the men, and Sophie stood on the porch for a few minutes watching them ride away.

* * *

As they rode back to the arena, James found himself preoccupied with his thoughts. His world was a blur of contradictions. He didn't recognize anything around him. The clothing seemed wrong, the speech didn't always make sense, and he found himself suddenly in the middle of a war he knew *entirely* too much about.

Over the past few months, he'd been having strange dreams that confused him even further. They weren't full dreams, just snapshots of visions. A woman without a face in an ivory dress, a woman without clothes. A large ship. A wedding by the ocean. Nothing that gave him any clue as to who he was, or what he was dreaming about.

James's attraction to Sophie overwhelmed him. She filled his dreams every night, and his thoughts every day. For whatever reason, he hated seeing her in pain and felt unusually protective. He wasn't certain why, but after spending a sleepless night thinking about her, he made the decision to explore his attraction to her. Richard Madden be damned.

Shaking his memories away, he looked back to see Sophie standing on the porch. She raised her hand and waved. He smiled as she walked over the threshold and closed the door.

* * *

Sophie woke the next morning, disappointed that James hadn't joined them for dinner the night before. Especially since Topper had spent the entire meal regaling them with stories of the hero that was Lieutenant James Emerson. She would have even accepted Richard's presence if it meant she could see the lieutenant again but she was left to entertain herself and spent the majority of the night staring into the fire in the library. Forcing herself out of bed, she got herself dressed and made her way downstairs.

As she entered the dining room, she was surprised to find James sitting at the table, tracing his finger up and down the scar on his left hand. Standing in the doorway a moment, she watched him. His hair seemed to grow longer every day, currently falling over his eyes, and she noticed him try to sweep it off his face. He had trimmed his beard but it was still bushy.

"Good morning."

James stood quickly and smiled. "Good morning."

"Is everything okay?"

"Yes, fine," he answered somewhat distractedly.

"Is there something I can help you with?"

"Hmm? Oh, no. Mitch—he's my sergeant. Anyway, Mitch took a group of men out early this morning. I ran into Mrs. Wade when I arrived back at the arena and she invited me to breakfast."

Sophie's heart raced as his gaze lingered on her, his blue eyes clear and familiar. "Um, will your sergeant be gone long?"

James nodded. "He's been called back to Averell's unit."

"Oh," she whispered. "Are you close friends?"

James smiled sadly. "Yes."

"Let's hope you'll see him soon, then." Sophie choked on the words, knowing there would be no guarantees.

James took his seat and smiled. "Thank you."

"May I offer you some coffee, Lieutenant?"

"Coffee would be wonderful, thank you."

Sophie poured him a cup, and on autopilot, put two lumps of sugar and some cream in his cup. "Oh, shoot, I'm so sorry. I should have asked, I just assumed. That's how Jamie likes his coffee, not that you care how my husband liked his coffee. Sorry I'm rambling. You probably like it black or some other way, don't you? I'll drink it."

She started to remove the cup, but James placed his hand over hers. The touch sent a shiver down her spine, making her heart race.

"Sophie, it's just how I like it."

As he stared up at her with his perfect smile, all Sophie could think about was how much she wanted to kiss him. She was shaken by the physical touch and desperately wanted more, but pushed her desire aside as she sat down, slipped her hand from under his, and placed it in her lap.

"I'd hoped you would be down here early. I wanted to make sure you were doing all right after that nasty incident at the ball. You seemed quite shaken by it at the time. Not that I don't think you can take care of yourself, of course," he added quickly.

She gave a quiet laugh. "No, I'm fine. Other than a little swelling, my lip is almost completely healed."

There was an awkward silence as they sipped their coffee.

"So, tell me about yourself, James. Where are you from?"

Slowly lowering his cup, his eyebrows puckered. "I don't know. I seem to have lost my memory of everything prior to several months ago."

"You don't remember anything?"

"I have flashes of things in my dreams, but I don't know what they mean."

Sophie raised her cup and sipped slowly. "That must be frustrating."

James nodded.

"How have you managed to engage Topper?"

James smiled. "He just needed a way to focus his anger and some minor instruction on how to do things with one hand. I started with simple tasks and have been moving to more difficult ones as he gets used to using his left hand."

Michael and Nona walked into the room, and Sophie forced away a frown. She wanted to continue their conversation, wanted to watch him eat, wanted to watch him smile.

Before their morning greetings were finished, Richard joined them. Sophie wanted to shrink into the corner when he walked over and kissed her hand. "Good morning, Sophie, how are you this morning?"

"I'm fine, Richard. How are you?" Pulling her hand from his, she shoved it in the folds of her skirts and forced a smile.

"Very well, thank you."

"Where's Topper?" James drew her attention again—by speaking.

Oh, and smiling.

Richard gave a civil smile. "I have him working with one of the horses this morning."

Sophie shook her head in an effort to force her thoughts away. Her mind felt suspiciously like overcooked oatmeal.

"What are your plans today?" Richard touched her arm.

She pulled away, stopping a hiss. "I'm scheduled at the hospital." She looked at James and smiled. "What about you?"

"We're going to be working without the horses for a few hours." Richard answered the question directed toward James, and Sophie rolled her eyes. Sophie was grateful when Michael took over the conversation, happy to sit and listen, choosing to observe the lieutenant in an attempt to block out Richard. Sophie was surprised how quickly everyone finished their breakfast, and when they were ready to leave, Sophie walked them out.

James and Richard moved toward the front door. Sophie hung back and let the men go ahead of her. As James passed her, he lightly touched her arm and gave her a smile. Almost as if he knew they had more to discuss and he would find a way to make it happen. Her stomach did a little flip. Sophie said good-bye and then made her way upstairs to finish getting ready and walk out to the hospital. The morning passed without incident, everyone relieved that there were no new injuries to tend to and the men were all resting comfortably.

By noon, her stomach grumbled almost loud enough to be heard. She had finally gained back most of the weight she'd lost during her illness, but now her body complained when she didn't eat at regular times. Sophie knew she'd need to take a break if she wanted to avoid a nasty headache.

"Sophie?"

Turning, she saw Christine motioning to her from the front of the tent. She made her way to her...and stalled. Richard walked in and stood behind Christine, a smile on his face as though he'd just done something benevolent.

Taking a deep breath, Sophie forced her feet to move again. "Hello."

"I have a basket full of food, and since I won't be able to eat it all myself, I thought perhaps you might join me," Richard said.

Her stomach betrayed her with its call for food, and Sophie tried to keep from wrapping her arms around her middle. "I suppose that would be all right."

"Excellent."

Richard escorted her outside, and Sophie turned when she noticed Christine wasn't following. "Isn't Christine coming?"

"Not this time."

Sophie suddenly felt a little nauseous, but before she could think about it, they heard pounding hooves and turned toward the sound. James pulled up and dismounted, his horse's nostrils flaring, and coat frothy from sweat. He pulled an unconscious soldier from the horse's back and rushed into the tent. Sophie followed.

James carried the man to one of the cots and gently settled him on his back. Christine and Dr. Palmer rushed over as Sophie made her way to James. "What happened?"

"He was shot," James said.

"Where?" Sophie lifted the man's head and laid it on a pillow.

James went quiet. Sophie took the hint but fully intended to get the story once everything calmed down. A groan from the soldier drew Sophie's attention, and she moved to help Christine hold him down.

"Sophie, you've been on your feet for hours. You should go on your picnic." Christine looked at her over her shoulder.

Dr. Palmer called one of the other nurses over and then forced Richard and James to leave, insisting that Sophie go with them as well. The three of them left the hospital, and Richard took Sophie's elbow as they walked towards the carriage. Pulling away from him, she had a sudden idea and turned back toward the lieutenant who was mounting his horse. "James!" she called. "Why don't you join us for lunch?"

"Sophie," Richard growled.

Sophie turned back to him, a serene smile on her face. "You did say you had too much food, did you not? It would appear that the lieutenant just saved that man's life, and I'd imagine he's very, very hungry."

"I'd be most grateful for the food, Sophie, thank you." James rode up to the couple.

Richard assisted her into his carriage, while James followed them on horseback. They arrived relatively quickly at the lake, and despite her reluctance, Sophie sat on the blanket Richard spread out for them. It wasn't lost on her that there wasn't much room for James, but she refrained from comment and started to unpack the picnic basket.

Pulling out fried chicken, potato salad, freshly baked bread, cookies, ripe peaches, and a bottle of wine, Sophie smiled. "This looks amazing."

"I tried to think of your favorites." Richard leaned back on his arm.

Ignoring the crawl down her spine, Sophie turned to James. "Lieutenant, may I prepare a plate for you?"

"That would be wonderful, Sophie, thank you."

* * *

James noticed the glare Richard gave him and raised an eyebrow. The glove appeared to have been thrown and James accepted the challenge. Sophie would be his, he didn't care who he had to step over to get to her. He'd spent every night since meeting her, tossing and turning, never achieving a full night's sleep. Every fiber of his being reached out for her, and he wasn't going to let anyone stand in his way.

CHAPTER SIXTEEN

RICHARD POURED WINE, but only two glasses. Sophie pointedly ignored Richard's childish act and handed her glass to James before turning back to Richard. "Richard, what can I get for you?"

"Before all of that, I need to speak with you privately about something. Would you join me on a little walk?" Richard stood.

"Now?"

"Yes, please."

"All right," she said cautiously and then looked over at James and mouthed 'sorry' to him.

James shook his head, and Richard helped her stand. Sophie followed Richard toward the lake. Sophie crossed her arms and tried to keep some kind of distance between him.

Richard smiled. "Over these past few months, I have developed a deep affection for you. I would like to explore a closer relationship."

Sophie took a deep breath. "Richard, please. I have said more than once that I can't commit to anything more than friendship."

"Sophie, you're all alone. I want to take care of you. What will you do without a man to provide for you?"

"You can't be serious. Didn't we just have this discussion? I have never needed, nor wanted, a man to provide for me."

Sophie moved away from him, but he took her arm to keep her from leaving.

"I could make you happy." He turned her to face him.

"Richard, I don't want a relationship. I'm sure that whomever you choose will be a lucky woman, but it won't be me. I can't just forget Jamie and everything that we shared. You need to forget about me, and move on."

Richard pulled her to him and kissed her. She frantically pushed at his chest, but he just held her tighter. "Richard, stop it. You're drunk."

* * *

James jumped up from the blanket, and began to make his way over to them.

"Relax." Richard bent to kiss her again. Sophie slapped him. Hard.

"Hey!" James yelled.

I'm going to kill him.

"Please, Richard. Stop. I don't want this." She backed away, visibly shaken.

"Has he already taken from you what should be mine?" Richard seethed.

Her head whipped up. "What are you talking about?"

"It's the lieutenant, isn't it? He didn't waste time getting to you, did he?"

"You're crazy." Sophie turned to walk away from him.

Richard reached for her, but James moved in between them and stood nose to nose with him. "What the hell do you think you're doing?"

"She's mine, Lieutenant," Richard fumed.

James pushed at his chest. "I believe she has made it perfectly clear that she is *not* yours. You keep your hands off her from now on, or you'll have to deal with me."

Sophie stalked back towards the stables.

"Sophie Ford, don't walk away from me," Richard yelled.

Sophie turned. "*Ford*, Richard! Remember that. I am Jamie's and no one else's."

Richard let out a string of curse words.

"Leave me alone!" she shouted.

"Sophie, get back here." He tried to walk toward her, but James kept himself between them.

"NO! Just go home Richard."

Richard turned to pack the supplies back into the carriage, and James waited until he was well on his way, then mounted his horse and took off after Sophie.

* * *

Fuming by the time she reached the stables, frustrated by how things were just getting more and more complicated, and growing angrier by the second, all Sophie wanted to do was kick something, or someone, as she made her way over to Samson's stall and peeked inside. He wasn't there.

Great. What am I going to do now?

Within minutes, James entered the barn, pulling his hat from his head and heading straight for her.

"I'm really sorry you were witness to that display." Sophie wrinkled her nose and sat back down on the bale of hay. "I don't know what came over him. He's never acted that way before. Lately, he's been getting really possessive and aggressive. I just can't seem to make sense out of anything right now."

James sat next to her and cocked his head in question. "What do you need to make sense out of, Sophie?"

Surprising even herself, she told him about Jamie and how much she missed him. She told him how much seeing him confused her. As he tenderly put his arm around her shoulders and let her vent it out, Sophie felt worse the closer he pulled her to him, the smell of horse and leather strangely intoxicating, and it took her several minutes to calm down. Laying her cheek on his chest, Sophie relaxed into his side.

"All done?" He swept her hair gently from her damp cheek.

"I don't know yet." Smiling as she took a deep breath, she realized her palm was squeezing his very muscular thigh. She pulled her hand away and stood. "I always seem to be crying all over you."

James leaned forward, his arms braced on his knees. "What can I do to help?"

"Talking helps." Sophie leaned against the wall. "Although, I think I'm letting my frustration overtake me."

James stood and walked over to her, laying his hands on her shoulders before gently lifting her face to look at him. "You have every right to be frustrated." He lowered his head and gently placed his lips on hers. She responded immediately, grasping his jacket and opening her mouth to allow better access. All too quickly, he pulled himself away. "I apologize. I shouldn't have done that. You've had a rough day and here I am adding to it. It won't happen again."

Sophie ran a finger over her still tingling lips, her stomach somersaulting. "Honestly, James, I hope it does happen again."

He smiled and took her hand, kissing her palm.

"May I ask you a personal question?" she asked.

"Of course."

"What the hell is going on here?" Richard's voice came from the doorway.

Sophie and James jumped apart like a couple of guilty teenagers.

"Richard," Sophie growled.

"You certainly didn't waste any time, did you?" Richard accused.

"Richard, you need to leave." James pointed to the door.

"Sophie and I have more to discuss."

"Like I'm going to let you get within a hundred feet of her." James stood in front of Sophie, his arms crossed, legs braced. Ready for a fight. "You've been here less than a week and you have the nerve to steal her out from under me. I won't allow it."

Sophie let out a squeal of frustration and approached Richard. James laid a hand on her arm and pushed her behind him again. Sophie wouldn't be silenced, and although she stayed behind James, she stepped sideways. "First of all, I was never yours to steal. Second, you have no right to say what is allowed, and what is not. Get it through your thick skull, Richard. I don't want you. Never have, never will."

Richard stalked her, his hands fisted at his side.

James stepped in front of her again. "Richard, I'm losing patience with you. You need to leave."

Richard attempted to push James aside but he grabbed Richard's hand and pinned his arm behind his back, rendering Richard immobile. "I told you to leave."

Sophie stared in shock at the classic martial arts move.

Something strange is going on here.

James pushed Richard out of the barn. "It stops here. If Sophie feels uncomfortable around you, or if you touch her again, I'll deal with you on my terms. Do I make myself clear?"

"You bastard." Richard took a swing.

James deflected the fist and swept his leg across Richard's knees. Sophie watched the fight from just inside the barn and her hand went to her mouth as Richard fell on his backside, unhurt but humiliated.

"Richard, just go," Sophie said as Richard scrambled to his feet. He finally strode off towards the arena, hands fisted once again at his sides.

"Where did you learn those defense moves?" she asked.

"I have no idea." He stroked her arm. "I seem to have always known them."

She knew now, without a doubt he was Jamie. She just needed proof.

Before she could ask, he took her hand. "Why don't I escort you home? I'd feel more comfortable if you and Richard were distanced a bit."

Sophie sighed. "Yeah, that doesn't always work."

"I noticed." James grinned. "I'll walk you back now and then we'll figure out what to do going forward."

"All right. Thank you." James slipped her hand into his arm and they began their slow walk back to the house.

"What happened to the soldier?" Sophie asked when she noticed him scan their surroundings.

"Which soldier?"

"Seriously?"

James adjusted his hat but didn't answer for several seconds. "He was shot."

"Nice try. Tell me what happened."

Before he could answer, and before Sophie could ask her very personal question, Christine came rushing out of the house. "Sophie!"

"Hi, Christine."

"Is everything all right? You didn't return from lunch and didn't retrieve the buggy."

"Yes, I'm fine, Christine. It's been a rough afternoon. I'll tell you all about it later if that's okay? I just want to curl up and take a nap."

Christine smiled. "Well, then you should."

Sophie nodded as the three made their way into the house and then turned to face James. "Thank you for everything, I'm so sorry you got caught in the middle."

He took her hand and kissed it and Sophie made her way upstairs and flopped onto her bed. She let out a sigh when she heard a quiet knock at her door. "Come in."

"Sophie? I have some food for you." Christine stepped into the room.

Sophie sat up and raised an eyebrow. "How did you know I was hungry?"

"The lieutenant said you didn't eat." Christine sat on the bed next to Sophie. "Now, tell me what's going on. You look as though the world is coming to an end."

"I've made a mess of everything." Sophie took a bite of chicken and sighed in pleasure, even if it was short lived. "Richard is the biggest jerk! I'd have never guessed he could be so abusive. I have forced James in the middle of my fight with him and some very strange things are happening."

"Like what?"

"He kissed me."

"Richard?"

"Jamie."

"Sophie," Christine said sadly.

Popping a grape to her mouth, Sophie groaned. "He's Jamie. I know he is, I just don't know how to prove it without getting his clothes off." Christine let out a choking sound and Sophie sighed. "Well, it's true, Christine."

Sophie continued to eat and gave Christine a minute to compose herself.

"I don't understand what's going on with Richard," Christine whispered. "He's never acted this way before. His actions simply don't fit the man I know. I'm sorry, Sophie, I know you two were getting close."

"I have no idea if we can salvage our friendship but right now, I don't want to see him. As far as James is concerned, all I want to do is spend every waking moment with him. There's something not quite right going on, and I feel like I need to figure it out and quickly. I'm sick of being confused."

They continued to talk until it was time for Christine to leave for home.

* * *

Once Christine left, Sophie made her way to her favorite spot in the library and curled up with a new book. Only a few minutes passed when she heard someone whisper her name. Peeking around the chair, she saw James standing in the doorway and jumped up, excited to see him.

"I don't want to intrude. I just came by to see how you were."

"I'm much better, thank you. What time is it?" Sophie slid a lock of hair behind her ear.

"It's almost five thirty."

"Oh! I thought it was much earlier." Sophie chewed her thumbnail as an awkward silence settled around them. "Thank you for telling Christine I hadn't eaten today. That was very thoughtful."

James smiled. "You're welcome. Now, I should probably get back."

Sophie walked over to him and put her hand on his arm. "Do you have to go? Can you stay for dinner?" She didn't want to beg, but she didn't want to miss time with him either.

James chuckled. "I am done with the training for today, so yes, Sophie, I can stay if you like."

"I'd like." He took her hand and Sophie could barely think straight. "How was it after I left? Was Richard a bear?"

He ran his thumb along her knuckles. "He disappeared. I haven't seen him in the past few hours and I have to admit, that's one of the reasons I came by so early. I wanted to make sure he wasn't here. I hope that's all right."

"Yes, it's fine." Sophie sighed in resignation. "I don't know what to do about Richard. He lost his ever-blessed mind today. I don't understand it."

"Lust can do strange things to a man."

Sophie snorted. "What makes you think Richard lusts after me?"

"Have you looked in a mirror?" Leaning down, he gently kissed her, and she slid her hands up his chest and linked them behind his neck. He broke the kiss, seemingly unable to catch his breath. "Sophie, we should talk."

"About what?"

"I can't sleep."

"You can't?"

"No." James raised his open palms to his temples in a circular, frantic motion. "Thoughts of you constantly run through my head."

"Really?"

James sighed. "Really."

"Well, what should we do then?"

"I'd like to spend time with you, privately, if you would be open to that."

Sophie grinned. "I'd love to spend time with you. Privately or otherwise."

The flitter of shallow footsteps sounded in the hallway, and Betty pushed the door open. "Dinner is almost ready, Miss Sophie.

"Thank you, Betty."

Sophie led Jamie to the dining room. It was empty, so the couple moved on to the parlor.

Nona and Michael were in the midst of an intense conversation with Richard. When Richard saw Jamie, he bellowed, "Get out!"

"Richard," Nona admonished.

"What the hell are you doing here?" Richard snapped.

"Richard, calm down. I asked James to stay for dinner," Sophie said.

Richard took a deep breath. "I require a private word with you."

"That will never happen," James said from behind Sophie.

"Sophie, there are things about this man that you don't know. Things I'm certain he hasn't told you."

James scowled. "What haven't I told her?"

Sophie stood between the two men and rolled her eyes. "Please. You two are snorting like a couple of angry bulls. Let's step outside. I'd rather not do this in the doctor's house."

Sophie turned and moved towards the foyer and out the front door. James and Richard followed her onto the porch and Richard reached over to take her arm. James quickly inserted himself between the two of them. "Don't touch her."

Sophie faced Richard. "Richard, I have nothing to say to you. I don't even know why you're here. I asked for space."

"I know. I've made a mess of everything. Sophie, please forgive me."

"Richard, this isn't a forgiveness issue, it's a boundary issue. I can forgive you for trying to force yourself on me, but I need to know it's not going to happen again."

"You don't seem to have any boundary issues with the Lieutenant."

"This is exactly what I'm talking about. You're sulking like a little boy who didn't get his way. I'm sick of it. The relationship I have with James is separate from the one I have with you and quite frankly, it's none of your business."

"You don't even know this man, Sophie. There are rumors that he is married and has abandoned his wife. Are you willing to test that?"

James clenched his fists and stepped forward. "I'd never abandon a wife."

Sophie placed a hand on his chest to keep him from hitting Richard.

"You should just leave and let her get on with her life!" Richard snapped.

"Richard, do you have proof that he's married, or are you simply trying to get rid of him?"

"Make him show you the wedding rings he wears around his neck and ask him why he keeps them hidden."

Sophie turned back to James. "Is that true?"

"Why don't you show her, Lieutenant? Put it to rest once and for all," Richard challenged.

James looked confused, but pulled the silken rope from around his neck and handed it to her. "I don't know who they belong to, Sophie."

Sophie inhaled sharply. "Where did you get these? They're mine!"

"What?"

"This is my engagement ring and this is the anniversary band you gave me on our fifth wedding anniversary!" Sophie's world began to spin as she stroked the New Zealand bone carving Emma's best friend, Hannah, gave Jamie for his birthday three years prior. "And this…" she held up the ring, "…is your wedding ring!"

"It can't be. If you were my wife, there's no way I'd forget you. There must be some mistake. Perhaps I found it somewhere or purchased it from someone."

Sophie closed her fist around the treasures in frustration. "No. You're Jamie."

Jamie shook his head. "I don't think that's possible."

"I designed this ring and gave it to you on our wedding day. I have the identical one. Look." She held her right hand out to him. A thinner version of his wedding ring was on her right ring finger. "See?"

He shook his head and turned away from Sophie. "I can't do this."

"What do you mean you can't do this?"

Turning, James mounted his horse, and galloped away, leaving her dumbfounded on the porch.

"Sophie."

"Not now, Richard." She ran into the house and up to her room.

Throwing herself on her bed, she used one of the pillows as a punching bag.

CHAPTER SEVENTEEN

SOPHIE WAS ONLY in her room for a few minutes when she heard a knock at her door.

Before she could answer, Christine poked her head in. "Sophie?"

Sophie chucked the pillow into the corner of the room with a frustrated groan.

Christine sat down next to her on the bed. "What happened?"

"He left—it's a mess, everything's a mess."

"What do you mean?"

Sophie filled Christine in on everything that happened. Once she was done telling the story, she took a deep breath and climbed off the bed. Before she could say another word, there was another knock at the door. "Come in."

Nona walked in.

Sophie chewed her lower lip. "Hi, Nona. I'm so sorry about all the drama. You have been so generous with your home and I don't want you to think I take any of it for granted."

"No need to apologize. We've needed something to shake off the cobwebs. There's been so much doom and gloom with the war. Having you here has made it a little more bearable."

Sophie sighed in relief. "Oh, Nona, I don't know what I'd do without you. I'd probably have to marry Richard." She shot a pointed look in Christine's direction and felt somewhat vindicated by her blush.

Nona hugged her, chuckling quietly. "Sophie, you don't need to worry about anything. You don't have to marry anyone you don't want to. We all consider you a part of this family and you are welcome to stay here as long as you like. Now, let's go downstairs and get something to eat. You must be famished."

Sophie pulled herself together and the three women made their way downstairs. They had a quiet dinner, and then Sophie and Christine decided to spend some time in the parlor, playing cards. The even got in a game of chess, but after a couple of hours, Sophie was getting more and more restless. She desperately wanted Jamie to come back but was afraid she had scared him off for good.

Christine sat down at the pianoforte. "Any requests?"

"If I give you a melody, do you think you could play it?" Sophie asked.

"Let's try."

Sophie started to sing a song she and Jamie wrote together. It took a few minutes, but Christine picked up the tune, and Sophie started to relax and let her voice go where it wanted to go. Singing for her had always been an outlet, and today that outlet was desperately needed.

Several minutes into their private concert, Christine stopped playing abruptly, and a strange look came over her face. Sophie turned to see Jamie standing in the doorway of the parlor, looking stunned. "Why do I know that song?"

Sophie made her way over to where he stood. "Because we wrote it together."

"I'll give you some privacy." Christine rose from the piano.

Jamie nodded to her in thanks as she made her way out of the room. He turned back to Sophie with a tormented look on his face, and she reached out to touch his arm, but he deflected the contact and walked over to the window. Sophie waited for him to speak, knowing he was working things out in his mind.

"I have strange dreams, snippets of memory, I think. But no sense of what they mean," he whispered.

"What kinds of things have you been dreaming?"

Staring out the window, he didn't speak for several seconds. "I see a woman in a wedding dress and she's walking towards me, but her face is covered with a veil." Resting his head on his arm leaning against the window frame, he continued, "I see the same woman rolling a stocking down her leg, but I still can't see her face. There's a young man sitting in a chair. He's getting something painted on his chest and I'm laughing at him."

"Lucas," Sophie whispered as she made her way to stand behind him.

"Lucas?"

"Your best friend." His head dropped slightly, and Sophie resisted the urge to wrap her arms around him.

"I don't remember him."

Sophie smiled. "You have a tattoo of a horseshoe, just above your heart. You and Lucas got them together."

He slowly unbuttoned his shirt and pulled it open just over his heart. "How did you know about the tattoo?"

"Because you're you." She placed her hand on his chest.

His eyebrows knitted together in a frown. "I don't understand."

"Neither do I fully but somehow, we have been brought to the same place." Sophie sighed. "You're James William Ford, you're twenty-eight years old, and you're my husband. You got that tattoo two weeks before our wedding. The scar on your hand was from slicing tomatoes and not paying attention. The woman rolling the stocking down her leg is me, and that was our wedding night." Sophie smiled in memory. "It was such a perfect wedding, Jamie. The man you see in your dream is your childhood friend, Lucas...Luke. He married my best friend, Alex, and the four of us went on a cruise for our honeymoons."

He pinched the bridge of his nose and shook his head.

Sophie squeezed his arm. "There's so much to tell, but I don't want to overwhelm you with information. You may have forgotten, but I remember every little detail."

She moved his hand away from his face and pulled his head down for a kiss. This wasn't the sweet, gentle kiss of the last couple of days. It was a kiss of desperation, passion, and promises of many more things to come. She moved her hands over his stomach and back up to his chest, relishing in the familiarity, yet overcome with brand new desire.

Sophie groaned when he broke the kiss, her breathing labored as she dropped her head onto his chest. His arms tightened around her. "That was unexpected."

"That's one way of putting it, I suppose." Sophie glanced up at him. "Can I please start calling you Jamie?"

He raised an eyebrow. "What's wrong with James?"

"It's what I call you when I'm mad at you." She grinned. "And, I'm so *not* mad at you right now."

He grimaced.

"Don't push it. I know who you are, and I know you'll remember eventually," she said. "And in the meantime, we get to explore a whole new relationship with each other."

Jamie kissed her quickly and then stepped away. "I should get back to camp."

"I'll walk you out." Sophie escorted him through the foyer and onto the front porch.

"I think tomorrow is going to be a really long day. Would you like me to join you for lunch? I'm not sure if I'll be able to break for very long, but I'll take whatever time I can."

Sophie smiled up at him. "I'd love that."

Jamie pulled her into his arms for a lingering kiss. "I'll try to watch for you when you visit Samson tomorrow."

"You noticed?"

Jamie chuckled. "You've been consistent with your schedule."

Sophie grinned. "I'm stuck in my ways, I'm afraid."

He kissed her forehead and then left for the Union camp. Sophie walked back inside and poked her head into the library. "He's gone, Christine, do you want the low-down?"

"I don't know what that means, but I'd like to know what's going on."

Sophie squealed with excitement and pulled Christine in for a hug. "Oh, Christine, he's back. He's really back and I'm going to make him remember everything. I can't believe I have him in my arms again. It's a miracle."

"Well, I have all night for you to tell me about, because Mama is staying with a friend. I told Nona I'd stay here tonight."

"Cool!" Sophie said.

The girls went upstairs and got ready for bed. It was a modern day pajama party in an old-fashioned era. Sophie wouldn't have traded it for the world. She felt so blessed that she had her husband back and had found a family she loved.

* * *

Sophie woke to darkness. Another vivid dream made returning to sleep impossible, so she slid off the mattress and pulled the curtains back. Still dark. She peered out the window and her gaze went to the arena. A lamp was burning by Richard's barn, and she could see men milling around.

She stared out past the training area, the white tents of the soldiers scattered over the terrain looking so similar to when she did reenactments. Even down to the occasional yellow flickering from a lantern lit inside or the cherry of a hand-rolled cigarette.

Grabbing a robe, she slipped it on and stepped into the hallway. The clock next to the guestroom read midnight.

Great. Too early to get up, and way too late to find something to do.
Stepping back into her bedroom, she stared back out the window and chewed on her thumbnail. After several minutes of watching a few of the soldiers close up the barn and douse the lamps, Sophie flopped onto the window seat and pulled her knees up to her chin. Men's laughter floated up to the window and she was drawn to a small group standing by the outside paddock. *Jamie.*

He stood with three of his men and appeared to regaling them with some kind of a story. They laughed and his hands moved like an honorary Sicilian as he talked. Sophie laid her cheek on one of her knees and watched.

It wasn't long before he shook his head and made a sweeping motion with one of his hands, causing the men to move toward the tents. Jamie paused and turned to glance up at her window. She didn't know if he could see her, but she smiled anyway. In the end, he shoved his hands in his pockets and made his way toward the tents along with his men.

Sophie straightened. She was done waiting. With a racing heart and shaking hands, she dressed quickly, sans corset, and snuck out of her bedroom and downstairs. She had a plan, and it would require seduction. She needed something sweet. Nona had a greenhouse just off the kitchen, so she gathered two oranges and made her way out to the tents. She knew in theory which one was James', but she'd never walked out here before. She was usually riding, and had the advantage of being up high, giving her a better vantage point.

Oh, for the love and glory be. Which one are you?

The occasional snore could be heard as she passed the tent flap openings, trying to notice any unique markings of the tents.

One of those wooden signs with an etching that said, "The Fords, established 2001" on the outside would do nicely right about now.

An arm wrapping around her waist and another covering her mouth, brought her back to the present and she let out a squeal, although the large hand pressing a little harder muffled it.

* * *

Jamie had heard the swish of skirts and peeked out to see Sophie roaming the aisle between the tents. She wasn't very good at subterfuge, and he couldn't decide if he was irritated or intrigued that she'd sought him out in the middle of the night.

"Sophie, what are you doing out here?" She relaxed immediately, sinking her back into his chest. He released her and turned her to face him. "It's past midnight, and it's not safe for you to be anywhere other than the house after dark," he admonished in a whisper.

She held up one of the oranges. "I woke up and couldn't go back to sleep. I thought you might want an orange."

"Come with me." He led her to one of the tents she'd just passed, and held the flap open for her. She dipped low and stepped inside.

Jamie lit the lantern that sat on a small table in the corner, but kept it low. Still, there was enough light to see each other relatively clearly.

"Don't you have a cot or something?"

He shook his head as he closed the flap and secured the ties. "No."

Sophie set one of the oranges on the table and started to peel the other. "It's not as bad as I imagined for a Civil War dwelling. At least you have blankets and a couple of chairs."

Jamie faced her. "Sophie. Will you tell me why you're out here? I'm assuming that since you're offering me an orange, there's no emergency."

She raised a finger and waggled at him. "Don't be so sure, Jamie. There are plenty of citrus based emergencies."

He crossed his arms. "Name one."

Sophie bit her lower lip. "Scurvy?"

He squeezed his eyes closed and the opened them again, a wary expression on his face. "Sophie."

She offered him a wedge of orange. "Want some?"

"No, thank you."

Sophie raised an eyebrow and sucked the slice through her lips and let out a quiet moan. "Heaven."

His stomach clenched as he watched a small drop of juice linger on her full lips. Her tongue darted out to lick it off. She smiled and handed him another wedge. "Have some. It's perfect."

He took the orange from her but didn't eat it right away. "Sophie, you need to go back to the house."

"Do I?" she whispered as she set the rest of the orange on the table and slipped the buttons from her blouse.

"Sophie, what are you doing?"

"Getting comfortable." She pushed her skirts from her body. "Much better."

"Put your clothes back on."

"I'm fully covered." She lowered her head and checked her appearance. "Chemise, pantaloons, stockings, and slippers. This is more clothing than I ever wore at home."

Dropping his head back, he stared at the low ceiling before taking a deep breath and meeting her gaze again. "This is entirely inappropriate, Sophie."

She shrugged. "Sue me."

Her lace chemise slid off one creamy, white shoulder.

"Sophie, we're not in private." He groaned as he turned his back. "We're not even in a place with a locking door."

"I. Don't. Care." She sighed. "More orange?"

He shook his head, but caught her smile as she popped another piece in her mouth. He turned around and stared at the tent flap.

"You're being gallant." Sophie giggled. "How about you turn around?" He shook his head. "I have a surprise for you. Turn around. I won't bite…well, not unless you want me to."

He turned and swore. Sophie stood before him in nothing but stockings and garters. He turned away again.

"Sir?" a quiet voice whispered from outside of the tent.

"Jack?" Jamie advanced on the tent opening.

"I heard arguing, sir."

Jamie sent a glare over his shoulder at Sophie. She grinned and popped another orange wedge in her mouth.

"Go back to your tent, Jack."

"Yes, sir."

Jamie pinched the bridge of his nose, but still fought the urge to look at her. "Get dressed."

Sophie moved to stand at his back. "You don't get to escape, love." She pulled his shirt from the waistband of his trousers. "I've waited a long time for this, and I don't care what you do and don't remember, I want my husband back."

He squeezed his eyes shut and groaned. "Sophie. Don't."

"Don't, what? I'll stop as soon as you say you don't want this." She slid her hands around the front of him and her hands slipped under his shirt.

Jamie clenched his fists at his side. "I won't do this."

"Why not?" Sophie kissed his neck.

Jamie tried to stay her hands. "Sophie, this is highly inappropriate."

Sophie chuckled. A low, throaty sound that made several muscles tense—muscles he didn't realize he had. In parts of his body he'd never really paid much attention to before. She kissed his back, in between his shoulder blades. "I don't care if it's inappropriate. I have certain needs."

Her tiny hands had now slipped up his back and she raked her nails gently over his skin. A low growl escaped between his gritted teeth. "Sophie."

"I want you naked, Jamie. I have been patient up till now, and I'm done being patient."

He squeezed his eyes shut with a grimace. "I don't remember you as my wife, Sophie."

"Oh, you're going to remember. I have no doubt. Now, turn around."

Turning to face her, he rasped, "Are you sure you want to do this? Even if I don't remember? Even if your reputation will be compromised?"

Her eyes, hooded with desire, seemed on fire as she smiled. "Surer than I have been about anything."

Reaching behind his back, he pulled his shirt over his head and then cupped her face and leaned down to kiss her. He slid one hand around her waist, pulled her body closer to his, and intensified his assault. He knew now that he was too far gone to do anything but make love to her. Laying her down on the makeshift mattress, he stroked her cheek.

"Make me yours again," she whispered.

As he made love to her, his visions began as a flash. The square pattern on a blue door, his hand knocking, and it opening to reveal the most beautiful woman he'd ever seen. The hallucination brought the memory of her disappearance and the confusion and devastation that followed.

"Shh, baby, I'm right here," she said.

He registered her voice cutting through the fog, and her fingers wiping wetness from his cheek. He pulled her closer and wrapped a blanket over her shoulders. "Sophie."

"What do you remember?"

"Flashes more than memories. You disappeared from our bed. You had wires attached to your body, but they were still there…everything, even what should have been inside of you." His voice shook as he relayed the night she disappeared. "I thought someone took you and that you were without your LVAD—" He grabbed his head, the pain sudden and excruciating.

Sophie laid a hand on top of his. "Don't force it, Jamie. It'll all come back. Just give it time."

He flopped onto his back, pulling her with him. "I don't know what I'm missing."

"Let me fill in some of the blanks." She ran a finger over his chest. "I was born in 1981, you were born in 1979. We met in 2000 and were married in June of 2001. In 2006, I was diagnosed with a failing heart. The last thing I remember was lying in our bed with you by my side. That was January 31, 2007."

"Over a hundred years in the future?"

Sophie sighed. "Yes."

"How is that even possible?"

She shrugged. "No idea."

Jamie nodded. "And Emma. My sister?"

"No." Sophie gasped quietly. "*My* sister. You remember her?"

Jamie frowned. "Sort of."

"Don't try." Sophie ran her palm across his cheek. "I need something other than your memory right now."

CHAPTER EIGHTEEN

THE NEXT MORNING began with a flurry of activity. Sophie was so excited she hadn't really been able to sleep. Jamie had snuck her back to the house at close to three, and spent another hour saying goodnight.

Up and dressed by eight o'clock, despite not having gone to sleep until dawn, Sophie rushed downstairs, decided to wait to eat breakfast, and made her way to the stables instead.

Samson was being used constantly for training, and as girlish as it might seem, she missed what she had become to think of as her horse. With great anticipation, she rounded the corner into the barn but stopped short. Richard was leaning against Samson's stall, obviously waiting for her to arrive.

"Richard." She moved slowly towards him. He said nothing, just stared straight through her. "Are you going to give me the silent treatment, or are we going to talk?"

He didn't look well. He hadn't shaved, his eyes were bloodshot, and she guessed he was more than two sheets to the wind.

"I'm guessin' there's not much to say," he grumbled, his southern accent heavier than she'd heard it before.

"Then why are you here? You know I come every morning to see Samson, so it can't be a coincidence that you are in your neighbors' barn, next to the horse that I visit every chance I get," Sophie said exasperated.

"Damn it, Sophie. You're mine. He can't have you."

Sophie stepped back, slightly nervous at his anger. "Richard, I never said I was yours or made a commitment. You know how I feel about Jamie. I have always been his and now that he's back, I plan to do whatever it takes to stay with him."

Richard glared as he advanced on her. He pushed her roughly up against one of the stall doors and leaned down to kiss her. She fought him but he wouldn't let her go.

"Stop, Richard. You're drunk. Please don't do this," she whimpered.

"You're supposed to be mine. One way or another, I am going to make you mine."

"Get your hands off her," Jamie ordered.

Richard turned, his forearm still firmly across Sophie's chest. "What the hell are you going to do about it?"

Grabbing Richard firmly by the collar of his shirt, Jamie pulled him off Sophie. Richard tried to fight, but he was no match for Jamie, especially drunk. Every move he made, Jamie countered with another that not only bested him but humiliated him as well. In the end, Jamie gave one good punch to the jaw and Richard was out cold.

Jamie turned to see Sophie slide down the wall of the stall, her face in her hands. "Sophie, are you okay? Did he hurt you?"

Sophie shook her head as Jamie hunkered down next to her and touched her shoulder. He gathered her in his arms and carried her to the bale of hay outside of Samson's stall. Settling her onto his lap as he sat down, he stroked her back. Samson stuck his head out of his stall and shoved his nose in between the couple.

Sophie reached up and stroked his nose. "I'm okay, boy."

Jamie took a ragged breath. "Did he hurt you?"

She shook her head and wrapped her arms around his neck. "No. He just scared me."

Jamie kissed her cheek. "Déjà vu."

Sophie looked at him. "What did you remember?"

"Chad the ass."

"Chad? My ex, Chad?"

Jamie nodded. "Remember the day I threw him out?"

Sophie put her hand on his cheek. "He thought he needed to save me from you. You thought otherwise and explained that to him." She smiled. "I fell in love with you that day."

He raised an eyebrow. "Oh, really? I thought it was when—"

Pain splintered as he tried to remember what he was going to say. He drew air in through his teeth and felt Sophie's grip tighten.

"Don't push it," she said.

He nodded and she laid her head on his shoulder. "What's on your agenda today?"

"It has changed slightly. We had a few new horses arrive, so Richard is going to work with them and the men." He looked over at the passed-out form of Richard. "Well, he *was* going to work with them. Ash can probably take over for him." Jamie rubbed his temples, his headache subsiding almost as quickly as it came. "Would you like to do something with me? A picnic maybe?"

"I'd love that. Let me organize the food though, okay?"

"Hardtack not appetizing enough?"

She laughed. "No, can't say that it is. Meet me at the house in a little while and I'll have everything ready."

"I'll take care of Richard and make sure he gets home to sleep it off." He gave her a little squeeze.

* * *

Jamie arrived an hour later and they took off toward the lake, hand in hand, Jamie carrying the picnic basket. When they arrived at the water, Jamie laid the blanket out, and Sophie went to work pulling out the food.

"How are you feeling?" Jamie asked.

"I'm exhausted."

He raised an eyebrow. "Well if you hadn't accosted me last night…"

Sophie grinned. "Yeah, I heard you complaining all night long."

"Watch the clouds with me."

She lay down on her back, and Jamie settled himself next to her. He took her hand in his and held it to his chest. She pointed to one above them. "That one looks like an elephant."

"More like a monkey, I think."

"What? You're crazy. Look at the trunk."

"No, that's his tail."

She laughed and he drew her hand to his lips. She turned her head, and as he leaned over to kiss her, he noticed the dark rings under her eyes. "Why don't you sleep, Sophie?"

"Do I have time to sleep? Shouldn't we be getting back soon?"

"We have time. Go to sleep."

She smiled. "I don't know if that would be entirely appropriate, sir."

He kissed her cheek. "A nap in the afternoon with my wife? What could possibly be more appropriate?"

She rolled on her side with a sigh, and he formed his body around hers. Jamie spent several minutes watching her sleep. He may not remember everything, but he remembered her as his wife, and he wouldn't let her go again. He closed his eyes and drew her body closer to him. Awakened by Sophie shivering, Jamie pulled her closer before leaning down, and kissing her cheek to wake her.

"Hi." She turned to face him. "How long was I asleep?"
"At least two hours. How do you feel?"
"Cold but otherwise okay. Did you sleep?"
"I did." He kissed her and then added, "But only until you started snoring."
She pushed him away with snort and sat up. "I do *not* snore!"
Jamie chuckled as he pushed her back down. "You do snore, and it's adorable."
He leaned down to kiss her but she turned her head. "Take it back."
"I'm only speaking the truth. Now kiss me."
"No." She moved her head to deflect his every attempt.
"Did you just deny me?"
Sophie giggled. "I did. What are you going to do about it?"
"You don't really want an answer to that, do you?"
"Ooh, I'm scared." He leaned down for one more attempt at a kiss, and at her deflection, grabbed her sides and began to tickle her. Sophie squealed. "Not fair!"
"Do you surrender?"
"Not on your life." She tried to roll away from him but he followed. Grabbing her around the waist again, he increased the level of torture and it didn't matter how much she protested, he wouldn't give up.
"Jamie! I'm going to pee."
"Say 'uncle,'" he ordered.
"UNCLE!" He tickled her one more time and Sophie gasped. "Hey! I said 'uncle.'"
"Sorry, love, I didn't hear you."
"You are such a sneak!" She laughed.
Jamie leaned down to kiss her and suddenly dirt splattered over them.
"What was that?" Sophie sat up and wiped the dirt from her skirts.
A whistle and then dirt kicked up again, and Jamie shoved her down and covered her body. "Stay down!"
"What's going on?"
"Those are bullets, Sophie, stay down!" Jamie rolled, grasping her around the waist and pulling her to relative cover. "Someone is shooting at us."
"Why?"
Jamie groaned. "I don't know, *why*, baby. Just sit there and stay out of sight!"
Sophie flattened herself on the ground behind a few large river rocks and watched as Jamie hunched down and began to move toward the lake. "What are you doing?" she squealed.

Jamie waved his hand to stay back and continued forward. Sophie couldn't breathe as she watched him inch further away from her and then, suddenly, a rider tore out from the cover of trees and took off—away from them.

Sophie jumped up and rushed to Jamie. "Who was that?"

Wrapping his arms around her waist, he pulled her close and kissed her temple. "I don't know, but I think it was the same man that shot Lund."

"The soldier you brought into the hospital?"

At his nod, Sophie squinted across the man-made lake. "Is he shooting at us on purpose?"

Sophie's skin crawled at the thought that the man was hiding in plain sight—close enough to get at them.

"I don't know but I mean to find out. Let's get you back to the house so I can find out what's going on."

Sophie's head whipped up. "What? No! Absolutely not! It's too dangerous."

Jamie chuckled as he cupped her face and kissed her. "I'll be fine."

"Famous last words," Sophie grumbled as they gathered their things and started back toward home.

Jamie took her hand, and she found herself distracted by the feel of his strong hand, now rougher than before, covering hers. The calluses were a heady feeling against her small, smooth palm and she smiled as she looked up at him. Without warning, she stumbled and went down hard. Luckily, Jamie had a good grip and was able to keep her from falling completely.

He dropped the basket and wrapped his free hand around her waist to help guide her gently to the ground. Grasping her ankle, the tears slid down her face as she tried to catch her breath.

"What happened?"

"Gopher hole, I think," she rasped.

Jamie knelt beside her. "Let's have a look." Pulling her boot off gently, he let out a quiet whistle. "This just hasn't been your day, has it?"

Sophie grimaced.

"Come here." He picked her up and started to move toward the Wades house.

"Jamie, if I get too heavy, you must tell me."

Jamie carried her back to the house and into the parlor so that Michael could look at her ankle. While the doctor examined her, Jamie gave her hand a gentle squeeze. "I'm going to grab the basket. I'll return soon."

She glanced up at him and smiled. "Okay. Thanks."

Her focus was pulled back to Michael as he squeezed her ankle. "Ouch."

"Sorry." Michael rose to his feet. "It's swollen but nothing appears to be broken. Rest for a few days and keep it elevated."

"Thanks, Michael." Sophie rested in the library, her foot elevated on a stool and packed with ice, per doctor's orders, grimacing at the constant throb.

Jamie came into the room and sat in the chair next to her. "How's your ankle?"

"I think I might have brittle bone disease."

"Excuse me?"

Sophie sighed. "I'm fine as long as I don't walk on it."

"So, don't walk on it," Jamie joked.

"Funny, ha, ha. Maybe I have cancer."

"I am reminded of your hypochondriac tendencies. You don't have cancer." Sophie opened her mouth to respond but Jamie cut her off. "*Or* brittle bones. You're just a little clumsy."

"I am *not!*" He raised an eyebrow and she wrinkled her nose. "Fine. What did you find out when you went to "retrieve the basket?""

Jamie rolled his eyes. "I really did retrieve the basket."

"Which would have taken you a lot less than an hour."

Jamie turned as he heard the library door open and stood when Christine entered the room. "I heard Sophie had an accident."

"You are so not off the hook," she whispered and then smiled at Christine. "Just call me gimpy."

Jamie chuckled and gave Christine his seat before sitting on the hearth facing the girls.

"What happened?" Christine asked.

Sophie filled her in on the day, leaving out some of the more personal portions.

"Richard did all that *and* you were shot at?" Christine exclaimed.

Sophie nodded. "Yep."

Christine frowned. "I've never known Richard to treat anyone like that."

"I think he objects to the competition I present," Jamie said.

"Can I get you anything?" Christine asked.

"No, thanks. I'm fine. Jamie's taking good care of me."

The butler chose that moment to interrupt the group. "Dinner is served."

Jamie and Christine stood. Jamie nodded toward the door. "I'll take Sophie in, Christine. You go on ahead."

Jamie picked Sophie up and carried her to the dining room. Settling her in her chair, he prepared a plate for her and then himself. Sophie smiled her thanks.

"How's your ankle, dear?" Nona asked.

"It's fine, Nona. I just have to stay off it for a few days."

"At least a week," Michael interjected.

Jamie rolled his eyes. "Won't that be fun?"

"Yes, Jamie, I'll look forward to our evenings filled with playing cards and great conversation." Sophie turned her head, and gave Jamie a mock scowl, before turning back to Michael with a serene smile.

Jamie sat next to Sophie and kissed her hand. "It'll be my pleasure."

Conversation swirled around the table as everyone began to eat. Sophie on the other hand, picked at her food. Unable to elevate her foot, the pain made her sick to her stomach and the strain of hiding it made it difficult to catch her breath.

Nona and Christine were discussing the strife a few of their distant neighbors were dealing with, while Michael interjected the occasional observation. All the while Sophie sat silent.

"Sophie, is it that bad?" Jamie whispered. She gave a stilted nod, so he laid his napkin on the table and stood. "Excuse me, Nona. Sophie is in a great deal of pain. I thought I'd move her back to the library, if that's acceptable."

"My word, yes, yes. I'll send Betty in with some ice."

"No, I'm happy to take care of that. Please, finish your dinner."

Jamie picked Sophie up and carried her back to the library. As they crossed the threshold into the room, Sophie burst into tears and took several deep breaths in an effort to push the pain away.

"Sweetheart," Jamie whispered as he settled her in her favorite chair and placed a pillow under her leg. "I'll be right back."

Sophie squeezed her eyes shut and nodded as he left the room. Lifting her skirt, she examined her ankle and grimaced at the sight. Twice the normal size and bruised, the longer she stared at it, the more it seemed to throb. She'd managed to convince herself she'd never walk again by the time Jamie returned with the ice.

"Here." Jamie sat on the hearth and wrapped the ice around her ankle. He handed her a glass of amber liquid, and Sophie raised an eyebrow in question. "Whiskey. It'll help dull the pain."

Despite the fact that she barely drank, she downed the liquid and sputtered at the burn.

Jamie chuckled. "You were supposed to sip that."

She shrugged. "Oops."

Jamie took the glass from her with a concerned frown. "What did you find out about the shooter?"

Jamie sighed. "Nothing yet. I have a few of the men on it. How's your ankle?"

"Bad." She dropped her head to the back of the chair. "Don't leave me here, okay?"

Jamie leaned over her and lifted her chin. "I'm not going anywhere. Would you like another drink?"

Sophie shook her head. "I want drugs."

Jamie stroked her cheek, catching a tear with his thumb. "Would you like Michael to give you laudanum?"

"No. I hated it when they gave it to me before."

"Before?" Jamie sat back on the hearth and handed her his handkerchief.

Sophie filled Jamie in on her arrival and the events that led up to her forced drugging. Admittedly, she purposely made it sound a little worse than it was, but was still taken aback by the vein pulsing in his neck.

"I'm going to kill him."

"Who? Richard or Michael?"

Jamie stood. "At this moment in time, I don't know."

Sophie had a sense of conviction and reached out to take his hand, tugging softly. "Sorry. I'm fine, and I'm sure Michael was just trying to help at the time."

Jamie squeezed her hand before kissing her fingers and sitting down again. "Richard, however, was a bully."

"Yes, you're right, but it's in the past, and quite frankly, I'm over it."

"Well, what can I do for you then?"

"Nothing." Sophie wrinkled her nose. "Just sit there and let me be pathetic."

CHAPTER NINETEEN

MAY AND JUNE found the couple growing closer. Sophie had shared the news of Jamie's recovery, albeit not complete, with Michael and Nona, and they had welcomed him into the family fold. He still slept most nights in his tent, but Sophie had managed to steal him away for a few nights in the privacy of her room.

The cavalry training was brutal, and Jamie found he didn't have as much time with Sophie as he'd have liked, but he spent every morning and every evening with her, which would have to be enough for now.

Although he and Richard formed a tentative treaty, Sophie wouldn't have anything to do with him, going so far as to limit her visits with Samson. Jamie was fine with her decision, but he did have to work with the man, so he tried his best to rise above the animosity to succeed in their mutual goals. He also spent a great deal of time working with Topper. The young man was becoming quite adept at using his left hand, almost to the point that people didn't realize he was missing his right.

One morning, when he didn't find Sophie at home, Jamie walked out to the Wades barn and as expected, found her standing outside of Samson's stall.

Jamie pulled her into his arms and kissed her. "Good morning, sweetheart. I should have just waited for you here."

Sophie smiled and kissed him back.

"You're up early. How did you sleep?"

Sophie looped her arms around his neck and crinkled her nose up in annoyance. "I wasn't with you, so I didn't sleep very well."

"I missed you, too."

She reached up again to kiss him, but they were interrupted by one of Jamie's men rushing in to say that there was word of General Lee advancing on Gettysburg.

* * *

Sophie went white. *What's today?*

She did a quick calculation in her head. "Jamie, it's July 1. Today's the first official day of the battle."

Jamie pursed his lips. "Gettysburg address?"

She nodded. "In November, but yes, now is the battle."

This battle would turn out to be the most famous and most important Civil War Battle. It occurred over three summer days, July first, second, and third. It started out seemingly small, but by the end of the battle it involved 160,000 Americans. Rubbing her forehead with her palm, her groan was audible, even over the rush of people moving around the barn.

Today the two divisions of Confederates will head back to Gettysburg. They run into Federal cavalry west of the town at Willoughby Run and the skirmish began. Events would quickly escalate. Lee would rush 25,000 men to the scene. The Union had less than 20,000.

The Union ends up winning the battle, but how do I warn the men without changing history?

Sophie would have to figure out a way to get the hospital ready for the wounded that would be coming through the doors—or tent flaps, as the case may be. She'd have to get Christine and the rest of the nurses prepared for the onslaught.

She gripped Jamie's arm. "Jamie, please be careful. I'll pray for you. Just know it will be over in three days, and I want you home immediately." She pulled him closer and whispered. "This is *my* battle. The one I spent the most time reading about, working with the team to reenact, and the one I *never* shut up about. Please try to remember what I told you. Do you hear me?"

He kissed her. "I promise."

Sophie took off running back to the house. Letting herself in the front door, she headed for the dining room. Michael, Nona, and Christine were sitting at the table eating breakfast.

"Sophie? Is everything all right?" Michael stood, a look of concern on his face.

"General Lee is attacking Gettysburg. All cavalry have been called up. Jamie and Richard have gone to help."

"Oh, my," Nona exclaimed.

Sophie looked at Christine. "We have to get the hospital prepared for the wounded. We need to make sure there are clean linens and boil all of the instruments. We should have fresh water and get together whatever medication we can." She used her fingers to check off the things she thought they would need. "We need to call in every doctor we can find, same with the nurses. Make sure the icehouse is packed—we can treat the minor injuries with ice."

"Sophie, slow down. I can't keep up with you," Christine said.

The next two days were spent preparing the hospital. Even Dr. Palmer joined in. He tried to fight her on some of her "insane ideas" but Sophie didn't care. If, God forbid, Jamie came in wounded, she was not going to let anyone butcher him.

Beyond tired by Friday night, Sophie was thankful she was able to sleep; however, she woke on Saturday morning with a feeling of dread. This would be the day the wounded and dead would arrive. Sophie got up, got herself dressed, and ate a quick breakfast. Opening the front door, she saw Christine coming up the driveway in her little carriage and barely waited for her to stop before jumping in.

"Good morning. Are you ready?"

"As ready as I'll ever be. Do you mind if we pray?" Sophie asked.

Christine shook her head and they said a quick prayer. Sophie would find herself praying several times over the trying day.

The wounded started trickling into the hospital at ten o'clock. They poured in at eleven. Sophie was frantic. She hadn't seen Jamie or Richard, and she was having a hard time concentrating on what was going on around her not knowing if they were safe.

She spent her time comforting the wounded and trying to keep the instruments as clean as possible. She knew it would be impossible for some of them to keep their limbs but tried to suggest splints whenever she could, for those soldiers who hadn't already been amputated in the field.

By four o'clock she was beside herself. It was so hot, the hottest it had been, some would say, and she wasn't sure if she would be able to stand up straight much longer. She felt sick to her stomach from not only the heat but also the worry. She told Christine she needed a break and had just walked outside when she saw Jamie walking towards her. She ran, throwing herself into his arms, uncaring that his body was filthy and covered in blood.

"Oh, God, Jamie? Are you all right? Where have you been? I've been worried sick." She started giving him the once over, looking for bullet wounds.

"I'm fine, Sophie." He grabbed her hands. "Sophie, the blood's not mine. I've been helping to gather up the wounded. How are you?"

She threw herself back into his arms. "I'm okay now that I know you're safe. Where are Richard and Samson?"

"Let's find somewhere to talk, all right?" Jamie said.

Sophie's terror grew as Jamie drew her over to one of the smaller tents set up for the doctors. Sophie grabbed the lapels of his jacket. "Jamie, tell me. Please."

"Richard was riding Samson, and a cannonball went off a few hundred feet from them. Samson sustained a nasty wound. Not only that, but Richard's leg was broken from the impact of Samson falling on him."

"Why was Richard even there? He's not a soldier!"

"He wanted to help."

"Did they shoot Samson?" Sophie's eyes filled with tears. The thought of such an incredible animal being killed was heartbreaking.

"The General was ready to, but Richard and I convinced them not to. We'll try and patch him up over the next few days and see how he does. We didn't shoot Richard either, although it was tempting."

Sophie gave him a sarcastic grin. "Thank you. So, where are they?"

"They'll be here. Don't worry."

"Did Samson get up?"

"Yes. He did remarkably well. However, he's limping severely and not happy to have anyone near him. We found a young private that Samson didn't object to quite as much, so he's leading him home." He smiled down at her and pulled her into his arms. "Let me hold you for a minute."

She buried her face in the rough wool of his jacket as his arms wrapped around her. "I was so worried, Jamie. Tell me everything that happened."

"Later."

Before Sophie could say anything, she saw Samson being led up the hill by a young man, a very young man. Samson's limp was severe, but it looked as though someone had tried to bandage his leg. He was giving the young soldier a devil of a time, so Sophie pulled herself away from Jamie.

"Samson," she called.

Samson turned his head toward her and trumpeted a greeting as she rushed toward him. Stopping in front of him, she put her palm out, and he nuzzled her hand as she crooned to him and moved her hand up his face. "Shhh, what a big brave horse you are. That's a good boy." She moved her hand down his neck and started moving her body to the rear of his to have a looked at his injury.

Jamie startled her, and the horse, as he grabbed her from behind. "Sophie, what are you doing? He's already kicked two men while they were trying to bandage him. You need to stay back. We'll have Michael look at him and then you can visit when he's all fixed up."

The horse nickered, almost in disagreement.

"Jamie, he's not going to hurt me, he knows me." She moved back to the horse's side and slowly moved her hand down his rear leg, crooning sweet words to him the entire time. He lifted his hoof automatically, but rather than kicking out as everyone expected, he held it still for her to look at more closely.

"Good boy." She pulled the bandage off and took a closer look, scrunching her nose up at the sight. Shrapnel and dirt were encrusted in the deep wound and a flap of skin peeled itself away from the leg, which would more than likely need to be stitched back. It looked painful and her heart broke for him as she took a deep breath and stood slowly.

"Sophie," Jamie warned.

"What?" she snapped in irritation. "He is not going to hurt me." She moved to his neck again and then around to the other side of his body. Other than the wound on his leg, the other injuries were somewhat superficial and would heal on their own. "Samson, you are such a brave boy." She stroked his nose as she kissed his cheek. "We're going to get that cleaned out and fixed up so that you can heal properly." The horse nuzzled and pushed at her shoulder. Sophie raised her eyebrow at Jamie in triumph. "I'm going to get some warm water and get this cleaned out so that Michael can suture it. Can you help me, or do you need to tend to the men?"

Jamie grinned reluctantly. "I'll help you. I'll check in with the doctors first and then we can look Samson over. I'll find Michael as well. It's his horse, so he'll probably want to know what's going on."

Sophie led Samson over to one of the smaller tents. She found Topper carrying bandages to one of the doctors. "Topper. You weren't fighting, were you?"

"No ma'am." A rare smile framed his face. "I have been assisting with the wounded. I heard Samson's injured."

Sophie nodded. "He is. I need to get a few things, but he won't tolerate anyone holding him."

Topper set the bandages on a table set up outside the tent. "He likes me, Sophie. Lieutenant Emerson and I have been working with him."

He made his way to Samson, reached his hand out, and Samson didn't bite him, which in Sophie's opinion was good enough.

"Great. Could you stand with him for me, then?"

He nodded, so she handed Topper the reins and made her way to the larger hospital tent. She noticed Christine standing over a patient, her face red with apparent anger. Sophie moved toward her. When Sophie saw who she was speaking with, she wasn't surprised. It was Dr. Palmer.

As Sophie approached, she saw that the patient was an unconscious Richard. "What's going on, Christine?"

"He wants to amputate Richard's leg."

Sophie frowned. "You can't take his leg, Dr. Palmer."

"Mrs. Ford, the leg is too far gone to save. It will be kinder just to amputate. If we don't, he'll be in pain for the rest of his life and probably walk with a limp."

"Please, Dr. Palmer. Think of Richard as your friend, rather than a patient. You have known each other for a long time, and you know he'd rather have you try everything, right? Can't you do that? What harm is there in doing everything possible to save it, and then if that doesn't work, you can amputate later." Sophie held her breath in anticipation.

"All right, ladies. We can wait." Both Sophie and Christine let out a collective sigh.

Sophie stared down at Richard. He looked so peaceful. His beard now completely full, he was dirty and bloody, but at least he was alive. She turned to Christine. "I have to tend to Samson, but I'll come back as soon as I'm done and help you with Richard, okay?"

"Yes, that's fine, Sophie. I'll sit with him for as long as I can. We seem to be slowing down now with the influx of wounded. I'll come and find you if that changes."

"Thank you. I'll see you later." Sophie gathered up several of the supplies she would need, trying to juggle them somewhat unsuccessfully. Jamie met her at the tent entrance and took her burdens from her, carrying them over to the horse. He appeared calmer than he had before and Sophie smiled as she thanked Topper.

Jamie and Sophie started to work on Samson's leg. At first, Sophie held him and tried to speak to him as Jamie went to work on his leg but he kept trying to kick him. He wouldn't let Jamie near him.

"Let me try," Sophie said.

"Sophie, he's in too much pain, he'll kick you."

"Or, maybe he'll let me near his leg because he knows me."

Jamie stood for a minute considering her argument. "All right, I'll hold him, but be careful. If he tries to kick you, even once, Sophie, that'll be it. Understand?"

She patted his cheek. "Yes, my big strong protector, I understand."

Stroking Samson's nose quickly, she moved her way slowly to his injury with a bucket of warm water and a soft rag. She was going to try and clean the wound out as much as possible, but she knew it would hurt. As she made her way to his back leg, Samson bent his head towards her and watched her intently. Jamie tried to pull him up straight.

"Let him look at me. It might help him accept the pain he's going to feel."

Jamie let the reins slack slightly but appeared ready to grab Samson if he tried to kick out. Topper stroked Samson's neck, also in an effort to keep him calm.

Sophie poured the warm water over the horse's wound and was able to get a lot of the debris out. Looking up at Samson, she said, "I have to clean this, boy, which means I need to get closer." She waggled a finger at him. "Do not kick me."

"Sophie!"

Ignoring Jamie, she climbed under the horse's belly, soaked the rag with clean water, and gently cleaned the rest of the dirt out. It wasn't as bad as she originally thought, which meant it would heal quicker. When she finished, she climbed out from under and chuckled when Jamie let out a long breath. "I was fine!"

Before Jamie could comment, they were both distracted as Michael rushed over to them. "I heard he has a nasty gash."

"He does. I just cleaned it, and he was an absolute champ." Sophie patted Samson's neck. Michael moved to the horse's side as Sophie stayed by his head and felt Jamie brush against her as he stood vigil. Samson skittered slightly the closer Michael got to his leg, and Sophie felt Jamie tense as Samson's ears went flat.

"Shh, boy," Sophie crooned, but the horse wouldn't calm and kicked out.

Jamie grabbed her arm and pulled her roughly away.

"What are you doing?" she screeched.

"He's kicking out."

"At *Michael*. Not me," she snapped as she pulled her arm away.

"Soph, stop."

She ignored him and rushed back to get Samson under control. Michael avoided another hoof, but Samson grew increasingly agitated, even with Topper trying to help. Ears back, eyes wild, and snorting as though he were a bull ready to strike.

Sophie tried everything to get him under control but he seemed too far gone, so she tried something she'd never done before…she sang to him. Although Samson threw his head a few times in frustration, she wouldn't give up. She continued to sing quietly until he lowered his head and nuzzled her shoulder.

"Good boy." She turned to Michael. "Try again."

The doctor sidled up to him, and this time, Samson let him examine the leg. Michael was efficient and smiled as he made his way back to Sophie. "Well, that doesn't look so bad. However, we are going to have to stitch him."

Sophie shook her head. "He'll never tolerate a needle. What if we bind his wound tight? Could the skin fuse back together, do you think?"

"I suppose that's a possibility. I'll make a poultice and we'll bandage him up. The leg isn't broken, so we'll watch it over the next few days to see if we need to go further."

Sophie stayed close to Samson as Michael prepared the special medicine and then they wrapped the wound tight. When Michael was finished, he went back to the soldiers.

"Can you come back to the house, Jamie? Then stay for dinner?" Sophie asked.

He nodded. "I'll check in with my men and meet you over at the house. Give me an hour or so."

Jamie left her and Sophie decided to check on Richard one more time. He was sleeping comfortably, and as several other nurses arrived to take over for the ones who had been there all day, Sophie found Christine, attached Samson's reins to the back of her carriage, and they made their way back to the Wades.

CHAPTER TWENTY

AFTER MAKING SURE Samson was cared for, Sophie went back to the house and found that Christine had organized cool baths for the both of them. After almost twenty minutes of soaking, she didn't want to get out of the water, but knew Jamie would be by to see her soon. She climbed out of the tub and found the coolest gown she had in her wardrobe and dressed quickly.

Making her way straight to the kitchen for a snack, she chatted with Mary who allowed her a fresh peach, and then she settled herself in the library. She'd been reading for less than an hour, when he heard Jamie in the hallway. "She's probably in the library, Daniel. I'll find her."

Sophie closed the book and set it aside. Rising to her feet, she arrived at the door just as Jamie opened it. "Hi."

Jamie wrapped his arms around her and pulled her close.

"What happened?"

Jamie straightened with a sigh. "We lost Ash and twenty of his men."

Her eyes filled with tears. "I'm so sorry. Any of yours?" He shook his head. She raised an eyebrow. "Because of…"

"Yes." He rubbed her back and then pulled her back to her favorite chair. "I remember you and two guys playing with model horses and watching you argue about the position of fake soldiers."

Sophie clapped her hands. "Oh, I remember that day. Wow. That's when we first met. Um, we had an assignment in history class to see if we could have done something different in any of the historic battles… we got to choose…and we had to chart it out and reenact it using models. I chose Gettysburg and forced Seth and Connor to team with me."

He rubbed his forehead as he sat on the hearth facing her. "Didn't Hannah choose Iwo Jima?"

"Yes." Sophie grinned. "You remember Hannah! That was a while after I graduated, but she and Emma worked on it together. Emma didn't do as well as Hannah, but she got into the code cracking side of it." She reached for his hand. "You're remembering."

Jamie sighed. "Little bits here and there, but I remember your presentation, because I ran your scenario with my men."

"You did not!"

"I did." He smiled. "No one even received so much as a scratch."

Sophie let out a little squeal. "That's so unreal. Do you think we changed history?"

Jamie shrugged. "It's certainly a possibility, but I don't feel as though I had much of a choice."

"What do you mean?"

He leaned forward, forearms on his knees. "If we *are* here for a reason, then I imagine we're supposed to survive, right?"

"Probably a good assumption."

"Just being here is a change in history anyway. So, maybe we're supposed to do something really big...and maybe we're not. Until it's clear, and until I can remember everything about life together, I'm going to focus on staying alive." He smiled. "And loving you."

She leaned in for a kiss. "I'm all for that." When he broke the kiss, Sophie leaned back and grinned. "I feel so vindicated right now! After the ribbing I got from Seth, and I was right after all."

Jamie raised an eyebrow. "He had a thing for you."

Sophie smacked his knee. "He did not."

He raised her hand to his lips and gave a gentle nip to her knuckles. "He absolutely did. I had to have a couple, "Come to Jesus" discussions with him."

Sophie wrinkled her nose. "I wondered why he started to avoid me."

Jamie kissed her hand again and then rose to his feet. "I really need to check in."

She followed. "Will you come back for dinner?"

"I don't know."

"If you don't, I'll bring dinner to you."

Jamie narrowed his eyes. "Make sure you bring someone with you. Topper or someone else of the male persuasion."

Sophie pursed her lips. "I've been living with these men for months now. I've formed friendships with many of them. If someone tried to do anything to me, and you weren't around, I'd have a dozen men defending my honor. And if Andrew's around..." She waved her hand in the air. "Well, the attacker would be dead, or maimed."

He grasped her upper arms gently and leaned down to kiss her cheek. "Bring Topper."

She nodded reluctantly and he turned to leave the room. She couldn't resist a gentle smack to his behind as he moved away from her.

* * *

Sophie woke the next morning and forced gritty eyes open. She stretched, her body sore, although not unpleasantly so, and sighed. "Jamie."

Needing to see him, she pushed herself out of bed and dressed quickly. Relieved to find no one about downstairs, she grabbed a slice of warm bread and took her morning walk to see Samson. Arriving at his stall, she heard commotion going on near the arena and cornered one of the men who had stepped into the barn. "Is Lieutenant Emerson working with the horses?"

The private shook his head. "No, ma'am, the lieutenant left at dawn."

"Where did he go?"

He grabbed a halter from one of the hooks near the entrance and shrugged. "Trouble at the border."

Sophie nodded and turned back to pet Samson, lost in her thoughts. She knew that the last Confederate stronghold on the Mississippi River surrendered to General Grant at Vicksburg on July 4, which was yesterday. The anti-draft riots would happen in New York, but not until July 13.

Sophie kissed Samson's muzzle. "He could have at least left a note, don't you think?" Samson nodded his head and Sophie smiled. "I can always count on you to agree with me."

She gave Samson one last pat, and then made her way back to the house to get ready to leave for the hospital. She decided to walk, and by the time she arrived, she had worked herself into such a mood, she was looking for a fight. Topper greeted her with a wide smile. He'd found himself a purpose, helping the soldiers, and his duties brought him to the hospital almost daily.

"Hi, Topper."

"Good morning." He handed her a note. "The lieutenant left this with me for you."

Her frustration was replaced with guilt as she opened the envelope.

Sophie, I'll be back in a couple of days. Sorry this is in a note. I love you - Jamie.

Sophie sighed. *I guess it's something.*

She found one of the other nurses who filled her in on the events of the morning and was relieved that for the most part, the day was slow. The men were all resting comfortably and no new wounded had arrived.

Sophie made her way to the cots and spent a few minutes with each soldier that was awake and lucid. She'd been in the tent for about thirty minutes when she arrived at Richard's cot. He was awake and appeared to be watching her intently. "Good morning, Richard. How are you feeling? Is there much pain in your leg?" He just stared at her. "Richard? Are you in pain?"

"No," he said bitterly and turned his head away from her.

"Is there anything I can get you?"

No response.

"Richard, are you having difficulty hearing me, or are you just being mean?" Sophie leaned closer to him. "Because if you didn't hear me, I'd be *happy* to repeat the question. However, if you're just being mean, then I'll move on and help someone who will appreciate it."

Another soldier overheard her comment and said loudly, "I appreciate you, Miss Sophie. You can come over here and help me."

A few of the other men laughed and Sophie couldn't help but smile. She started to move away, but Richard reached out and grabbed her hand. She turned around and sat down in the chair next to his cot. "Richard, I know a lot has happened, but I'd like to help you if you'll let me."

"I'd appreciate some water, Sophie."

"Okay, I'll be right back." She brought it and helped him sit up to drink. "Do you think you could try to walk around a bit today? I'm sure your leg is killing you, but it would be good to get some circulation going."

He nodded.

"Good. I'll finish making the rounds and then come back and help you, okay?"

Sophie finished checking on the men and then made her way back to Richard. She helped him stand and handed him a pair of crutches. "Okay, bud, let's get you moving. I'd like you to make one entire circle around the room, do you think you can do that?"

Richard hobbled up and down the main aisle of the hospital. He refused to let her walk with him, so she stayed by his bed and watched. Despite a nasty break, Richard was better off than some. Dr. Paxton had fashioned an impressive cast that would have rivaled modern day medicine in her opinion, and she figured Richard would regain mobility in a few weeks.

She had to give Richard credit, he didn't complain, despite the fact that he must have been in a great deal of pain. He stopped a few times but seemed to be doing all right.

When he turned around to make his way back to his cot, Sophie noticed sweat pouring from his body and his face tight with pain. She quickly went to assist. "Richard, you did great. Let's get you back to the cot. Are you in terrible pain?" He didn't say a word but the grimace spoke volumes. "You're incredibly brave, Mr. Madden. Let's try and get you comfortable and then I'll see if we can find you something for the pain."

"No laudanum," Richard whispered

Sophie went to find one of the doctors. Lucky for her, Dr. Palmer wasn't on duty today. She found Dr. Mickel, who came to check on Richard before deciding what to give him. While the doctor was examining Richard, Sophie went to check on a few of the other patients who were awake. After successfully changing several dressings and soothing a few frayed nerves, Sophie made her way back to Richard for one more quick check. "What did the doctor say?"

"He wanted to give me laudanum. I told him I'd rather live with the pain."

"I don't know if that makes you smart, crazy, or stupid." Sophie sat in the chair. "But if you can live with the pain, then you're a bigger man than most. Would you like me to read to you?"

He stared at her for several seconds before rasping, "What I'd really like, Sophie is for you to sing for me."

"I don't know if that would be a good idea." She glanced around the room. "Several of the men are resting and I don't want to wake them."

"Please, Sophie, it would distract me from the pain," Richard implored.

"You're very good at the guilt trip, aren't you?" She smiled down at him. "All right. Let me think."

Sophie didn't remember many songs of the era, or at least ones that would have been considered historic in the twenty-first century. She wracked her brain for something to sing; in the end, she decided to sing one of Jamie's originals. The song was suited for either electric or acoustic, so she thought she might be able to pull it off a cappella.

It was a challenge for her not to do things to change history. It's not like she could pull out a Trisha Yearwood tune. She'd end up feeling guilty of any impact it might have in the future. She finished singing and realized there was complete silence. With a grimace, she glanced around the room. "Sorry, gentleman, did I disturb you?"

"Don't be ridiculous, Sophie. That was incredible." Richard grabbed her hand.

"Yes, Miss Sophie. I've never heard anything like it," one of the other patients called out.

Then, after a moment of silence, the room erupted in applause. Sophie blushed and then stood and took a curtsy. "You're all very kind."

"Will you sing for us tomorrow, Miss Sophie?"

"Yes, Miss Sophie, please sing for us again."

"All right, gentleman. I'll sing for you tomorrow."

Christine arrived about an hour later and pulled her aside for a moment alone. "How is your day so far?"

Sophie sighed. "Jamie left."

Christine ushered her away from the men. "What do you mean?"

Sophie made a point of studying the table of surgical instruments in front of her. "He took off early this morning, trouble somewhere. One of the borders, maybe?"

"Are you all right?"

Sophie nodded. "Yes, I'm just not good at the inability to find him on a second's notice."

"Stay busy. Did he say when he'd be back?"

"Couple of days...I hope."

Christine dropped the subject and the girls got to work on changing dressings and soothing soldiers. Waylaid by one of the men who had a nasty infection and had developed a fever, they tried everything to bring his fever down but weren't having much luck. Sophie sang quietly to him as Christine laid ice-soaked cloths over his body.

The day moved quickly and Sophie ended up staying later than expected. Christine offered to drop her at home so she didn't have to walk. Sophie was relieved to have a ride, her exhaustion both physically and mentally overwhelming. That night, Sophie let out a sigh as she snuggled under the covers of her bed and fell asleep as soon as her head hit the pillow.

* * *

Sophie spent the next two days simply trying to function, unable to stop worrying about Jamie's safety. Without cell phones and the ability to find him quickly, she had to distract herself in mundane ways. She decided to check on Samson after her shift at the hospital one particularly hot afternoon, and Christine offered to join her.

They made the quick trip from the center of town and Christine pulled her buggy in front of the Wades home and secured the horse. Once the girls made their way out to the stables, Christine stopped at the arena to observe the training.

"Ahhh."

Christine's eyebrows furrowed in confusion. "Is something amiss?"

Sophie giggled as she peered over the railing. "I wondered why you were so eager to join me today."

Dr. Stephen Paxton knelt beside a young soldier who appeared to have been thrown from one of the larger horses.

"Don't be ridiculous," Christine retorted. "I don't even know that soldier."

Sophie laughed at her deflection.

"If you happen to notice, my brother is also inside," Christine said indignantly.

"Yes, yes he is. And Andrew is the reason you came out to the stables with me."

Christine huffed, so Sophie had mercy and left her friend to fawn over the handsome doctor.

"Sophie, wait!"

She turned to find Andrew jogging toward her. "Hi, Andrew."

He smiled as he stopped beside her. "How are you?"

Sophie raised an eyebrow. "Fine. Why?"

Andrew shrugged. "I haven't seen the lieutenant around in a few days."

"Some trouble at the border."

He smiled gently. "Whatever you need, you let me know."

She grinned up at him. "You're good at being an overprotective brother."

"I've had lots of practice."

Sophie let out a quiet snort. "Yes, you have. I'm fine. I'm going to hug my horse now."

"Your horse, huh?"

"A girl can dream."

Andrew left her, and Sophie made her way to Samson's stall. Thinking a little exercise would do him some good, and wanting to have a closer look at his leg, Sophie grabbed a halter and let herself into his stall. Singing quietly to him as she slipped the leather over his head, she patted his neck before leading him out of the barn and into the open.

She didn't want to tie him down, so she loosened the lead and moved to his rump. Running her hand down his leg, she felt light heat, but the swelling appeared to be dissipating. She slid her hand along his side as she made his way back to his head. "What a clever boy you are," she crooned as she stroked his nose.

Despite her quiet voice, he was still a bit skittish. His eyes widened, wilder than she would have liked. Without warning, she heard a whistle and then a loud crack. Sophie spun around to find what had hit the side of the building. But before she could react with any kind of urgency, Samson's ears went straight back and he pulled away from Sophie. She tried to calm him, and a soldier rushed over to try help. However, he only managed to spook Samson even more and Sophie got caught up in his lead.

Samson went into the air, and as he came down, his hoof caught her in the head. She went down hard and fast, letting go of the rope and setting Samson free. He bolted before anyone could stop him.

* * *

Christine watched the scene unfold in front of her too fast to react.

"Andrew!" Christine screamed and then made a run for her fallen friend, kneeling beside her and cradling her head gently in her hands. "Sophie? Sophie, wake up."

Sophie's skin, now a grayish pallor, alarmed Christine, not to mention the nasty bruise forming on her temple. Tenderly moving Sophie's hair aside, not an easy task with the blood from the wound caking it to her temple, Christine let out a sigh of relief when Andrew and Stephen rushed toward her.

"What happened?" Stephen knelt as he removed his jacket and folded it for a makeshift pillow.

Christine glanced up at the doctor. "I heard a loud crack and then Samson spooked. His hoof grazed her temple."

Stephen nodded. "All right, we need to get her out of this dirt."

Andrew made his way to a group of soldiers who stood vigil over Sophie. "Was it a rock? Did someone throw it?" His voice was low and lethal.

No one knew—or admitted that they knew.

"We need to get her away from here," the doctor called.

Without further discussion, one of the men grabbed a small wagon and hitched a horse to it. Dr. Paxton bent down and picked Sophie up, laying her gently in the back. "I'll take her home."

"Would someone please try and find her horse? I'll return as soon as I know she's all right," Andrew added.

Christine sat with Sophie in the back of the wagon as Stephen maneuvered it back to the house. Once he set the brake, Christine held her head as Andrew lifted Sophie and carried her through the front door, yelling for Nona. Stephen followed close behind with his medical bag.

"Oh, no. Drew, what happened?" Nona bustled into the foyer.

"Samson kicked Sophie and she won't wake up."

Nona pointed to the stairs. "Please take her up to her bedroom. It'll be more comfortable to examine her there."

Andrew gingerly carried his burden up the stairs and entered Sophie's bedroom. After he laid her on her bed, he stepped outside so that Stephen could examine her. Stephen poured water from the pitcher into the bowl and found a soft cloth. Christine loosened her clothing and then stepped back. Stephen laid the cool, wet cloth on her forehead, making sure not to put any pressure on her bruised temple.

Rummaging in his medical bag, he located the smelling salts and Sophie jerked when he waved them under her nose. Nona entered the room with fresh water steeped in ice, just as Sophie tried to push Stephen's hand away.

"Sophie. I need you to wake up for me. Can you hear me?" Stephen lifted her into the sitting position.

"Sweepy. Want to sweep," Sophie slurred.

Christine helped Stephen get Sophie up and off the bed as she called for Andrew to help. Stephen lifted her arm and settled it around his neck so that he could steady her. "Sophie, you need to stand up. Can you try for me please?"

Andrew rushed through the door and moved his sister aside in order to assist Stephen.

CHAPTER TWENTY-ONE

SOPHIE SLOWLY SLID off the bed as Stephen and Andrew held her from each side. She was confused, her head hurt, and she felt sick to her stomach. The men lowered her onto the chest at the end of the bed.

"Gonna be sick," Sophie rasped.

Christine grabbed the bowl and put it under her chin. Just in time.

She rubbed sore eyes. "I'm so tired. What happened? I want to sleep."

"Samson kicked you and you have been unconscious. It's important to stay awake. Can you do that for me?" Stephen's voice was soothing and brother-like.

"Samson kicked me? He wouldn't do that. What happened?" Sophie slurred.

"He got spooked. He didn't do it on purpose." Andrew squeezed her shoulder. "Sophie? Sophie, wake up. You can't go to sleep."

Stephen picked her up again and he and Andrew started moving her around the room. Sophie stumbled. "But I'm so tired."

Andrew gripped her waist tighter. "I know you are, but we need to keep you moving."

As the men continued to walk Sophie around the room, Christine made her answer questions. She became lucid about fifteen minutes into their little exercise session and was also able to hold herself up. Stephen took a moment to take another look at her and felt that the danger had passed, however, she was informed she needed to stay awake for the next four to five hours to be sure.

"Can I at least lie down? My head is throbbing." Sophie grimaced.

"You may lie down, but don't sleep." Stephen leaned forward. "Do you understand?"

Sophie nodded, but groaned at the motion.

"I'll sit with her, Dr. Paxton. Perhaps we can sit in the parlor. That way there will be noise to help keep her awake," Christine suggested.

Stephen paused briefly before nodding. "All right."

The men helped Sophie down the stairs and into the parlor. Stephen got her situated on the sofa and went to find her something to drink.

"I'll check on Samson." Andrew left quickly.

Stephen returned with hot tea and a couple of cookies, not happy with Sophie's dazed appearance, despite Christine's vigilance. "Sophie, you need to wake up."

Sitting up slightly, she rasped, "I'm awake. I'm awake."

"I have some tea and cookies for you." Stephen held a cookie out to her.

One hand went to her mouth, the other to her stomach at the thought. "I don't know if I could eat anything. My stomach is churning."

"I'm sure it is but I'd like you to try please."

"Your bedside manner sucks," she retorted. Stephen didn't comment as he handed her the tea and stood guard while she took a sip. She took a small bite of one of the cookies but pushed the uneaten portion away with a grimace. "Where's Samson?"

Stephen set down the discarded teacup and cookie. "Andrew went to find out. He bolted after he kicked you and we're not sure where he ran off to."

Sophie grabbed his arm. "They won't hurt him, will they? They understand it wasn't his fault, right?"

Placing his hand gently on hers, Stephen smiled. "Yes, Sophie, I'm sure they understand. They will put him back in his stall and you can visit him as soon as you're feeling up to it."

Sophie nodded and went back to her tea. She and Christine sat in the parlor and talked for over two hours. Michael and Nona checked on her periodically but for the most part, they left her to rest.

Andrew returned in time for an early dinner and Sophie asked Stephen to stay as well. She knew Christine would never ask him and wanted to help in her own way.

"How's Samson?"

"He's well, Sophie. Your pet is back in his stall," Andrew assured her.

Sophie raised an eyebrow. "My pet?"

Andrew chuckled. "That's what the men have begun to call him."

"Funny." Sophie rolled her eyes.

"Which is *why* Jimmy and Frank spent four hours tracking him down and coaxing him back to the barn."

"Really?"

Andrew nodded and her heart swelled. Once the nausea and sleepiness finally subsided, she convinced Christine to take a walk with Stephen, and Nona insisted she rest before dinner, so she reluctantly made her way upstairs.

As she walked through the foyer, she heard a knock on the door and reached to open it.

"What happened to your head, Sophie?" Jamie growled. She narrowed her eyes at him. "Sophie, answer me, please." He walked in and quietly closed the door.

"Maybe if you'd been here, you wouldn't need to ask," she snipped.

"Sophie, don't be difficult. I want to know what happened to your head." She burst into tears and he pulled her close as tears flowed unchecked down her face. "Sweetheart," he whispered. "Tell me."

She gave a halfhearted shrug. "Samson kicked me."

Jamie cupped her face in his hands and leaned down so that he was nose to nose with her. "What do you mean, Samson kicked you? How did that happen?"

She pulled back slightly and took a deep breath. "He got spooked while I was walking him—"

"Why were you walking him alone, Sophie?" Jamie growled.

Sophie stomped her foot. "Because you weren't here!"

He dragged his hands down his face.

"Anyway, he reared. When he came back down, his hoof grazed my head."

Jamie scowled. "Who spooked him?"

"I don't know."

He continued to stare at her.

"Stop looking at me like that," she muttered.

"Did you lose consciousness?" She lowered her head without answering, but he tipped her chin back up with his finger. "Sophie Jane Wellington Ford, answer me. Did you lose consciousness?"

She squeezed her eyes shut. "Yes, I lost consciousness. But I've been forced to stay awake for the past three hours. Dr. Paxton was out at the arena when it happened, and Andrew and Christine have been hovering."

Jamie frowned. "Maybe you should be in bed, resting."

"But you just got home."

"I'll stay with you tonight." He slipped her hair away from her temple. "This does not look good. What did Dr. Paxton say?"

"That I had to stay awake."

Jamie smiled gently. "Anything else?"

She frowned and then shook her head. "Nothing else."

* * *

"Okay. Let's get you up to bed. I'll let everyone know where you are." He wrapped an arm around her waist and led her upstairs.

She pushed open her door and took a deep breath. "Oh! Going to be sick." Pulling away from Jamie, she only just made it to the pitcher.

"Better?" Jamie grasped her around the waist and stroked her back. When she nodded, he lifted her and laid her on the bed. Gently sweeping her hair away from her face, he leaned down and kissed her forehead. "Sweetheart, you're very warm. Are you feeling all right? Can I get you anything?"

Staring up at him, she shook her head. "I'm so tired. Sleep."

Jamie sat back. "I don't think you should sleep, sweetheart."

"I'm hot."

He rubbed her cheek and sat up further. "Sophie?"

Her words slurred and her eyes closed as she whispered, "Jams, tired, sweep."

"Sophie, you need to stay awake."

Her eyes fluttered and then closed. "Sweep."

"Sophie?" No response. "Sophie, you need to wake up." Still no response. Alarm hit him as he laid her down gently before leaving her to find either Stephen or Michael, rushing downstairs. Stephen had already left, so Jamie made his way to Michael's office. "Dr. Wade?"

Michael looked up from his desk.

"Sophie's upstairs in her room and I can't wake her."

Michael grabbed the smelling salts and led the way to her room. Neither one of them could wake her with verbal stimulation, so Michael put the vinegar under her nose. No response. "Lieutenant, I think this is much worse than we originally thought. Her temperature appears to be rising and she's unresponsive. We must get her fever down and try to get her to wake up."

Jamie went to work immediately. He started to unbutton her jacket. Michael left to find Nona, who arrived quickly with Betty in tow and immediately shooed him out of the room. He was left in the hall pacing and praying. Terrified she wouldn't wake up. It must have only taken a few minutes for the door to open, but to Jamie, it seemed like hours before Nona stood in the open doorway.

"She's resting, dear. We're going to get ice, so you may sit with her if you like."

Jamie went back into Sophie's room and sat down on the bed. Laying his hand on her cheek, he felt the heat, and as he leaned over to kiss her forehead, tears filled his eyes. The thought of her in pain was almost his undoing.

Michael returned, and Jamie coughed in an effort to clear his emotion. They went to work, laying ice soaked linens over her body and changing them every twenty minutes. On the third change, she started shivering.

"This is a good sign," Michael said.

Within minutes, Sophie began thrashing around, trying to take off the strips of cloth. "Jamie, don't leave me."

Tears streamed down her face and she appeared to be in the midst of a dream. Her breathing was labored, which concerned Michael, so Jamie climbed onto the bed and pulled her into his arms. "Shh, Sweetheart, I'm here. I'm not going anywhere."

Sophie began to scream, "Jamie, please don't go. I promise, I'll be nice, just don't leave me again. Jamie, where are you? Oh, God, Jamie, NO!"

She tried to sit up, but Jamie pulled her tighter to his chest and whispered, "Sophie, honey, listen to my voice. I'm right here. I'm not leaving you."

As Jamie sang quietly to her and stroked her back, she calmed, so Michael put more cold cloths on her forehead and arms. Jamie wasn't prepared to let her go, regardless of the fact the wet compresses were soaking him.

It took several hours for her fever to drop, and Jamie was forced to leave her once more so that Nona could change Sophie's bedding and nightgown. He hated being relegated to the hallway and paced in frustration as he waited to be let back in.

He turned as Andrew limped up the stairs and stopped briefly. "Lieutenant. What's happening with Sophie?"

"Her fever spiked and she's been unconscious."

Andrew raised an eyebrow. "Did Nona kick you out of the room?"

Jamie nodded and sighed.

Just then, Nona opened the door. "Drew, how are you feeling?" Glancing to his knee, she frowned. "Did you overuse your leg?"

Andrew shook his head. "I'm fine, Nona, thank you. How's Sophie?"

"Michael says she feels cooler, and her bedding has been changed, which will make her more comfortable, but she hasn't woken up yet."

Relief spread through Jamie as he pushed past her. "Thank you. Excuse me, Nona." Jamie walked into Sophie's room and over to her bedside. Laying his hand gently on her cheek, he leaned down and kissed her forehead, grateful that she felt cooler.

A knock came at the door, and Christine poked her head inside. "How are you feeling?"

Sophie turned her head toward her voice. "Much better now, thank you. What are you doing here so late?"

"I was worried about you, so I'm going to stay here for a few days." Christine moved further into the room as she said, "I keep joking with Mama, that maybe I should move in here. I seem to be here every day as it is."

Sophie giggled again. "Ow."

"Sorry," Christine said, looking guilty. "Can I get you anything?"

"I'm hungry. Am I allowed to eat anything?"

Jamie patted her hand. "I'll check with Michael, sweetheart. Christine, you stay and visit." He kissed her again quickly and then stepped into the hallway. Andrew pushed away from the wall.

"Lieutenant? I think someone tried to hurt Sophie."

"Walk with me." Jamie motioned towards the stairs. "What happened?"

"There was a loud bang, which we all thought was a rock of some kind, but it appears to have been a bullet. It was not an accident. In fact, I believe they were aiming for Sophie."

Jamie frowned. "That's twice."

"What do you mean, twice?" Jamie filled him in on the attempt by the lake and Andrew swore. "You take care of Sophie, and I'll see what I can find out."

Jamie nodded and went to find Michael.

Pinching the bridge of his nose to ward off the headache approaching, he retrieved the approved bowl of soup, and made his way up the stairs. He juggled the tray and pushed Sophie's door open. "You're allowed to have some broth."

"Lucky me," Sophie said sarcastically as she turned her head toward him.

"Do you need help to sit up?" Sophie shook her head and leaned against the headboard. Jamie laid a napkin across her lap and then set the tray in front of her. "Michael says the danger has passed and it's safe for you to sleep after you eat."

Jamie sat with her while she ate and then forced her to climb deeper under the covers and rest. He lay down beside her and stroked her back until she fell asleep, although her sleep was fitful, and she jerked awake less than an hour later. Sitting up, she called for Jamie, who was no longer in the bed with her.

He rose from the chair in the corner and made his way over to her. "I'm here, Sophie. Did you have a bad dream?"

She rubbed her eyes and laid back down. "No, I just thought I might have imagined you were here. Have you been here the whole time?"

"Yes." He chuckled. "I wanted to make sure you rested, and I was having a difficult time lying next to you, so I thought I'd move to the chair. Can I get you anything?"

Sophie nodded. "Some water, please."

He rose to his feet and brought her a glass of water. Leaning over, he felt her forehead. "Your fever has broken. How do you feel?"

"I'm still sore but I don't feel as though my head is going to split open."

"Why don't you roll over and I'll rub your back."

"All right." She handed him the glass and moved to her stomach. Jamie started to massage her shoulders and Sophie sighed in pleasure. "You were always so good at this."

He leaned down and kissed the back of her neck.

Sophie gave a quiet laugh. "You didn't say it was going to be one of *those* massages."

"That's just a bonus."

She reached up to move her hair away from her face and pain shot through her head. "Wait, Jamie, I think I'm going to be sick." She rolled over and sat up. Taking several deep breaths, she squeezed her eyes shut.

"Did I do something?"

"No. Ugh, it hurts."

Jamie stood and found a cool, wet cloth, and then made his way back to her side. "Here, put this on, it should help." He laid it gently over her eyes.

She laid down on her back again and sighed. "Hmm-mm, yes, much better. Thank you."

Jamie stared at her while she was essentially blindfolded. Her nightgown had ridden up her thighs and, despite the fact that the buttons at the front were fastened all the way to her neck, the delicacy of the fabric didn't distract from her full breasts. Sitting slowly back down on the bed, he took one of her feet in his hands and started to massage it, working his way to her ankle.

"You're *so* getting brownie points for this," Sophie said behind her blindfold.

Jamie stretched out beside her. "How's your head?"

"Improved, I think."

He leaned down to place his lips gently on hers. The kiss became more urgent as his hand moved from her cheek to her neck. He loved the feeling of her body beneath his fingers. She'd lost so much weight over the course of her illness, but now, she was healthy and regaining her lush figure.

Jamie reached his hand to the bottom of her nightgown and pushed it up her body. When he reached her hips, he rolled her onto her back and pushed the nightgown higher, noticing her birthmark just below her navel, shaped like the state of Texas.

He chuckled, remembering when he wanted to venture south of the border, he'd shout "Remember the Alamo!" or make a corny joke like not remembering the state of Texas being so close to Virginia. Sophie's quiet moan forced him back to the present and he pushed himself up from the bed.

"Did I do something wrong?" she asked.

Pacing the small space next to the bed, he whispered, "No, sweetheart. I'm sorry."

Sophie sat up and glared at him, a little irritated with the stopping and starting. Well, really just the stopping. "Don't be sorry, come back to bed."

Jamie shook his head and held his hands up. "No. You need to rest."

Sophie slipped her nightgown off her shoulders. "Nooo, I need my husband to make love to me."

Jamie had to turn away from the sight of her full breasts rising and falling with her quick breaths, begging to be touched and tasted. "Later. When you're feeling better. Please put your nightgown back on."

"No."

Jamie sat back down on the bed, his back to her, and Sophie knelt behind him and laid her cheek on his shoulder. "I feel fine."

He glanced at her. "Sophie, you need to rest and this is not open for discussion."

Sophie pursed her lips and then gave him a slow smile. "How about just a kiss?"

Jamie raised an eyebrow. "One kiss. I mean it."

Kissing her as he laid her back down on the bed, his hand seemed to find its way under her nightgown and up her thigh. She gasped as he moved further up her leg. "Yes, just one kiss—ohhhh."

Jamie forced himself to pull away from her once again. "I'm sorry, sweetheart, we need to stop."

"Wha-what? Why?"

Sitting up, he rested his elbows on his knees and ran his hands through his hair. "You got kicked in the head by a horse today, were unconscious, and fought off a really nasty fever. I think that making love to you might just overwhelm your body."

"You have that much faith in your abilities, do you?"

"Ten-Cow," he admonished. Sophie burst into tears and Jamie pulled her close. "What did I say?"

"You called me Ten-Cow."

Jamie pushed a curl behind her shoulder and smiled. "Yes."

Sophie sniffed, and Jamie chuckled as he wrapped his arms around her waist and settled her head on his shoulder. Letting her soak his chest with her tears, he waited until she calmed, and then he swept her hair off her forehead. "How's your head?"

Sophie stared up at him and sighed quietly. "It hurts."

"Why didn't you tell me?" He stood and made his way to the bureau. "Honey, don't do that again, okay? I don't want you in pain." He grabbed the cloth, rinsed it, and laid it gently on her forehead. "How's that?"

"Good, thank you. What time is it?"

"I think it's almost midnight." He sat next to her again and kissed her cheek. "And you need to rest. Time to go back to sleep." He leaned down and kissed her then stood and moved away from the bed.

Sophie grabbed for him. "Where are you going?"

"Nowhere. I'll stay right here but in the chair."

Sophie grinned at him. "Chicken."

"It's called self-preservation."

CHAPTER TWENTY-TWO

"GOOD MORNING." CHRISTINE drew the curtains. "How do you feel?"

"Where did you come from?" Sophie opened her eyes and glanced around the room.

"James is currently in the dining room."

"Why didn't you say so?" Sophie jumped out of bed.

"Careful." Christine steadied Sophie. "How's your head?"

"It's definitely better."

"The bruise looks a bit worse today, but I think you're on the mend. Let's get you dressed and downstairs to meet your man."

Christine helped Sophie into a yellow skirt and white blouse. The colors suited her light hair and skin, and once the yellow satin ribbon was added to her hair, she felt a little less like she'd been kicked in the head by a horse. Sophie rushed downstairs, and as she turned the corner into the dining room, she stopped short. Jamie and Andrew stood as she came in the door.

"Good morning, gentlemen," she said as brightly as she could.

She took her seat and Jamie brought her a cup of coffee that he'd already prepared for her and she smiled as she took her first sip. "Perfect, thank you."

As Andrew stood at the buffet putting together a plate of food, Jamie leaned down and whispered in her ear, "Meet me in the library."

Before Sophie could respond, Christine walked in, so Jamie used the distraction to quietly leave the room, and Sophie smiled to her as she stood and followed. Walking into the library, Sophie jumped slightly when Jamie stepped out from behind the door and pulled her into his arms. "Good morning." He kicked the door shut.

"Good morning." Sophie sighed in pleasure. "When did you leave my room? You must be exhausted."

"I left at six, but got an hour of sleep in my tent." He kissed her again and then examined her forehead. "Your bruise looks worse, sweetheart. Are you in any pain?"

"I still have the headache, but I think it's better." She linked her arms around his neck. "Thank you for staying with me last night."

He leaned down and kissed her nose. "Get used to it."

"What do you mean, get used to it?"

"I'm not leaving you again. The men will just have to live without me." He pulled her over to one of the high-backed chairs and sat across from her on the hearth.

"In bed...*with* me, right?"

"Maybe."

Sophie sank into her favorite chair and raised an eyebrow. "So, let me get this straight. You plan to sneak into my bedroom every night and fall asleep in the *oh so not* comfortable chair, just so you can keep your promise of never leaving me?"

"Something like that." He took his left hand and linked his fingers with hers, the clink of their rings sounding in the quiet room.

"You're wearing your wedding ring."

Jamie nodded. "Of course I am. I'm your husband."

"Not sure if we are in this century," Sophie said. "Don't we need something written in a bible?"

Jamie chuckled. "Probably. I suppose we should rectify that."

"Oh, really?"

"You don't agree?"

"Hm."

"What do you mean, 'Hm'?"

She patted his chest, leaned down, and kissed his cheek. "That one's for you to figure out."

"Sophie, what is that supposed to mean?"

"Love you!" She rose to his feet and raced out of the room.

Jamie jumped up off the chair and chased her. "Sophie, get back here." Almost halfway down the hall when he caught her from behind, he pulled her back into the library, laughing.

"Ow," she said.

"Did I hurt you?" He turned her around to inspect her forehead.

"No, I'm fine. I just forgot about my head." She leaned against him and put her arms around his waist.

"No more jarring movements, all right? You really need to take it easy for a little while." He dropped his chin onto the top of her head and continued to hold her for a few minutes.

She looked up at him. "We should probably get back. People will be wondering where we are."

He gave her one last kiss, and then they made their way back to the dining room. After a quick lunch, Jamie forced Sophie back to bed with a promise he'd wake her in plenty of time to check on Samson before dark.

* * *

Sophie freshened up and then made her way to the barn, heading straight for Samson's stall. He whinnied when she called him before poking his head out and pushing at her shoulder with his nose. "Yes, boy, I know you didn't mean to hurt me." She gave him some sugar and kissed his muzzle before checking his leg. Satisfied his healing was right on course, she left him and headed back to the house.

She passed the arena, and heard yelling coming from Richard's barn. She peeked around the corner and scowled. Richard, leaning heavily on crutches was nose to nose with Jamie.

After several obscenities were delivered to each side, Jamie tapped Richard's shoulder, hard enough that Richard had to fight for balance. "She's my wife, and you'll go nowhere near her."

Richard swore. "You aren't worthy of her."

"You're a very sore loser, Dick."

"What did you just say?" Sophie snapped.

Both men whipped their heads around, surprised to see her.

Jamie rushed toward her. "Sophie—"

"You did *not* just refer to me as something you won, as though I was a prize to be competed over, did you? Did you?"

"Sophie, don't be ridiculous. Of course not," Jamie said.

"Oh, so now I'm ridiculous." She threw up her hands. "I've had enough of you two. Why don't you just fight to the death? Have at it. Jamie, you can pretend it's a cage fight. You love those. You're both jackasses." She stormed off toward the house.

"Don't come near my wife again, do you understand me?" Jamie didn't wait for a response as he took off after Sophie. "Sophie, stop," he yelled.

"No," she yelled back.

"*Stop*, baby." He'd almost caught up with her just before she reached the house, when she stopped suddenly and grabbed her head. "You need to relax," he warned as he grabbed her waist from behind, kissing her neck and giving her a squeeze.

"No." She tried to pull out of his arms but he had her firmly in his grip.

Jamie laughed. "You're not going to relax, sweetheart?"

She pushed at his arms. "Don't 'sweetheart' me, especially when you're laughing at me."

"Sophie, I'm not laughing at you."

She turned to face him and poked him in the chest. "Is this how it's going to be? A man looks sideways at me and you go off the deep end because you think he's competition? You were never like this before! I won't be competed for Jamie." She went for his chest again but he grabbed her hand quickly before raising it to his lips.

He wrinkled his brow. "I was defending your honor."

"I can do that myself."

He frowned. "But then I'd have nothing to do."

She dropped her head into his sternum. "Jamie, stop teasing, this is serious. I don't want to be someone's trophy."

"Look at me." She didn't respond, so he lifted her chin with his fingers. "You're so much more than that and I know you know that. Where is this coming from?"

"I don't know. I'm sorry." Her palm settled on her forehead. "My head hurts and I just feel overwhelmed with everything right now. It probably doesn't help that you and Richard are acting like a couple of fighting cocks. And he's injured." She smacked his chest. "You should have a little more compassion."

"I think I know what's going on." Grabbing her hand, he pulled her towards the house, through the front door and back to the library. "Sit here, please." He gestured to one of the high-backed chairs.

"What are you doing?"

"I'll be right back," he said mysteriously.

Her head throbbed from all the exertion, so she rested it against the high back of the chair and closed her eyes. She heard Jamie come back into the room but didn't look up.

He leaned down and kissed her forehead. "Are you all right?"

She smiled and opened her eyes. "Yes, my head just hurts. Why? Do I look that pathetic?"

He chuckled. "I have something for you. Have a look."

She turned her head and on the little table between the two chairs, Jamie had set down a pot of tea with milk. Next to it was a chocolate bar. Sophie squealed in delight.

"Chocolate, Jamie? Where did you get chocolate?" Milton Hershey was only about six years old at this point in history, which meant Hershey, Pennsylvania wouldn't exist for several decades. Taking a bite, she let out a sigh. "Ohhh, this is amazing."

"Mary helped me put this together. They had a few blocks that they were going to melt to drink and she let me cut a piece for you. If your head wasn't bothering you, I'd have brought red wine instead of tea, but I didn't want to take any chances. Now, enjoy your treat. I'm going to get something for your head, I'll be right back."

Sophie reached out and grabbed his hand. "Jamie, this was very thoughtful. You have no idea how much I needed this."

"Once a month it's the same thing, so I'd say I did know." He leaned down and gave her a lingering kiss. Leaving her to her chocolate, he went off to find something for her headache, returning with an ice-soaked cloth and gently laying it over her head.

"Thanks." Sophie closed her eyes.

They spent the next few hours talking about their wedding and their future. The future they had already experienced and the one on the horizon.

"Dinner is served," Daniel said from the doorway.

Jamie stood and helped Sophie from her chair.

After dinner, the couple spent time with Christine and the Wades in the parlor. Sophie was amazed at the bond already forming between Jamie and Christine, and it brought back memories of how he and Alex had been extremely close. Not just because Luke was his best friend. She had become a sister to him, right alongside Emma and Hannah, and it seemed as though Jamie was adding another one to his family.

When it was time for the evening to come to a close, Sophie walked Jamie out. She had a feeling Christine knew he would probably sneak back in, but she never said a word. As they stood on the porch, Jamie pulled Sophie into his arms and kissed her. "How's your head?"

"It's much better. I think the chocolate helped."

He chuckled. "Well, I'm glad. I'm going to leave now," he said a little louder than necessary but then whispered, "I'll see you later."

She giggled at the wolfish smile on his face before waving goodnight and then making her way inside. She said goodnight to the Wades and went upstairs to get ready for bed. She and Christine spent some time talking as they assisted each other out of their hoops and corsets.

Christine said goodnight and was ready to walk out the door, when she turned and whispered, "I left the front door unlocked."

"You did? I do declare, Miss Christine, you are a very, very naughty friend! And I *love* you for it."

Christine laughed and Sophie gave her a hug before she left.

* * *

An hour later, Jamie walked into Sophie's room and found her pacing. "What's wrong?"

She threw herself into his arms. "I thought you'd be here much sooner. I can't believe you made me wait this long. Just what were you doing?"

"Shhh, sweetheart, someone will hear you." He chuckled softly. "I have something to show you, but you're going to have to let me go."

She kept her hands around his neck and looked at him. "I'm not ready to yet."

"Oh, really? So, you're not the teeniest bit curious to see what I brought you?" He raised an eyebrow at her.

"Kiss me first and then I'll tell you."

He smiled down at her before kissing her breathless.

"You are so very good at that, James William. Now, what did you bring me?" He pulled a pair of pants from behind his back.

Sophie took them from him and held them up to the light. "You brought me pants?"

"Not just any pants, Sophie. Breeches." She looked at him in confusion, so he continued, "I thought you might like to go riding in a day or so, and these will be thin enough to hide underneath your skirts so you don't have to ride sidesaddle. Just don't wear your hoops and I think they'll work."

"Oh!" She threw herself back in his arms again. "You are the most wonderful, fabulous, unbelievable, incredibly gorgeous man I have ever known."

"That's all you can come up with to describe me?" He lifted her hand and kissed her palm. "I'm disappointed."

Sophie giggled and settled herself in one of the chairs in front of the fire.

"Wait, Ten-Cow, I have an idea. Stand up for a sec."

Once she stood, Jamie moved the chairs to face each other and then gestured for her to sit again. After she took a seat, he lifted her legs and laid them on his lap. He began to massage her feet and was rewarded with her sigh. Sophie sunk further in her chair. "What made you think of the breeches?"

"Well, when Samson is better, you're going to want to ride, and I thought of that movie you made me watch, remember, where this girl had, like, a fake leg to put over the pommel?"

Sophie laughed. "The Anne Hathaway one."

"Yes. I can't imagine you riding sidesaddle, so if you have pants, maybe we can fake it."

Sophie smiled. "I did it, you know."

"Did what?"

"Rode sidesaddle."

Jamie's eyes widened. "You didn't!"

Sophie laughed as she shared her experience, even the part when Richard came to her rescue. Seeing Jamie's body tense, Sophie smiled. "You have to give him credit for that one. He could have been hurt pulling me from Samson. Even if he was a total tool in the end, he still came to my rescue."

Jamie ran his finger across the top of her foot. "How do you think this time travel thing happened?"

"I don't have any idea. I just remember feeling your tears on my hand, and then saw a few strange things. Then I'm freezing and being carried into the parlor by Richard." Jamie gave her ankle a squeeze and Sophie raised an eyebrow. "Do you remember more?"

Jamie frowned. "The library seemed to disappear, replaced by a huge expanse of land and then I felt pain. When I woke up, I was in the home of a farmer and his wife and they informed me I had been shot."

Sophie pulled her feet from his lap and rose to her feet. "What?" she shrieked. "Where? Show me!"

Jamie stood and pulled his shirt aside. Sophie frowned when he turned slightly for her to see the jagged scar across his side. She ran her fingers over the puckered skin. "How did I *not* notice that before?"

"Strategery."

"Okay, Will Ferrell. Seriously, how did this happen?"

Jamie sighed and took his seat again. "All I can remember is pain *before* I blacked out. What I can't quite figure out is if it came from here, as in this time, or home. It was weird."

"Very weird." Sophie sat and leaned forward. " How did you come up with Emerson?"

Jamie grimaced. "Guess what I was listening to all night?"

Sophie leaned back in surprise. "No! Seriously? Tonic? Wow, you really are a glutton for punishment. My poor, precious sweetheart. Have you remembered everything now?"

He shrugged. "I don't know. I'm remembering more every day. You'll have to fill me in on the rest."

Sophie smiled. "It'll be my pleasure."

"Do you miss our life?"

"I miss aspects of it." Sophie slipped her feet back onto Jamie's chair. "I miss Emma and worry about how she's handling life without us. I miss Alex, but at least I know she has Luke. I miss air conditioning. Actually, I *really* miss air conditioning. But with you here, I have everything. I guess I'm comforted knowing Emma will be taken care of by Alex and Hannah."

Jamie rose to his feet. "Let's go to sleep, sweetheart, you need your rest."

She followed him to the bed and climbed under the blankets. She rolled to face him when he joined her. "I love your hair."

"You do?" He chuckled. "You always were a sucker for the hair bands."

"Ah, so true."

"Which do you prefer?"

"I like them both, but I think I like the longer look right now." She stroked his cheek. "It suits you. I have to admit, though, if you want to shave the beard off, I won't be hurt."

"You don't like my beard?" He rubbed his whiskers in mock offense.

"It's not that I don't *like* it, I just prefer your face clean shaven. You have such a gorgeous face, why hide it under all that hair?" She leaned over to kiss him.

Jamie cupped her face and reluctantly broke the kiss. "You need to sleep, sweetheart. I want your head to heal quickly."

She ran her hand down his chest. "Are you sure sleep is what you want me to do? I can think of several other things that would help my head heal."

"I'm sure you can." Jamie kissed her and she pulled his lower lip into her mouth and gave it a little nip. "Sophie, you're going to drive me crazy."

"That's the plan." Her fingers traveled down his chest. "I've missed you so much. Are you really going to deny me? Especially with this mysterious healing of my heart? I want to experience everything."

Rolling her onto her back, he kissed his way down her throat. In the distance, shouts and an alarm of some form sounded. He raised his head to get a better listen. "Sophie, did you hear that?"

Rapid footsteps moved quickly down the hallway.

"The shouting and the running? No, I didn't hear anything."

CHAPTER TWENTY-THREE

A FIRM KNOCK sounded and Sophie groaned as Jamie jumped off the bed and went to stand behind the door. "Come in."

"Jamie, Sophie, come quick. There's a fire in the stables." Christine poked her head inside.

Sophie flew to the window. "Oh, *no*. Samson!" She quickly threw on the pair of breeches Jamie had brought earlier.

"How did Christine know I was here?" Jamie whispered.

"Who do you think left the front door unlocked?"

"Door?" Jamie swore. "I climbed up the trellis, onto the roof, and through the window at the end of the hallway. Next time, clue me in would you?"

If Sophie weren't so worried, she would have laughed. Jamie had already donned his shirt and boots, so they met Christine at the bottom of the stairs and ran to the stables.

Richard's barn and one side of the arena were completely engulfed in flames. Although the Wades' stables appeared to be untouched, there was a small breeze, and they were all concerned it would carry embers to other structures on the property.

Sophie and Jamie arrived to find everyone working quickly to get all of the horses out and the fire under control. Without thought, Sophie ran into the barn and straight for Samson's stall. Jamie took off after her. "Sophie, no!"

Samson panicked, smelling the smoke. He pounded his front hoof on the ground as he threw his head around with a snort. Sophie was about to swing open the stall door when Jamie caught up to her. "Sophie, don't. He'll bolt."

"But he's scared, Jamie, I just want him out of here."

"I know, honey, but let's be smart about this."

Jamie let himself inside the stall, grabbed his handkerchief and secured it around Samson's eyes. Sophie put a halter on him and Jamie pulled him out the barn doors. Leading him into an open pen further away from the other buildings, Jamie removed both the halter and the handkerchief and then jumped out of his way. As the horse reared and paced up and down the large area, Jamie kept his body between Samson and Sophie as they made their way out the gate. Sophie didn't want to leave him and fought to stay.

"Have you forgotten your injuries?"

Sophie stood her ground. "He's not going to hurt me."

"Don't make me force you, Sophie. Your safety comes first."

Samson reared and Jamie pulled Sophie closer to him, but as if to prove him wrong, the horse calmed and meekly made his way to Sophie. As he nuzzled her, Sophie giggled. "See? He's harmless."

"Hmm-mm," he grumbled. "We have bigger issues right now, sweetheart, so please come with me."

Richard and Christine were standing outside of the arena, and Jamie went to work with the other men to get the blaze under control. Sophie and Christine removed the remaining horses from Michael's stables, and just to be safe, they put them in with Samson before making their way back to the men.

Many of Jamie's unit had come to assist with the fire and were able to get it contained, but it took several hours to get the fire completely out. Nona, Sophie, and Christine organized fresh water and food for the men, and then could only stand around and wait.

"Where on earth did you get those trousers, Sophie?" Christine asked.

"Jamie found them for me, so that I could ride astride. Aren't they great?"

Just then they heard gunshots. A few minutes later, Sophie saw Jamie walking toward her. Her eyes filled with tears as she rushed to him. "Please tell me you were able to get all the horses out."

"All but two," he said sadly, and Sophie winced but let him pull her into his arms. "They were in so much pain, baby. We had to put them down."

"I know."

Jamie put his arm around her shoulders and kissed her temple before joining the others. "Richard, do you know what happened?"

"The only thing we know for sure is that it was deliberate." Richard leaned heavily against his crutches. "Probably the Rebels."

"I'm sorry about your horses, Richard," Sophie said.

"They got the majority of them out," he responded curtly.

"You know you're welcome to house the rest of the horses in my stables until you're able to rebuild," Michael said.

Richard nodded. Sophie separated herself from Jamie and walked over to Richard's side. "Richard, how is your leg?"

"It's fine." Richard's tone laced with an edge.

"I would have thought it would be quite painful with all of the running and lifting you have been doing over the past few hours. Are you sure you're all right?"

"I lifted a crutch and pointed with it," he snapped.

"You shouldn't even be on your leg right now, let alone assisting with an emergency."

"I'm not your problem, *Mrs*. Ford. Leave it alone."

"Don't speak to her that way," Jamie growled.

Sophie laid her hand on Jamie's chest. "Jamie, I can speak for myself." She turned back to Richard. "Richard, why don't you come back to the house with all of us and at the very least, let Christine take care of you for a little while." Then to Christine, she said, "Sorry, I should really ask you before I volunteer you for things, shouldn't I?"

"No, it's fine." Christine smiled. "Sophie's right, Richard. You should let Michael give you something for the pain and allow us to take care of you for a little while. We're your friends and we'd like to help."

"All right," he grumbled.

Jamie pulled Sophie back over to him, and they both went to check on the horses. After determining they were unharmed, Sophie spent a few extra minutes with Samson, then they started walking back to the house.

"How's your head?" he asked as he took her hand in his.

"I have a little bit of a headache but nothing severe. How are you doing?"

"I'm fine." He pulled her hand to his lips and kissed it. "I like the way you look in those breeches. You have the most incredible backside. Kind of like the way your Old Navy jeans look on you."

"Why, Mr. Ford, are you flirting with me?"

He stopped walking and pulled her into his arms. "You decide."

Covered in soot, he couldn't help but transfer some of the black onto Sophie's clothing.

"As sexy as you are, my love, you smell a bit like an ashtray. I think we should organize a bath for you."

"You don't like ashtray? This happens to be the newest cologne. Eau de soot."

She laughed and then wrinkled her nose at the smell. "Maybe Michael has some extra clothes you could borrow."

He pulled her closer in an effort to transfer more of the dirt onto her, but she pulled out of his arms, turned on her heel, and started to run. He ran after her but without her skirts, she was quite fast and made it all the way to the porch before he finally caught up with her, grabbing her from behind and kissing her neck. She squealed with laughter.

"I win!" she said, doing the *Rocky* dance.

"Maybe the breeches weren't such a good idea. Especially if I can't catch you." He picked her up and swung her in a circle.

"You are such a sore loser!"

"I'm not used to losing."

Sophie patted his cheek. "So true, my love. Next time, I'll let you win."

"There won't be a next time." Jamie kissed her.

"We'll see. Now, let's get you cleaned up."

They walked into the foyer and found Betty speaking with the butler.

"Betty, the men are covered in soot, would you please organize baths for them? Also, send someone to fetch Richard fresh clothes."

Betty went off to take care of everything, and Jamie gave Sophie quick squeeze just as the rest of the group started filing into the foyer. Richard was limping quite severely and looking miserable, so Michael quickly went to prepare a syringe of Morphine for him.

Betty informed them that three tubs were set up in the room just off the kitchen, so Jamie helped Richard back to the bathtubs while Sophie went to find towels. Stephen had managed a pretty significant cast for Richard, however, he'd need help to keep it from getting wet.

Sophie and Christine needed to get cleaned up as well, so they made their way up to their rooms once they knew the men were settled. Sophie walked into her room to find a small bath waiting for her. Good old Betty.

After finishing her bath, she dressed quickly and went downstairs. Richard and Christine were in the parlor, and Michael was preparing the Morphine. She went looking for Jamie, and after not finding him in the dining room, made a beeline for the library. His back was to her when she walked into the room. "Hi, baby, how was your bath?"

When he turned, Sophie gasped, her knees buckling, and she had to grab the chair next to her for support.

"That good?" he asked as he moved toward her.

Her eyes filled with tears and her hands were over her mouth in disbelief at the Jamie of her future.

"Sophie, are you all right?"

"You shaved! You look amazing." She threw her arms around his neck, kissed his cheeks, and rubbed her hands down his face. He had left the goatee and kept his sideburns long.

"Michael helped me achieve the look. It's kind of freaky shaving with a single blade, but I think it worked. Are you sure you like it?"

"I like it so much, I want you in my bed and naked."

"Sophie Jane, is that appropriate conversation for mixed company in the nineteenth-century?"

"Oh, there is so much more I could say, however, I'll wait until we are alone and you are in my bed and naked." She drew his head down and kissed him.

Jamie laughed and kissed her back. "It's almost three o'clock. You really should get some rest, especially since you're still healing."

"I *am* tired," she admitted and leaned her forehead against his.

"I'm not surprised." He settled her into her favorite chair and then sat across from her. "It's been a very long night."

"I just don't want to sleep without you."

"I know, honey but I think it would be best just for tonight. I have to organize the men first thing tomorrow morning to find out who did this."

Sophie sighed. "Can't you sneak in? Michael and Nona know you've recovered your memory. They know we're married."

Jamie shook his head. "I don't think that would be a good idea. I can't seem to keep my hands off you when we're alone and you need to rest."

"I take it riding is off for a while?"

"Sorry, sweetheart. As soon as we get the person who set the fire and has been firing shots at you, we'll go riding. I promise. You'll want to wait until Samson's well anyway, right?" At her reluctant nod, Jamie smiled. "Why don't you walk me out and then you can go to sleep."

"Will I even see you tomorrow?" she asked as they reached the porch.

"If I don't see you during the day, I'll make a point to come by at dinnertime." He pulled her into his arms for a lingering kiss.

"Okay. Be careful tomorrow, won't you?"

"I will. Don't worry."

He took her face gently in his hands. "I love you."

"I love more. I'll miss you tonight."

"Me too."

Jamie mounted his horse and took off toward camp. Sophie went inside, closed the door and headed to bed.

* * *

The following day proved frantic. People constantly moved throughout the house. Nona and Michael fed the soldiers who were helping to remove debris and rebuild what they could. Sophie and Christine put in a few hours at the hospital, but they were really needed closer to home, so ended up returning in time for lunch.

Sophie hadn't been able to fall asleep until almost four and then was awakened at eight with all of the activity. Feeling as though she got a brief reprieve at the hospital, she almost wanted to go back as soon as she got home and found herself right back in the thick of it all. Sneaking her way into the library, she fell into her favorite chair. Closing her eyes, she tried to relax while debating whether she was hungry enough to brave the crowds.

"Hiding?" Christine strode into the room and closed the door.

Sophie chuckled. "Sort of. What about you?"

Christine grinned. "Sort of. Are you hungry? They're starting to set the food out in the dining room."

"Yes, but I'm also tired and don't feel like facing a large group of people. What about you?"

"I feel the same way." Christine sat in the chair next to Sophie's. "Let's just stay here for a little while and we can eat once the crowd thins."

"That's a great plan."

A few minutes later, they heard the door open, and the girls poked their heads around the chairs. Jamie stood in the doorway trying to juggle plates of food.

Sophie jumped up and went to help him. "What are you doing?" Taking a couple of the plates from his hands, she smiled and lifted her face.

He leaned down to give her a quick kiss. "I had a feeling you might be hiding."

Christine laughed.

"Neither of you is funny," Sophie retorted.

Jamie had done a great job of getting enough food for all of them and even a wide range of choices.

"James, this is wonderful. Thank you." Christine grabbed a sandwich.

Sophie kissed him. "This was very sweet, thank you."

"You're welcome," he said. "I have news."

"Oh?" Christine asked.

"We found the men who set the fire."

"Who?" Sophie raised her eyebrow.

"The ringleader was the man who accosted you in the stables. He had three other disgruntled soldiers who assisted him."

"Oh, my goodness." Christine's hand flew to her neck. "Did they say why?"

"They targeted Richard because of our altercation. They are being held at the jail until they can be court-martialed."

Sophie studied his face. "What aren't you telling me?"

"Neither of them is the man who has been shooting at you."

Sophie sighed. "What are we going to do?"

"*We* aren't going to do anything. *You* are going to stay in this house and I'm going to find the man." Then under his breath, "And he'll experience pain beyond anything he has before."

"Jamie." Sophie frowned. "You don't know what this man is capable of, or even, if there's just one. So, let's not rush to jump into the fire, okay?"

"Of course, sweetheart. Wouldn't think of it."

"Jamie."

"I should get going."

"This conversation isn't over."

"I know, sweetheart." Jamie gave Sophie a quick kiss and left them to help with the cleanup process.

"Stubborn man."

Christine raised an eyebrow.

Sophie smiled. "They say you're supposed to marry your opposite, but Jamie and I just had to be different."

"Who are these people who give all this sage wisdom?"

"Good question."

Sophie giggled and the ladies went back to their food.

* * *

Jamie made his way out the back door and to the arena. Michael met him halfway and shook his hand. "Son, I believe we need to have a conversation."

Jamie grimaced. "Yes, sir."

"The climbing up the trellis to sneak into Sophie's room needs to cease." Jamie groaned, and Michael chuckled. "You *can* use the front door, James."

Jamie's eyes widened. Not quite the reaction he had expected. "Dr. Wade, I'm sorry if I have offended you or your wife."

Michael chuckled. "You haven't. You've both been through quite an ordeal, so please consider our home yours. You are welcome anytime."

"Thank you."

Jamie followed Michael back out to the stables, internally shaking his head at Michael's very modern reaction.

* * *

Sophie smiled as she felt soft lips on her cheek. "Mmmm, hi."

"Wake up, sleepyhead." Jamie kissed her nose.

She smiled up at him. "What are you doing here?"

"The debris has been dealt with, so we're done for the day. We'll start repairing and rebuilding tomorrow."

"What time is it?"

"It's almost four o'clock, why?"

"I came up her to change and thought I'd just lie down for a minute. I've slept for hours." Sophie grinned. "And now there's only two hours before dinner."

"So?"

"So, I have plans for you." She climbed off the bed and pulled him to his feet.

"What kind of plans?" he asked suspiciously as she gave him her famed Cheshire grin, walked over to her door, and locked it. "Sophie, the house is full of people."

She stopped in front of him and began unbuttoning his shirt. She slipped her hands inside and slid it off his shoulders. "We'll be really, really quiet."

He chuckled and bent down to pick her up, carrying her to the bed.

CHAPTER TWENTY-FOUR

"THAT WAS THE most magnificent, incredible...I'm at a loss for words." Sophie turned and found him staring at her. "Jamie, are you okay?"

"Hmm? Yes, I'm fine." He gave her a strange smile as he climbed off the bed and poured a glass of water. "I need to do something. I'll try to be back by dinner."

"What?"

She never got an answer. He was dressed and out the door before she could say anything else. Sophie stayed on the bed, simultaneously reveling in their lovemaking and slightly concerned about where Jamie went. Before she knew it, it was past five o'clock, so she forced herself to get up and get dressed. Downstairs, Christine and Nona were in the parlor playing cards. They motioned her in when they saw her.

"How are you feeling, dear?" Nona asked.

"Very well, thank you."

Christine gave her a wink. "I'll bet."

Sophie raised her eyebrows in response and Christine smiled. The butler announced that Adam and Elizabeth had arrived, along with Richard, so Nona suggested they make their way into the dining room.

"Do you mind if we wait for Jamie? He should be here any minute." Sophie stood and made her way to the window.

"I don't think he'll be joining us this evening," Richard said.

"Of course he will. What a ludicrous thing to say."

"Sophie, he left over an hour ago."

"What do you mean, 'he left,' Richard?"

"He packed up a few things, got on his horse, and rode off. Looks like he's made his choice."

"Richard, don't be cruel," Christine admonished and then grabbed Sophie's hand. "Come with me."

Sophie followed Christine down the hall and into the library. "What's going on?"

Christine closed the door. "Jamie went on an errand."

"What? He didn't say anything about an errand."

Christine sighed. "He was supposed to, but he must have been sidetracked."

"Well, what do you know of it, then?"

"I can't tell you. Just know that he's coming back."

Sophie crossed her arms. "I already figured he was coming back."

"Good." Christine smiled. "Let's have dinner."

Sophie reluctantly joined the rest of the group for dinner, although, she picked at her food. By seven o'clock, Jamie still hadn't arrived. By eight o'clock, she was frantic. Richard left and Michael and Nona went to visit with some friends, so Sophie retreated back to the library.

At nine o'clock, Christine came in to check on her. "Sophie, I think we should turn in."

"I don't think I'll be able to sleep."

"I understand but you need to at least try."

Sophie reluctantly followed her up the stairs and once she was free of her stays, she climbed into bed. She tossed and turned for what seemed like hours, finally falling into a fitful sleep. Christine woke her early the next morning and they went downstairs for breakfast.

"I really thought he'd show up during the night. I swear, Christine, I'm going to kill him," Sophie snapped.

The butler came in and whispered something to Christine. She got up and walked outside, telling Sophie not to go anywhere. Christine rushed back into the dining room a few minutes later and grabbed her hand. "Sophie, you have to come outside now."

"What? Why?" Sophie asked.

"Just come and see."

Sophie walked out on the porch and almost passed out. Jamie stood in the front driveway of the house. Gathered around him were dairy cows. Ten of them.

"Jamie?" Sophie asked cautiously.

"Good morning, sweetheart."

"What are you doing?"

Jamie met her on the porch and went down on bended knee. "Sophie Jane Wellington Ford, you are my ten-cow woman. Will you do me the honor of marrying me—again?"

Sophie stood before him, tears streaming down her face. "Yes! Absolutely."

Jamie lifted her into his arms and kissed her. "I love you."

"I love you, more." She laughed and cried at the same time. "How did you do all this?"

"I called on Mr. Powell, the farmer who took care of me when I first got here. He let me borrow the cows. It took a relatively short train ride to get to the farm, but a little longer to get back here. And I have to return them tomorrow."

"You scared me to death!" She punched his arm.

"Sorry. It was harder than I thought to wrangle…they kept getting separated. A cowboy – I am not."

She laughed. "You really didn't have to do this, you know."

"I wanted to make a statement."

"Well, you certainly did that."

Sophie pointed a finger at Christine. "I cannot believe you didn't tell me."

Christine shrugged. "I made a promise."

Jamie leaned over and gave her a chaste kiss on the cheek. "And I appreciate it."

Christine hugged them both and then made herself scarce. Miriam and Andrew joined them for dinner that evening. Everyone was in high spirits with the exciting news and much wine and champagne was served. After hearing the story of Jamie's journey, Andrew graciously offered to help him return the cows the following day.

It turned into a late night, and Sophie was exhausted but couldn't sleep with the excitement of the past few days.

Jamie found her pacing her bedroom floor when he snuck in shortly after midnight. He pulled her into his arms. "Hi."

"Hi." She lifted her head for a kiss. "How long will you be gone tomorrow?"

"Andrew is going to meet me here at four."

"A.M.?"

"Yes. I'm hoping we'll be home by dinner."

"I can't believe I have to watch you leave again!"

"I'll be home before you know it." Jamie kissed her again.

"You better be. However, since you're here now…"

"Since I'm here now, what?"

Sophie unbuttoned his shirt as Jamie cupped her face and gently kissed her. She didn't want gentle and proceeded to show him exactly what she expected.

They made love all night and fell asleep in each other's arms.

Jamie woke her just before he left. "I'll see you at dinner."

"I love you," she said sleepily.

"I love you more." He gave her one last kiss and Sophie fell back to sleep as he closed the bedroom door.

* * *

Waking at eight, Sophie dressed quickly and met Christine in the dining room. They ate quickly and then headed off to the hospital. The women worked for several hours before calling it a day and making their way home. By dinnertime, Jamie and Andrew still hadn't returned. Sophie was beyond worried, but Christine assured her that they were fine. They tried to kill some time in the parlor since Michael and Nona had places to go and people to see and said not to wait up for them.

The girls once again chose music as their distraction. Sophie had Christine play "Amazing Grace" and "Star Spangled Banner," both songs Sophie knew the words to. Singing became a problem when Sophie started to pace, so Christine stopped playing. "When you get to the pacing stage in your thought process, nothing else registers."

Sophie didn't hear her or even notice that the music had stopped; she just continued to pace up and down the parlor. Christine stood and made her way across the room. She sat on the sofa and picked up the book she had left there earlier. She knew she was in for a long night.

There was no way Sophie would go to bed until Jamie arrived home, safe and sound. Ten o'clock rolled around and they still hadn't arrived. Sophie had chewed her fingernails to the quick, nearly worn a hole in the carpet, and made the poor butler hide with her constant, "Are they here yet?"

"Not yet."

"Where are they?"

"It might have taken them longer than originally expected and they probably ended up staying at the Powell Farm," Christine reassured.

"What if something happened?"

"I'm sure they're fine. Let's turn in. We'll leave the front door unlocked so that Jamie can get in."

Sophie reluctantly acquiesced, and the two headed for their rooms. Sophie climbed into bed after watching out her window for over an hour in an effort to see them in the distance somehow. It took her another hour to finally fall asleep. Jamie came into the bedroom at three thirty and quietly got undressed.

"Where have you been?" Sophie whispered.

Jamie eased into bed and pulled her into his arms. "Sorry. Andrew and I were ambushed on our way back. We were able to outsmart and outrun them but we had to take the long way around."

Sophie sat up. "You say that like, 'Andrew and I went down to the store to get milk'! What happened?"

"Rebels intercepted us. Luckily, we saw them before they caught up to us. I probably should have worn civilian clothes but I'm limited on what I have here, so I was in uniform. They fired at us, but fortunately, they had Civil War guns and not gangs in the hood guns, or we probably wouldn't have made it back," he said, trying to lighten the mood.

"*So* not amusing. Where's Andrew?"

"He's downstairs. We thought it would be better if he stayed here tonight. Andrew's a really great guy by the way. He reminds me a lot of Luke."

"I know, right? That's what I thought, too."

* * *

Jamie watched the sun stream through the windows of the bedroom and turned to the sound of Sophie's snoring. He'd never gone to sleep, and now he was too pent up to try. He slid from the bed as gently as he could, dressed, and went downstairs to check on Andrew. He found him in the dining room, already making a dent in breakfast.

"Good morning, James," Andrew said with a mouth full of food.

Jamie laughed. "Do you not get fed much, Andrew? Good morning, by the way."

Andrew smiled. "I only get fed when I come here. Well, I only get fed this well when I come here."

"Yeah, Mary's pretty phenomenal."

Christine walked in a few minutes later and helped herself to breakfast.

"Where's Sophie?" Jamie asked.

Christine raised her eyebrow at him as if to say, 'Seriously? You expect *me* to know that?'

Jamie chuckled. "Never mind. I'll check on her." He ran up the stairs and opened Sophie's door. She was still asleep, so he went over to the bed and leaned down to kiss her.

"It's time to wake up," he whispered as he ran his lips across her jaw line.

Sophie groaned. "I don't want to."

Jamie poured some water from her pitcher into the bowl on the dresser. He pulled the covers off her and kissed her again. "Come on. Wash your face and make sure you put your breeches on under you skirts. I'll meet you downstairs. You have ten minutes."

"Breeches?" Sophie perked up. She jumped out of bed, splashed her face with water, and rushed to get dressed. She made it in record time, even though she had to have Betty help her with her corset.

When she arrived in the dining room, Jamie had already prepared a plate for her and gone to get the horses ready. Beyond excited, she practically inhaled her food. Jamie arrived a few minutes later to collect her. "Ready? I have Gentle Ben outside for you."

"Christine?" Sophie asked.

"Hmm?" Christine smiled, mid-chew.

"He's your horse, are you sure you don't need him?"

"Not at all." Christine wiped her mouth with her napkin. "I'm taking the buggy this morning, which means I can use one of the other horses."

Sophie gave a little squeal. "Thank you!" Jumping from her seat, she followed Jamie out the front door. "Hello, boy. Are you ready?" Gentle Ben, although just as large as Samson, was much calmer. His black coat shone in the sunlight.

Jamie laid his hand on her back. "Christine assured me he is sound and calm."

"No wonder you're letting me ride." Sophie smiled.

"Do you need a leg up?"

"Yes, please. I'm not quite sure how I'm going to do this in these darn skirts. I wish I could have just left them off."

Jamie helped her up, and after a few tries, she was able to get her leg over the saddle. She did her best to wrap the skirts in a way that wouldn't interfere with her or the horse. Jamie then mounted and they took off towards the lake. He had put a few snacks in saddlebags so they could ride for longer, but he had other plans than just eating.

He grimaced when she shot him a look and then dug her heels in. Gentle Ben responded immediately. They flew over the beautiful green hills and valleys of the Wades' property. As they were coming up to a fence, Sophie didn't hesitate. She put Ben's head into it and he jumped it with feet to spare. Sophie let out a holler and slowed him down to a walk. Jamie caught up with her a few seconds later. "You scared the crap out of me."

Sophie laughed. "Oh, baby, that was incredible. You have no idea."

They reached the lake but decided to walk the horses for a few extra minutes to cool them down. Jamie found a secluded area at the edge of the water and dismounted. He helped Sophie down and they led the horses to a tree nearby and tied them to a low hanging limb.

Jamie had secured a blanket to Sophie's saddle, so she grabbed it and laid it on the ground at the edge of the water. Sitting on the blanket, she removed her boots, stretched out, and waited for Jamie to gather the food.

"Did you enjoy that?" He sat next to her and leaned down to kiss her.

"Are you kidding me? It was the most magnificent thing I've ever experienced. Well, since last night, anyway. Thank you for finding these." Sophie indicated the breeches.

"My pleasure. I wonder if we should try and have some more made for you at some point."

"I'd love that. Of course, underwear that I could wear under them would be a good idea as well."

Stretching out beside her, he raised an eyebrow. "Oh? What are you wearing now?"

"Wouldn't you like to know?"

"How about I investigate?"

"Under what authority, sir?"

Jamie reached over to pull her into his arms. "There's a law called, I want to get into my wife's pants. Of course, you are innocent until proven guilty. However, there is reason to believe you are in violation of section eight fifteen, code eighty-one."

Sophie laughed. "I'm in violation of my birthday? Very clever."

Jamie kissed her and kept kissing her as he unbuttoned her blouse. "No chemise?"

"No, too much clothing. Although, the corset's scratchy without that extra layer. I wonder if I could design a bra in this century. It would be so much easier. You should have seen Betty's reaction when she saw I wasn't wearing a chemise. She was mortified."

"Mmm, but so unbelievably sexy." Jamie went to work on freeing her body from the corset stays.

Sophie laughed and stood up, letting the corset slip from her waist and then pulling off her blouse.

Jamie sat up. "What are you doing?"

"I'm going for a swim." Pushing her skirt from her waist, she went to work on her breeches. She waded into the water and swam to the middle to wait for Jamie. With a smile, he quickly undressed and swam out to meet her. He wrapped his arm around her waist and drew her into a tight embrace.

Sophie pushed away from him. "Up for a race?"

Jamie chuckled. "Always."

The competition wasn't a fair one. Jamie had been on the varsity swim team, and lapped her multiple times. Sophie met him in the middle and looped her arms around his neck. "I'm once again impressed."

"Oh, you should be. I'm impressive."

Sophie smiled. "I'm hungry, are you?"

Jamie gave her a quick kiss. "Yes, starved. Let me get out first."

She nodded and waited for him to wade out onto the bank. He took a look around to make sure it was safe and then motioned for her to come out of the water. He had just put his pants on and grabbed the blanket to wrap around her, when they heard horses approaching in the distance.

He grabbed her clothes and boots, and handed them to her in a bunch. "Take these and hide just in case they're not friendly. They're riding awfully fast, which makes me think they might be up to no good."

Jamie pushed Sophie behind a small grove of trees next to the lake. She'd had the wherewithal to grab Gentle Ben and lead him into hiding with her. She watched as Jamie rushed to get his socks and boots on and her heart raced as the riders approached. Jamie had one arm in the sleeve of his shirt when he stopped. He glanced at her hidden behind the covering of a large boulder. She raised an eyebrow and he gave her an imperceptible shrug.

She realized he didn't recognize the men.

His scowl of irritation also spoke volumes, so she ducked further out of sight. The men weren't in uniform, and Sophie had no idea if they were friend or foe.

Jamie slid his arm through the remaining sleeve but instead of attempting to button it, he crossed his arms over the open shirt. "Gentleman," he began slowly. "Is there a reason you're on private property?"

The man who seemed to take the lead sent a shiver down Sophie's spine. His badly pockmarked face held eyes that resonated evil. "Well looky here, Carl, we got us a bona-fide Yankee."

Confederates, maybe? Southern accent, definitely.

Carl was dressed in nondescript tan pants and black boots. His shirt and jacket, although worn, appeared to be clean and neatly pressed. Sophie noted that everything about him seemed somewhat average. His dirty blond hair, short back and sides, and his height, which even in the saddle looked quite a bit shorter than Jamie's.

The only thing Sophie took as distinguishable was the way he held his gun. No different than anyone else, she supposed, yet, it was. She couldn't quite put her finger on it.

"Ain't he one of the ones we was trackin' the other night?" Carl droned.

If that guy's southern, I'm Miss America.

"I do believe you're right, Carl."

Meanwhile, Sophie frantically tried to get dry enough to get her clothes on. Good old Ben stood next to her, not making a sound. It was almost as though he knew they needed silence. She got her breeches on and realized she wouldn't get her corset on without assistance, so she put her blouse on with nothing underneath.

She was able to get her socks on and one boot when she heard the conversation get louder and more intense. She took the blanket and tried to wrap her thick hair up in it, just to keep it from soaking her clothes. She was having a difficult time not tilting her head to one side with the weight of it, however. She successfully got her second boot on and then found a small opening in her makeshift hiding place to see what was going on.

"What are ya doin' there, son?" Carl asked Jamie.

"I was taking a swim. Now, gentlemen, would you please answer my question?"

Carl's cohort sneered. "This ain't your property, so it don't matter to you none."

"No, you are correct, this is not my land. However, it is Richard Madden's, and I don't think he would appreciate you trespassing."

Sophie watched Jamie turn slightly, as though he were going to pick up the remains of his lunch. When they were first married, they had volunteered to build houses with a group of deaf students, and they'd gone through a quick but rigorous American Sign Language course. Most of it stuck. They used to sign to each other whenever they weren't in a quiet area, or not within shouting distance. Jamie was signing now. Sophie didn't like what he was saying, but Jamie was insistent.

Get Richard and a few of my men. Take Ben and hurry back.

Sophie left her skirts on the ground so that with just her breeches on she was able to mount Ben without aid. The fancy turban holding her hair bobbled, and she tugged it off, dropping it to the ground. She quietly made her way from the trees in the opposite direction of the intruders. When she knew they wouldn't be able to catch her, she dug her heels in and Ben flew.

They had more than one fence to jump this way, and Sophie was grateful he was so responsive to her. She got to the arena and saw that Richard and a few of the men were working the horses. Andrew was also there.

"Richard! Andrew!"

They turned quickly at her terrified voice.

"Come quick, please! Jamie needs help. He's out at the lake and the two men that you met on the way back from Mr. Powell's are with him. Get guns."

Richard and Andrew didn't waste any time and, as luck would have it, several of the horses had already been tacked up, so they grabbed two and mounted. They were handed pistols and took off toward the lake. Sophie was hot on their heels.

Richard pulled up. "Sophie, what do you think you're doing? You need to stay here."

"Like hell I will. You're the one who shouldn't be on a horse with that leg!"

"I'm fine."

"Good. Follow me." She dug her heels in. "If you can keep up."

The men had no choice but to follow. The threesome arrived at Sophie's starting point. Richard motioned for her to stay where she was and he and Andrew walked their horses towards Jamie.

Sophie dismounted and then snuck to her original hiding place. Hunkering behind a rock, she had a sweeping view of the scene unfolding before her. Jamie had his hands up, and Sophie could tell he was doing his best to keep the men talking. The two men, still mounted but now pointing guns at Jamie, turned their heads toward Andrew and Richard.

"Gentlemen, you are on my land without permission. Perhaps you could tell me what you're doing here," Richard said.

Carl apparently didn't want to answer Richard's question and fired his gun in the air. Andrew ducked. That's when all hell broke loose. Both Richard and Andrew fired. Uglier than Carl, hit in the middle of his forehead, was dead on impact. Carl was able to avoid a bullet, but his spooked horse threw him and he ended up sprawled on the ground. Recovering quickly, he jumped up and rushed at Jamie, gun drawn.

It didn't matter that Carl had a gun. Jamie had several years of mixed martial arts on his side. He was able to wrestle the gun from Carl's grip and had him on the ground in a chokehold in a matter of seconds. Richard and Andrew jumped from their horses and came to assist Jamie with his captive.

Sophie didn't stick around to find out what might happen next. She stumbled out of her hiding place, her heart in her throat. "Jamie!"

She saw his head whip around, but then she went down hard. She'd tripped over Carl's partner and fell flat on her face. Jamie rushed over to help her up and she fell into his arms.

"Sweetheart, we're all okay." He held her close. "Look."

She took a moment to compose herself and took a couple of deep breaths, turning to see that Richard and Andrew had Carl well in hand and they appeared to be unhurt. They had him tied to a tree. She ran over to Andrew, and he lifted her off the ground in a bear hug.

"You scared me to death!" She punched him as he walked her back to Jamie. Then the three men started to gather up the horses. Jamie's horse had bolted, and she was pretty sure Ben probably had as well, so they prepared to walk back to the stables. Andrew gave Sophie his horse and then joined Jamie and Carl.

"I think I'll take Carl's horse back to the barn. We'll make him walk, what do you think?" Jamie said.

"Excellent idea," Richard said.

"I have information!" Carl yelled as they tied his hands together.

"Save it," Richard snapped.

Richard mounted his horse and pulled Carl by a rope attached to his secured hands. Jamie cornered Andrew. "Let's leave this guy where he is and send a coroner's wagon back for him. I don't want Sophie to have to think about a dead body close to the house."

Andrew nodded. "I'm going to stop in at the jail, so you take Sophie back, and I'll meet you at the house later."

Jamie helped Sophie mount and then climbed up behind her. Sophie glanced over her shoulder with a concerned frown. "Where's Andrew going?"

Jamie pulled her close. "He's stopping at the jail. Don't worry, sweetheart, he won't be long."

She leaned back against him with a sigh and let him take the reins. Arriving back at the barn, Sophie handed Andrew's horse to the groom.

"The large black horse made it back, ma'am."

Sophie smiled at the groom. "Thank you, Jimmy. Is someone seeing to him?"

"Yes, ma'am. Topper is brushing him down."

Sophie nodded. "Thanks."

She made her way to Samson's stall. She needed to check his injury and she needed to hug her pet. Jamie came in to check on her about an hour later. Sophie stood inside his stall with her arms looped around his neck.

Jamie pulled her into his arms for a kiss. "Should I be jealous?"

She smiled up at him. "No, you're a better kisser."

"Are you ready to go? We'll just make it in time for dinner."

"I need to change first. I can't wear these breeches to dinner. Poor Nona would faint from embarrassment." She added in a whisper, "I also don't have a corset on, which would probably kill her."

Jamie chuckled as they started back to the house for dinner. "I'm sure everyone will wait for you."

They ran into Andrew on the way out of the barn.

"Are you coming up to the house for dinner?" Sophie asked.

"Yes, I'll be there shortly."

"Invite Richard, would you please?"

Jamie took her hand in his and led her to the house. They let themselves in, and Sophie rushed up to her room to change. She found Christine at the top of the stairs. "Hi! You are not going to believe the day we had. Can you please help me back into a corset?"

Christine followed Sophie into her room and assisted her with her dress. Sophie filled her in on everything that happened, Christine laughed at the animated way Sophie flailed her hands the more excited she got.

The girls made their way down to dinner. Nona was already seated, but Michael stood as the ladies walked in the room. Jamie waited by the door for Sophie, greeting her as though he hadn't just seen her twenty minutes ago. He bent down and gave her a quick kiss and then escorted her to her chair. Once she was settled, he sat next to her. Andrew and Richard arrived a few minutes later.

Dinner was a highly animated affair, as everyone talked at once. Now that the danger was over, they could relax and focus on the positives of the day. Andrew and Jamie regaled the table with their confrontation, embellishing more and more as they added to the story. Sophie noticed that Richard didn't do much other than drink. He picked at his food and rarely interjected into the conversation. He'd look at her on occasion, but she couldn't read what was behind his eyes.

"Are you okay?" Jamie leaned over and whispered as he squeezed her hand under the table.

She nodded and forced a smile. He raised an eyebrow, but she shook her head and took a sip of her wine. Dessert came and Sophie couldn't stomach the bread pudding. She pushed her plate aside and laid her hands in her lap.

Dinner wrapped up, and rather than the men and women separating, they decided to congregate as one in the parlor.

Jamie took Sophie's hand in his, lifting her palm to his lips as they left the dining room. "We'll talk later, baby. I know something's bothering you."

She smiled up at him, but before she could respond, Andrew grabbed her elbow. "Sophie, you and Christine must perform for us this evening."

"Only if Jamie sings with me." Sophie sent him a pointed look. "I even taught Christine one of the songs we wrote together."

Jamie nodded, so Christine sat down at the pianoforte. Sophie started out strong and Jamie joined her with his harmony. By the end, you could have heard a pin drop. Then Andrew jumped out of his seat and started clapping. The rest of the group followed suit.

"Incredible!" Andrew clapped Jamie on the shoulder and gave Sophie and his sister a kiss on the cheek. "I can't wait to hear more."

The rest of the night was filled with chess, cards, and pleasant conversation. Sophie noticed that Jamie and Christine had their heads together a few times in frantic whispering. At that moment, she was too tired to care.

* * *

The next morning, Jamie almost didn't make it out of the house in time for the cavalry drills. He'd overslept, obviously due to his complete comfort in the Wades home. Dressing quickly, he kissed Sophie and then made his way out to the arena. Andrew met him halfway, anger written across his face.

"What's going on?" Jamie asked.

"The prisoner says he has information that will be of great interest to you and the Union, but he will only speak to Sophie."

Jamie frowned. "What the hell does that mean?"

"He won't elaborate."

"Well, he's not getting anywhere near my wife."

"I explained that to him, but he believes what he has to say will be of great interest to you—" Andrew stalled.

"And?" Jamie pushed.

"And will also save Sophie's life."

Jamie cursed as he ran his hands through his hair. "Take me to him."

"I had a feeling you'd say that."

Andrew led him to horses that were ready to go and the two mounted and took off toward the town jail. Jamie's mind raced with what this lowlife could possibly have to say that would save Sophie's life. By the time they pulled their horses to a stop outside the small, brick building that housed the occasional drunk, Jamie shook with anger.

"Do you need a minute?" Andrew asked as they stepped onto the wooden walkway.

Shaking his head, Jamie pushed the front door open and was met by Joe Roberts. The sheriff reminded Jamie of a bulldog. Stocky, with not one ounce of fat on his body, just solid muscle, Joe was the perfect enforcer.

"Sheriff." Jamie held out his hand.

Joe shook his hand and then led the men to the room that housed several holding cells. Carl had been placed in one of the middle cells, bars on three sides, brick wall at the back, with a window large enough to see outside but not big enough for a body to escape. A small cot sat against the back wall and a bucket next to it. Watching Carl closely as Joe led them into the anteroom, Jamie waited for him to demand release but was taken aback by his smugness and appearance of absolute confidence.

"Where's the woman?" Carl stood and approached the bars.

Jamie shook his head. "What's this information you have?"

"I'll only speak to the woman."

Jamie's fingers twitched, aching to form a fist. "That's not going to happen."

Carl laughed. "Well, then. She'll die."

Jamie rushed the bars, but Carl moved too far back for him to reach him. "Open the door, Joe."

"You don't want your pretty wife to die, do you, James William Ford?" Carl taunted.

Jamie scowled. "How do you know my name?"

"Sophie Jane Wellington Ford is your pretty little wife, and her baby sister, Emma, is a dead ringer for her."

Jamie whipped his head around. "Joe, open the door."

"I'll tell you how I know what I know, but then I talk to your wife." Carl crossed his arms. "You may want everyone else to leave, don't you think?"

Jamie turned to the men. "Joe, Andrew, give us a minute." Once the men left, Jamie moved closer to the cell. "What do you think you know?"

"Your wife is in danger."

Jamie took a deep, silent breath, his heart beating rapidly as he glared at Carl. "Explain."

"I know where you're from, I know why you're here, and I know who doesn't like it."

"You're speaking in circles." Jamie scowled. "What do you want?"

Carl stepped closer to Jamie. "You are not from this time. Your wife is not from this time," he whispered.

"Excuse me?"

"Trains, planes, and automobiles are all familiar forms of transporttation for you. Our president is George W. Bush."

"*Our* president?" Jamie whispered.

"Now, I need to speak with Sophie."

"Who the hell are you?"

Carl stepped back to the tiny cot and sat down. "Get your wife."

Jamie swore as he yanked the door to the main office open and stormed away from Carl. He mounted his horse and took off toward home, somewhat surprised to hear hooves barreling down on him seconds later.

"Jamie!"

"I'll explain later, Andrew. I have to find Sophie," Jamie shouted back without slowing.

CHAPTER TWENTY-FIVE

ARRIVING BACK AT the Wade house, Jamie dismounted almost before the horse stopped moving and ran inside. "Sophie!" He rushed through the house, ending his search at the library. His breath caught in his throat as his eyes scanned the room and found her up on a ladder, reaching for a book. "Sophie Jane, what are you doing?"

Sophie let out a quiet screech, grabbed for a rung on the ladder, and only just caught her foot from slipping as the book she was holding fell to the floor.

Jamie climbed up behind her and drew her back against his chest. "What the heck are you doing?"

"I needed to return this book and Daniel's busy."

"Sophie, you should not be climbing ladders, especially without someone to spot you."

"Oh, please. I was fine. If you hadn't come in here and scared the dickens out of me, you would have never known." Sophie pushed back against him. He didn't budge. "Jamie, move, baby. I can climb down without you." Rather than acquiescing, Jamie kept a firm hold around her waist and stepped down with her. Sophie giggled. "Overprotective, much?"

Turning Sophie to face him, Jamie kissed her. She slid her hands up his chest and sighed when he broke the kiss. "I love kissing you."

"Me, too."

"What are you doing here, by the way? I thought you were going to be at the arena all day." Sophie smiled and added quickly, "Not that I'm not thrilled to see you."

Running his hands through his hair, he let out a groan.

Sophie placed her palm on his chest. "What's wrong?"

Taking her hand, Jamie led her to a chair, settled her down, and then sat on the hearth facing her.

"What's going on?" Sophie asked.

Jamie filled her in on his conversation with the prisoner, and Sophie slumped back in the chair in shock. "What does he want to talk to me about?"

"He won't tell me. Only you."

"Okay, so take me to the jail."

"Ten-Cow, this is serious, and could even be dangerous."

Sophie snorted. "The man's in jail. Danger doesn't apply."

"Jamie? Sophie? What's going on?"

The couple turned as Andrew rushed into the room.

"Hi, Andrew." Sophie smiled. "We're on our way to the jail. Did you want to join us?"

Andrew's eyebrows went up in surprise.

"Sophie is not really treating this lightly, Andrew. Are you, *sweetheart*?" Jamie gave Sophie a warning glance.

"No, you're right, I'm not."

Jamie led Sophie out to the Wades barn and made her stand where he could see her while he and Andrew hitched up a small buggy.

"All right, sweetheart. We're ready."

Sophie smiled as Jamie helped her into the buggy. He had to stop himself from lifting her out again and locking her up. He climbed up beside her as Andrew mounted his horse and then the three took off toward town.

Sophie squeezed Jamie's thigh. "Jamie, I'm going to be fine."

His grunt was the only response.

Arriving at the jail, Jamie lifted Sophie down and followed her into the building, Andrew following close behind. Joe reluctantly let Jamie and Sophie into the room housing Carl and then closed them in.

Carl stood and made his way to the front of the cell. "I thought I was clear. I'll only speak with your wife...alone."

Jamie laughed without humor. "Not going to happen."

Carl turned and walked back to his cot. "That's too bad."

Sophie faced her husband. "Babe, the man is locked up. Just let me talk to him."

"No."

"Jamie," she growled. "He has answers to several questions, it would seem, and I'd like to know what he knows. You can stand right outside the door and watch through the window."

Jamie took a deep breath. "I don't like this, Sophie."

"Noooo!" Her mocking earned her a frown from her husband. "He can't hurt me. Give me five minutes." Sophie gently pushed Jamie toward the door, and he hovered just outside. Sophie made her way back to Carl and stood close to the bars.

"Sophie," Jamie warned.

* * *

Stepping back slightly, she sent a smirk in his direction and then turned back to the prisoner. "So, Carl. Tell me what this is all about."

Carl stood. "You're in danger."

"I heard you, but what does that mean?"

"You're the key to a much bigger plan, Sophie. You're not the only person who has traveled here," he whispered.

Sophie gasped. "Traveled?"

"Yes. You're the key to a larger plot and they do not want you to succeed."

Sophie narrowed her eyes. "Who?"

"You must be careful, Sophie. He has brought men back with him who have resources."

"Back?"

"In time."

Sophie grasped the bars and leaned forward. "How is that possible?"

"That's complicated and entirely beside the point."

"But I don't understand why I'm here or who this man is. How did I get here?"

"His name is Victor Cary, and he's—"

Without warning, the glass in the window above Carl shattered and she heard Jamie swear. Turning at his voice, she found herself on the floor, and Jamie covering her as all hell broke loose around her. "What happened?"

"Sweetheart, are you okay?" Jamie began to run his hands over her face and body.

Looking down, Sophie let out a screech at the sight of blood and brain matter covering the bodice of her dress and glanced back up at Jamie, frantically wiping her face with his handkerchief. "What happened?"

"Are you okay?" Jamie cupped her face.

Sophie nodded slowly and leaned around him to look at the cells but Jamie blocked her view. "What happened? Why can't I see?"

"Sophie, Carl has been shot."

"Shot? How?" Sophie tried to sit up. "Why didn't we hear it?"

"Sophie, *stop*," Jamie growled. "I need to make sure you're okay."

Sophie stilled his hands and grasped his lapels. "Jamie, I'm *fine*. Can I please get up? You're crushing me."

Jamie stood quickly and then lifted Sophie from the floor, ushering her out of the room and settling her in one of the chairs in the main office. Sophie was surprised when Andrew rushed through the door, out of breath, with a look of relief on his face. "Sophie, are you well?"

"Yes, I'm fine. Where did you come from?"

"What did you find out?" Jamie stepped in front of Sophie.

"Nothing. Whoever did it is long gone."

Jamie swore, and Sophie stood and pushed him aside. "*What* is going on? One of you needs to tell me."

"We'll talk at home, Ten-Cow."

"Joe and I can handle everything here, Jamie," Andrew said. "Take Sophie home."

Jamie assisted Sophie into the buggy, drove back to the house, and then ushered her silently up to her bedroom.

"Jamie?" Grabbing his hand, she led him to the trunk at the end of the bed and pushed him down. Cupping his cheek, she leaned down and kissed him. "I'm fine, sweetheart. No injuries, no failing heart, nothing. So tell me what is going on."

"I think the person who shot Carl might be a sharp shooter," Jamie said. "From our time."

"Seriously?"

"Yes. Carl said someone is after you. The reason the shot was so accurate is because it came from a high powered rifle—I think."

"Did you tell Andrew?"

Jamie shook his head. "No."

"Why didn't we hear the shot?"

"I can only guess the rifle would have a silencer attached."

Sophie sat next to him and leaned her head against his shoulder. "This is like something out of a movie. Time hopping, sharp shooters, intrigue."

Wrapping an arm around Sophie's waist, Jamie pulled her closer to him. "What did Carl tell you?"

"He said someone was after me, that I'm the key to a larger plot, and that a man named Victor Cary has brought men back to kill me. At least, that's what I think he was trying to tell me. He didn't finish his sentence."

Jamie swore as he stood and began to pace the room. Sophie stared at him and then down at her bloody dress. She began to shake as reality set in, and she dropped her face into her hands only to be met with filth. Dried blood and caked-on dirt covered her fingers, so unusual on her perfectly manicured hands.

"Gross!" She dug her palms into the folds of her dress and wiped as hard as she could. "Jamie, help me get the blood off."

Sophie rose to her feet and ripped at her clothing. Jamie grabbed her hands. "Shh, Sophie, it's okay. Let me help."

Sophie nodded and tried to stand still as Jamie made quick work of her buttons. She couldn't stop shaking. Placing her hand over her mouth, she took several deep breaths and squeezed her eyes shut. "You know, I see blood all day long, but the fact this man's brain is mixed in is beyond disgusting!"

"I'm sorry, honey." Jamie loosened her corset and pushed it over her hips then led her to the bowl on the bureau and dampened a towel.

Sophie slid her hands into the bowl of water and did her best to remove the blood and dirt as Jamie gently wiped her face.

"Do you think the person was aiming for me?"

"The one who shot Carl?" Jamie asked.

Sophie nodded.

"I don't think so."

She shuddered. "You don't think so, because if he was aiming for me, I'd be dead, right?"

"Sophie."

"What did I do that would make someone want to kill me?"

"I don't think it's personal, sweetheart." Jamie tipped her chin up. "I'm going to figure this out. I promise. You just need to be careful now."

Sophie sat on the bed. "How am I supposed to be careful with a freakin' gun pointed at my head from a hundred miles away?"

Jamie stroked her cheek. "Melodrama aside, I think it would be a good idea for you to stay inside for a while."

"The house?" She crossed her arms.

"I don't want you out in the open. It's too dangerous."

"I have work, Jamie. The hospital, Samson, among other things."

"Until we know exactly what's going on, you'll have to find other things to occupy your time. Act the quintessential Victorian lady."

Sophie snorted. "When did you become such a chauvinist?"

Jamie shrugged. "I want you safe, Sophie. If you feel that makes me a chauvinist, then so be it."

"We need help," she whispered.

"I know." Jamie let out a deep sigh.

Sophie looked up at him. "You're going to have to tell someone in order to get it."

"I know."

"Which means you're going to have to trust someone with our lives."

"I know."

Sophie wrapped her arms around his waist. "Andrew."

"Yes, Andrew," Jamie said with a humorless smile.

"When?"

"No time like the present, I suppose." Jamie cupped her cheek. "Will you be okay if I leave you?"

She shook her head. "No."

His eyebrows puckered. "You won't be okay?"

"Jamie, I want to be there when you tell him. It might help if Christine is there, too."

"That's a lot of people, Ten-Cow."

"No, it's not. Christine already knows about us and Andrew is the only other person who will know. I trust them."

"I hate the thought of waiting."

"They'll both be here for dinner. I'm sure we can find some time alone."

Jamie pinched the bridge of his nose. "You have an answer for everything, apparently."

Sophie kissed his chin. "I think the fact that you are worried about me might be clouding your judgment a bit."

Jamie smiled. "You might be right."

"Why don't I make things clearer for you?" Sophie started to unbutton his shirt. "Because I happen to need a distraction, and I'm thinking you're the perfect person to provide it."

"Oh, really?"

"Yes. Are you up to the challenge?" Sophie slipped her hands under the waistband of his trousers and chuckled. "It would appear that you are."

Jamie laughed as he pushed her to the bed and then spent the rest of the afternoon distracting her.

An hour before dinner, they heard a sharp rap on the door.

"Yes?" Sophie called through it.

"Sophie, are you all right?" Christine asked.

Sophie opened the door slightly and smiled. "Yes, I'm fine. Did you talk to Andrew?"

Christine nodded. "Yes, he came to the hospital to find me. Are you certain you're not hurt? You have something in your hair."

Sophie reached up, felt the roughness of dried blood, and shivered in disgust. "Yuck."

"Shall I organize a bath?"

"That would be much appreciated. How long until dinner?"

"One hour."

"Jamie wants to tell Andrew everything after dinner," Sophie whispered. "We need some help to figure out what's going on."

Christine gasped. "My word. I didn't realize it was that serious."

"I know. We'll fill you in after dinner, okay?"

"Of course." Christine smiled. "You can trust Andrew, as you can trust me."

"Why do you think we're telling him?"

"I'll send Betty in with your bath."

Sophie nodded and closed her door. Jamie sat in the chair and started to pull on his boots. Sophie raised an eyebrow. "Where are you going?"

"I need to check on a few of the horses." He rose to his feet. "Can I leave you to your bath?"

Sophie nodded. "Sure. Don't miss dinner."

Jamie chuckled. "I'll be back in plenty of time."

"Oh, wait. I need to check on Samson."

"You're not leaving the house, remember? I'll check on him for you, and will even give him sugar and remind him that you love him."

"You better," she warned as Jamie opened the door. "I love you."

"I love you more, Ten-Cow," Jamie whispered and then he was gone.

Sophie wrapped a robe around her body and waited for Betty, who arrived just a few minutes later. Once she felt clean, she dressed quickly and made her way downstairs, surprised to find Jamie had beaten her to the parlor.

"How did you do that?" she asked as he met her at the doorway.

Jamie chuckled as he leaned down and kissed her cheek. "Everything was in order, so I visited with Samson and then had a quick swim."

"How is he?"

"He's good. He thanks you for the sugar."

Sophie giggled as she leaned her head against his shoulder and. "Mmm, you smell good."

"How was your bath?"

"Lonely," she whispered.

"Naughty."

"How are you, Sophie?" Andrew rushed forward and raised her hand to his lips.

"Hold that thought," Jamie whispered.

"I'm fine, Andrew." Sophie smiled. "I promise."

Andrew stared at her briefly and then lifted his head to Jamie. "I understand we need to have a conversation?"

Jamie nodded. "We're hoping we can steal some time after dinner."

"I think that'll be fine."

The butler announced dinner, and as her plate was set in front of her, Sophie thought she'd never survive the evening. With stomach churning and heart racing, she couldn't eat, so she stared at her plate and occasionally moved her fork around.

"Relax, sweetheart," Jamie whispered as he reached under the table and squeezed her thigh. Sophie nodded but continued to push the food around on her plate.

"Sophie?"

"Hmm?"

"You're distracted, dear. Is anything amiss?" Nona asked.

Sophie shook her head. "Sorry, Nona. I'm fine. It's just been a long day."

"Perhaps you should turn in early. We'll go for a walk tomorrow morning, bright and early."

"I think Sophie should stay in tomorrow. She hasn't been feeling well, and I'd like her to rest," Jamie said.

"I'm sorry to hear that," Nona said.

"Is there anything I can do?" Michael asked.

"No, it's just a headache," Sophie said quickly. "I'm sure a day or two of rest will suffice."

"Well, if you don't feel better in the next few days, let me know."

"I will, Michael. Thank you." Sophie glanced at Jamie and then back at her plate.

"Shall we move to the parlor?" Nona asked.

"Actually, I need to speak with Jamie." Andrew stood. "Do you mind if we take a few minutes?"

"Not at all."

"I'd like Sophie and Christine to join us as well, but it won't take long," Jamie said.

"We'll meet you in the parlor shortly," Christine said, and the foursome stood and made their way into the library.

"So, what's this all about?" Andrew asked as Christine closed the door for privacy.

Sophie slipped her hand into Jamie's for silent support and smiled encouragement.

"Someone is targeting Sophie and they want her dead."

Christine gasped. "Whatever for?"

Andrew crossed him arms and waited.

"Andrew, I am about to tell you something that can never leave this room," Jamie said.

"All right."

Jamie looked at Sophie and then back at Andrew. "Sophie and I are not from this time."

"What do you mean?"

"We are from the future."

Andrew raised his eyebrows and Christine stepped in front of him. "It's true, Drew."

"Explain, please."

"I don't think we can explain. Exactly. We're just as confused."

Jamie filled Andrew in on everything they did know, ending with Carl's warning and the name of the man after Sophie. Andrew sat on the hearth and rested his forearms on his knees, waiting several minutes before speaking. "I don't know why, but I believe you."

"You've both accepted this quickly." Sophie said. "I don't know that I would have if I were in your shoes."

"After knowing me, you wouldn't believe me if I told you something like this?" Christine asked, surprise in her voice.

"I guess I didn't look at it that way."

"Sophie, we know that neither of you are mad, and having spent so much time with you these past few months, there are things that didn't make sense, other than this."

Andrew nodded.

"Really? Like what?"

"Your strange speech, for one," Christine said.

"The fact you know so much about the war," Andrew added and then looked at Sophie. "*Before* things happen."

Sophie shivered. "Have I really been that loose lipped?"

Christine wrapped an arm around her shoulders. "With me, you have, and on occasion I know that Andrew has overheard." She sent a look of admonishment in his direction for his eavesdropping and frowned when he shrugged in response.

"I need to watch that." Sophie sighed. "*You* need to help me watch what I say."

"I will," Christine promised.

"What if this man, Victor Cary, is part of the Confederacy?" Andrew ran his hands through his hair.

Jamie let out a low whistle. "He could be posing as the enemy and providing crucial information to the other side."

"I didn't even think of that." Sophie rubbed her temples. "And I don't really want to think of it now."

"We should contact Clayton."

"Who is this Clayton person?" Jamie asked.

"Richard's brother," Christine provided.

Jamie shook his head. "Absolutely not!"

"I agree," Sophie said quickly. "Especially a relation of Richard's."

Andrew stood. "He should know this information. He and Christopher run the war offices and would be highly interested. Clayton can also help us."

Jamie paced the room, and Sophie gripped the back of one of the chairs in an effort to stop herself from mirroring his motions. The ramifications of bringing another person into their secret circle could be huge, and the fact that Clayton was related to Richard made it even more difficult to believe it would be a good idea.

"Jamie, it's the only way. I trust Clayton," Andrew said.

Jamie stalled once as if to say something and then ran his hands through his hair. It was a tense several minutes as the only sound in the library was the sound of Jamie's heavy footsteps on the hardwood floors.

"Can we let Clayton know about the threat without letting him know about us?"

Andrew shrugged. "Possibly."

"What if we can't?" Sophie asked.

"If you have to tell Clayton, Sophie, you can trust him," Christine said.

"Because his brother is evidence of that?"

Christine smiled sadly. "No, because Clayton is, and always has been, the pillar of honor."

Jamie wrapped his arm around Sophie's waist and pulled her close. "Well, if you think it's the only way, Andrew, then send the wire."

"Are you sure?" Sophie glanced up at him.

Jamie kissed her temple. "It might be the only way."

Andrew nodded. "I'll send it first thing in the morning."

"I'm really tired." Sophie yawned. "Does anyone care if I turn in?"

"Could you give us a minute, please?" Jamie waited for Andrew and Christine to leave the room and then turned Sophie to face him and stroked her cheek. "Are you okay?"

Sophie's eyes filled with tears but nodded her head. "I'm just really tired and a little overwhelmed."

Jamie caught a tear with this thumb. "Baby, everything's going to be okay, I promise."

"What if it's not? What if you get killed, or I get killed?"

His hand shook. "That's not going to happen."

"Promise?"

Jamie kissed her and then leaned his forehead against hers. "I promise. Nothing is going to happen to either one of us."

Sophie allowed herself to take comfort in his arms, albeit briefly, and then pulled away and forced herself to climb the stairs with Christine.

CHAPTER TWENTY-SIX

THE NEXT MORNING Christine knocked on her door, and the two made their way down to breakfast. Jamie had left before dawn, and Sophie wasn't sure she'd see him again before dinner. Nona sat at the table with a cup of coffee and smiled when the girls walked in.

Shortly after they took their seats, the butler showed Jamie in. He walked straight over to Nona and kissed her hand, followed by a kiss on the cheek for Christine and Sophie. He wouldn't allow the girls to get up and prepared plates for each of them before getting his own.

"How would you two feel about a party?" Nona asked.

Christine chuckled. "You may want to rephrase that, Nona."

"Yes, of course. We are hosting an engagement, or perhaps even better, a reunion party for the two of you on the fifteenth."

Sophie gasped. "Are you sure, Nona? You really don't need to do this. The fact that you have allowed us to stay in your home has been a huge blessing."

"Nonsense." Nona waved her hand dismissively. "I always like an excuse to throw a party."

"Thank you, Nona." Jamie laid his fork down and smiled.

"Do you have any requests, Sophie, before I get started?"

"No. Thank you, Nona. Please let me know what I can do to help."

Nona chuckled as she left the room

Christine pushed her plate away. "Sophie, you and I have an appointment with Madame at eleven."

"Oh? Why?"

"She's going to make your wedding dress."

"What?" Sophie dropped her fork. "We're already married!"

Christine giggled. "Renewal of your vows, then. Nona insisted."

Sophie grimaced. "I'd hoped we could just write something in a Bible and be done with it."

"As Nona said, she likes an excuse to throw a party."

"Christine, I don't think I need a wedding gown. I'll simply wear what I have."

Christine tsked. "That'll never do." She turned to Jamie and said, "Covered buggy, I promise."

Jamie set his cup down. "Could the dressmaker come here?"

"I suppose I could ask." Christine shrugged. "It's highly unlikely, but I can try."

"I would appreciate that."

Sophie let out a groan of frustration. "I hate this."

"I know." Jamie leaned over and squeezed her hand.

Christine rose to her feet. "I'll check with Madame and see you later."

Sophie nodded and watched her walk out the door. "I can't believe all of this."

"It's pretty overwhelming, isn't it?"

Sophie nodded.

"I hate to say this, but I have to leave you." Jamie set his napkin on the table.

"Can I please walk you over there? I really want to visit Samson."

Jamie shook his head. "Not yet, Ten-Cow. I'll check on him."

"This sucks," she whispered.

Jamie stood and pulled her into his arms. "Not for long, sweetheart." He gave her a lingering kiss before going their separate ways for the morning.

Sophie spent time in the library, reading and contemplating, which is where Christine found her two hours later.

"Sophie? Madame has arrived."

Sophie stood with a smile and followed Christine up to her room. Sophie's bedroom had been transformed into a dress shop. Two assistants stood beside a mirror, a step stool in front of the looking glass, and material was spread across the bed. The dressmaker was an elegant woman, who was either truly French, or did a very good impersonation. She was warm and helpful, and when Sophie described what she wanted, Madame seemed to know exactly what she was asking for.

* * *

Jamie had a moment of solitude and decided to check on Sophie. He made his way back to the house and up to her room. Knocking on the door, he let himself in before bid and found Sophie in a robe, surrounded by mounds of fabric and ribbon.

"What are you doing here?" Sophie stepped over the pile and rushed to greet him.

Jamie leaned down to kiss her. "I had a few minutes and thought I'd see how you were. I also missed you."

"*Madame* Ford, I have the perfect fabric."

Jamie raised his head at the sound of the French accent and nearly lost his hold on Sophie. "You!"

"*Pardonnez-moi?*"

"What the hell are you doing here?" Jamie bellowed.

"Jamie?" Sophie's voice held concern and confusion.

"*S'il vous plait,*" Madame whispered as she indicated to her assistants to leave them.

"What's going on?" Sophie grasped Jamie's arm.

"This is the woman from the grief counseling center who came when we couldn't find you."

Sophie gasped. "What?"

"What are you doing here, Bernadette?" Jamie's tone held warning. "*How* did you get here?"

"Perhaps you are thinking of someone else?"

"No way, lady. You better tell me who you really are."

"You don't understand," Bernadette stuttered.

"Then I'd highly suggest you start explaining."

"It is *très compliqué.*"

"Why don't we start at the beginning?" Jamie crossed his arms and glared. "How did we get here?"

"I don't know what you mean," Bernadette said evasively.

"You know exactly what I mean!" Jamie snapped.

"Jamie." Sophie laid her hand on his shoulder.

"No!" He slammed his palm against the wall and then turned back to Bernadette. "You were the one who held my hand and tried to convince me to let her go. *You* were the one who said nothing about the fact she might be alive. *Nothing*! You tried to make me believe I'd never see her again. You tried to make me believe she was lost to me forever."

Tears streamed down Sophie's cheeks. "You were in our home? Did you know what was going to happen?"

Bernadette's hand covered her mouth. "*Non*, I didn't know."

Jamie seethed. "You lying bi—!"

Sophie gasped. "Jamie. Stop."

"No, Sophie. I lost you! She could have stopped it," he railed.

"I could not have stopped it," Bernadette said.

"You could not have stopped the thing you know nothing about?" Jamie countered.

"I cannot tell you anything."

Sophie caught Jamie's arm and pulled him back.

Jamie forced himself to take a deep breath. "You've just admitted you know something, and I'd suggest you start talking, lady, or you may not walk out of this room alive."

Bernadette took a deep breath but did not speak for several minutes. Jamie took a step forward, but she held her hand up to stay him. "There is a time portal."

"And?"

Bernadette laid her hand across her ample bosom. "A ripple in the time, space continuum."

"You better start telling us something we haven't already figured out!" Jamie's anger vibrated through his body.

"Baby, let her speak." Sophie squeezed his shoulder.

"My husband and I are the facilitators of the portal."

"Facilitators?" Sophie whispered.

"Yes. Caretakers, if you will. We ensure that the wrong people don't end up where they don't belong."

"I don't understand." Sophie frowned. "Why are *we* here?"

"It is so complicated."

Jamie advanced on Bernadette. "Start explaining."

Bernadette turned to Sophie. "There is a threat in this time that could affect the future, and you have been chosen to counteract it."

"Excuse me?" Jamie growled.

Sophie pushed him behind her and faced the seamstress. "What is this threat everyone keeps talking about?"

"Pardon?"

"Someone has been trying to kill Sophie." Jamie scowled. "Do you know anything about that?"

Bernadette gasped. "No!"

Sophie's hand flew to her chest. "What?"

"He has found you."

"*Who* has found me?"

Bernadette began to pace, her fingers pressing into her temple. *"Monsieur* Cary."

"Why would this Cary fellow want to hurt me?" Sophie pinched the bridge of her nose. "What did I do?"

"*Madame* Ford, you know more about this war than most, and have been chosen in order to counter the Cary family's influence in the south."

Sophie held her hands up. "I don't know *that* much!"

"You know more than he does, and he has traveled back to further the cause of the South. You must ensure that the North prevails."

Sophie gasped. "How the heck am I supposed to do that?"

"You simply need to make certain history continues as it is written in the future and to assist with others that might come after you."

"More time travelers?" Jamie asked.

Bernadette nodded.

"Who?"

"I cannot tell you that. I don't know yet. I am not shown who is to travel until right before I am to assist them. But you will be the key to make certain they are safe."

"Piece of cake." Sophie snapped her fingers and gave Jamie a worried look.

Jamie hissed. "Why Sophie? Why my wife? Surely, there are others with far more knowledge than her, who would be more equipped to succeed."

"*Oui*, however, he didn't know about Sophie. We needed someone that he would not suspect." Bernadette took Sophie's hands. "Your heart was failing in the future. Being sent back ensured you would live. We felt that you would be able to counteract Cary's influence and live a long, healthy life."

"What did you plan to do about Jamie, then? Why didn't he come with me?"

Bernadette sighed. "He wasn't part of the plan, Sophie. We thought you'd fall in love with someone else and life would continue."

Jamie's face heated with rage. "You thought she'd *replace* me?"

"I admit we did not take into consideration the effect her disappearance would have on you, which is why we sent you back. I apologize for that."

"What about Cary?" Sophie asked.

"He was not supposed to know who you were." Bernadette frowned.

"I don't know how he found out. I'll have to investigate."

"Can we go back?" Jamie asked.

Bernadette paused for several seconds. "*Oui*. However, if you choose to do so, Sophie's heart will fail again, and you won't be able to return."

Jamie ran his hands through his hair. "Some choice."

Bernadette grimaced. "If you kill him, this will all be over."

Jamie scowled. "You seriously want me to murder someone in cold blood?"

She shook her head. "Non, it would be self-defense. You could even say it was part of the war."

One of Bernadette's assistants knocked on the door and requested a moment with the dressmaker.

Jamie stepped forward. "We're not finished here, Bernadette."

"I'll return in a moment."

Before Jamie could say anything further, she moved out of the room and closed the door. Jamie rushed to open it and found the hallway empty.

"Bernadette!" Jamie called.

Sophie poked her head out the door. "Where did she go?"

Jamie let out a litany of expletives.

"Jamie." Her tone indicated admonishment, but he couldn't help but catch her slight smile.

"She's gone." He ran his hands through his hair.

Sophie grabbed his arm. "Does that mean she can just 'poof' her way out of places?"

Jamie shrugged. "I don't know. All I know is I don't like it, and we need to figure out what this woman is up to."

"You need to get back to the men and I need to think."

"Ten-Cow."

"I'm fine, Jamie. I promise. I just need to process." At his raised eyebrow, she reached up and stroked his cheek. "Go. I'm fine."

Jamie reluctantly left Sophie, and since she was suddenly starved, she headed to the kitchen. Finding Mary elbow deep in a large bowl of dough, Sophie wished she had a camera.

"Hi, Mary."

Mary gave her a warning glance. "You should not be here."

"But if I wasn't here, you and I couldn't talk."

Mary tried to hide a smile as she pulled the dough out of the bowl and slapped it onto the butcher-block table.

Sophie grinned. "Will you let me help?"

Mary rolled her eyes. "You can slice the peaches."

"That means you're making your succulent peach pie, aren't you?" At Mary's slight nod, Sophie clapped her hands. "Yum!"

Sophie washed her hands and then went to work on the fruit. Perched on a wooden stool at the large table in the middle of the room, she peeled and sliced, occasionally sneaking one of the slices into her mouth and sighing at the taste of the sweet, juicy fruit.

Mary brightened up as she and Sophie talked and joked, and Sophie was grateful for the distraction. She wasn't sure she could spend another day in the library, even if it was her favorite place.

"Sophie?"

Hearing Jamie's voice, Sophie's heart skipped a beat. "In here," she called.

Jamie walked into the room, his hair disheveled and dust covering his boots and she grinned as she raised her chin to receive his kiss. "Hi."

"Hi. How has your morning been, sweetheart?"

"Good. Mary and I have been having a great time."

"Are you making peach pies, Mary?" Jamie grinned in anticipation.

"Yes, sir."

"Ah, you are a goddess." He grabbed a slice from the table.

Sophie smacked his hand. "I'm helping."

Jamie grabbed her palm and kissed it. "And you're doing an exemplary job."

"What are you doing back here so early?" She narrowed her eyes. "Are you checking up on me?"

"Absolutely. I'm also starving." Jamie sent a hopeful look toward Mary.

Mary wiped the flour from her hands and cut two slices from a loaf of fresh bread, handing them to him with a jar of strawberry preserves.

"Thank you," Jamie said appreciatively as he slathered the bread and took a bite. "Perfect."

Mary gestured to the kitchen door. "You two need to get out of my kitchen."

Sophie raised an eyebrow. "One more peach?"

Mary handed her the fruit and shook her head. "Shoo."

Sophie giggled as she grabbed Jamie's hand and led him from the kitchen. Jamie caught her around the waist and pulled her close. "I missed you today."

"Back atya." She pulled him into the library. "Come and tell me all about your day. How's it been?"

Jamie closed the door and then pulled Sophie to the window bench. "Better now."

"Charmer."

"Andrew managed to get hold of Clayton."

Sophie raised an eyebrow. "And?"

"He arrives tomorrow."

Sophie sunk deeper into the cushions. "Wow. That was fast."

Jamie linked his fingers with hers. "I know, right? Thank God for the railroad."

"How's Samson?"

Jamie chuckled. "He's ornery. He did let me take him out of his stall this morning and check his wound. It's almost completely healed."

"Good. I really miss him." Sophie let out a sigh. "Can I see him tonight? After dinner? If I wear all black, a sniper won't be able to find me in the dark."

"Unless he has infrared."

Her body sagged. "I didn't think of that."

"But if you want to give it a try, we can."

"Seriously?"

Jamie smiled. "Yes, sweetheart. I doubt they'll shoot randomly, so I think the cover of night will be safe enough."

Sophie leaned against him and laid her head on his shoulder. "Thank you."

Jamie held her for several minutes and then squeezed her hand. "I can't stay, Soph. I need to get back."

She wrinkled her nose. "I wish I had a television or something."

"I know what you mean." He kissed her cheek. "But, I'll see you in just a few hours, and dinner will come sooner than you think."

Sophie's snorted in disbelief.

"You seem tired."

"I am, actually."

Jamie stood and cupped her cheek. "Are you sick?"

"A little nauseous."

"That's two days in a row. You should talk to Michael."

Sophie shook her head. "No, I'm just tired. I'll sleep, and I'm sure I'll be fine by dinner."

"Okay. If you're sure."

"I am. Come on, I'll walk you out."

* * *

Sophie felt soft lips on her cheek, and her husband's hypnotic voice whispering in her ear. "Time to wake up, beautiful."

Sophie swam through the clouds, and forced her eyes open. "Hi."

"Are you okay?"

"Going to be sick." Sophie jumped out of bed, reaching the bowl on her bureau just in time.

Jamie handed her a glass of water and helped her back to the bed. "What's going on?"

"I'm just tired." Sophie sipped her water. "It's passed. See? I'm fine."

"Are you saying that just so you can get out of the house and see your pet?"

Sophie smiled. "Yes."

Jamie groaned.

"I'm kidding, sweetheart. I feel much better." Sophie stood and gathered up the gown she had been wearing earlier. "Now, help me with my clothes."

Sophie knew Jamie watched her closely as he tightened her corset and then helped her button her dress. She took several deep breaths in an effort to control another wave of nausea and then forced a smile when Jamie turned her to face him.

He cupped her face. "You look green."

"I'm fine."

Jamie kissed her forehead, took her hand, and led her toward the dining room. "If you feel sick, Kermit, you tell me right away."

"You're funny." Sophie was grateful dinner passed quickly and that she was able to eat something with no further bouts of nausea. After dinner, Jamie excused them so that he could take her to see Samson, and Andrew decided to join them. Sophie could tell Jamie was relieved to have someone else to keep guard as they made their way out to the stables.

Sophie kept her head down as the men flanked her and led her into the barn. Once inside, Andrew closed the doors and Sophie took a few minutes to check on Samson. He whinnied for her as she approached his stall and stuck his head out for some attention. "Hi, boy. Would you like to come out and play for a little while? I can't ride you today but I will tomorrow."

"Careful, Soph."

"I'll just bring him out here, at least he can walk the length." Opening Samson's stall, Sophie realized she'd forgotten to grab his halter, so she stepped back from the opening to grab one a few stalls down. Samson followed her out, stopping when she stopped, and walking when she did. Rather than putting the halter on him, she walked the length of the barn, Samson following behind her like a dutiful puppy.

Andrew laughed. "I cannot believe what you have done to that horse. You've ruined him for anyone else."

"I didn't mean to! Do you think Michael will be mad?" Sophie asked a little concerned.

"Honestly, Michael felt he'd served his time with the injury he received in battle and has no intention of putting him back into any battles. He is officially retired as an army horse."

"Seriously?"

"Yes." Andrew sighed. "I may have ruined his little surprise for you. When he tells you, act like you didn't know, all right?"

"I will."

Samson nudged Sophie's shoulder for more attention, so she leaned back into him, patting his neck. Jamie moved to his side. "I need to check him."

"Can I do it?" Sophie stood up and stepped under his neck.

"Yes, as long as he stands still."

Sophie turned and stroked Samson's nose. "Do not kick me. Do not even flick your tail or Jamie will think you might hurt me." Samson's ears followed her movements and then when she moved to his back leg, he turned his head to watch her. Sophie felt for heat and then picked up his back hoof and checked his range of motion. Samson stood next to her, perfectly still the entire time. "He looks great." She ran her palm across his side as she moved back to his shoulder. "He's probably ready to ride."

"No way to tell until we can get him into the arena," Andrew said.

"Ooh, could I ride in the arena?" Sophie asked hopefully.

"Nice try." Jamie shook his head. "Until we locate and eliminate the threat, you're housebound."

Stroking Samson's cheeks, she pulled his head toward her and kissed his muzzle. "Sorry, boy. I'll ride you soon. I promise."

"Time to get back, Ten-Cow." Jamie stood outside Samson's stall.

She reluctantly led Samson back to his stall, gave him some sugar, and then followed the men out of the barn. No one was around when they got back to the house, so Andrew said goodnight and left for home Sophie followed Jamie up the stairs to their room. Once Jamie closed and locked the door, Sophie wrapped her arms around his neck and kissed him. Jamie slipped her hair off her forehead. "What was that for?"

"Just because." She settled her hands on the waistband of his pants.

"I thought you were sick."

"Let me show you how untrue that statement is."

Jamie chuckled and carried her to the bed.

CHAPTER TWENTY-SEVEN

CLAYTON MADDEN ARRIVED at his brother's home just before noon the next day. Jamie knew Sophie wasn't happy when he left her at the Wades' to meet with Clayton. She never wanted to be out of the action, but she conceded that he was doing it for her own good, so he kissed her and made his way next door to the Madden's home, confident she would stay put.

Jamie expected Clayton to be much like his brother, but he was the polar opposite. When Jamie walked into Richard's office at the back of the house, he tried to hide his shock as the tall, blond man stood and held his hand out in greeting.

"Jamie, this is Clayton. Clayton, Jamie," Andrew said.

"Nice to meet you, Clayton."

"You, too." Clayton indicated one of the chairs. "Please, have a seat."

Clayton didn't look much like his brother, other than height and build. He reminded Jamie of blond Orlando Bloom with a soul patch. His hair was longer than Richard's, much lighter, and where Richard's features had a coldness about them, Clayton appeared friendly. Jamie sat in the chair next to Andrew, facing Clayton, and the men began to strategize.

The meeting took over an hour. Jamie had to admit he enjoyed both men's conversation, which might have been why he didn't leave earlier. Clayton's sense of humor, although subtle, was almost as wicked as Andrew's, and the three of them spent less time coming up with a game plan for the prisoner than laughing about various anecdotes.

After leaving the meeting to make his way back to Sophie, Jamie let himself into the house and went looking for his wife. He found her asleep on the parlor sofa. He stood and watched her for several minutes, amazed that he had been blessed all over again. He knelt next to her and kissed her forehead, her nose, her lips. It didn't take long for her to wake up and start to kiss him back.

"Where have you been?"

"It took a little longer than expected."

Sophie sat up and stifled a yawn. "Did it go well?"

Jamie pulled her off the couch and cupped her cheek. "Very well. You look tired, baby. Are you okay?"

"I'm fine now that you're back."

Jamie narrowed his eyes in disbelief, but changed the subject anyway. "Andrew, Clayton, and Richard are joining us for dinner tonight and it's almost ready. Shall I escort you?"

Sophie's lip popped out in a mock pout.

"It won't be a late night, grumpy pants."

"I want you all to myself."

"And you'll have me…after dinner." Jamie raised an eyebrow. "You're not still PMSing are you?"

Sophie shrugged and grinned. "Probably."

"Well, let's have some dinner and wine. You'll feel better once you eat."

Dinner passed quickly, and rather than everyone hanging out after the meal, they seemed to scatter to the four corners of the earth. Before retiring, Michael pulled Jamie aside. "James, I'd like to have a word with you tomorrow if you don't mind. Would you come to my office before breakfast please?"

"Of course."

Jamie looked at Sophie and shrugged at her raised eyebrow.

"Good night, you two. Enjoy the rest of the evening." Michael and Nona went off to bed, leaving Jamie and Sophie to their own devices, so they chose to spend some time in the library.

Jamie pulled Sophie onto his lap and kissed her.

"We need to talk about what we're going to do once we're married. Where will we live, what will we do for work? Can you stay with the army and actually make a living?"

Jamie chuckled. "One question at a time, love."

Sophie wrinkled her nose.

"I see your wheels turning, Ten-Cow. Let's not borrow trouble, all right?"

"We're in a strange place in a strange time. I don't know how any of our skills will translate to the nineteenth-century. We're really good at a few specific things, namely computers, which don't exist here. It's not like I can go into human resources when no one has ever heard of it. You don't have the Internet to tap in this century, so what are we going to do?"

Jamie raised his hands in surrender. "Sophie, stop. I'll talk to Andrew tomorrow about options. Christine would be a great resource for you, especially considering she knows the whole truth. She's smart, honey, I know she'll have some great ideas."

"Despite your irritating logic, I can't help but be worried. You have always been the glass half full guy."

Jamie laughed. "Sophie Jane. You were dying and God made you whole in an entirely different century. *Then,* He made it so I joined you, and you're worried about a little thing like money? You don't think He's going to take care of us?"

Sophie sighed. "I suppose you're right."

"Of course I'm right." He kissed her nose. "I'm always right. Now, let's go to bed and concentrate on other, much more pleasant things."

* * *

Before breakfast the next morning, Jamie went to Michael's office. "You wanted to see me, Michael?"

"James. Good morning. Yes, please sit down." Michael indicated a chair.

Jamie entered the room and sat in one of the chairs facing Michael's desk.

"As you may or may not be aware, I have plans to sell off a portion of my property to the east of the lake. I have always felt the land we have now is too much to take care of, and I'd like to offer you the option to purchase that section of forty acres. I'll give you a fair price, and we can work out payment details that will work for you."

Jamie's eyebrows went up in shock. "Thank you, Michael. I'll definitely speak with Sophie about this, and let you know quickly."

"Now, I have one other request. You have been instrumental in the training of the men, and Nona and I'd greatly appreciate it if you and Sophie would live in our home for as long as it takes to build yours."

"Michael, this is very generous of you."

"Nonsense, you would be doing us a great service. When we built our home, we thought it would be filled with family, however, the war and life have changed things slightly, and Nona and I feel as though we're rattling around in wasted space. We have both come to view you and Sophie as our family and would very much enjoy the company."

"Are you sure, Michael?"

The doctor laughed and rose to his feet. "I promised Nona that I'd somehow convince you, and she will not be happy if I come back with a 'no.'"

Jamie stood and shook Michael's hand, suddenly at a loss for words. They walked together down to the dining room and found the ladies waiting for them. Once the meal was over and the rest of the group dispersed for their various duties, Jamie pulled Sophie into the library.

"What?" Sophie whispered.

"You are never going to guess." Jamie relayed the conversation with Michael.

"What does this mean, Jamie?"

"It means, my sweet pessimist, that apparently God has plans for us. So, do I accept?"

"Well, gee, Jamie, I don't know. What do you think?"

Jamie chuckled as he pulled her into his arms and kissed her breathless.

* * *

The next few days were a blur of Nona and party planning. Sophie felt as though she'd worn a hole in every carpet in the house with the amount of pacing she'd done in an effort to stop herself from pulling her hair out. She wasn't allowed to lift a finger and it drove Sophie nuts. Waking on the morning of her "reunion, slash, engagement" party to an empty bed, she punched the pillow in frustration.

She sat up and noticed several boxes neatly stacked in the corner of her room. Climbing out of bed, she made her way to the pile and knelt down to investigate. Before she could open the first box, a knock sounded on her door. "Come in."

"Good morning." Christine poked her head in.

"Hey there, what are you doing here so early?"

"Early? Have you forgotten how long it takes to wash your hair?"

Sophie laughed. "Good point."

Christine laid a large box on Sophie's bed. "Betty is arranging baths for both of us."

Sophie leaned over to investigate the delivery. "What's this?"

"Have a look." Christine stepped away from the bed.

Sophie opened the box, and inside was yet another exquisite gown. Ivory chiffon with tiny green flowers embroidered into the fabric. Sophie lifted it out and let out a quiet whistle. "You guys are spoiling me." She hugged Christine. "Thank you."

"I can't take the credit."

"You can't?"

Christine shook her head. "Read the card."

Sophie located the card just as Betty came in with a few of the male staff carrying the large copper tub. Christine directed the filling of the bath and then left her alone to read her letter.

Christine returned to find Sophie in tears on the edge of her bed. "Sophie, what's amiss?"

"I'm just married to the most amazing man."

Christine smiled. "In that case, are you ready for your bath?"

After her bath, Sophie let Christine assist her with her hair before leaving her again to get ready next door. Sophie worried she would be late to her own party, but no one else seemed concerned, so she tried her best to relax. Her stomach clenched with nervousness, and she felt a little under the weather.

Christine returned to help with her corset, and then Sophie stepped into the hoops, petticoats, and finally her gown. Sophie put the finishing touches on her hair, leaving it to hang in flowing waves. Just the way Jamie liked it.

Christine gave her shoulder a squeeze. "You look beautiful."

Sophie looked in the mirror and felt her heart swell as she stared at the gown that was almost identical to the one she used to wear for reenactments. Sophie ran her hands over the fabric and sighed. Jamie remembered every detail, down to the size of the flowers, and the feeling of the overlay. Once Christine's hair was styled, the girls made their way downstairs. Jamie paced the foyer, his hands shoved deep in his pockets.

"You okay?" Sophie reached for his hand.

Christine left the couple to enter the ballroom.

"Yes. I just hate that I couldn't run up the stairs and get you myself. Too many people around." Jamie leaned down and kissed her cheek. "You look incredible, love."

"Thank you for the dress. I can't believe you remembered all the details."

Jamie chuckled. "I'm observant. Did you forget?"

Sophie slid her hands under his jacket and kissed his neck. "Never." "I also put it on you a hundred times."

"And took it off me a hundred times, if I recall," Sophie said with a secret smile.

Jamie kissed her quickly and then presented his arm. "Are you ready to face our new families, Ten-Cow?"

Sophie slipped her hand into the crook of his elbow and leaned against him for support, suddenly dizzy.

He squeezed her hand and she heard the concern in his voice when he whispered, "Honey, are you okay?"

"Just feeling a little sick." She dropped her head onto his shoulder. "I think I got a little overheated today."

"Can I get you anything?"

She took another deep breath and forced a smile. "No. It's passed. Let's go."

They found Nona and Michael standing by the ballroom doors waiting to escort them in. Sophie's nerves seemed to get the better of her, and she clung to Jamie for support. He kissed her cheek and whispered, "Relax, baby. I'm right here."

The moment the foursome entered the ballroom, they were confronted with a sea of faces.

"Surprise!" everyone shouted in unison.

She looked at Jamie. "What did you do?"

Before he could answer, the butler came in with a cake and twenty-seven candles.

"Make a wish, sweetheart." Jamie pushed her gently forward.

"There's only one thing that would make this life perfect." She closed her eyes and blew out her candles. They fluttered out after one blow, and the crowd applauded as Jamie kissed her and helped her cut the cake.

"Thank you, everyone! This is a wonderful surprise." Sophie beamed at the crowd. "Please," she motioned to the dance floor, "dance and enjoy."

The musicians took her cue and started up a lively quadrille. Jamie took her hand and squeezed it. "How are you feeling?"

Sophie grinned. "Perfectly fine." Her nausea had gone as quickly as it had come.

"Your ladies are waving you over."

Sophie glanced at the tables by the French doors and waved back. Elizabeth and Christine were giggling and conspiring like teenagers, motioning for her to join them. Jamie kissed her cheek and whispered, "I'll find Andrew."

She made her way to the table. "What are you two conspiring?"

Christine laid her palm on her chest. "Us?"

Sophie smirked as she took a seat between them and thanked the man who laid a piece of cake in front of her. Before she could take a bite, however, Michael pulled her aside and handed her a piece of paper.

Sophie raised an eyebrow in question. "What's this?"

Michael smiled. "It's a transfer of ownership."

She unfolded and read the note, and her eyes filled with tears instantly. "Michael, I can't accept this."

Michael gave a little chuckle. "Sophie, you have to accept this. You have ruined him for anyone else. I have been told that he pines when you're not around, and I can't have a horse that doesn't act like a horse."

Sophie leaned over and kissed his cheek. "This is incredible. I love that horse more than you could ever imagine. Thank you."

"It's my pleasure. And, of course, I hope you'll keep him in our stables until you can build your own," he said.

Sophie saw Jamie and Andrew approaching. Jamie's face showed concern, so she wiped her tears and plastered a smile on her face. Jamie reached her side and Sophie handed him the note. Michael excused himself and Sophie noticed a smirk on Andrew's face. "Did you know about this?"

"Yes, as a matter of fact I did." Andrew chuckled. "I almost let you in on the surprise the other day. Did I cover it up well enough?"

"I had no clue, Andrew. You did well."

Andrew lifted her hand and kissed her fingers before leaving them to find his siblings.

Jamie pulled Sophie into one of the alcoves for a moment of privacy. "What are you doing, Mr. Ford?"

"I am accosting you, Mrs. Ford." Jamie leaned down and kissed her.

"Sophie?"

Hearing Christine's voice calling for her, she dropped her forehead into Jamie's chest. "Just when it was getting fun."

"Give me a second before you answer her," Jamie requested.

Sophie grinned up at him. He got half a second before they were pulled from their hiding place at the insistence of Christine. "Time to toast the happy couple."

Nona waved the couple to the center of the room and insisted on a few speeches. Sophie blushed under the wonderful things everyone had to say and generosity of their gifts. The family spent the next few minutes congratulating them, and then it was time for everyone to leave and the group made their way to the door.

Sophie followed the group out onto the porch, Jamie's hand firmly linked with hers. They waved as the buggies disappeared down the drive. Andrew and Christine stood with them, intending to stay for a bit longer. The evening grew cooler as the sun set and Sophie sighed as Jamie guided her toward the front door. "Time to go, sweetheart."

"Just one more minute? I don't want to go inside just yet."

Jamie shook his head. "Ten-Cow, it's not safe. Come on inside."

"Okay." As she turned, she heard a sudden whoosh, then excruciating pain in her arm, and the sound of her own voice screaming.

"Sophie!" Jamie threw her to the ground and covered her body.

Andrew jumped over the porch railing and ran in the direction of the threat, as Christine knelt beside Sophie and cradled her head in her lap. "What was that?"

Jamie climbed off Sophie to assess the situation. Blood oozed from her arm. He pulled out his handkerchief and pushed it against the wound.

"Jamie," Sophie moaned. "What happened?"

"You've been shot," he replied as he frantically tried to get the bleeding to stop.

Sophie pulled away from his hand. "It burns."

"I know, sweetheart. Christine, can you get Michael, please?"

Christine nodded and rushed inside.

"Sophie, I need to get you in the house. I'm going to lift you, okay?"

"I think I can stand."

Jamie's eyebrows puckered. "Are you sure?"

Sophie nodded and braced her uninjured arm around Jamie's neck. With his hand around her waist, he lifted her, stopping when he heard her whimper. "I'm going to be sick." Jamie held her until her stomach settled. "This really, *really* hurts."

He lifted her into his arms. "I know, sweetheart." Jamie carried her upstairs, his voice shaking as he settled her gently on the bed and said, "I need to get your clothing off you."

Sophie stood and braced her good arm against the bedpost so that Jamie could unbutton her gown. She dropped her forehead against her arm and took a deep breath. With shaky hands, Jamie tugged and tore at the corset, in an effort to give her breathing room. As he pushed the garment from her hips, Sophie stumbled. Jamie caught her as she lost consciousness and laid her on the bed, his heart racing in fear.

The door flew open, bringing Michael, followed closely by Christine.

"She's been shot," Jamie said. "And now, she's unconscious. I don't know how bad the wound is."

"Step aside, son."

Jamie felt Christine's hand tugging gently on his arm. He looked up and stepped back to give Michael space to work. Pacing the room, Jamie felt as though his world was slipping away, reminders of their future and Sophie's disease slowly ripping the life from her.

"James?"

"Hmm?"

"It's a flesh wound. There is no bullet and with a few stitches, Sophie should be fine." Michael patted his shoulder.

Jamie rushed to her side and stroked her cheek.

Michael caught his eye and said, "I think I should try and stitch the wound while she isn't lucid."

Jamie nodded. "All right, will you please hurry?"

At Jamie's insistence, Michael washed his hands and then prepared a needle for Sophie's wound. "You're both going to have to hold her down in case she wakes up."

Jamie stretched out beside her, pinning her good arm behind his back. He wrapped one arm under her neck and the other around her waist, while Christine sat at her feet just in case she began to kick. Michael pulled a chair next to the bed and got her arm into position.

"Ready?" Michael asked Jamie.

Tears filling his eyes, he nodded and held Sophie a little tighter. As soon as the needle hit her flesh, Sophie woke with a scream, and tried to pull her body away. She pounded Jamie's back with the arm trapped behind him in an attempt to get him to move.

"Shh, sweetheart, it's okay. Michael has to close the wound."

Sophie screamed again, her head thrashing against the pillow.

Jamie grimaced. "Hurry, Michael."

Christine sat on her feet to keep them still, and sweat beaded her forehead from the effort.

"I'm almost done." Michael kept his head down and inserted the needle again.

"Jamie!" Sophie begged.

"Just relax, Ten-Cow, it's almost over," Jamie whispered.

"Make it stop! Make it *stop*!"

Michael stepped back. "I'm done."

Jamie loosened his hold and Sophie rolled toward him. She threw up, and her sobbing grew uncontrollable. Jamie watched her agony, certain the pain would be overwhelming. Jamie held her hair and stroked her back until her spasms subsided. Christine cleaned the blood from her arm and bandaged the wound, tight enough to stop the bleeding, while Jamie climbed off the bed and followed Michael to the door.

"I'll make a poultice," Michael said. "We'll begin putting that on her in the morning. For now, I can give her laudanum or morphine for the pain and to help her sleep."

"No," Sophie groaned.

Jamie winced. "I'll find you if her pain worsens."

Michael nodded and then left them to tend to Sophie. A tense twenty minutes passed as they worked to control Sophie's pain and calm her frayed nerves. Jamie lifted Sophie from the bed and carried her to one of the chairs.

"Jamie, you should get cleaned up." Christine gathered the dirty rags. "I'll retrieve fresh linens."

He shook his head. "I'm not leaving."

"It's okay, Jamie," Sophie rasped.

Jamie leaned over and stroked her cheek. "I don't want to leave you, sweetheart."

"You have puke all over you." Sophie took a deep breath. "I'll be fine. I think the worst is over, and you really need to change.

Jamie sighed. "All right. But I'll wait until Christine returns with sheets."

Christine took the cue and left the room.

"I can live with that." Sophie squeezed her eyes shut and reached for her arm. "This really, really hurts."

Jamie pulled her hand away. "I know."

Christine returned with Betty in tow, and Jamie leaned over and kissed Sophie's cheek. "I'll be back soon."

"Fine."

Jamie left the room and made his way out the front door. As he stepped off the back porch on his way to the stables, he was met by Andrew. "We got him."

"The shooter?"

Andrew nodded. "Clayton is interrogating him now."

Jamie slapped his shoulder. "Thank you."

"How's Sophie?"

"The bullet clipped her arm." Jamie grimaced. "She needed stitches but I think she'll be fine."

"What happened to you?" Andrew pointed to the stain on the front of his shirt.

"Sophie was sick."

Andrew stepped back slightly. "Do you have a change of clothing?"

"I do. I think I'm going to make a stop at the lake and then check in with Clayton."

Andrew nodded. "Well, if you need anything, let me know."

Jamie grabbed a horse and made his way out to the lake. After cleaning up, he rode back to the Madden's. Met by their housekeeper, Jamie was shown into the parlor, and instructed to wait. He didn't have to wait for long.

"Jamie?"

Turning, he reached his hand out as Clayton walked in. "What did you find out?"

"The man said his name was Victor Cary."

"*Was*? What happened?"

Clayton nodded. "He's dead."

"How?"

"I don't know what happened. He was speaking and then white foam spilled from his mouth. He fell from the chair and didn't move again."

"Poison," Jamie whispered.

"What was that?"

"Nothing." Jamie pinched the bridge of his nose. "Are we sure he was the shooter?"

"Yes. Andrew confiscated his gun—"

"Where is the gun?" Jamie interrupted him.

Clayton frowned. "Andrew said he disposed of it."

Jamie relaxed. "Ah, well, great."

"Is there something you want to tell me?"

"No, it appears you and Andrew have everything in hand. Please let me know if you need anything from me." Jamie forced a smile. "I should get back to Sophie. I'll let myself out."

Jamie jogged back to the Wades house and rushed inside. Climbing the stairs, he met Christine on the landing. "How is she?"

"In pain," Christine said. "She seems more comfortable since we changed the bedding and put her in a nightgown, but she's putting up a brave front."

Jamie smiled and squeezed Christine's arm. "Thank you. I'll take over from here."

"I'll be back to check on her in an hour."

"You're a good friend, Christine." Jamie let himself into the room and found Sophie teetering at the edge of the bed. Rushing to her side, he settled his hands on either side of her hips to steady her. "What are you doing?"

"I'm thirsty."

"Sweetheart, get back into bed. I'll get you a glass of water, and anything else you need."

She nodded and sat on the mattress.

He handed her the water. "Clayton interrogated the shooter."

"And?" Sophie took a sip.

"It was Victor Cary—and he's dead."

"How?"

"Poison, as far as I can tell."

Jamie filled her in on his conversation with Clayton.

Sophie gasped. "That sounds so very secret black ops or something."

He chuckled. "I know."

Sophie shook her head. "How did the shooter get the poison?"

"He must have hidden a cyanide capsule in his mouth."

"Wow." Sophie bit her lip. "How do you think he knew about me?"
Jamie paused for a minute.
"Jamie?"
Jamie sat heavily on the bed. "Do you remember that secret donation to the company last year?"
"The one you had to have your accountant track?"
Jamie nodded. "Yes. It was from the Cary family."
Sophie sat up with a gasp. "*The* Cary family?"
"Yes."
"The 'let's buy up every political seat in Washington State' Cary family?"
"Yes."
"Holy cow, Jamie. That's huge." Sophie frowned. "Is that why Brian was so freaked out when he called?"
Jamie nodded. "He wanted to keep the money, but I made sure it was all returned with a note of 'thanks but no thanks.' "
Sophie rubbed her forehead. "Do you think Cary knew the connection before they sent the money?"
Jamie shrugged. "I don't know, but it would seem so."
"Bernadette says I'm to make sure history stays the same. Granted, I know a lot about the war, but I don't know everything. I suppose if Victor Cary is dead, I won't have any trouble keeping things on track, will I?"
Jamie frowned. "Nope, and it means I don't have to kill him."
"James William," Sophie admonished. "When did you become so violent?"
Jamie shrugged. "Probably when you got shot."
"I'm going to be fine." Sophie sighed. "I wonder what Andrew did with the gun. I'm dying to know if it's from our time."
"I'll ask Andrew tomorrow to fill in the blanks. For now, I want you to rest."
"I feel like that's all I ever do." Sophie raised her hand to her bandage.
He caught her hand and pulled it away. "Don't touch it, sweetheart."
"It burns."
"Do you want me to get you something?" Jamie frowned when Sophie squeezed her eyes shut and nodded. "Why didn't you tell me it

was that bad?" Sophie burst into tears, and Jamie pulled her into his arms briefly. "I'll be right back."

Once he found the doctor, he rushed back to the bedroom. "Michael's bringing morphine."

She nodded with a whimper. Her door opened, and Michael walked in, holding a syringe that reminded Jamie of several horror movies he'd seen. "Is that a new needle?"

Michael raised an eyebrow. "As a matter of fact, it is. They're good for several uses, but this one is new."

Jamie relaxed. "Good. Please promise me you will only use this needle on Sophie. No one else."

The doctor frowned. "Seems like a waste to me."

"Michael, please. It's important to me."

"Well, I suppose, if that's your wish." Michael administered the morphine and then left them alone again.

Jamie watched her eyes turn to glass. "How's the pain now?"

"It's still there but I don't care."

Jamie chuckled and pulled her close, sweeping her hair away from her cheek. He held her until she fell asleep and then joined her.

* * *

Jamie woke the next morning to find Sophie climbing back into bed. "Sophie Jane, what are you doing?"

"I was thirsty." Placing her hand on his chest, she pushed him back onto the bed. "No, don't get up. I'm perfectly capable of getting some water."

"How's your arm?"

"It hurts."

Jamie sat up. "Do I need to get you more pain meds?"

Sophie grimaced. "No. My headache is almost as bad as my arm, so I'd rather refrain."

"I'm sorry, honey."

"I wish we had some milder pain meds."

"Wasn't aspirin invented in this century?" he asked.

"Yes, but the buffered version isn't created for another thirty years or so, and in Germany, which won't help Americans for several years. Plus, at the beginning it did more harm than good, so it wouldn't be an option anyway."

Jamie chuckled and kissed her head.

Sophie raised an eyebrow. "What?"

"Your brain's ability to hold that much information astounds me."

Sophie smiled. "I do love to astound you."

"Baby, your arm's bleeding through the bandage." Jamie pushed himself from the bed and pulled her with him. "Come sit in the chair so I can look at it."

Sophie sat by the fireplace and Jamie unwrapped her blood-soaked bandage. "It's puckered and red. Do you feel sick? Like, fever sick."

Shaking her head, she swallowed but didn't respond.

"I'll be right back." Jamie dressed quickly and rushed to find Michael, who followed him back to the room, bandages and poultice in hand.

Jamie knelt next to Sophie's chair and waited, rather impatiently, for Michael to examine her arm. At Sophie's groan, Jamie took her hand and held it to his lips. "Just look at me, Ten-Cow."

She nodded and turned tear-filled eyes toward him.

"It doesn't appear to be infected." Michael squinted to get a better look. "Yet. The poultice should help with the pain, Sophie, and also help ward off infection."

Jamie stood and took the supplies from the doctor's hands. "I'll take care of her."

Michael nodded. "All right. Sophie, if you need more morphine, let me know."

"I will. Thanks, Michael."

Jamie waited for him to leave the room and then went to work on her arm. "You can break down now, Ten-Cow."

"I'm fine."

Jamie raised an eyebrow, but didn't contradict her. When he finished cleaning and bandaging her wound, he lifted her and settled her onto his lap. "I've got you."

Sophie leaned her cheek against his shoulder and cried.

* * *

One week later, Sophie's arm was almost healed. The pain subsided, and an annoying itch replaced it. Christine and Nona focused on her wedding celebration, asking on occasion for her opinion but telling her she was in the way if she tried to help.

With Jamie at the arena and her morning visit with Samson completed, Sophie wandered the house, uninterested in holing up in the library again. Just before lunch, she heard Jamie call her name. "In here, Jamie."

He rushed into the parlor and pulled her off the couch. "You need to change."

"Huh?"

"Go put your breeches on and then meet me outside."

"Riding?"

Jamie kissed her and then grinned. "Yes."

Sophie took the stairs two at a time and changed quickly.

As she stepped onto the porch, she heard a trumpeting hello. "Samson?" Shielding her eyes from the sun, Sophie saw Samson saddled and sidestepping, as Jamie tried to keep him from rushing the porch to get to her. Sophie let out a squeal of excitement and clapped her hands as she ran and threw herself into Jamie's arms. "I get to ride him?"

Jamie grinned as he caught her. "You do. Michael gave the okay. Are you ready?"

Samson nudged her back with his muzzle and Sophie laughed. "Okay, boy, I'm coming." She turned and stroked his face. "Will you fly with me?"

"No flying, baby. Slow and careful," Jamie said as he helped her mount. She'd worn light skirts over her breeches, and she adjusted them for modesty while Jamie held Samson. Once she told him she was ready, Jamie jumped onto his horse and then led them toward the lake.

"Race ya," Sophie challenged and dug her heels into Samson's side. Her heart soared as Samson responded. With a yell of pure joy, Sophie guided him to a fence, leaned her body forward, and gripped with her thighs. His front hooves rose and flew over the hurdle, clearing it with several feet to spare.

The sound of pounding hooves barely registered behind her as she set Samson toward another fence. Once he cleared it, she slowed him to a trot and then a walk, and turned in surprise to find Jamie right next to her. "Hi."

Jamie smiled, despite the look of fear on his face. "Are you okay?"

"Are you kidding me?" Sophie grinned. "I am the happiest I have been in a while."

"Well, could you please be happy and slower in the future?"

Sophie laughed. "Probably not."

"Samson looks quite happy as well."

"I love this horse and he knows it." Sophie slapped Samson's neck and his ears went back to hear her voice. Sophie turned to Jamie. "Your riding has improved."

He smiled. "I'm in the saddle every day; I would hope it would have."

"Well, I'm impressed. And in love." Her head dropped back and she smiled at the sky. "And happy."

"I have another surprise. Follow me." Jamie led them to the lake and dismounted.

He lifted Sophie from Samson and then gathered the supplies he'd attached to their saddles.

"What have you got there?"

Jamie took her hand and pulled her closer to the water. "I have food, blankets, and the rest of the day off to love you."

Sophie's joy bubbled out with a laugh. "Well, then, let's not waste any time."

* * *

Several hours later, as the sun rose in the sky, Jamie suggested they head back for dinner but this time, their ride back was slower and filled with conversation.

When they arrived back at the barn, Sophie spent some extra time to shower attention on Samson. He was dozing when she finally left his stall. Sophie took Jamie's outstretched hand and followed him to the house. Dinner included Andrew and Christine, but Michael and Nona were with friends, so the four of them lingered over their meal.

"I have what you've been asking for," Andrew said to Jamie.

"Where?" Jamie whispered.

"Perhaps we could have drinks in the library." Andrew stood. "We can discuss it in there." Andrew led them into the library before closing the door and slipping the lock.

Sophie raised an eyebrow in Christine's direction, but her slender shoulder rose in a shrug. The three watched Andrew make his way to the window seat.

Throwing the pillows to the ground, he pulled out a rather large knife and pried a loose board of wood from the top. Reaching inside, he pulled out a gun. Jamie whistled as Sophie gasped.

"That's the gun?" Jamie asked, despite the obvious.

Andrew nodded. "Yes, it's the most incredible piece of artillery I have ever seen."

Jamie removed it from Andrew's hands. "It's some kind of Beretta."

Sophie moved closer and ran her hand over the serial number. "It kind of looks like a gun made in this century, don't you think? In fact, it's a little uncanny how much it looks like a Union issue rifle."

"Yes," Andrew said.

"That's probably why they chose it." Jamie raised it to eye level.

"No, Jamie. Look. It's been modified." Sophie pointed to the trigger mechanism.

As Jamie and Andrew studied the rifle, Sophie watched her husband's face flicker with several emotions, including appreciation. "This is genius."

"Why?" Sophie asked.

"They've essentially taken a Beretta and put it inside a Union issue rifle shell. Unless you were really looking at it, you probably wouldn't know the difference."

Andrew's breath came out in a whoosh. "The army could use this."

Sophie shook her head. "That would be dangerous, Andrew. We have to keep this hidden."

Andrew frowned. "I know. I just wish there was a way to utilize this for our side."

"Without ammo, it's pretty useless anyway," Jamie pointed out.

"Why the window seat, Andrew?" Sophie asked.

"You seem to be here more than most, so I figured it was the safest place."

Sophie grinned. "Smart."

Jamie handed the gun back to Andrew and sat on the edge of the hearth. "Tell us what happened with the shooter."

"He let it slip that he was Victor Cary, and was angry that he had failed." Andrew placed the gun back in its hiding place.

"Did he slip, Andrew, or do you think he was trying to throw us off track?"

Andrew sat on the window seat and settled his forearms on his knees. "He convinced both Clayton and me, and I doubt he could have done that if he weren't who he said he was. He had documentation proving who he was, as well."

"What kind of documentation?" Sophie asked.

Andrew pulled something from his pocket. "I had never seen anything like this, so I confiscated it before Clayton could see it. I assume it's something from your time?"

Jamie stood and took it from him. "It's a license for Washington State. Most definitely from my time."

"The photograph was accurate."

Jamie slapped the plastic against his fingertips. "Thank God this is over."

Andrew nodded. "I assume you'll want to keep that."

"Yes, thank you."

"I'll take my leave, then."

"I'll walk you out," Jamie offered.

"I'll meet you upstairs, okay?" Sophie said.

She hugged Christine and made a dash up the stairs while Jamie saw them out. She only just made it to the bowl on the dresser.

Jamie joined her not long after. "Honey, what happened? Are you okay?"

Sophie groaned. "I don't know. I've been feeling sick for about an hour."

Jamie rushed to unbutton her dress and unlace her corset to give her some breathing room. "You're probably just hot and overwhelmed with everything. Come on, let's get you into your nightgown."

Sophie was sick once more before Jamie helped her into bed and crawled in beside her. It didn't take her long to fall asleep, but she didn't stay that way for very long.

* * *

Jamie, kept up all night with her, worried more with each passing hour. She finally fell asleep for good at three o'clock, so he stole a few hours of sleep. Woken at six by Sophie's groan, he reached for the bowl. "I'm getting Michael."

He found him at the dining room table. Michael grabbed his medicine bag and followed Jamie upstairs. He was forced into the hallway and paced the aisle while Michael examined her.

After what seemed like hours, Michael opened the door and patted Jamie on the shoulder. "You can see her now."

Jamie bolted into the room, relieved to see Sophie sitting by the window, looking much less green. "Baby?"

"Hmm-mm." Sophie smiled.

"So, what's wrong? Why are you sick—" Jamie stalled. "Sophie, why are you smiling?"

"Well…" Sophie laid her hand on her stomach. "We're going to have to build a bigger house."

"Why?" Sophie stared pointedly at him. It took him a minute. "Seriously? NO way."

"Yes, way. You're going to be a daddy."

He sat down and ran his hands through his hair. "Wow." He jumped up and pulled her into his arms. "WOW!"

Sophie laughed as he continued to repeat the word and hold her tighter with each passing minute.

"Everything's perfect." Sophie reached up and cupped his cheek. "We're staying."

He kissed her palm. "We're staying."

The decision was made to stay in the past and do their best to guide any further travelers that might arrive, keep the history as accurate as possible, and to finally live the life they'd dreamed of as a young couple.

As they spent the rest of the night coming up with baby names and planning their future, Sophie sent up a silent prayer of thanks. She'd been reunited with the man of her dreams, her heart was working better than it ever had, and she had wonderful friends surrounding her.

Her price truly had been paid in more ways than she could count.

I was born and raised in New Zealand, and that's where my love of horses was formed. My grandfather taught me to ride at four years old, and I couldn't get enough.

My love and passion for Abraham Lincoln and the entire Civil War era might have come from my American father; however, he lays no claim to influencing me. My mother used to tell me I was simply born in the wrong place in the wrong time.

I haven't always wanted to write. It took me a long time to get started, but now I don't seem to be able to stop, the joy of escaping to the 1860s is too much fun. I've been happily married and gooey in love with my husband for sixteen years. We live in the Pacific Northwest with our two sons.

I hope you've enjoyed The Bride Price.

Made in the USA
San Bernardino, CA
11 February 2015